For
Jennifer Kavanagh

AUTHOR'S NOTE

With the exception of obvious historical characters referred to in the text, all the people who play a part in this novel are products of the author's imagination and bear no resemblance to any real individuals living or dead.

ACKNOWLEDGEMENTS

Many people helped me while I was writing this book and I should like to thank them all. Among them are the late Robert Belgrave and Sir Donald Logan, who shared their memories of the Suez crisis with me, and Mr James Turner and his colleagues at 1 King's Bench Walk, who allowed me to watch the Bar at work.

None of the opinions expressed by the characters in this novel should be taken to represent those of any of my advisers.

DREAMS OF ANOTHER DAY

Also by Daphne Wright:
THE DISTANT KINGDOM
THE LONGEST WINTER
THE PARROT CAGE
NEVER SUCH INNOCENCE

DREAMS OF ANOTHER DAY

Daphne Wright

LITTLE, BROWN AND COMPANY

A *Little, Brown* Book

First published in Great Britain in 1992
by Little, Brown and Company

A CIP catalogue record for this book
is available from the British Library.

ISBN 0 356 20780 3

Typeset in Baskerville by Leaper & Gard Ltd, Bristol
Printed in England by Clays Ltd, St Ives plc

Little, Brown and Company (UK) Limited
165 Great Dover Street
London SE1 4YA

CHAPTER 1

Two people were watching a young woman sitting in the shade at the foot of a massive lotus-headed pillar. Her eyes were shut and she was leaning against the stone as relaxed as though it were made of something soft, comfortable. A sharp-edged shadow lay over her and so she had taken off her hat, letting it lie in her lap.

One of the watchers was a man in a long, pale blue gown and dusty turban, who squatted unblinking in the shade opposite her, intent as a lizard waiting for its prey. He was waiting until the patch of shade, which had been slowly changing shape as he watched, moved far enough for the sun to reach the woman. He hoped that she would start and stumble up. With luck she would drop her bag or her camera or forget her hat.

Although she was very thin, he thought that she was rich, even beyond the usual, incomprehensible richness of all the foreigners who came to walk about the ruins. He had noticed the way the others had treated her with deference and allowed her to move away from them and be alone. He always watched the foreigners and rarely misjudged their resources.

The woman was dressed in a white drill skirt and a loose shirt of fine linen caught in at the waist with a wide belt of polished blue leather. There were white canvas shoes on her narrow feet and the hat she held loosely on her knees was made of local straw with only a simple blue ribbon round the crown. But her watch was gold and so was the heavy bracelet on her other wrist, and there were pearls around her slim neck.

Her name was Mary Alderbrook and she was English, single and thirty-one years old. To her friends, among whom she would have counted the other watcher, she was known as Ming.

The man waited patiently, ignoring the shrill cries of the other foreigners at the far end of the temple.

Ming heard them, but she ignored them too. There was a luxurious pleasure in sitting alone, feeling and thinking and not having to be polite. She had a guide book in her bag and had already read the description of the place, so she had a framework of facts into which to fit her own observations.

A sudden warmth reached through her skirt to her bare thigh, and she opened her eyes to the pale dazzle of the sun and smiled. Of all the places where they had stopped, Kom Ombo was the one she most liked.

Perched on a low promontory above the river, the temple was much less oppressive than the others she had seen on the stately voyage up the river, and the reliefs on its pale golden walls were clearer and more accessible than most of the others.

A white-sailed felucca slid into view against the low green trees on the farther shore. Ming watched it until it had passed out of her line of sight and then tilted her head back against the pillar, staring upwards at a broken section of the temple roof. She had not looked at it when she had chosen her shady seat and was amazed to see that it was not only carved but brightly coloured, too. The turquoise and black paint on the great outstretched wings of the eagles was fresh and clear, even after thousands of years.

So much had survived, she thought, and yet it was all so very dead. She had hoped vaguely that by coming so far and by searching the relics of a civilisation so utterly alien she might arrive at some knowledge or even intuition that would help her to find her own way, but so far nothing had happened. She had recovered her health in the astonishing air and revelled in the dry heat that seemed clean and invigorating after London's grubby dampness, but she had come to no conclusions about herself or her life.

With the others from the boat, Ming had marvelled at the tombs and temples, relished the clarity and colour of the wall paintings, smiled at the optimism of a religion that portrayed all its gods as young, beautiful and happy, tried to decipher some of the hieroglyphs, and been interested in everything she saw. But the things that had moved her had been incidental.

A group of children playing on the edge of the river and risking bilharzia had caught her eye one day and she had watched them for at least ten minutes as the boat cruised slowly past their little beach between two fields of sugar cane. There had been both boys and girls there, and the girls were dressed in ragged gowns of bright cotton. The pinks and greens, purples and oranges of their clothes lit the monotonous landscape of dirty-green water, grey-brown earth and dull green palms as brightly as the children's smiles illuminated their thin, brown faces. Ming had stood on the top deck wondering how those girls must feel when they reached the end of their childhood, when their hair was covered with black veils and their bright cottons were exchanged for the ubiquitous long black gowns the adult women wore.

The second watcher, a tall dark-haired woman with a very straight back and a commanding manner, saw that Ming was properly awake and moved forward out of the deep shadows cast by the temple forecourt.

'Ming!' she called. 'Ming, are you there? We ought to go back now. The boat's due to leave in fifteen minutes.'

'Coming, Connie,' said Ming a little wearily as she stood up, clasping her bag and hat and camera. The hat slipped just as Constance Wroughton appeared between the vast pillars, and Ming left it where it had fallen as she moved forwards. There were two patches of golden dust on the back of her skirt and her thin shirt, but she ignored them. The man who had been waiting moved as quickly as any lizard, picked up the hat and followed her. He reached

Ming just as she realised that she was missing something and turned. Her gentle face hardened as she saw what had happened. The man offered her the hat and for a moment she refused to take it. Then she shrugged, reached out for the hat and waited for the familiar words and action. The man held out his cupped hand in a gesture that ought to have been supplicating, but to Ming expressed a predatory threat.

'*Baksheesh*,' he ordered.

Ming understood the customs of the place and knew that compared with the men who held out their dusty, calloused hands wherever she went in the country she was rich beyond any dream of avarice, and yet she hated being coerced into endless tipping. Throughout her life she had done everything that was expected of her and buried the few rebellious feelings she had allowed herself to recognise, but suddenly her temper snapped.

'*Imshi!*' she said almost viciously and let her hand drop to her side, leaving him with the hat. The man looked at her as though he could not believe what he had heard. Ming turned away and began to walk fast towards the shore. Constance opened her bag, found a suitable note, and handed it to the man who gave her the hat and went muttering back to the shade.

'I'm sorry, Connie,' said Ming when the other woman caught up with her. 'I don't know what came over me.'

'It doesn't matter at all,' answered the older woman. 'But do put your hat on; the sun's hot.'

Ming obeyed.

'I don't know what's the matter with me,' she said hopelessly. 'I keep getting furious for no reason at all.'

'The perennial demand for *baksheesh* is terribly. . . .'

'That's not what I mean.' Ming sighed. 'It's not just out here. It was happening in London, too, although I usually managed to hold it back. Poor man!' She laughed sadly. 'It's rather unfair that the dam should have burst over him.'

Connie slid her hand into the crook of Ming's elbow and urged her forward, thankful that the first crack had appeared in her defences.

'Come and have tea,' she said. 'We mustn't miss the boat.'

'I don't think I'll bother with tea,' said Ming. 'I think I'll go and lie down. I must be what Nanny used to call "over-tired and fractious and silly".'

They walked along the dusty yellow path, screwing up their eyes against the sun's brilliance, until they reached the boat. As they crossed the rickety gangplank that connected it to the shore, Connie said:

'Don't you think you've rested enough, Ming?' There was kindness in her voice but a certain implacability, which the other woman heard with an odd combination of dread and relief.

'Perhaps,' she said with her usual polite deference. 'But I still seem to get so appallingly tired all the time. The doctors warned me I would.'

'Come and have tea,' said Connie again as she led the way to the upper deck of the boat. It was furnished with long cane chairs and cheerful striped canvas awnings. Several of the other passengers were already installed on the far side of the deck and Connie chose a pair of chairs well away from them all.

Ming lay back in one of the chairs and closed her eyes. Connie ordered tea from the smiling waiter on duty and sat back in silence, lighting a cigarette. As she drew the smoke into her lungs, she watched the still face of her friend with its fine bones, charming nose and slightly short upper lip. It was an extraordinarily pretty face but recently it had become lifeless, as though it was no more than a mask for an unhappiness that had been growing worse for a long time.

A different waiter appeared with a tray of tea and Connie tipped him. Accepting the money he said, in an accent so strong as to make the words barely comprehensible:

'You are sisters?'

'No, not sisters,' answered Connie as patiently as though it were not the fortieth time she had answered that question since they had embarked at Cairo.

'You are her mother?'

Connie shook her head and waved him away, almost losing patience herself. She was only twelve years older than Ming, and they were not related at all, although they shared a brother-in-law. After Connie's sister, Diana, had died her husband had married one of Ming's sisters and the two families had merged.

Hearing the waiter walk away to the opposite end of the deck, Ming opened her dark blue eyes and smiled at Connie with the familiar sweetness that seemed to express both attentiveness and a charming acquiescence. It was a smile that had attracted innumerable people over the years and it was backed by a gentleness that had kept them enslaved. Only Connie and a few other deeply concerned friends had begun to suspect that it was a gentleness that was also keeping Ming herself enslaved.

'Shall I pour?' asked Ming, swinging her slim legs over the side of the chair. 'You mustn't pay any attention to me,' she added as she handed Connie a cup of tea and poured out her own. 'It's only a bad case of self-pity, and I'll deal with it. I'm miserably discontented and yet I have every-thing anyone could reasonably want.'

'I'm not so sure about that,' said Connie as she stubbed out her cigarette.

Ming looked up at her, surprised.

'I have friends and family, and since my godmother died enough money to make me independent of everyone else,' she said, adding in an attempt at lightness, 'I am as free as anyone could ever expect to be.'

Ming paused and drank some tea to control her slightly quivering voice.

'I'm healthy enough now and I've no grounds whatso-ever for complaining or being angry. I ought to be happy.'

The boat's engines started up their familiar, comforting throb, the crew unhitched the ropes, and the boat slid out into the middle of the river again. Ming put down her cup and turned to Connie, unaware of the other tourists on the deck.

'But I'm not. What am I going to do? What's wrong with me?'

'There's nothing wrong with you,' said Connie with an energy in her voice that startled Ming. More slowly she added: 'And as for what you ought to do, I'd say: "Be a bit selfish. Say what you actually think occasionally. Cause trouble."'

At that Ming laughed and all her intelligence and humour showed through the distress.

'Oh, I don't need any urging to be selfish.'

'I think you do,' said Connie seriously. 'Not only do you always try to make peace between warring factions, which is admirable enough I suppose – although I suspect sometimes people want to go on warring for a bit ...'

Ming managed to smile at that.

'But you also expend most of your energies suppressing everything in yourself that you are afraid will upset someone else. Don't you think you ought to use your brains and your strength for something a bit more constructive?'.

'Such as?' Ming was taken aback at the thought that she could be so much criticised for something that seemed to her to be basic common sense.

'Something that makes you use everything you've got instead of burying it. I'm not a religious woman, Ming, but I can't help thinking of the parable of the talents whenever I look at you. Your godmother's legacy has done you no good.'

'Except freed me from the work I'd come to detest.' Ming smiled slightly. 'You can't imagine how awful it was to realise quite how much I hated it when I'd once loved doing it. And what a revelation it was to discover that I could just dump it. That was selfish, if you like.'

'Why did you hate it so much?' Connie finished her tea and put the cup back on the wicker tray. She felt in her bag for her cigarettes. 'I'm not suggesting you were wrong; I'm just curious as to why you should have loathed it so.'

Ming pulled herself out of the long chair and went to lean against the rail, looking out at the slowly passing shore. All the manifold irritations of the job she had done as secretary to a Member of Parliament were too petty to have given rise to the unbearable frustration that had driven her away after so long.

'I suppose the feeling that everything I did was to help Roger achieve things for himself,' she said eventually, keeping her eyes on the figure of a turbanned man riding through the sugar cane on a donkey that looked far too small to support his weight. His green-and-white striped gown was hitched up to his knees, revealing long, thin bare legs and leather slip-on shoes with heels at least an inch and a half high.

'All my satisfactions were second-hand,' Ming went on when the man had ridden out of sight. 'The things that had once excited me – like drafting his speeches, sorting out his constituents' problems, inventing parliamentary questions for him to ask – became so many dreary chores.'

'I'm not surprised,' said Connie, but Ming was not listening. In her mind she was back in the House of Commons. She no longer saw the palms and the passing feluccas; only the green leather benches and the endless coming and going of dark-suited men.

'I found myself listening to his speeches sometimes and getting furious when he put the wrong emphasis on what I'd written for him, or noticing where he'd changed it because he had missed the point. You see, you're wrong. I'm not the sweet, helpful, dutiful, unselfish creature you seem to think me.'

'Good.' Connie's quietly satisfied voice reached through Ming's preoccupations and she went back to her chair. Connie twisted her neck so that she could look at Ming and saw that her eyes were narrowed and her pointed chin looked stubborn.

'You are all those things, Ming,' she declared. 'But there's much more to you than that. I think all that's happened is that you've discovered what most of us knew from the moment you started working for Roger Sillhorne: that you're twice as clever as he and could do his job standing on your head. It's no wonder that you were frustrated by playing second fiddle to him all the time. You ought to be doing a job of your own.'

'But I've had no education,' protested Ming, coming back to sit down. 'What with the war getting in the way.' Connie poured her another cup of tea.

'Did you never think of training for anything?'

'No. Even though my sister went to London University in 1946, somehow after all that had happened the idea of sitting about learning things seemed ... irrelevant, and by the time I'd come to my senses it was too late. But you're right: I must find something to do. I feel so pathetic!'

Connie almost laughed. Anything less pathetic than Ming's incisive voice just then would have been hard to imagine. Before Connie could say anything they heard something bang into the side of the boat and then fall into the river with a heavy splash. She swung her legs over the side of her long chair and stood up to see what was happening, shading her eyes. A group of young men were yelling and gesticulating at the boat. Some were stooping to pick up stones from a pile at their feet; others were actually throwing them. To Connie there was something dream-like and unreal about the big, white boat gliding so slowly past the furiously shouting Egyptians on the shore.

One stone, pitched more efficiently than the rest, landed on the deck only feet away from them.

'They're stones,' said Ming, horrified. Then her voice rose in a warning: 'I say, Connie, do be careful.'

As she spoke yet another stone was sailing through the air towards them. Connie, blinking against the glare, ducked in the wrong direction. The heavy stone hit the side of her forehead with a noise that forced Ming out of her chair. As Connie collapsed on to the deck, bleeding and unconscious, Ming lurched forwards, feeling a sharp pain in her side. Afraid that her scar might have started to leak, she knelt over Connie's felled body, trying to shield her from the stones. Ming felt a hard glancing blow on her own shoulders and arched closer to Connie's head, trying to tuck her own out of the way too. She felt faint and rather sick, but she hung on, desperately afraid that Connie might be badly injured.

'Can't someone help them?' a frail voice called from

further down the deck. Through her dread, Ming recognised it as belonging to a Mrs Sutherland, the wife of an elderly vicar who had conducted a service in the saloon on the previous Sunday morning.

'Coming, my dear.'

Ming half-lifted her head to see the parson and his wife hurrying towards her through the crowd of shocked passengers. The sound of stones landing on the deck had stopped, although there were splashes to the stern of the boat and the angry shouts were still echoing over the water. Stewards were standing at the rails of the lower decks, shouting insults at the men on the shore.

'Can we get her away from that rail?' asked Mr Sutherland, taking off his panama hat as he arrived at Ming's side.

'I don't think we need to actually,' she said, realising that the boat had at last glided out of the range of the stone-throwers. As Ming moved away a little and tried to ease her shoulders, Mrs Sutherland caught up with her husband and lowered herself painfully on to the deck. She started to dab the blood away from Connie's face with her handkerchief.

'I don't think your friend is too badly hurt,' she said, looking up at Ming. 'Just stunned.'

'Oh, thank goodness.' Ming leaned against one of the chairs and wiped the back of her hand against her forehead. Slowly the other tea-drinkers came to offer their help and advice.

'It's a mercy the cut is so near her hairline, Miss Alderbrook,' said Mrs Sutherland. 'Nothing will show even if it does scar. Let's straighten her out. William, will you keep her cool? She'll be all right in a moment.'

The parson knelt on the deck beside Connie and took off his buff linen jacket. He rolled it into a pillow which he slipped under her head, and then energetically plied his hat above her face, smiling at Ming.

'That was awfully brave,' he said shyly. 'Weren't you afraid of being struck?'

Ming, holding her right side with both hands, shook her head. It was clear that the scar was still intact, but it hurt and brought back horrible memories of the night of complete powerlessness and terror when her appendix had burst.

'There didn't seem much point worrying about it,' she said, touched by his approval. 'It had to be done. Was anyone else hurt?'

'It doesn't look like it. Just jolly bad luck that you two were on this side of the boat where they could get you. I say, they have hurt you, haven't they? You look awfully pale. My dear....'

'No, it's all right. I've just stretched a recent appendix scar a bit. It's healed now, but I'm still not quite used to it. Don't you think we ought to get some stewards to carry Connie to her cabin out of the sun?'

'She'll be coming round in a moment,' said the vicar's wife with certainty. She had taken some eau de Cologne from her capacious bag and was dabbing the unwounded side of Connie's face with it. 'Here we are.'

Ming saw that the muscles around Connie's mouth were tightening and her eyelids beginning to move. She groaned and lifted a hand to her forehead. The vicar's wife murmured reassurances as Connie felt the still-oozing blood and brought her fingers close to her eyes, obviously trying to focus on their redness.

'It's not too serious, Miss Wroughton,' said the vicar, just as Ming was trying to explain what had happened.

'I expect you've a horrid headache,' said his wife more practically. The other two fell guiltily silent and the onlookers began to drift back to their chairs.

As soon as Connie was fully conscious the vicar helped her back into her chair and insisted that she drink some tepid tea. Connie, looking faintly amused despite the obvious pain in her head, obediently took the cup he held out. When she saw that Ming was frowning, she said:

'Are you all right? Did they get you too?'

'Not badly,' she answered slowly. 'But I can't help wondering what it was all about. Surely it couldn't have been because I refused to tip that man?'

'Don't be silly.' Connie sounded both tired and

impatient. 'I tipped him for you. I expect they were just boys having a lark.'

She closed her eyes and put her free hand to her forehead again.

'I shouldn't touch it,' said the vicar's wife. 'As soon as you've had your tea we ought to disinfect it and bandage it up. It's important to cover it especially in this climate.'

'I don't think it was just a lark,' said her husband. 'There's a lot of anti-British feeling about just now.'

When he caught his wife's eye he flushed slightly. 'Sorry, my dear. Mustn't get on my hobby horse, I know. Why don't you take Miss Wroughton down and see to her face?'

Ming was about to go with them when she turned back to the vicar to ask him what he meant to say. He looked at her and smiled.

'My wife tries to stop me boring on about it all, and not many of our fellow-passengers agree with me, but I don't think you can really blame these people for resenting us. After all, they are catastrophically poor and a lot of the population is frighteningly unhealthy as well as half-starved. The one undeniable asset they have is the Suez Canal and we and the French have made sure that the lion's share of its profits comes to us. Who wouldn't be angry?'

'Yes, well, but,' said Ming, who had often listened to her father's views about the country, 'we did buy the majority of shares in the Canal in eighteen-something and they had the money then. It is ours.'

'That rather depends how you look at it,' said the vicar. 'But I mustn't bore you – and I must go and dress for dinner.' He smiled his charming, self-deprecating smile, leaving Ming frustrated and rather worried.

She went down later to see whether Connie needed anything and found her with a tray of soup and biscuits on her knees.

'Are you really all right?' asked Ming, pulling up the only chair in the cabin.

'I'm fine. My head aches, but sweet Mrs Sutherland has given me some pills. She used to be a nurse, you know.'

'Really? What luck! They're both awfully nice. Well, if

you really don't need anything, I suppose I'd better get ready for dinner.'

'You do that. But, Ming?'

'Yes?'

'When those louts interrupted us I was about to ask whether you'd consider giving us a hand with the magazine until you've settled on your new career of trouble-causing, whatever it might be.'

Ming stopped, half-way to the door of the wood-panelled cabin, and turned. She looked eager but a little doubtful.

'Max and I have found that editing and organising it take so long,' said Connie casually as though she had only just thought of it, 'that we need more freelance contributors than we'd expected, but finding and commissioning them take yet more time away from our own articles.'

'You mean you want a secretary,' said Ming, her voice flattening as she spoke.

Connie laughed, wincing and laying her hand gently on her bandaged forehead.

'I keep forgetting this. We don't need any more secretarial help, but we do need more articles.'

'But I've never written anything.'

'Except speeches and letters and, I suspect, most of those articles that appeared under Roger Sillhorne's name last year.'

As Connie spoke she watched Ming's face and saw that she had been right. 'Precisely! Why not start now and write me a few thousand words about cruising up the Nile? I'm supposed to be doing it, but after this afternoon's performance, I'm not sure I'd find the right lyrical note.'

'No,' agreed Ming. 'I don't suppose you would. Perhaps I should try. You'd have to be ruthless, you know, if it wasn't any good.'

'Ah yes,' said Connie with a smile that disguised her determination, 'I can promise you that.'

'Then I will have a go. Thank you. I'll leave you in peace now. But do send for me if you need anything. I'll look in before I go to bed.'

'Thank you, Ming.'

CHAPTER 2

While Ming was in her cabin after dinner anointing her bruised and stiffening shoulder with witch hazel, her two elder sisters and a friend were talking about her as they listened to the rain splattering down on London.

All three of the sisters had the same fine bones, fair hair and remarkable dark blue eyes, and yet none of them could have been mistaken for either of the others. Margery, the eldest, who was always known as Gerry, hardly bothered about her clothes and tended to look preoccupied and often rumpled, while Felicity had an air of seductive confidence that made her seem more substantial than the others and added a touch of glamour to her good looks.

There were a few grey threads in Gerry's hair but it had never occurred to her to have them dyed blonde again. Flixe, who believed in improving on nature whenever she could, was exasperated by her sister's waste of her looks but rarely said so.

'Have you heard from Ming yet?' asked the third woman as she watched the two of them, amused by the differences between them and envious of the obvious affection they shared.

'I doubt if the mails from Egypt will get us anything before Ming's back herself,' said Gerry rather crossly.

She liked Julia Wallington well enough and admired the fact that she was a successfully practising barrister, but she could never understand quite why Flixe was so fond of Julia or wanted to see so much of her.

They were sitting in the conservatory of Flixe's house, which was comfortable and enticing despite the depressing weather outside. Instead of the usual white, Flixe had chosen a pale apricot paint for the woodwork, and the floor was covered in terracotta tiles. A selection of tattered but colourful Persian carpets added to the warmth, as did several efficient radiators. They enabled Flixe to grow a spectacular selection of luxuriantly flowering sub-tropical shrubs among the well-upholstered wicker chairs. There were even productive orange and lemon trees in huge unglazed terracotta pots, and the sweet spicy scent of their flowers filled the conservatory.

Flixe picked up a thermos jug of iced coffee and refilled their glasses.

'I do hope the poor girl is recovering,' said Julia, well aware of Gerry's hostility but unable to do very much about it.

She was a tall woman with silvered dark hair and an attractive face that could look severe until her interest or her sympathy were engaged. Then her wide mouth would relax and her brown eyes lose some of their acuteness. There were people who were afraid of her, but others, like Flixe who knew her well, saw beneath her façade to the warmth and vulnerability that she usually kept hidden.

'My husband had a burst appendix a year or two ago and I know how ghastly it can be,' she went on, still trying to placate Gerry. 'He was laid very low; couldn't face the House of Commons for weeks. But he recovered in the end, and I'm sure Ming will too.'

Gerry smiled at her, grateful for her concern for Ming but irritated that she was there at all. She drank a little of the sweet, cold coffee and said nothing.

'It seems so unfair that Ming should have had to put up with that as well as everything else,' said Flixe, wishing that the other two could relax.

'I'm sure she'll cope with it,' said Julia tentatively. 'I've hardly ever met her, but she's always seemed thoroughly in control, and I've never really understood why you're both so protective of her. After all, she's over thirty now.'

The two sisters looked at each other. For once there was an identical expression in their dark-lashed blue eyes. It was Gerry who answered.

'That's part of the trouble. She is far too much in control.'

'Mmm,' said Flixe, her eyes looking far beyond the luxuriant plants in front of her. 'Ever since her twin was killed in the war, Ming's kept all her difficulties to herself, and ...' She broke off and turned, almost helplessly, to her elder sister.

'And they eat away at her,' said Gerry quickly. 'I know that sounds melodramatic, Julia, but it's horrible to know that she's miserable and not even be able to ask why, let alone do anything to help.'

Julia's straight eyebrows twitched and she looked at Gerry with more sympathy – and more respect – than before.

Flixe got up from her chair again as though she were too restless to keep still. She picked up a long-spouted copper watering can and started to water her plants.

'She's hardly ever spoken about Annie since then. But it wasn't only that: the war damaged other things in her, too.'

'Poor Ming. And yet it's ten years since it ended.'

'I know,' said Gerry, sounding heartfelt. 'It's a different world.'

'Different, and yet ...' Flixe's voice was almost dreamy. 'And yet not such fun.'

'Flixe!'

'Don't sound so disapproving, Gerry,' she said with a laugh. 'Horrible though lots of it was, we did have fun – even you.'

A smile was Gerry's only answer to that before she turned back to Julia.

'But Ming didn't see any of that side of it. It seems desperately unfair; she's much nicer than either of us, but we always seem to have better luck.'

'Speak for yourself,' said Flixe over her shoulder as she stood picking the dead flowers off a tall camellia. 'I don't think it's luck as much as good management.'

As though to follow her sister's lead back into frivolity,

Gerry smiled as she put down her empty glass.

'As the eldest I'm always right. You ought to know that by now, Flixe.'

Flixe turned back. The glossy dark leaves and bright pink flowers made a wonderful foil for her as she stood there in her full-skirted dress of cherry-coloured wool, but she seemed quite unconscious of the effect.

'Not always, but this time you are right. There is something different about Ming. She's ... oh, kinder and a lot less selfish than either of us. But perhaps we do over-mother her.'

Julia, who had known the full warmth of Flixe's compassion, smiled at them both as she stood up.

'I ought to go. You two must have lots of things to talk about.'

Gerry heard an oddly wistful note in Julia's voice and pulled herself together.

'Not on my account, Julia,' she said, looking down at her watch. 'I must go and do something about dinner tonight. My husband's got some old naval friends coming and they need more formal food than I usually cook. It was good to see you.'

She held out her hand and Julia shook it before lowering herself into the long wicker chair again. Flixe left her gardening to kiss her sister.

'You may be the eldest,' she said, brushing a hair from Gerry's green jersey, 'but sibling hierarchies don't exist past twenty-one. Take care of yourself, old thing. You're looking rather worn.'

'Thanks a lot,' Gerry said ironically. 'Bye, Flixe. You've made a blissful garden here.'

'I'll see you out. I won't be long, Julia.'

Julia lay back in the long chair and thought about the two sisters.

'She was a bit spiky, wasn't she?' said Julia when Flixe came back after a long interval and stood beside her chair. 'Was it just because I was here?'

'No, I don't think so,' said Flixe, looking concerned. 'I see her every weekend; she knows I hardly ever see you without either the children or the husbands.'

After a moment's thought Flixe added: 'If she sounded stiff, it was probably at the suggestion that we're over-protective of Ming.'

Julia's wide mouth twitched into a rueful smile.

'Did I sound sharp? I am sorry. I suppose it's because I have such a passionate desire for people to be what they really are instead of what other people think they should be.'

Flixe looked down at her with affection.

'D'you see what I mean?' Julia went on earnestly. 'I didn't want to annoy either of you, but I can't help wondering whether your treating Ming as though she's fragile will make her so. There must be real force concealed in her somewhere and it seems a pity that she should be protected against it. But I didn't mean to criticise.'

'I know.' Flixe picked up the thermos jug and offered Julia more coffee, adding as she poured: 'You spent a lot of time fulfilling other people's expectations in the old days, didn't you, Julia?'

Flixe put down the jug and went back to her fading camellia so that Julia would not feel compelled to answer. Piling the shrivelled flowers into a wide, flat basket, Flixe added:

'And you're probably right. We may overdo it. Having spent our early years furious that our mother had no interest in us as anything except products to do her credit, I suppose we've tried to give Ming what we missed.'

'But she's considerably more than grown up now.' Julia's common sense made Flixe smile ruefully.

'I know. Sometimes it is difficult to remember that.'

Flixe bent down to retrieve a dead flower from the floor. 'But if we're to talk of spikiness, you don't seem altogether serene yourself.' She straightened up. 'Trouble in chambers? Or at home?'

Julia gave a short unhappy laugh and recrossed her long legs.

'Fair comment,' she said as lightly as she could. 'You always do see through me.'

From long experience Flixe knew that her friend wanted to tell her something but was so anxious not to bore that she could not begin. Flixe applied a prompt.

'Well?'

'You could say it's home.' Julia spoke reluctantly. 'David in fact. He's not happy either, and I can't seem to do anything to help.'

Flixe, hearing a note of real sadness in Julia's voice, put down the basket and went to sit beside her. She had seen the difficulties Julia and David had had to surmount before they married and could imagine the depths of her feelings for him.

'It's agony, isn't it?' Flixe put a hand over Julia's for a second. 'But it's just part of life. We all go through it. You're not happy all the time: you can't expect that your husband will be. And there's nothing you can do except wait until he is himself again. Just like us with Ming.'

'You're so sensible.'

'You don't sound as though you admire that very much,' said Flixe, amused.

Julia's brown eyes lightened and her eyebrows lifted.

'I do really,' she said, sighing, 'but like a child I suppose I want to be told that everything's all right.'

She looked sideways at Flixe's lovely, glowing face and almost reached out to touch it.

'There's something about you that makes us all come to you for mothering. Do you mind?'

'It's my stock-in-trade.'

The words ought to have been light, but somehow they were not. When she saw Julia looking at her, Flixe added:

'I ought to be good at it since it's all I ever do.'

'That sounds as though Gerry's been lecturing at you to get a job again. It's none of her business.'

'Elder sisters are always bossy. They can't help it. But I'm in no position to get any kind of work just now,' said Flixe, rather enjoying the loyalty of Julia's protest. 'How does David's misery manifest itself? I can't imagine him sulking.'

Julia's eyes dulled again and she turned her head away.

'No. He could never sulk or snap or anything like that. But it's obvious all the same. He's lost his ... zest, and everything – even me and the children – seems to need much more effort from him than before.'

Her wide lips thinned and her eyes were full of pain. At last she looked straight at Flixe.

'It's horrible to know that he's having to work so hard to be interested in us.'

There was no answer to that. The sound of the front door opening made Flixe look down at her watch.

'Five o'clock: time to go and be a mother again.'

'I know.' Julia got out of the long chair. Standing, tall and distinguished, she looked down at Flixe and said seriously: 'I think I'd give anything to have him happy again. Anything at all.'

'He will be, Julia. Don't torment yourself or there'll be two of you miserable instead of only one.'

'Ah, Flixe!' Julia was able to laugh again. 'I'm not sure what I'd do without you. You keep me going.'

'It's a two-way process,' said Flixe truthfully.

CHAPTER 3

Ming's flat was cold when she got back to it late the following Friday evening, and it smelled stale. She dumped her luggage in the hall and went into each room to fling open the windows and let in the chilly air of the April evening. Smelling the mixture of damp, dust and petrol as she stood at her bedroom window, she missed the dry, intoxicating warmth of Egypt.

'But no one throws stones in London,' she said to herself, turning back into the pretty room, 'however angry they might be.'

Despite the stuffiness, the whole flat was immaculately tidy and the post was neatly stacked in a fat heap on the hall table with a short note from the charwoman Ming had inherited from the people who had sold her the flat. The few lines explained where Mrs Crook had stowed the provisions she had bought to 'see you through till Monday, Miss' and hoped that the holiday had been a success. Ming smiled at its friendliness and went into the kitchen to make herself a pot of tea, which she took with her letters into the pale drawing room.

There was very little furniture, because she was still not sure how she wanted the flat to look and did not want to clutter it up with mistakes, and the few things there had nothing in common with each other. The only memorable feature apart from the single painting was the colour of the walls.

Ming had persuaded the decorator, much against his will, to paint them a glowing coral colour and then to apply drastically thinned coats of successively paler and paler colours until he had achieved a pearly finish, through which the original coral appeared like the flush on the inside of a seashell.

The picture was an oil painting, hung over the white chimney-piece, of an unpopulated curving beach on some Scandinavian coastline. It must have been painted during one of the white nights of summer when the sun never really set. The dusky light made the whole scene look strange and still in its restrained lavender and grey-blue colour scheme. Ming had seen the painting in an obscure gallery miles away from Bond Street and loved it for its quiet and lonely peacefulness.

As she did every time she came into the room, she let herself look at the painting and felt soothed by its emptiness. Despite the horrible stoning, she had enjoyed the cruise and revelled in Connie's company, but she felt curiously satisfied to be on her own again. After a while she went to sit down at the desk and began to deal with her post.

Among the typed envelopes, which all looked as though they were concerned with the legacy her godmother had left her, was one addressed in the distinctive handwriting of a civil servant called Mark Sudley, whom she had met six months earlier in Gerry's house. Ming opened it at once.

> Dear Ming,
> Welcome back! Was it wonderful? Did you see egrets and Nile kingfishers and swallows swooping through the temples? I'd love to hear all about it. Could I drop in and see you? There's something I'd like to ask you about, too. Would you telephone when you've got a minute spare?
>
> Mark

Ming smiled. The letter was so like Mark, relaxed, affectionate and wholly unthreatening, that she picked up the telephone at once. Dialling his number, she quickly invited him to share a scratch supper with her that evening.

When he had accepted, she retreated to the kitchen to see what Mrs Crook had left for her. Having looked at the store cupboards, she decided that Mark would have to put up with bacon and eggs. Flixe, she knew, would rustle up some wonderfully aromatic Mediterranean dish from one of Elizabeth David's recipes, but her own cooking was much less advanced.

She laid the table and took the eggs out of the fridge before going back to her post to deal with the official-looking letters. As she had expected they were mostly about the money she had inherited and she decided to answer them later. The money had been made available to her only four months earlier and she had still not become accustomed to it, although its very existence was giving her a sensation of power that she had never had before.

Several of her personal letters included helpful suggestions from friends of her mother who ran various charities and wanted donations or free labour, but none of them offered Ming the kind of work she wanted. She threw the envelopes into a wicker wastepaper basket and piled all the letters to one side, before looking at the last three envelopes. Two were addressed in her sisters' handwriting and one in Roger Sillhorne's.

Taking a gulp of tea, Ming decided to throw Roger Sillhorne's unopened letter straight into the basket with the empty envelopes. He had written to her frequently since her resignation, and all his letters had been filled with a mixture of bullying and cajolery that she had come to find detestable. Just before she had left for Egypt, she had asked him not to write again. Since he had ignored that request, she decided to be ruthless. The letter was torn into four pieces and thrown away.

Brushing her hands together as though to remove some sticky dust, Ming returned to her desk to open her sisters' letters, and found two invitations to dinner.

'What can we do about poor little Mingie?' she asked herself sardonically, mimicking her eldest sister's voice: 'We really must find someone for her.'

Ming took a moment to remind herself of the fact that

she cared a lot for both her sisters and that they interfered in her life only out of the highest and most generous of motives. By the time she telephoned first Gerry and then Flixe her voice held nothing but affection. She thanked each of them, accepted their invitations, answered questions about Egypt and asked about their affairs.

Gerry, childless, talked about her husband, about the undergraduates to whom she taught Russian at London University and about the tricky translation she had just been commissioned to make of a novel that had been recently smuggled out of the Soviet Union. Flixe, on the other hand, had plenty to say about her three children, the youngest of whom was nearly two, despite the fact that Ming had seen them all only a month earlier.

'She's growing huge and pretty,' said Flixe, eventually summing up her enthusiastic account of the family. 'I'm sure it's because she's the only one who's never had a ration card.'

'Oh, good.' Ming was genuinely fond of her nephew and nieces. 'And clever too, I hope?'

'As a bagful of monkeys. Peter's delighted with her ... and with me: I'm going to have another one.'

'Heavens! I mean, congratulations. Did you ... did you mean to?'

'Ming, really! Of course we did. I'm not sure what I'd do without a baby,' said Flixe. 'You can't imagine how lovely they are. You ought to try it for yourself.' There was a short pause, before Ming asked about her brother-in-law.

'Peter's the same as always: funny and generous and unknowable and fascinating ... just himself.'

'Good,' said Ming with a laugh. 'I'm glad. Well, I'll see you both on Tuesday week. Thanks, Flixe.'

She put down the telephone, thinking about her sister's husband. Like both Flixe and Gerry, Ming had met Peter Suvarov during the war. He had been kind to her when her twin had been killed, with an intelligent, slightly astringent, kindness that had helped far more than other people's more sentimental sympathy. Later he had gone out of his way to make a friend of her, despite the huge gap in their ages. As soon as she had left school he had given her a job in the secret research group he had run all through the war.

Inevitably Ming had fallen in love with him. When he had married Flixe after the war Ming had minded desperately, but she had done her best to keep her feelings hidden.

Her misery had quickly dulled and her feelings had changed from passionate hero-worship and dependence into a slightly cynical liking, which had left her feeling lost. None of the men who had wanted to marry her since the war, and there had been several, had been able to make her feel one-tenth of what Peter had aroused in her. Since even that had gone, she had come to the conclusion that she was incapable of love.

When Mark came to the flat a little later he professed himself delighted to share her bacon and eggs and leaned against the red-painted kitchen dresser while she cooked, talking idly of his colleagues and the occasional frustrations of his work at the Ministry of Defence.

He was a big man, very broad in the shoulder and attractive without being at all conventionally handsome. His skin was smooth and slightly tanned, which made the whites of his eyes very bright; his nose was straight and his jaw pleasantly square. His best feature was definitely his grey eyes, which were full of intelligence and usually lit with laughter. Despite the strength of his chin, his mouth was gentle.

'You hardly ever talk about your job,' Ming said, turning from the cooker with the big frying pan in her left hand and a spatula in the other. 'I've often wondered what made you become a peace-time civil servant.'

'Here, let me help,' he said, pushing himself away from the dresser. He found two white plates and held them out.

'I suppose,' he went on when they were sitting on either side of the grey-and-white formica table, 'that I was flattered when they offered to keep me on after the war. I thought then that it was the most important job I could possibly do. I still think so, actually.'

'Why?' asked Ming, her fair head on one side. 'I don't mean that I don't agree, but I am interested.' She poured a little pile of salt on to the edge of her plate and began to eat.

Mark smiled at her serious face and tried to concentrate on her question instead of the one he had come to ask her.

'Because I can't imagine anything more important – or interesting – than being involved in the running of the country,' he said at last, cutting off a piece of bacon and plunging it into the glistening softness of the egg yolk. 'Does that sound fearfully pompous?'

'Yes,' said Ming with a wicked smile; then her eyes softened. 'But understandable, too. Why not politics? Were you never attracted to the House?'

'Good God! No!' Mark's protest was immediate and heartfelt. Then he remembered Ming's long-held job. 'Not that I meant to denigrate people who follow that road,' he said. 'But their skills are quite different and their preoccupations, too. In fact, I'd say ...'

'With the greatest respect.' Ming's interpolation was spoken quietly but with an oddly formal edge in her voice. Mark looked up in surprise and saw that behind the sweetness of her smile she was still laughing at him.

'Yes,' he said, laughing back and showing his very white, even teeth. 'With the greatest respect, I'd say that most – but by no means all – of them are more interested in keeping their seats than in ensuring that the best policy is adopted. I should hate to have to work under that constraint.'

'But you must have constraints of your own,' said Ming as she thought about what she knew of him.

His long training in the art of presenting balanced arguments on the most intricate aspects of defence policy had made him into not only a fluent talker but also a man able to subdue his own emotions in the interests of reason. Ming had never seen him angry or even impatient and, although that was one of the reasons why she felt so safe in his company, she occasionally wondered what he would be like if he let emotion rip.

'What were we talking about?' she asked when she saw him looking at her much more intently than before.

'Politics, and the Civil Service,' said Mark, pushing away his plate. 'I'd hate to leave the subject with your thinking that I'm pompous. I think the main reason I like the work so much is that it's interesting and I've some colleagues I both like and admire.'

The softness in Ming's dark blue eyes as she listened to him brought Mark quickly back to his real reason for being in her flat.

'Ming, there is something I need to ask you.'

'Yes, of course,' she said, taking her elbows off the table and sitting up straight again. 'You said so in your letter. What can I do for you?'

Mark licked his lower lip, took a breath and then laughed.

'I've rehearsed it so often that the words I'd planned to use sound all wrong,' he said.

Ming pushed herself further back in her red-painted Windsor chair. She had an inkling of what he was going to ask and wanted to stop him. Before she could do anything, he said with a whimsical smile that was supposed to disguise his anxiety:

'You see I very much want you to marry me.'

For a moment she could not say anything or even think. A kind of panic paralysed her mind. As it ebbed, she put her knife and fork tidily together on her egg-smeared plate, looked up at him and said quietly:

'Mark, I can't. It never occurred to me that you might be coming to ask something like that or I'd have told you straight away.'

'But ...' Before he could put words to his question, Ming rushed on.

'I thought we were just friends. When I saw you before I went away you seemed just as you always have done. And your letter was so ordinary. I would never ... I'm so sorry.'

Her distress was so obvious that Mark made himself ignore his own desperate feelings. He reached across the table and took one of her hands in his. Hers was icy cold.

'Ming,' he said, really upset. 'I never meant to worry you. Lots of people must have asked you that question at one time or another.'

'A few,' she began, 'but I've never ... I can't. ...'

'You're afraid, aren't you? You can't think that I would try to force you to do anything.' Mark found it hard to believe that the cheerful affectionate companion of the previous half hour could have put on such nervous stiffness just because she did not want to marry him.

'I don't think anything like that,' she said more firmly, letting him keep hold of her hand. In the circumstances she could hardly tell him that what frightened her most at that moment was the thought of losing his friendship.

'And it's not that I don't like you,' she said as directly as a child. 'I do – more, I think, than anyone else I've met. I trust you, too. If I could, Mark, I would marry you, but I can't.'

'And I thought we got on so well,' he said with spurious casualness, looking down at their clasped hands.

'We do,' said Ming, sounding almost despairing in her need for him to understand her. Marriage to Mark would solve many of her problems, and delight her difficult parents, but she could not bring herself to accept that the sisterly liking she felt for him was love, and she was not prepared to commit herself to anyone without loving him.

'Then why?' His question forced her to try to put into words some ideas about herself that she had never articulated before. She found it difficult.

'Because much as I'd like to, I don't love you,' she said by way of introduction. At the expression on his face, she felt impelled to add: 'I like you enormously, but there isn't any more to it than that.'

'I see,' said Mark.

He took his hand away. Ming winced; her instincts always ordered her to agree, to accept and to please people, but for once she disobeyed. 'I don't seem able to feel more than liking: not just for you but for everyone,' she said, trying to make him understand so that he would be less hurt.

'It's as though something was left out of my character ... perhaps there was some bad fairy at my christening.' She smiled, but there was neither amusement nor pleasure in her eyes.

Mark was watching her face again, his grey eyes intent and worried but not at all angry. When she stopped speaking, he said:

'I don't think any of that's true. You seem to me to be capable of enormous affection.'

'It's an illusion: all part of the bad fairy's gift,' Ming answered. She had never told anyone else what she really felt and was surprised at how difficult she found it.

'I can be kind to people and look after them, listen to them and mind about them, and they think that's love, but it isn't. I have tried to get it right and I can't. I feel as though – at thirty-one – I've only just discovered that I'm seriously handicapped.'

Mark sat in silence for a while, but then he stood up and walked round the pale grey table to hold out both hands to Ming, saying with determined cheerfulness:

'Handicapped or not, you're much the nicest person I know. Even if we can't be married we can still be friends, can't we?'

Ming accepted his hands and let him pull her up out of the red chair.

'I'd like it so much, but would you really?'

'Yes, Ming, I would like it.' He put one of his hands to her cheek. 'I'd be a fool to lose you – on whatever terms you set.'

She was astonished by his generosity and filled with gratitude. As though to prove that he could keep within the bounds of friendship, Mark insisted on staying to help her with the washing up.

When he had gone Ming retrieved the four pieces of Roger Sillhorne's unread letter from the wastepaper basket, extracted the letter itself from the envelope and pieced it together.

Ming,

I can't accept your prohibition on letters. We worked together for eight years and I've asked you to marry me. You owe me more than a cold letter telling me to leave you alone. If you felt like that why did you lead me to think that you wanted me? Why did you always smile at me and pretend? It's bloody unfair.

I miss you so much. Your successor smells of cheap face powder and can't deal with the constituents as you could. She's lazy and slummocky and I dislike her. Come back, Ming. If you won't marry me, at least come back to the office. I need you.

R.

The contrast between the two men could not have been more marked if they had belonged to different species. Mark's generosity gave Ming the confidence to tell Roger Sillhorne for the first time exactly what she meant:

Dear Roger,

My smiling at you in the office never constituted an invitation. I smile at bus conductors, too.

Your asking me to marry you gives you no rights over me.

My having worked for you for eight years gives you no rights over me either. You paid for my work. You did not pay for my lifelong devotion. It is not for sale.

I have told you that I cannot marry you. You and the constituency will have to find an alternative wife. Please do not write any more letters to me. If you do, I shall not read them.

Ming Alderbrook

She put the letter in an envelope, addressed and stamped it, and then burned Roger's in the empty grate. In all her life she had never been so blunt with anyone and she found herself shaking. But she decided that Connie was right: there was no immutable law that said that she had to swallow everything everyone else said to her and never show what it did to her.

On that thought, she went to deal with her unpacking, washing her stockings and sorting the rest of her clothes for the laundry and the dry cleaner's. For some reason she had always hated writing laundry lists and was half tempted to leave that chore to Mrs Crook, but she made herself do it and packed everything up in the laundry box for the van driver to collect on the following Monday morning.

When everything was in its place, Ming took the sheaves of notes she had written in Egypt back to her desk and set about trying to batter them into the shape of an article for Connie.

A week later she had rewritten the resulting piece six times and was still unhappy with it. In despair she telephoned Connie's partner, Max Hillary, and asked whether she could talk to him about it. She did not know him well, but, having read what he had written in the magazine, she was prepared to trust his judgement.

'Of course,' he said down the telephone. 'Any time. I'd love to see you. Connie says your cruise was quite entertaining.'

'Does she? I'm glad. I enjoyed most of it, but I'm surprised she didn't take against it after what happened to her.'

'She's tough,' said Max with a smile in his voice. 'Will you come down here?'

'Thank you, Max; I'd love to. Have you got troops of people staying at the moment or could I come right away? Connie wanted the article tomorrow and I just can't get it right. I don't want her to see it in this state.'

'Are you frightened of her?' Max's penetrating question made Ming laugh.

'No,' she said firmly, lying. 'But I don't want her to have to be kind about this – and she's far too kind to be honest. I need an honest opinion. Will you give it to me?'

'Yes,' he said, sounding absolutely serious for once. 'I can certainly promise to do that. Look, why not drive down now and stay overnight? That way we'll have plenty of time to get your article right and you can give it to her yourself when she comes here tomorrow morning.'

'May I really? That's sweet of you. I'll see you in a couple of hours then.'

'Drive carefully.'

'I will.' Ming put down the telephone and went to pack an overnight bag.

Max lived in a small seventeenth-century cottage on the

estate near Etchingham in Sussex that Connie had inherited on her elder sister's death. Taxes and Diana's huge bequest to Peter Suvarov had ensured that the big house and most of the land had had to be let, but Connie had kept the Dower House, in which she and her sister had lived during the war when the big house was requisitioned, several cottages and enough land for a market garden. That was run for her by a young graduate of Cirencester agricultural college who was by inclination a botanist. Connie took a considerable interest in his work and together they experimented with unusual fruit and vegetables and new varieties of the more familiar sort.

Ming reached the small estate after a slow crawl through the traffic that was leaving London for the south coast, and drove past the impeccably tidy rows of vegetables and salads to Max's cottage. When she knocked on the plain wooden front door, he flung it open and held out his hand to her.

He was a thin man of about fifty with a clever, serious face. Someone who did not know him might have put him down as a don were it not for the indefinable style of his shabby, well-cut clothes and an equally indescribable sense of withdrawal in him. His fine-featured face was lined and his light blue eyes could look as cold as steel when he was angry. Seeing Ming, they warmed and brightened.

'I've been so dull,' he confided as he ushered her into the drawing room. 'It's wonderful to see you. Connie's been away in London and won't be back until tomorrow and I've been working so hard I'm cross-eyed. Come on in.'

Ming stood in the doorway entranced. The drawing room was long and, despite its low ceiling and mullioned windows, it seemed to be filled with light, which fell on bowls of flowers, piles of typescript, stacks of magazines, pictures, old tapestry cushions and bits of Connie's huge collection of antique Delftware. Fires burned at both ends of the room and scented it with woodsmoke and warm ash.

Apart from various chairs and sofas swathed in pale loose-covers, the furniture was mostly well-polished oak. There was an oval gate-legged table at one end, at which

Max had obviously been working. Two pewter candlesticks and a blue-and-white bowl of late narcissi had been pushed to the farther edge, and his spectacles lay beside a neat heap of annotated typescript.

Oak bookshelves lined the walls between the windows and a variety of small coffers did duty as occasional tables and as supports for piles of books. What little could be seen of the walls was white, as were the plain cotton rep curtains, but the window-seats were upholstered in Delft blue and there was a variety of old rugs in different purplish-red tones on the polished floor.

It was a chaotic room but full of glorious things, and Ming felt immediately at ease in it.

'How lovely!' she said.

Max turned, pushing his grey hair away from his face, and smiled at her.

'I'd forgotten that you hadn't seen it before. It is nice ... but hellishly lonely sometimes.'

'Poor Max,' said Ming, wondering why he did not live in London.

'Would you like a drink?' he asked.

'I'd rather talk to you about this wretched article first,' she answered, and he laughed.

'Don't worry so much,' he said. 'I'll get you something to drink while I read it. It'll take me a minute or two to do that anyway. What would you like? What about sherry? It's nice and dry.'

'All right. Thank you.'

She drank it sitting in the corner of a sofa near one of the fires while Max read her work at the table. He seemed to take ages and Ming could not help listening for sighs of boredom or despair. She felt like a child waiting for a vaccination.

At last Max pushed back his chair. Ming got up from the sofa, but he made her sit down again and came to sit beside her, his spectacles pushed up on to his high forehead.

'You're right,' he said calmly. 'It won't do like this.'

'No, no. I realise that,' said Ming, her tongue tripping over the words in her haste to assure him that she had no inflated ideas of her own competence.

'Calm down. It won't do, but that doesn't mean that you can't change it. You were too tense when you wrote it. It reads as though you were writing a ... oh, I don't know: Perhaps a report for a sanitary inspector.'

'Thanks!' said Ming, regaining some of her sense of humour. Max grinned at her.

'That's better. After we've had lunch I'll bring down my typewriter for you to have another go. If I explain exactly what I want, will you try?'

Ming waited a moment before she agreed, and then after they had eaten a simple cold lunch, she did her best to carry out his instructions. She found it very difficult and wasted sheet after sheet of paper before she was prepared to let him see any of it.

He had shut the white curtains by then and switched on the lamps, before piling more logs on each of the fires. While he read, she walked up and down the long room, alternately rolling and stretching her shoulders to ease the stiffness out of them.

'Much better,' said Max after a while.

Ming breathed deeply, as though she had just swum forty feet under water.

'Really very much better. You need to do a bit more to this description of the egrets at Kom Ombo. Otherwise, apart from a little tidying up here and there, it'll do.' He smiled at her eager face. 'I like the old man in the high-heeled shoes.'

'I'm glad,' said Ming. 'Thank you for helping me, Max. I'd never have done it without you.'

'Well, it's not quite done yet,' he said, looking at his watch. 'Why don't you finish it now and I'll vanish into the kitchen to do something about supper for us.'

'Now, Max? You're a slave driver!' Ming's tone of voice was light, but it carried a genuine protest. She felt as though exhaustion had drained most of the blood out of her body, but she did what he wanted and was rewarded with both praise and a dish of superb *osso bucco*.

'So what's next?' said Max, piling up their plates and

offering Ming cheese and wrinkled apples.

'Next?' she asked, looking up from the apple she was peeling. 'What do you mean?'

'Didn't Connie talk to you about the next issue and what you might write for that?'

'No,' said Ming, her face pink with pleasure. 'No, she only asked me to do the Egypt piece. Do you mean that you think I ... ?'

'Yes. Connie does too. Even before you went on your trip she was talking about getting you to do something for us. You'd better stay on for tomorrow's editorial conference,' said Max with a smile that disconcerted Ming.

'That sounds a bit above my station.' She cut a piece out of her neatly peeled apple and began to eat.

'Not a bit. It's just Connie and me and a pot of coffee at eleven o'clock. Do stay. We need a fresh eye.'

'That's very kind of you, Max. Thank you.'

When she had finished the apple and complimented him on the *osso bucco*, which he had cooked quite as well as Flixe would have done, Ming asked Max how he and Connie had come to set up the magazine.

He looked at her with such a sardonic lift of his dark eyebrows that she realised she had broken some unspoken rule.

'It was an idle question,' she said quickly. 'I wasn't trying to pry into your friendship.'

Her innocent face and dark blue eyes looked so worried that he believed her and answered more fully with less implied reproof than he would otherwise have done.

'She was a friend of my wife,' he said, surprising Ming, who knew nothing of any wife, 'and she felt responsible for what happened – unnecessarily in my view – and once it was all over, she set about housing me and finding me something to do. I needed her help too much to reject it.'

'Oh,' said Ming, riven with curiosity but quite unable to ask any of the questions. Her mind ranged over car crashes, love affairs, suicide and all sorts of melodramas. Knowing that she could never ask Connie if she felt responsible for whatever happened, Ming thought of Peter Suvarov, who

always knew everything about everyone and could sometimes be persuaded to tell it.

Max watched her and wondered whether she could
possibly not have known his history. Aware that he was still
morbidly sensitive, he found it hard to believe that anyone
could have missed the newspaper reports and the subse-
quent gossip. On the other hand he knew Ming to be
honest and too gentle for her own good and he had been
horribly surprised that she should have asked such a
question.

CHAPTER 4

Connie arrived at precisely eleven the next morning, by which time Ming and Max had breakfasted and read through some of the immense bundle of newspapers and periodicals he had had delivered. Ming had been accustomed to reading the bulk of the serious press for Roger Sillhorne and marking anything he might need to know, but she had never seen such a range of trivial and highly specialised periodicals as the ones that Max took. Since she had also read through several back issues of his own magazine before she went to sleep the night before, she felt almost drunk with words and took a moment to focus on Connie's tall figure in the doorway. Max stood up at once, saying that he would make the coffee.

Although she was dressed in a comfortable old tweed skirt and a dark green twin-set, Connie had obviously had a new perm while she was in London and the shape of her hair did something to disguise the yellowing bruise that surrounded the cut on her forehead.

'How good to see you, Ming! How's the piece on Egypt coming along?'

'Finished at last. Max lashed me all yesterday to have it rewritten for today,' said Ming. 'He's asked me to sit in on your editorial meeting, but I really don't want to get in the way.'

'You won't,' said Connie briefly. She looked at Ming with a kind of helplessness that was quite foreign to her and added: 'It'll be good to have someone as a buffer to stop me telling Max how near the brink we are.'

'I don't understand. I thought people spoke very well of the magazine.'

'They do.' Connie's mouth twisted. 'But admiration doesn't pay the printer. We're not selling nearly as many copies as I'd expected and it's all costing more than I had planned. I simply can't afford to keep the magazine going for much longer than two or three more issues unless we can bring in more from subscriptions and the advertisers.'

She suddenly gripped the bridge of her nose as though she had a bad headache. Ming waited, not sure whether to offer comfort or comment, or just keep quiet.

'And I need to keep it going,' said Connie when she looked up again.

Ming wondered why. Connie had plenty of other things to do and her interest in the magazine was clearly not profit. She breathed carefully as though to quell a rising panic.

'Don't tell Max. I don't want him to have to worry about it, since there's nothing he can do. I'll tell him that we need you because you're just the age we're aiming at. In fact you would be the ideal person to persuade your contemporaries to take the magazine. Might you be prepared to try to drum up subscriptions for us?'

'Yes,' said Ming, almost before she had thought about it. Selling Connie's magazine seemed a more alluring prospect than standing in the street selling flags for a charity or getting up bazaars for her mother's friends, which were the only other jobs she had been offered.

'We can't pay you much,' Connie began, but Ming interrupted her before she had a chance to finish her sentence.

'Don't worry about that. I've got Anna Kingsley's money, which is far more than I need, and you clearly need all yours at the moment.'

'You are sweet,' said Connie.

Ming smiled and straightened her shoulders. 'Then I'll do whatever I can for whatever you can afford to pay me for the moment and then if the circulation improves, you can pay me more and perhaps I could even put in a bit of capital. If things don't get any better, you can wash out any idea of owing me anything.'

'Ming, you ...' Connie hesitated.

The younger woman looked so puzzled and so willing that Connie was filled with the kind of protectiveness that Ming's sisters displayed all too obviously.

'I have been determined to make you less good-natured so that fewer people will exploit you, and here I am joining the crowd.' Connie sighed and pushed the heavy dark hair away from her forehead. Ming saw how badly bruised she was and how painful the jagged-edged cut must still be.

'But I need you too much to refuse your offer. Keep a note of your expenses and I'll reimburse those, and obviously pay you for any articles you write, and ... Ah, Max,' Connie added in a cooler voice as she looked up and saw him, 'Ming has just agreed to become our subscriptions manager.'

'Wonderful news!' Max put down the heavy tray on a low oak chest and picked up the pewter coffee pot. 'White for you, Connie?'

'Yes, please.'

'How was your meeting yesterday?'

'Interesting.' Connie accepted a large blue-and-white cup from Max and added two lumps of sugar. Stirring the coffee, she turned to Ming. 'I went to talk to one of the account managers who takes quite a lot of our space to find out what we ought to do to get more women to buy the magazine. He introduced me to the psychiatrist who advises the agency, and ...'

'What?' said Ming, too startled to notice that she was interrupting. 'A psychiatrist in advertising?'

Max poured Ming a cup of coffee and then one for himself.

'Yes. Apparently most of the big agencies are using people like him now. In America they call them "motivational researchers". They're needed to advise on the best way to push people into buying things. Without some mental manipulation it seems that no one would ever buy anything.'

'Come on, Connie. Don't exaggerate,' said Max, looking amused. 'Buying things is a natural human instinct. No one needs to be pushed into it.'

'Well, they definitely do need to be forced to buy the magazine,' said Connie, sounding irritable enough to make Ming wince.

It seemed to have no such effect on Max, who sat peacefully drinking his coffee. Connie turned to Ming.

'You see, we need to make more intelligent, married women aware of our existence and persuade them to subscribe. I am absolutely convinced that there are plenty of them who would like what we're trying to produce, but we haven't reached them yet.'

'Part of the difficulty must be that the women you most want are spending what little money they have on their homes and children,' said Ming slowly. There was more that she wanted to say, but she felt too uncertain of her position to start criticising.

Connie's rather hard, handsome face was transfigured by a smile of mixed ruefulness and satisfaction.

'That's rather what the advertising man said, and his suggestion was to make the women feel guilty about losing touch with "the world beyond the nursery". He said that that's how all the most successful advertisements work. You make the potential customer feel unsafe so that she buys security with your product.'

'How horrible!' As the other two laughed at her exclamation, Ming felt absurdly naïve and was glad that she had said no more.

For the next hour she sat in silence, listening to Max and Connie in growing frustration. They discussed the recent news and talked about commissioning articles on all sorts of subjects from the proposals for a common market in Europe to the significance of the mixed reviews of *Look Back in Anger*; from the cost of Grace Kelly's wedding to Prince Rainier of Monaco to the recent state visit of Krushchev and Bulganin to Britain and the strange disappearance of

Commander Crabbe, who might or might not have been murdered by the Russians as he dived beneath their ships in Portsmouth Harbour.

Listening to them, Ming felt increasingly sure of one reason why they were having trouble selling the magazine, but the memory of their mockery and the knowledge of her inexperience in their world kept her quiet. After a while, Max noticed her stillness and a certain stubborn twist to her gentle mouth.

'What's up?' he said. 'Something's the matter, Ming. What is it?'

Connie turned her dark head to look impatiently at Ming.

'Aren't you feeling well?' she asked in irritable concern.

'I'm feeling perfectly all right,' answered Ming. 'It's just ... well, don't you think that all the things you're talking about are a bit uninteresting?'

Connie's dark eyebrows closed over the top of her nose and her mouth tightened. Max tilted his head to one side.

'Uninteresting how?' he asked. 'International relations, domestic politics, the first new directions in the theatre for a generation: they're all fairly important subjects, you know.'

'Yes, I know they are.' Having started to speak, Ming knew that she was going to have to explain herself, however much she irritated the others. She remembered the advice Connie had given her in Egypt and spoke as steadily as she could.

'But they've all been written about in every newspaper and most of the other magazines that touch on anything more than knitting patterns and ... and how to make cheap jam for the nursery.'

'That's a fair point, Connie,' said Max with a laugh that made him seem much younger than usual. 'Go on, Ming.'

'Well,' she said, crossing one slim leg over the other and leaning forward in her eagerness to make them understand what she meant, 'you've said that the whole point of the magazine is to make young married women realise that there is a world beyond the nursery.'

'Precisely!' said Connie. 'Several worlds in fact: of

politics, science, the arts and so on. That's why we're tackling all those sorts of subjects so that our readers are better informed. And our articles are not the same as all the others; we're producing serious analysis, not news.'

'Yes, I know, but people can get most of it from the news-papers or the wireless. The problem isn't that women don't know there are all those worlds out there, but that they're cut off from them. Isn't there some way of showing them how to join in?'

Connie got out of her chair and paced in front of the fire. With an expression of exaggerated patience on her long face, she started to speak.

'Ming, we're in the business of widening people's mental horizons, not listing advertisements for vacancies in offices.'

Trying not to let Connie's biting voice make her sound defensive, Ming said carefully:

'I do understand that. Please don't be angry, Connie. I'm not being deliberately obtuse. Listen: the articles I've read so far are intelligent and important but rather worthy – if you see what I mean – and a bit austere. I think they'd appeal more if they were more fun. I don't mean comical, but entertaining and even a bit controversial.'

'Thank you,' said Connie with cold sarcasm. 'I'm glad you think that they're intelligent.'

Looking up at the older woman, Ming began to wish that she had never started on her protest. She liked Connie and they had always got on well with each other, but her anger was making Ming feel wobbly. She looked at Max and saw a smile of pure amusement on his thin face, which helped.

'Don't intimidate her, Connie,' he said. 'I think she's got a point.' Ming smiled gratefully at him.

'Oughtn't the magazine to be going behind the scenes and showing how things are orchestrated?' She looked back to her long years assisting Roger Sillhorne. 'Most of us just carry on through our lives doing as we've been taught and putting up with things we don't like because they're "facts of life". Couldn't the magazine do something about that? Show who has the power, for example, and how they got it?

What happens if they abuse it and who controls it and therefore who controls us all?'

Max got up to fetch the coffee pot, which was keeping warm in the hearth, and poured more into each of their cups. Sitting back in his chair he drank. There was a gleam in his grey eyes that had not been there earlier in the morning.

'For example,' said Ming, her face increasingly pink with enthusiasm, 'what about an article on the way the advertisers are using psychology to manipulate us all into feeling guilty and buying their stuff? Wouldn't that be more useful – and more interesting – than yet another analysis of the balance of trade and what the government plans to do about it?'

'Perhaps,' said Connie, slowly getting over her surprise that her pliant and gentle protégée was making so fundamental a criticism of her ideas. 'But it's important that we write seriously for our women readers. It would be a disaster if we started to write down to them and assumed that their only interests were jam and knitting.'

'Yes, but there's more to life than international relations.' With a vivid memory of the power that her inheritance had given her Ming went on: 'What about money? That's crucial and jolly interesting, too.'

Connie went back to her chair and sat down in silence.

'What about starting with a series of interviews, say, with women who were earning large amounts of money, to show that it is possible?' Ming went on.

Max looked amused but Connie clearly disapproved.

'Isn't that rather vulgar?'

Ming flushed slightly at the disdain in Connie's voice, but she stood her ground.

'Money is considered vulgar only by those who have plenty and therefore don't need to think about it or those who haven't quite enough and therefore can't bear to think about it.'

'Perhaps.' Connie still looked unconvinced.

She took her gold cigarette case out of her bag and offered it to the other two. Ming shook her head. Since her illness she had lost the taste for smoking. But Max took a cigarette.

'It's certainly true, Connie, that without money one is also quite without power,' said Max, no longer amused. 'With it, worlds do open. And it would mark out the magazine as being different from any other around.'

'I suppose it's a possibility, but I had certainly never considered money as being a particularly desirable subject for the magazine.'

'Perhaps because you've always had it,' said Max. 'The only difficulty that I can see, Ming, is whether there are enough women earning significant amounts to make a series.'

She sat up straighter. 'The only way we'll discover that is by looking for them. And there are other financial things we could tackle, too. For instance all this criticism from the church about premium bonds and how they'll turn the people of this country into gamblers.'

'Yes?' Max looked interested but sceptical. 'So what?'

'Well, think of the Church of England's investments. All that money in blue chips is being gambled on the prospect of the shares' value rising. If that's good enough for the church, why shouldn't the populace have a go too? I detest hypocrisy.' All the energy was back in Ming's voice and she no longer looked tentative.

Max roared with laughter and even Connie's set lips relaxed enough to twitch into a smile.

'Bravo!'

'All right,' said Connie, taking the necessary decision. She tapped the ash off her cigarette into a flat pewter dish that Max used as an ashtray. 'You'd better try to discover some suitable women, Ming. If you can find anyone, we can discuss it later. It might offend people, but ...' She broke off.

'But, we have to be prepared to do that,' said Max, watching them both with a sardonic look in his light eyes. 'Otherwise we might just as well be publishing – what was it you said, Ming? – knitting patterns and recipes for cheap jam for the nursery.'

Ming laughed in relief. On the few occasions when she had met Max in the past he had seemed cool and rather difficult; she had never expected him to take her part or to have a sense of humour.

'Very well,' said Connie. 'What else, Ming? You seem to have some surprisingly radical ideas.'

There was still enough sarcasm in Connie's voice to make Ming want to shrivel into the depths of her chair.

'I haven't any more at the moment,' she said, lying but determined not to cause any more trouble.

For the rest of the morning she merely listened as Max and Connie went through the books publishers had sent them, deciding which ones should be reviewed and by whom. Just as the small grandfather clock struck one, Connie shuffled her papers together and stood up.

'That's that, then. Ming, you'll draft something on your advertising idea and look for women earning high salaries. Now, we'd better leave you in peace, Max. Coming, Ming?'

Obedient, but a little reluctant to face Connie's wrath without the support of Max's amused peacemaking, Ming went to fetch her luggage and then said goodbye to Max.

As soon as she had shut Max's front door behind them, Connie said abruptly:

'You're looking much better, Ming.'

'Thank you. I didn't mean to be tiresome in there.'

Connie smiled and shook her head.

'You weren't. It was a fair point and gutsy of you to stick to it. I don't know that I entirely agree with you about the dull worthiness of what we've been publishing, but I do see what you mean. I'm sorry if I sounded obstructive. Now, I think I'd better give you some lunch,' she said.

'That's sweet of you,' said Ming, feeling too tired to stand up for anything at all any more, 'but I ought to get back to London. I'm having dinner at Flixe's tonight and I need to have my hair washed.'

'All right. I'll walk with you to your car,' said Connie, tucking a hand in Ming's arm. When they were well out of earshot of the cottage, she added: 'Ming, can I ask you not to talk to anyone about Max? He doesn't sign all the things he writes for us and it would be better if it were not generally known that he plays such a large part in the magazine.'

'Certainly, but why?'

Ming was surprised to see her friend's face flush as though with embarrassment or perhaps anger. After a long silence, Connie eventually said:

'There are a lot of people who disapprove of him – mainly people who don't know him – and so it's better that his connection with the magazine is played down.'

Suppressing the obvious question because Connie seemed so reluctant to talk, Ming loyally assured her that she would say nothing to anyone of Max's presence at the meeting or the part he played in the magazine.

As she drove back to London, stopping at a café for a sandwich and another cup of coffee about half-way, Ming could not help speculating about Max and the part he and Connie played in each other's lives.

That evening Ming changed into a suitable little black dress and drove round to her sister's big, comfortable house in Kensington.

Peter Suvarov opened the door when she rang the bell and kissed her. He looked almost exactly the same as he had done when she had come round in her hospital bed during the Blitz and seen him for the first time. There were deeper lines on his face and his hair was more heavily streaked with grey, but his glinting dark eyes were the same, and his beautifully shaped mouth, which could look wholly generous one moment and frighteningly bitter the next, had not changed at all. He was as slim as he had been then, and few people would have realised his true age.

Before she could say anything he urged her into the drawing room.

'You're looking a lot less washed-out than before the cruise,' he said. 'It must have helped, despite the unfortunate incident. I'm glad.'

'Thank you,' she said, smiling up at him. Cynical she might have become, but his approval still warmed her and he could still make her feel enveloped in protection. Looking around the big drawing room, she was relieved to find that no other guests had arrived and that Flixe herself was still cooking or dressing.

Peter poured her a gin and tonic and settled down to ask about Egypt. He watched her over the rim of his whisky glass, enjoying the renewed brightness in her eyes and the lift to her lips. Thinking that she looked as lovely as she had as a girl, but a lot more interesting, he listened to her descriptions.

'Why did you choose Egypt in the first place?' he asked when she had finished. 'It always seemed odd when you could have gone to all sorts of good – and safer – places at this end of the Mediterranean.'

'Oh, it was my father's idea,' she said, sipping her drink. 'He wanted me to see it before the last of our troops leave this summer. It's been so much part of his life that he can't really bear the thought that it doesn't actually belong to the British Army. I don't think it occurred to him that there could be trouble – or that Connie and I might actually be stoned. Doesn't it sound biblical?'

Peter thought that he heard the faintest hint of sarcasm in Ming's voice.

'And you did what he wanted, just like that?' His mouth twisted as he spoke, but his eyes were quite kind. Ming nodded.

'It seemed easier,' she said after a while. 'It usually is. And I didn't really care where I went. The doctors said I had to go somewhere warm and dry. What did it matter? And I suppose I was quite curious. I have a few random memories of coming back from India through the Suez Canal, but as I was only three then, they don't mean much. I'm glad to have seen it – and even to have seen all that bottled-up rage exploding.'

She drank and then added: 'I hated that, but in an odd way I identified ...'

Peter watched her with a faint smile in his eyes. It reminded her how easy it was to confide in him and how much she still needed to protect herself against him.

'In any case,' she said hurriedly, 'it was well worth it. I enjoyed the trip and we saw lots of lovely places.'

'Good. Ming . . .'

'Who's Flixe producing for my inspection this evening?' she asked before he could put his question into words.

At that Peter laughed, ignored what he had been going to say and leaned forward to kiss her cheek.

'I keep telling her to stop it,' he said, 'but she likes doing it, and I know you're too strong-minded to succumb to the wrong one. You are, aren't you, Ming?'

'Oh, I think so,' she said, laughing with him.

'Mingie, darling!'

Flixe's voice from the door made Ming push herself up from the downy depths of the sofa.

'Hello, Flixe,' she said. 'You look glorious. Aren't you even feeling sick?'

'Certainly not,' said Flixe, smoothing the violet silk dress down over her still-slim waist. 'Only Andrew made me the least bit sick. I'll get tired later on and my wretched ankles will swell, but I feel wonderful now. How are you?'

She looked so anxiously at her sister that Ming held her off with a hand against her shoulder.

'I'm perfectly all right again now,' she said firmly. 'Something smells superb. What are you cooking?'

'*Bœuf bourguignon*,' said Flixe. 'But never mind that. I've asked a frightfully nice stockbroker this evening, and he ought to be here any minute now. He's called Charles Bederley and he's much brighter than a lot of them, so don't dismiss him just because he's in the City.'

Ming promised that she would behave, which made Peter Suvarov smile because in all the years he had known her she had never been anything but impeccably polite.

Later, as they were all sitting around the candlelit table eating Flixe's casserole, he watched in increasing amusement as Ming cross-examined the young man about his work, his clients, his own opportunities for making money, and the possibilities of women doing the same job. At that question the young man laughed and laid down his knife and fork.

'I shouldn't have thought they'd want to,' he said. 'The Stock Exchange is a cross between a bear garden and a prep. school. Much better stay at home and spend the profits. Hah! Hah!'

Peter Suvarov, who had been listening without contributing anything to the conversation, watched Ming's face in the dim but mellow light of the six white candles and saw her delicate features harden. Interested in the measurable changes in her, he wondered what Constance Wroughton could have been saying to her in Egypt and decided that it was time to take part again.

'Have you been reading *Le Deuxième Sexe*, Ming?' he asked with a smile.

'Not for ages,' she said, turning away from the stockbroker to face her brother-in-law. 'I bought a copy in Paris years ago, but I never managed to stagger through more than about a third of it, although I did read the conclusion. Did you ever read it, Flixe?'

'I browsed through the translation when it was first published here. My French isn't up to the original. I found quite a lot in it that interested me – relations between mothers and daughters mainly.'

'Ah yes,' said Ming, who had been an unhappy witness to some quite vicious arguments both her elder sisters had had with their mother. 'I think the things that stuck in my mind the most were her pointing out that girls are brought up never to expect to take responsibility for themselves and that Balzac advised men to treat women as slaves while persuading them that they are queens.'

'Oh, I say,' protested Charles Bederley with a jolly laugh. 'Isn't that going a bit far? I mean, hardly any men nowadays treat women as slaves. It's the other way round, really. My poor brother-in-law beavers away at his job while my sister swans around buying things – and criticises him for not making enough money.'

'Poor him,' said Ming with her usual sweet smile. Charles Bederley was quite deceived by it and smiled back in warm approval until she added: 'What did your sister do before they were married?'

'She was at Central Office for a bit; you might have known her. Sarah Bederley.'

'I think I do remember her. Very efficient and well thought of. Why did she stop?'

'She got married,' he said as though talking to a rather stupid child.

'And so,' said Ming, feeling as though something in her brain might swell and swell until it split her skull if she did not get it out in words first, 'although you resent the idea of women "swanning around spending money earned by men" you assume that they will give up their own jobs and salaries on marriage. That seems rather unfair.'

'Ming!' said Flixe crossly before Charles Bederley could bring himself to answer.

Before Ming could either protest or justify herself, Charles, who was finding it hard to equate her slender figure and extreme prettiness with her ideas, asked her whether she worked.

'As you know, I used to be a secretary in the House of Commons,' she said as calmly as though the little scene had never happened. She felt ashamed of her small outburst but was still too angry to make herself apologise. 'And then I had to leave when I was rather ill. I'm just setting off on a new career – I hope – as a journalist.'

'Ming! What good news,' said Flixe. 'Writing for Connie's magazine? That's terrific. What are you going to do?'

'Oh, a variety of things,' said Ming, having scooped up the last of her beef. 'Possibly television reviews when I've bought a television; the odd political piece; and I want to do something on women and money ...'

'Oh, I see,' said Charles Bederley, sounding relieved, 'no wonder you're in a state about women spenders.'

'Hardly a state,' said Ming, 'but I do worry that so few women are in control of anything more than pocket money. I want to write about women who make it for themselves, only I don't know any.'

'I don't think I do, either,' he said. 'Of course we've got lady clients with family money.'

'There's always Julia,' said Flixe, getting up to fetch the

pudding, while her husband cleared the plates. 'She makes quite a lot at the Bar. Why not go and talk to her? Her children are growing up most peculiar,' she added over her shoulder. 'I really don't think it can be good for them to have a mother who is so preoccupied with other things even when she can spend time with them at home.'

Left alone with Charles, Ming pre-empted any more argument by asking him whether he was planning to go abroad in the summer and talking about Egypt. He found travel a much easier subject to discuss than the right of women to be taken seriously and by the time Peter was handing round plates and Flixe was offering a chocolate-and-chestnut pudding Charles had relaxed.

When they had finished the pudding Flixe whisked Ming up to her bedroom for a gossip while the two men drank their port. Ming, determined to forestall any criticism of her attack on Charles Bederley, asked Flixe about Julia.

Interested, as always, in working out why people behaved as they did and the effect their behaviour had on themselves and their families, Flixe described her friend's career and the deleterious effect it was having on her two children.

'I always rather liked her husband,' said Ming, who had known him slightly when she worked in the House of Commons. They had not often met because David Wallington was a member of the Labour Party, but they had occasionally run into each other in the corridors.

'It must be difficult for him having a working wife,' said Flixe, 'particularly in that world, where wives have such a big part to play.'

Ming laughed.

'I don't suppose there are many garden fêtes to open in south London,' she said. 'Look here, hadn't we better go down? I can't imagine poor old Peter wanting to spend hours with that pompous young man.'

Flixe raised her smooth eyebrows and shrugged.

'I did so hope you'd like him,' she said. 'You are horribly picky, you know. And you're missing out on such a lot.'

Ming only smiled. It was not a subject she was prepared to discuss with her sister.

'By the way,' said Flixe as she reached the door of her bedroom, 'have you been injected against polio yet?'

'No. I thought there was only enough of the vaccine for children so far.'

'There isn't even enough for all of them yet,' said Flixe drily, 'but that's on the Health Service. You can get it privately. I do think you ought.'

'I probably will in the end, but there's no real urgency.' Ming stopped for a second to look at her reflection in the long pier-glass by the door and twitched the hem of her straight-cut black dress.

'Haven't you heard about Caroline Hazeldene?'

Flixe's voice distracted Ming from her critical appraisal of her own reflection and she turned round at once.

'No. She hasn't got it, has she?'

'She had it,' said Flixe slowly. 'She died last week.'

Ming put a hand against the wall, feeling suddenly dizzy.

'Poor Jack,' she said, thinking of the man she had known since childhood. 'He loved her so. Oh, Flixe, it's too cruel. They've only been married four years.'

'I know; it's ghastly. And there are the children, too. He'll have to bring them back from Cyprus and if he stays in the army they'll have to be parked with one or other lot of grandparents. It doesn't really bear thinking about.'

As they went silently downstairs to join the men in the drawing room, Ming thought about Jack Hazeldene. His father had been in the same regiment as hers and since the two families had shared many of the same postings they had seen a lot of each other. Ming and her twin had played with Jack, ridden with him, danced with him and grown up with him, almost as though he had been their brother.

Since the war her life had diverged from his and they had met less often, but she still minded about him. The thought of what he must be feeling horrified her.

Ming was still abstracted when they reached the drawing room and she sat on the sofa beside Charles Bederley without speaking. Puzzled but still impressed by her lovely face, he set himself to charm and entertain her. She did her best to reciprocate, but his assumption that as a woman she would be both predictable and uninterested in anything much beyond her own social life irritated her more and more until she snapped at him.

When he had said goodbye and left the house, Flixe took Ming to task for being 'beastly' to him, and making him feel uncomfortable.

'I'm sorry,' said Ming. 'I didn't mean to do that. I was thinking about poor Jack and that must have made me angry. But it was a nice party, Flixe. Thank you.'

'Are you all right?' her sister asked, helping Ming into her coat. 'You don't seem yourself at all.'

'To tell you the truth,' said Ming, settling her shoulders into the coat and doing up the big black buttons, 'I am beginning to believe that I have never yet been myself.'

'Hurrah!' said Peter from the drawing-room doorway. Flixe turned round and made a face at him. He grinned at her, shook his greying head and said: 'Keep it up, Ming.'

She also turned to look at him, her fair head framed in the big, upturned collar of her black coat. Watching his saturnine face, she remembered that he had always known more about her than anyone else and she walked back down the hall to kiss him.

'Goodbye, Peter,' she said.

'Goodbye, my dear. It's wonderful to see you breaking out of the chrysalis. Don't let anyone try to make you stay inside.'

Ming laughed.

'I'll try not to, but I hope the butterfly turns out at least to be a painted lady and not just a cabbage white after all this time.'

CHAPTER 5

The first thing that Ming did the next morning was to write to Jack Hazeldene. It took her hours to produce a letter that was neither sickeningly sentimental nor too cold to show him how much she sympathised with him, but eventually she found a way to put what she really felt into words and hoped that he would understand.

The letter written and posted to the British Forces Post Office in Cyprus, she set to work for Connie and Max, telephoning all her old friends and acquaintances to find out whether they could introduce her to any successful professional women who might help with her article. She also took the opportunity to tell each friend about the magazine and tried to persuade them all to subscribe.

Ming knew perfectly well that to get enough new orders she would have to range far beyond her own circle, but she thought it would be useful to hear the reactions of people she liked before she drafted any press-releases or advertisements.

One or two of her friends agreed to take the magazine at once but others not surprisingly wanted to see what they would be buying and so Ming went to lunch or tea with them, taking back issues with her and explaining the ways in which the new version would be different. During her first two visits Ming stressed the magazine's power to alleviate the boredom that all her friends agreed was an inevitable part of the life of a mother at home with small children, but she quickly discovered her mistake.

'Oh, I can see that it would,' said one of her friends with immense feeling. 'And I could really do with it, but we just couldn't afford it, Ming. Four bob a month! John hardly makes a thousand a year and we're going to need every bit for school fees. I'll have to get it from the library. Do all libraries have it yet?'

Making a mental note to find that out from Connie, Ming revised her plans and at the next house she visited she reluctantly followed the advertising psychologist's advice.

'You see, Serena,' she said to an old school friend, who was anxiously trying to teach her eighteen-month-old son to build a tower of coloured wooden bricks while a red-headed four-year-old rampaged at the other end of the nursery, 'I know how easy it is to get cut off. Flixe is so busy with her brood these days that she hardly even knows who's in the Cabinet, let alone what is going on abroad or who's writing or painting the best things now. The magazine will have lots of political articles as well as the arts.'

The baby, whose bright dark eyes and wide smile had made Ming want to pick him up and cuddle him, suddenly lost his temper with the red and green bricks he was trying to balance and hit them down on his half-built tower.

'I'm not surprised she's cut off,' said Serena just as four blocks tumbled to the floor. 'No, Robin, not like that. Put it on carefully. No, if you hit it, you'll knock all the others down. Try again.'

His cheerful face trembled and then creased and he let out a roar of frustration.

'It's all right; don't get cross. Mummy will help build it up.'

Serena raised her head again, pushing her lank, unwaved hair behind her ears. Watching the effort she was making with her younger child, Ming realised exactly why she looked so tired.

'I occasionally try to read serious books, but by the time I've put them both to bed and dealt with supper I'm worn out. I sometimes wonder if our mothers weren't more sensible having nannies for us,' Serena said.

Before Ming could answer the elder boy uttered a war
cry, seized the striped curtains and swung himself in a
wide arc to crash against the radiator and collapse in a heap
on the floor. Serena left Robin in Ming's care and went to
attend to Eric.

Ming tried to mop up his tears and then to help with the
building, but her efforts were spurned and so she simply
waited for Serena's return.

'I don't know,' Ming said then. 'Flixe has frequent arguments with friends who have nannies because she thinks
that nannied children tend to be slower, besides being
damaged by not having enough maternal attention. She's
an avid reader of people like Dr Spock and John Bowlby,
you see.'

Ming watched the two lively, bright-eyed but tiresome
boys who were absorbing so much of her friend's attention.
Smiling slightly, she added: 'Perhaps she's right: the
children I've seen with nannies are much duller than yours.'

'Are they? That's something I suppose. But doing it
oneself does mean one gets so boring. Sometimes when
George comes home wanting intelligent conversation to
amuse him after the office I can hardly string two words
together and all I want to tell him is what happened in the
fish queue and how infuriating the boys have been all day.
And,' Serena added, looking almost demented, 'the most
infuriating thing is that as soon as they see him they behave
angelically and he assumes that it's been my fault all day
that they've been unspeakable. Of course I do love them.'

'Of course you do,' said Ming, seeing for the first time
exactly how much guilt there was in such women for advertisers to use. She suppressed her instinctive desire to
comfort her old friend and said: 'But *The World Beyond* isn't
a book – it's a slim magazine and it has a vast amount of
interesting stuff in it. You'd ...'

Eric threw a fluffy duck straight at the fire. The duck
bounced off the wire guard and landed in the shaky tower.
Almost before Robin had noticed it, Serena whisked it
away.

'That's my duck,' said the child.

'I know, Robin. And I'm keeping it safe for you. See, here it is in the chair.' Over his head she raised her shaggy eyebrows. 'You see, Ming?'

'I see.' Ming's answer was quite sincere. 'I can't imagine how you ever have time to do anything else at all.'

Robin, bored with his building at last, heaved himself to his feet, grabbed the duck from his mother's chair and carried it carefully towards the other side of the room. His red-haired brother was investigating the inner workings of some clockwork toy he had found in his toybox.

'But at least if I did manage to read your mag. I'd have something to talk about apart from nappies and potty training ... Robin, no! Come away from the fire. Eric, stop that; you'll break it. You must be careful. Here, come and help Robin build his tower again. Sorry, Ming.'

'It's a shame to distract you, Serena. I'm probably making them more rumbustious than they would otherwise be. I'll leave you in peace.'

'God no! Don't go. It's wonderful to have an adult to talk to. You can't imagine how I long for one. Day after day, walking round the park and coming back to this,' said Serena. 'I must say, I do think perhaps I'd better take your magazine. I might even have something to discuss at the rare dinner parties we go to. Would I have to commit myself for a whole year?'

Ming shook her fair head, feeling a sickly mixture of guilt and triumph. Having made her first sale face-to-face, she stayed to drink a cup of tea. Before she left she asked her friend to write to the magazine whenever she disagreed with any of the opinions in it and to Ming herself if she thought of subjects she would like to have covered in it.

'We need to know, you see. Otherwise we're just guessing what would be interesting, because none of us has children or knows quite what it's like to be stuck at home with them. And we don't always agree with each other's guesses; but perhaps I shouldn't say that.'

'All right,' said Serena, holding her younger son back from the open front door by his collar. 'Have you written to Rosie?'

'Rosie?'

'Yes, you know. Miss Roseheath from school. She always adored you; I'm sure she'd take a subscription for herself – and probably the school too. And she could talk about it to parents and leavers, which might help.'

'Good heavens! Is she still there? I'd have thought that she would have moved on to something more interesting years ago,' said Ming, remembering things that she had not thought about for years.

'She's headmistress now – quite a lot of power – and doing great things for the school. If we ever have a girl, I'll definitely send her there. I must go and get these creatures bathed. It was lovely to see you, Ming. I'm sorry I look such a wreck.'

'You look like a woman struggling to keep two voracious children occupied,' said Ming with obvious admiration in her voice. She kissed her friend and said goodbye.

Ming went straight from that meeting in her friend's nursery to one with Julia Wallington in chambers, which produced a contrast that made Ming ache with sympathy for Serena.

Julia, who had not been in court at all that day, was dressed in a plain suit of some smooth indigo-coloured cloth and a heavy cream silk shirt. Her hair was pinned back into a neat roll and her makeup was so discreet that it was almost invisible. She too looked tired, but, unlike Serena, manifestly in command and rather frightening.

Julia seemed to approve of what Ming was trying to do with her articles for *The World Beyond* and answered most of her questions about the money that women could earn in the professions and the difficulties they tended to encounter at the bar. Ming, who had never known her well, was very careful in the questions that she put at the beginning of the interview and was pleasantly surprised by Julia's frankness.

As they talked the questions became more searching and Julia's answers both longer and more interesting. The more they discussed Julia's work and its rewards and costs, the more Ming admired her and the more she wanted to know, but there were some questions about its effect on her family life that Ming did not think she could possibly ask.

The article began to take shape in her mind as she worked around those difficult points and Julia's encouragement gave her the confidence to believe that she would be able to write it in a way that would satisfy Connie and yet avoid all the worthiness that Ming had disliked so much in the magazine's first few issues. When she got up to go, thanking Julia for giving her so much time, Julia stood up too, saying:

'Try not to give the impression that it's easy, won't you?'

Ming stood with a hand on the door knob, surprised.

'I don't mean that I'm exceptional or anything vain like that,' Julia went on with a smile that made her look much more approachable, 'but it wouldn't be fair to make your readers think it's easy. It's tough for anyone and for women it is still very much harder than for men. It would be irresponsible not to point that out. All right?'

'Yes,' said Ming. 'I quite see that. Thank you for all your help.'

'It was a pleasure. I like the idea of your magazine and I'll do what I can to get it better known,' she said, adding: 'Flixe is right, you know.'

'In what?' asked Ming, wondering what on earth was coming. Julia smiled again.

'She once said that you've a great gift of sympathy and I see what she meant. You can make one feel that you know exactly where the scars are and that you'd never poke them. That is both rare and valuable, particularly in your profession.' She raised her hand in farewell and even before Ming had crossed the threshold, Julia had gone back to the brief on which she was working.

Inspired by her example and approval, Ming worked extremely hard for the rest of the week, both planning her two articles and pursuing possible subscribers. She used the same technique of persuasion in person, on the telephone and in letters, and by Friday had taken firm orders from twenty women. It was a start, but it depressed her: she needed thousands of new subscribers, not merely tens.

Sorting through the immense piles of paper on her desk,

she came upon the heap of letters from her mother's friends that had accumulated while she was in Egypt. Guiltily aware that she had not answered any of them, Ming quickly wrote to each woman to explain why she was unable to take up the kind offer of work for charity because she had a full-time job, and then went on to try to sell them the magazine. Most of the women to whom she was writing were well beyond the age range that was Connie's target, but it seemed worth trying.

Ming also wrote to her old teacher, to the headmistresses of a number of other girls' schools, and to the various women's colleges at the universities asking whether they would be prepared to let her have lists of their graduates or at least include a leaflet about the magazine whenever they sent out material.

By that stage she was well on the way to composing an impersonal letter that could be duplicated in hundreds to save time and would allow her to add a personal post-script where it was appropriate. While she was typing out a fair copy of it, she heard the flap of the letter box and went out into the hall to pick up her post. There was a gratifying number of envelopes and she carried them back to her desk, hoping that several would contain subscriptions. Before she could open any of them, the telephone rang.

Ming answered and heard Mark Sudley sounding oddly tentative as he asked her how she was. Ming smiled at the sound of his voice, delighted that he still wanted to talk to her.

'I'm very well. Hard at work again and really revelling in it. What about you?'

'Not half bad,' he said. 'I was wondering whether I could persuade you to come and see *Salad Days* with me. I seem to remember your saying you hadn't seen it yet. Perhaps we could have some dinner in Soho first. Would you like that?'

'Very much indeed,' she answered truthfully. 'I've missed you.'

'Really? Good. How would next Tuesday suit you?'

'Tuesday's tricky, actually, because I have to go down to Etchingham. Monday or Wednesday would be better,' said

Ming, taking it as a matter of course that she would attend the weekly editorial meeting.

'I'll try for Monday then and telephone you if they've got tickets,' said Mark, adding with some feeling: 'It'll be really good to see you.'

'Thank you. Goodbye,' she answered, wondering whether it would be unfair to try to make him take out a subscription. She was pretty sure that he would if she asked him.

Picking up the first envelope in the pile, she slid her forefinger under the flap and ripped it open. There was a single sheet and no enclosure. Assuming that it was a rejection of one of her selling letters, she unfolded the sheet and read the short, typed paragraph:

Ming,
You are a cold-hearted bitch. I know that you are trying to ruin everything I'm doing. You won't succeed, but if you go on doing it, I'll simply have to find a way to stop you. I am not going to sign this because we both know there's no need.

The first coherent thought in Ming's mind was a determination not to be sick. She sat heavily down on the chair by her desk, trying to control the nausea that pumped hot saliva into her mouth. Breathing deeply, she brought her body under control again and then carefully read the letter once more.

'But I'm not,' she said aloud.

She looked out of the window at the newly green trees, read the letter once more and desperately searched her conscience for anything she might have done to cause such a misunderstanding. Slowly self-justification turned first to fear and then to real anger. There was a sour taste in her mouth and a ringing in her ears.

'Ming,' she said aloud, looking down at the letter again. 'Who calls me that who could possibly have written it?'

Only her family and her very close friends used the nickname. Could any of them have written such a letter? If it had even addressed her as 'Mary', it would have seemed less vicious.

The faces of people she knew that she had annoyed or upset began to swim into her mind. There seemed suddenly to be an awful lot of them; and she knew there could have been others who had hidden their rage or hurt at whatever she had done. She sat shivering as she tried to think which of them could hate her enough to write like that.

Eventually, she forced herself out of her chair and went into the kitchen to make herself something hot to drink. Her hands were shaking and her teeth chattering although it was not cold. She told herself that it was absurd to mind so much about a few lines of words on a page, but she did mind.

'It couldn't be Connie,' she murmured, thinking of the unmistakable anger she had aroused at the meeting. She poured boiling water on the tea leaves, and provided her own answer. Connie had no need to write her an anonymous letter. If she had disliked Ming's suggestions for the magazine, all she would have had to do was refuse them.

Lurching between sickening suspicion of one friend after another and horror at her own disloyalty, Ming went back to the drawing room to retrieve the envelope in case it gave her any clues. Postmarked from London SW1 at half-past five the previous day, it was plain and white: the kind of envelope that could be bought from any supplier of office stationery. As she was staring at it the telephone rang and she picked it up automatically. Not until she tried to give her number did she realise how badly her voice would shake.

'Ming? What's the trouble? You sound ghastly,' said the familiar voice of her eldest sister. It held all sorts of childhood memories: of teasing and bossiness; but also of comfort. Ming relaxed a little and loosened her hold on the receiver.

'Hello, Gerry. I've had an anonymous letter.' Her voice cracked on the last word and she breathed deeply in an effort to control it. 'It's extremely trivial, but it seems to have affected my voice.'

'You poor old thing. How utterly beastly. Don't pay any attention to it.'

'It's a bit hard not to.'

'Why? What does it say?'

Ming read it out, her voice still shaking over some words.

'It's obviously been written by some lunatic,' said Gerry firmly. 'There's nothing relevant to you in it except for your name and all sorts of people could have got that. If I were you, I'd telephone the police at once and then forget about it.'

Gerry's common-sense advice helped to steady Ming and there was the beginning of a smile on her lips as she said:

'That may not be terribly easy.'

'No,' came the astringent answer, 'but you'll have to do it; otherwise you'll brood over it and wonder who wrote it and the whole thing will come to seem even more beastly than it is. And if I were you, I wouldn't tell anyone else about it.'

'No,' said Ming. 'I suppose not.'

'That's probably superfluous advice,' said Gerry when she thought about what she had said, 'since you never do tell anyone what bothers you. But I'd have thought it worth keeping this to yourself in case the writer gets to hear how much you hated the letter. You don't want to give him any satisfaction or encouragement.'

'God forbid!' said Ming. 'But who on earth could it be, Gerry?'

As she heard desperation in her sister's voice, Gerry wanted to rush straight round to Chelsea, but she remembered Julia Wallington's disapproval of her unsuitable protectiveness of Ming and tried to offer what comfort she could down the telephone.

'It's probably someone you've only met once or twice in your life; someone who's jealous of you. Perhaps its someone Anna knew, who thought he had a better right to Anna's money than you. Whoever wrote it is obviously unbalanced.'

'That sounds sensible,' said Ming, still not quite able to keep her voice steady. 'I'm sorry to be so wet about it, but it was rather a shock.'

'I'm sure it was,' said Gerry, hating to hear Ming trying to justify herself for so reasonable a reaction. 'You ring the police now, and if you need me ring me up. You've got my new number at the university, haven't you?'

'Yes, I have. But it seems a very trivial thing to bother the police with.'

'Nonsense, Ming. They're there to protect us – ring them up.'

Eventually Ming agreed and Gerry rang off without explaining why she had telephoned. Ming dialled the number of her local police station and was told firmly but politely that there was nothing the police could do about anonymous letters unless they contained physical threats. She was warned that there would probably be more letters and advised to keep them all just in case there were ever anything that could lead to an official investigation.

'If they did ever threaten you, miss, or there were any signs of more physical action we could look into it,' said the voice at the other end of the telephone, making Ming start shaking again. 'And the more information you could give us about the letters the better it would be. Keep them and don't worry about them until they get nasty.'

Actually frightened instead of merely appalled for the first time since she had opened the envelope, Ming had an impulse to shut all the curtains and see that the front door was locked. Footsteps sounded in the doorway and she whirled, dropping the small sheet of paper.

'All right if I do in here now? Then I'll leave you be,' said the charlady, leaning her broom against the wall and flapping a yellow duster out of her apron pocket.

'Yes,' said Ming, holding one hand flat against her neck. 'Yes, that's perfectly all right.' She bent down to pick up the letter, folded it up and slid it back into its typed envelope, which she put in the bottom drawer of her desk.

Her enthusiasm for writing to distant acquaintances on her own writing paper to solicit subscriptions for the magazine had dwindled and she decided to ask Connie for some specifically magazine-addressed paper. Ming was perfectly well aware of her absurdity – whoever had written her the letter already had her address – but she was prepared to pander to it.

The horror of the anonymous accusation stayed with her, but during the next two weeks there were plenty of other things to distract her. Most of the people to whom she had written about the magazine responded and a lot of them agreed to take a subscription.

One was Miss Roseheath from Ming's old school. Her reply was warmly enthusiastic, both about the magazine itself and about Ming's own part in it:

> *I often think of you. I used to watch you when you were here and wonder how you would turn out. You had so many talents and yet you were afraid of so many things as a child. Then what with your sister's death and even the war itself, I felt that you had rather lost your way. This new departure is very exciting and I wish you the best of luck with it.*
>
> *Yours ever,*
>
> *Janet Roseheath*

CHAPTER 6

Ming tried to remember Miss Roseheath's letter, just as she tried to remember all the other affectionate things people had said to her, when the second anonymous letter came exactly two weeks after the first. Its accusations were very similar, although there was one new one: that Ming was dangerous.

That made her laugh aloud, which helped, but as more letters came on the same day each fortnight she ceased to be able to find anything amusing in them at all. They were all typed on the same machine, posted in the same kind of envelope, at the same time of day and in the same postal district of London.

The message in each was much the same as the first, but as the series continued the letters began to include references to things that Ming had been doing or articles that had appeared in the magazine under her name. She began to feel as though she were being watched wherever she went and there were times when she could hardly bear to leave her own flat. Whenever friends, or even her sisters, telephoned her, she could not help wondering if they were capable of such letters and whenever she noticed someone in the street staring at her – or caught someone's eye on a bus – she was afraid that she had come face to face with her correspondent.

She used her work for the magazine as a distraction and whenever she could stayed overnight with Max before the

Tuesday meetings, feeling much safer away from her own flat. But the letters continued to come and they began to make her feel persecuted.

It was a relief one day in June when her mother telephoned from Gloucestershire to say:

'We haven't seen you for months. Won't you come down for a few days?'

'I'd love to,' said Ming quickly, both conscience-stricken at having neglected her parents and delighted by the prospect of getting out of reach of her nameless antagonist for a while. 'I've just been working so hard on Connie Wroughton's magazine that I haven't been away for the weekend for months.'

'So I gather,' said Fanny Alderbrook drily. 'But come for next week. Do. There's nothing special on, although the garden's looking lovely.'

Ming agreed and the following Friday drove herself down to the grey-stone house at the edge of the village where she had grown up. It looked prettier than usual in the low golden light of the late-June evening, and Ming felt a welling of delight that surprised her.

Her father, a retired general in his sixties, came out on to the gravel drive to welcome her. Tall and broadly built, he stood waiting, surrounded by his three black labradors, who were all named after characters in *Winnie the Pooh.*

'You look fearfully tired, old thing,' he said as he kissed her and took her suitcase. 'Come and have a drink. Your mother's in the drawing room.'

'You look well,' said Ming, meaning it.

'Country air. It would do you good, too, instead of stewing in London when you don't need to work at all now.'

Ming smiled and said nothing as she preceded him into the sage-green drawing room where her mother was waiting.

It was from Fanny Alderbrook that her daughters had inherited their delicate, fair good looks and remarkable eyes, but her face was so marked by discontent that the prettiness was disguised. Her hair had lost its brightness years earlier and was thinning as it grew white. Beside her large, bluff husband, she looked very slight and delicate. Ming had often noticed that the strength of her mother's character came as a shock to the unwary.

'Hello, darling,' she said, getting out of her chair to kiss her youngest daughter. 'You look awful, really pale again, and there are dreadful bruises under your eyes. You really shouldn't be working so hard, you know. Thank you,' she added as she accepted a glass of sherry from her husband.

Ming took one too, and tried to explain why she was so absorbed in her ill-paid job for Constance Wroughton. Neither of her parents seemed convinced by her explanations and she went on trying to get them to understand what she wanted to do with her life. Eventually she gave that up and instead talked about the pleasure she found simply talking with Connie and Max.

'They're so interesting, you see,' she finished, 'and have done so many things beyond my own experience.'

'I'd really rather not hear about it,' said her father, pouring his wife some more sherry.

'What on earth do you mean?' Ming asked, startled out of her traditional submissiveness. 'What's wrong with Connie? Or is it the magazine itself?'

The general threw another log on the unnecessary fire with such force that it sent a mass of orange sparks spurting up the chimney.

'I don't like its tone, I must say.'

'Why on earth not?' Ming was as much surprised as angry. 'What's the matter with it?'

'Spiteful,' said the general shortly. He kicked one of the dogs out of his way and went back to sit in his chair.

Ming saw her mother's shoulders tauten in their Wedgewood-blue twinset.

'I don't read it any more,' the general went on, moving in his chair and sticking his legs out. 'But the bits I looked at all seemed to be trying to make people discontented with their lot, criticising the accepted ways of doing things.'

'Daddy, you can't really mind that so much.' Ming's protest was half drowned in the bark of the dog he had kicked for the second time. 'What is it that really bothers you?'

'If you must have it, it's that man,' he said burying his nose in his whisky glass. He looked up at her again and she was surprised by the earnestness of his expression. 'I hate the idea of your being ... forced into contact with a man like that. And I'd rather no one else knew about it.'

'Are you talking about Max Hillary?' Ming asked, her own drink forgotten.

Even the general could hear the perplexity in her voice.

'What on earth is the matter with him? Connie told me that people do disapprove of him, but why? What has he ever done to you?'

'Darling, please don't,' said her mother from the opposite side of the fireplace. 'We'd so much rather you didn't.'

'I'm sorry if I'm being very stupid, but I just don't understand.'

'Better not to talk about it then,' said the general in a softer voice. 'I'm glad you don't understand.'

'But why?' asked Ming, determined not to be left frustrated.

'Darling, don't.' The minatory note in her mother's voice was enough to make Ming want to change the subject. She fell back on one of her favourite techniques for dealing with her father's anger.

'What do you think is going to happen in the Middle East now that the last of our forces have left Egypt, Daddy?' she asked and was rewarded when her mother turned to smile at her in approval.

'It's disastrous. The Prime Minister may say that in the event of trouble there he can send in troops from Cyprus,' said the general, sounding both relieved and irritable, 'but that's simply not practical. The Canal is our lifeline and without the security of our chaps actually there in the Canal Zone, who knows what will happen? Nasser wants control of the whole area and I don't trust him an inch.'

'But surely he won't get control. It's owned by an international company.'

'I'm not sure. He's already started putting himself up against us by getting poor Glubb dismissed.'

'I thought General Glubb was commander of the Jordanian forces,' protested Ming. 'Nothing whatever to do with Nasser – or the Canal.'

'Nasser was behind the sacking, and we haven't been able to do a thing about it. Glubb's given everything to the Arab Legion and to be thrown out like that at no notice … it's an outrage. And it'll get worse and worse.'

'Let's go and have dinner,' said his wife pacifically. 'It should be ready.'

They went into the dining room and spent the meal discussing Flixe's children and the sadness of Gerry's inability to have any. When she had done the washing up, Ming pleaded exhaustion and went up to her room, feeling much less delight than when she had arrived four hours earlier.

A bed had been made up for her in the room she had had as a child, and she was depressed to see that all of her old books and even a once-loved doll were still ranged about the room as though she had never left home. She was dismayed by her urge to burn the lot to show her parents that she was no longer the sweet, dutiful creature who once used all her energy to make peace between them and her sisters.

Reminding herself that she was a guest in their house, and that she had come there for sanctuary, she piled the toys and books in the bottom drawer of the big white-painted chest and resolved to behave as compliantly as she could.

With that in mind she set her travelling alarm clock so that she was up and dressed in time to lay the breakfast table while her mother made fishcakes from the previous evening's left-over haddock and potatoes. Ming even ironed the *Daily Telegraph* so that she could refold it in the shape her father preferred.

When he came down from his dressing room and saw what she was doing, he patted her shoulder.

'You're a good girl, Ming,' he said cheerfully. He had obviously decided to ignore their inconclusive discussion about the magazine. 'Neither of your sisters bother with that these days. What's for breakfast?'

'Fishcakes, I think.'

'Jolly good.' He sat down and picked up the paper. 'Your mother's fishcakes have improved a lot. Good and crisp. Any coffee yet?'

'I'll go and fetch it,' said Ming with a smile.

Her good resolutions lasted all through breakfast and persuaded her to offer to arrange the church flowers, a task which her mother loathed but dutifully did whenever it was her turn.

'That would be lovely. And perhaps while you're picking them, you could get some for the house too. There are plenty of roses. Could you do a big vase for the drawing room and something small and low for in here?'

'Yes, if you like,' said Ming, a little puzzled. 'Are we having people to lunch?'

Looking self-conscious, Fanny Alderbrook said lightly:

'Only the Adamsons and poor Jack Hazeldene. Didn't I tell you?'

'No, you didn't,' said Ming coolly. 'I thought he was in Cyprus.'

'They're very pleased with him there,' said her father. 'He's a good chap. It's a bad business.' He coughed and rattled his newspaper.

'Why? Has he left the army?' asked Ming.

'No, darling. Of course not,' said her mother. 'He's just brought the children back to his parents.'

'It must be awful for them, to lose their mother and then be sent away from their father, too.'

Ming looked at her mother as she spoke and was surprised to see a faintly satisfied expression on her face. Ming's own face began to stiffen.

'His mother will bring them up well,' said Mrs Alderbrook quickly fussing with the coffee pot. 'So long as she's able. But she's in despair about what will happen to them if she gets ill – or worse. He'll have to marry again, don't you think? More coffee?'

'Thank you, Fanny,' said the general, pushing his cup forward. Ming decided to say nothing more about Jack Hazeldene's predicament and talked brightly about the garden.

When he had finished his breakfast the general dropped his napkin on top of the newspaper and left Ming alone with her mother.

'I've often thought,' Fanny began as soon as he had shut the door, 'that you and poor old Jack got on awfully well.'

'Yes, I always liked him,' said Ming pleasantly, adding as though to send her mother a warning, 'and Caroline, too. She was very sweet. I'm not surprised that he adored her so. It's horrible that this should have happened to them.'

Mrs Alderbrook was silenced for a few minutes. Then she poured herself another cup of coffee, which she obviously did not want since she merely stirred it round and round without drinking any of it.

'Yes, awful,' she agreed, 'for Jack and for those children. It would be so wonderful if . . .'

'Mother,' said Ming at last, 'please don't say it.'

'What, Ming?'

'Don't tell me that it would be a good idea for me to marry Jack.'

'But, darling,' said her mother, holding out one small perfect hand, palm upwards. 'It's just that he would be so terribly suitable for you. And you could do so much for them all. And time is getting on, you know: you are over thirty now.'

As a child Ming had been frightened of her mother and, in doing her best to satisfy all her demands, had never questioned her motives. For once she began to look at Fanny Alderbrook as one adult to another and did not like everything that she saw.

'Don't you think it's indecent to try to thrust me into the arms of a man whose wife is hardly cold in her grave?' Ming was rather surprised to hear how chilly her own voice sounded.

'Darling, really! What a thing to say. I only want what's best for you. It's all I've ever wanted for any of you girls; that you should marry suitably and be happy.'

There was a great deal that Ming wanted to say then, but she saw what appeared to be bewildered distress in her mother's face.

'Never mind,' Ming said gently, not certain whether the expression was genuine but not prepared to test it. 'I'll go and do the flowers.'

An hour later she was standing in front of the altar of the small grey-stone church with a wide trug of flowers at her feet. The green altar cloth had already been covered with a fine white linen cloth and the heavy silver vases polished and filled with water by one of the other ladies of the parish. All Ming had to do was achieve two perfectly matching flower arrangements that would satisfy her mother.

Feeling as though she had reverted to the dutiful school-girl she had once been, Ming took some sprays of silvery *pittosporum* leaves from the basket. She quickly built up a framework into which she inserted pink and white roses and a few sprays of honeysuckle to add scent and a hint of informality.

She heard the west door open and felt a draught on the back of her neck.

'I won't be much longer,' she called over her shoulder without properly turning round, assuming that the newcomer was another of the parish ladies, there to set out the hymn books or replace a worn hassock. There was silence until a man's voice said hesitantly:

'Ming?'

Then she did turn. Standing in the aisle, with the old military banners hanging in colourful mockery either side of him, stood Jack Hazeldene. From where Ming was standing, he looked like a man defeated. His thick hair was streaked with grey and looked dried out, and there were lines around his mouth and eyes that made Ming wince. His shoulders were as straight as ever but he seemed diminished and desperately thin. He looked much older than his thirty-three years.

'Ming?' he said again. 'It is you, isn't it? I didn't realise you were down here.'

She walked down the chancel steps, both hands held out. He came towards her and took them.

'Jack,' she said, trying to find words that would not add to his burdens. 'I am so sorry about Caroline.'

Still gripping her hands he tried to speak, shook his head and then coughed.

'Sorry,' he said. 'I'm no good at being graceful and saying things that let people off. Thank you for your letter. It was one of the few that said something real. I'm sorry I haven't answered it yet.'

'It didn't need an answer,' Ming said at once. 'I'll clear up later and get out of your way.'

'No, don't do that,' he said, at last finding a smile. 'It's good to see you. I didn't come here to ... well, er, pray or anything like that.'

'Just to be alone for a bit, I expect.' Ming smiled. 'That's why I want to get out of your way.' She pulled her hands out of his and moved towards the door.

'Ming, don't go,' he called. 'Not unless you have to, I mean. It wasn't solitude I wanted; just to get away from the endless well-meant but impossible advice people pour over me all the time.' He smiled again and added: 'You never bossed me, not even when we were children.'

'I was too little to do that,' she said with a smile, 'and you were much too strong. Besides, Annie did all the bossing for both of us.'

'She did, didn't she?' he said more easily. 'I'd forgotten. I'm sorry. It's too easy to think that no one has ever felt anything like this before. Look, why don't I help with the clearing up while you finish the vases? Then we could go for a walk together.'

Ming came back to him, pleased that he had understood what she had meant to tell him.

'All right. That would be lovely if you don't mind the thorns.'

She slid the rest of her flowers into the gaps between the branches while he picked up the dropped leaves and discarded stalks that lay in a half circle round the altar.

'There,' she said at last, putting her secateurs on top of the rubbish in the trug. 'That'll do. It's not up to my mother's standards, but she can always explain that she didn't do them herself. I'll chuck this lot on the compost heap and then I'd better go and see if she needs any help with lunch.'

'Do you know who's coming?' he asked, picking up the basket and going to open the church door for her. 'I thought it was just going to be your parents. I'm not sure I can cope with a party.'

'You won't have to. It's only the Adamsons and me,' said Ming. There had been enough desperation in his voice to make her add, more frankly than she had planned, 'And I'm no danger to you, Jack.'

He looked at her carefully as she stood in the stone archway of the porch. Her dark blue eyes were clear and kind and very honest. For almost the first time since he had returned to England he felt able to speak his thoughts aloud:

'They don't see how unbearable it is to be told all the time − and sometimes in as many words − that I must marry again.'

'I know,' said Ming with a vivid memory of her mother's campaign that morning. 'It's all done with the best of motives but that doesn't unfortunately stop one wanting to scream and yell and hit them.'

'My God,' said Jack Hazeldene staring at her, 'you really do understand.'

'Yes, I do. They do it to me, too, and for quite different reasons I find it just as hard.'

They set off through the churchyard past the horrible pink granite of the modern graves to the old ones with their lopsided, lichened stones and indecipherable lettering. There was a seat there backed by yew trees. As they sat down he gestured to all the graves.

'It's not as though it's never happened to anyone else before,' he said. 'I could just about cope with having lost her, even with thinking about the last weeks when she was so afraid and in such pain, if they'd just leave me alone for a bit. But they can't. They're sorry she's dead, but they're too embarrassed by me to talk about it, and they're trying to find a successor as though she was just part of a machine that can be replaced when it's worn out. It's ... grotesque.'

Ming sat beside him in silence, thinking that what he most needed was to be able, at last, to let out some of his desperation. He talked, with the words pouring out of him like poison from a lanced boil, about Caroline's illness and his children, about the unendurable thought that if the vaccine had been discovered even a year earlier she would not have died, and about his terrifying loneliness. At one moment he said bitterly that he wished he had never even known Caroline, let alone loved her.

Ming listened without interrupting or trying to comfort him until at last he fell silent. Then, dredging her own experience, she tried to help. Jack wept a little and clung to her hands with a grip that was so tight it hurt her, but slowly he grew calm again.

They were very late for lunch and it shocked Ming to see the delighted approval on the faces of her parents.

CHAPTER 7

When Ming got back to the flat, hot and tired a week later, it was to find another anonymous typewritten letter amongst her post. Once again she read it to learn that the writer thought her jealous, incompetent, snobbish and at risk of offending beyond bearing. The writer did not spell out what would be done to Ming if that happened, but there was an implicit threat behind almost every word.

Ming's effort to ignore the loathing was particularly difficult when she was tired, but she worked at it and told herself that the letter-writer was probably inadequate and unhappy, and should be pitied rather than feared. At least, she told herself briskly, the anonymous malice was of minor importance compared with what Jack Hazeldene was suffering. She added the letter to the pile in the bottom drawer of her desk and tried to forget it.

Among the remaining letters was one from Mark Sudley, saying that he had been unable to get her on the telephone, wondered whether she was going to the Attingers' later in the month and if so whether she would like to dine with him first. The Attingers were distant relations of her mother and had indeed invited her to their dance, which was to be a combined celebration of their silver wedding, their eldest son's twenty-first birthday and their daughter's coming-out. Ming had accepted the invitation out of a sense of family duty, but she had not been looking forward to it and had even considered having a diplomatic migraine.

She thought that if Mark were to be there too it might be more entertaining than she had expected, made a mental note to buy something to wear and rang him up to accept his invitation to dine.

The last letter in her morning post was from Julia's husband, David Wallington. With the approval of Connie and Max, Ming had written to ask him whether he would agree to be interviewed for *The World Beyond*. She wanted him to lay bare the realities of life as a Member of Parliament, but she also wanted to find out what it was like to be the husband of a successful barrister.

He had written a pleasant note, suggesting that Ming should come to his house in south London for lunch the following Sunday. They could eat with Julia and the children, he wrote, and then retire to his study for the interview. Ming accepted both invitations and then telephoned Max to report.

'Good,' he said energetically. 'David Wallington is one of the few really civilised men in the House of Commons. I shall be interested to see what you make of him. Don't be too straightforward: like every other interviewer, you will need to ask about how he squares his socialist principles with owning thousands of acres of Scotland, but there are more interesting questions as well.'

'You don't have to tell me, Max. I'd love to know what it's like to watch your wife being so successful in what really is a man's world.'

'She's older than he, isn't she?'

'I'm not sure,' said Ming. 'She could be. Does that matter?'

'Heaven knows. I'd have thought that some men might find it tough. See what you can do. Oh and by the way, didn't you say that you're short of furniture in Chelsea?'

'Yes, I did. Why?'

'Because there's a quite lovely house near here whose owner has died and whose heirs are selling up. The contents are going under the hammer tomorrow afternoon. Tempted?' Max sounded as though he hoped that she was so Ming quickly said:

'Yes. Would you come with me, Max, and advise?'

'I hoped you'd ask. I'd love to. You'd better come down first thing in the morning to give you time to see what there is. With luck it'll be raining.'

'I can't think why it should be,' said Ming, peering out of her windows at the clear turquoise evening sky, across which only a few threadlike, pale pink clouds were sailing. 'It's been glorious for the last week.'

'Rain stops a lot of bargain hunters,' said Max. 'Pray for rain.' He put down his telephone, leaving Ming to smile at his enthusiasm as much as his pragmatism.

The next morning, as she woke to pouring rain, she was less amused. The prospect of driving through south London in such weather was so unpleasant that she almost rang him up to say she would not go. Looking round her bleak rooms, which by then were filling up with piles of letters, back copies of the magazine and cuttings from other periodicals, persuaded her to set out.

When she eventually reached the auction, having collected Max on the way, Ming thought that the hours of peering through her flooded windscreen and the headache that had induced had been worth it. The big red-brick house had been built in the late seventeenth century and was one of the prettiest Ming had seen for years.

'Goodness, how lovely!' she murmured. 'But who could possibly buy it?'

'No one, alas,' said Max. Ming looked surprised at the bitterness in his voice. 'It's too big for anyone to keep up as a private house, not suitable for a school or hospital. What can they do? It would cost a fortune even to mend the roof, let alone repoint the brickwork, replace the rotting window frames or even heat it adequately. It's going to be demolished.'

'How sad!'

Inside they found a mixture of junk and glorious furniture of almost every period since the house had been built, all numbered and arranged into convenient batches for the auctioneers. With Max's enthusiastic instructions ringing in her ears, Ming banished her regret for the house, picked up a catalogue at the door and proceeded to walk slowly round the entire ground floor, marking her catalogue whenever she saw anything she liked. He tagged along just behind her, drawing her attention to particular pieces and occasionally criticising her choices.

At last she turned and, deliberately smiling, said:

'Max, please! I know that you're far more knowledgeable than I am, but I'm looking for things for my home, not for a museum. Will you let me walk round on my own?'

There was a moment's resentment on his thin face, but that was quickly banished behind a smile as kind as her own.

'Sorry. I was getting carried away. It's so long since I've been able to buy anything that I let my enthusiasm get the better of me. You carry on. I'll window shop on my own.'

'Thanks, Max,' she said, laying one thin hand on his arm for a moment. 'Perhaps you can divert the dealers.' He laughed and let her go.

Ming herself sought him out just before the auction began and asked whether he would be prepared to sit with her.

'It's ages since I came to this sort of sale,' she said, 'and I need someone to keep my feet on the ground.'

'I'll do that. Have you fixed your top prices?' Max asked. 'Good.'

They found their way to the centre of the third row of chairs. Ming was glad to see that at least three-quarters of the seats were unfilled. The auctioneer, a youngish man with an extraordinarily plummy voice and a well-cut dark suit, mounted the rostrum in front of them and began his patter. The first fifty lots were of no interest to Ming, being mainly kitchen furniture and linen, but lot fifty-one was a ravishing eighteenth-century *chaise longue*. She had tried it and discovered that it was just as comfortable as her second-hand sofas and much better looking.

As the auctioneer reached number forty-nine, Ming felt her blood beginning to race and the palms of her hands began to sweat. She rubbed them on her handkerchief and did not even notice Max looking at her out of the corner of his eye with a highly amused smile on his face. Lot fifty was two dozen monogrammed linen sheets, which went for an absurdly small sum, and then the auctioneer raised Ming's blood pressure still more.

'The first of our really important lots this afternoon, ladies and gentlemen, a fine eighteenth-century sofa, upholstered in the original silk. It needs some repairs but is in really remarkable condition. Very rare that a piece of this quality reaches a sale room. Worth at least five hundred pounds. Who will start me at three hundred and fifty?'

Ming's top price was fifty pounds less than that and she gripped her hands together to force herself to stop waving her bidding card. No one spoke. The auctioneer started again and eventually wrung a bid out of somewhere for fifty pounds. Breathing again, Ming raised her own card.

'One hundred and twenty-five pounds,' said the auctioneer an instant later. Any advance on one hundred and twenty-five pounds? I must have more, ladies and gentlemen. There's no chance that I can sell such a superb piece for such a derisory sum.'

Ming's handed fluttered upwards, but Max caught it and forced it back down on her knee.

'It's your bid,' he hissed. 'Don't be a fool.'

'But he says he can't sell for that,' Ming hissed back. Max raised his arched eyebrows even higher and shook his head at her.

'Come on, ladies and gentlemen,' the auctioneer was still trying to flog his dead horse. 'You can hardly buy a new sofa in the Tottenham Court Road for that much.'

Ming felt sorry for him, but a wild hope was making it difficult for her to breathe.

'Sold for one hundred and twenty-five pounds. Number, please!'

Hands shaking and a broad smile on her lips, Ming held up her number.

'Well done!' Max whispered. 'What next?'

'Nothing until sixty-nine,' she said, holding out her catalogue.

By the end of the afternoon, she had spent just over one

thousand pounds, but she had acquired, besides the sofa, a Regency breakfast table and four chairs for her little dining room, an elegant satinwood sofa table and a dressing mirror for her bedroom, a walnut chest of drawers, two armchairs, a painting and a Crown Derby dinner service. She had not planned to buy any china at all, but when she saw the auctioneer prepared to knock it down for a tiny fraction of its worth, she had broken all her rules and bid for it.

Max went with her to arrange for payment and delivery and then persuaded her to go back to his cottage for a drink. When he invited her to stay for supper and spend the night in his comfortable spare room, she declined.

'I can't. If I'm to be in Kennington for lunch tomorrow with the Wallingtons, I really must go back.'

'You don't need to, Ming,' he said. 'Kennington's nearly as far from Chelsea as it is from here. And I'd love some company. The evenings are the worst.'

Watching the naked loneliness in his eyes, Ming almost asked him about his past, why he was hiding in Connie's cottage when he obviously pined to be in London, and what he had done to make people like her father disapprove of him so much. But if he had wanted her to know he would have told her.

'Max,' she said as kindly as she could, 'if I'm to make a decent job of the interview I need to prepare it properly. I must go home, and soon, or it'll be dark as well as raining. Thank you for coming with me today. I don't know that I'd have had the courage to buy anything if you hadn't been there.'

'Nonsense,' he said, recovering his usual sardonic voice. 'You've all the courage in the world, Ming. You've just let those sisters and friends of yours persuade you for years that you're fragile. You're not; you're as tough as they make 'em.'

'Too tough?' In the old days that question would have been voiced with serious anxiety, but Ming was coming to realise that toughness was a talent that she needed to acquire. Her dark blue eyes sparkled.

Max shook his head, laughing with her. But his voice was serious: 'You can't be too tough in this wretched world.'

'Don't be unhappy, Max,' she said and then quickly added, 'sorry. It's none of my business.'

'I can't ... I can't talk about it,' he said. 'I'll get your coat. Don't ...'

'It's all right. I shouldn't have said anything. It's just that I hate seeing anyone so ... oh, you know,' said Ming as she buttoned up the grey-blue mackintosh and pulled open the cottage door. Max could not help smiling at her inarticulate sympathy.

'You're a generous soul. I'll see you on Tuesday. Good luck tomorrow.'

'Thanks, Max,' said Ming, wondering why her anonymous correspondent's criticisms were so much easier to remember than the sort of things Max had just said. 'Good night.'

The following day Ming set off for her interview with David Wallington by taxi. Never having been to Kennington, she was not confident of finding her way to the house or of leaving her car parked outside it while they ate. The driver of the taxi she hailed tried to persuade her that he couldn't go south of the river, but she insisted and with very bad grace he drove her along the Embankment and across Lambeth bridge.

It was hard to remember the previous day's rain, for the sun was blazing down and there was not a cloud to be seen anywhere. The light seemed to accentuate all the broken-down murkiness of the streets through which the taxi took her. Looking out of the windows, Ming was full of misgivings and found it hard to imagine the impeccably dressed Julia Wallington emerging from such a place. Quite soon the taxi turned left off the main street, right and then left again and pulled up outside a large Georgian brick house with clean windows and freshly painted window frames. Relieved to see the bright brass number on the black door, Ming paid the taxi driver, tipped him and ran up the shallow steps to ring the doorbell.

A moment later the door was opened by a small girl wearing a blue-and-white checked dress with bands of red and blue smocking across the front and the tops of the puffed sleeves. She had dark hair in pigtails, each one tipped with a red ribbon, and she was wearing red calf shoes over her short white socks.

'Hello,' said Ming, amused by the unexpected apparition. 'I've been asked to lunch.'

'Yes, I know,' said the child. 'You're Miss Alderbrook. I'm Amanda and I'm letting you in because Daddy's working still and it's Janice's day off and Mummy's in the kitchen, getting cross.'

'Goodness me!' said Ming, feeling inadequate in the face of such comprehensive information. 'Well, it's very kind of you to let me in.'

'Yes, but it's all right; I wasn't doing anything else. If you come into the drawing room, I'll pour some sherry, too,' said Amanda, leading the way.

Ming shut the heavy front door behind her and followed the child into a large, sunny room furnished with comfortable-looking chairs and an immense sofa covered in dark blue-green velvet. Mounds of cushions in a selection of paler greens and blues – stripes, checks, tapestry and even old-fashioned patchwork – filled its corners and made it look at once less formidably big and enticingly comfortable.

'How old are you, Amanda?' asked Ming as the child efficiently poured her a glass of pale gold sherry from a tall decanter.

'I shall be exactly eight and a half next Tuesday,' she said, handing Ming the glass.

'Thank you. Are you going to have something to drink?'

'No, I don't think so. We always have orange squash for lunch at weekends and I'm not thirsty now. What's your real name?'

'I was christened Mary, but people I like call me Ming,' she answered. 'Would you like to?'

The child beamed and lost some of her frightening sophistication.

'Yes, I would,' she confided, coming to stand closer to Ming, 'but Mummy doesn't let me call grown-ups by their Christian names. She thinks it's precocious.'

'Does she?' asked Ming, trying to keep the laugh out of her voice. She could well imagine Julia's fear of her daughter's precocity and assumed that Amanda must once have overheard her talking about it.

'We're having chicken for lunch and then apple crumble. Mummy used to be able to make apple pie, but something's happened to her pastry these days and it simply won't work.' Amanda pulled one of her dark plaits over her shoulder and began to fiddle with the ribbon. 'Janice makes lovely pastry. She's a much better cook than Mummy; I wish she was here all the time at weekends. I don't like ...'

The door opened before she could finish and Ming was rather relieved to see a faint blush staining her plump cheeks.

'Ming! I'm sorry I was stuck in the kitchen when you came. It's wonderful to see you here,' said Julia, her voice warm with welcome.

'Amanda looked after me very well,' said Ming, smiling and for the first time feeling some pity for Julia.

She was wearing a simple shirt-waister of beige-and-pink striped cotton with a pair of flat-heeled sandals. Her hair was bundled into a loose knot at the back of her head and she was wearing neither stockings nor make-up. She looked much less frightening than usual and Ming hoped that she had not heard her daughter's criticisms of her cooking.

'How are you, Julia?'

'Busy, but then I nearly always am. Darling, why don't you go and tell Daddy that lunch is nearly ready and see if Jonathan has washed his hands yet?'

'Because I want to stay and talk to Ming,' said Amanda with an expression of conscious naughtiness on her face. To Ming's admiration, Julia achieved a cheerful-sounding laugh.

'Yes, it was very silly of me to put it like that when what I meant was: please, Amanda, go and fetch Daddy and Jonathan. Off you go, darling.'

To Ming's surprise the child went, dragging her smart red shoes across the polished parquet. Julia turned to her guest.

'Sorry, Ming. It's difficult to judge the right line with Amanda just now. She's very conscious of the fact that I'm not with her as much as her friends' mothers are and so she likes to punish me for it when I am here – and to demonstrate that she considers herself mistress of the house, because she's in it so much more than I am.'

'You sound admirably calm about it,' said Ming. 'Most of my friends with children seem to find them – particularly their daughters – a source of apparently endless unhappiness and rage, except for Flixe, of course.'

Julia laughed. 'Flixe is a natural mother. To me both those feelings are perfectly familiar. But Amanda is only a child. It's not ... well no, it is deliberate, but she doesn't understand why she wants to get at me all the time. It would be absurd to let myself get sucked into playing emotional games with her. She's only eight, after all, and I know she must often feel horribly frustrated.'

Thinking that it was refreshing to hear a mother talk so frankly about her child, Ming was about to ask about Julia's son, but before she could phrase the question, Julia pre-empted her by asking whether she would like to see the garden before lunch.

'I'd love to,' said Ming. 'This is such a surprising house to find in a place like ... like Kennington.'

Julia's twinkling smile told Ming a lot more than her diplomatic answer.

'When David first brought me down here on a house-hunting expedition after we were married I was taken aback. But it's part of his constituency, and so it's right that we live here. The only real problem is the local schools. We had a bit of a fight over that. But I've insisted that Amanda goes to one run by the Girls' Public Day School Trust.'

Julia held open the door to the hall and ushered Ming ahead of her. They crossed the polished floor of the hall and went into a large, functional kitchen with a shiny, bright green linoleum floor. In the middle of the opposite wall were a pair of tall french windows, which led to an iron staircase down into the garden.

It was large and wonderfully overstocked with curved beds stuffed with shrubs, roses and annuals in a glorious muddle of colour and shape. The grass was rough, starred with daisies and rather long. A small grove of apple trees stood about half-way down the garden, already hung with swelling fruit. Climbing roses frothed over the fences at either side and hung in white-and-yellow festoons across to the nearest trees. Two sturdy swings were suspended on ropes from the branches of an immense cedar, and there was even a hammock swaying gently between two of the apple trees. Behind a low hedge at the back of the garden Ming could see the white pitched roofs of a group of beehives and rows of what looked like vegetables.

'Do you make honey?' she asked in delight.

'David does. He says he finds looking after the bees relaxing after the frustrations of the House – and the children like it for tea. In theory David does the vegetables, too, but they got so neglected that he's recently given in and we have a jobbing gardener twice a week.'

At the sound of a step behind them, Julia turned. Ming was aware of her making some kind of effort.

'David, how did it go?' she asked in what sounded like a deliberately cheerful voice. Then she turned and added in explanation to Ming, 'He's been writing a tricky speech.'

'Not too bad, although it reads very dully. Hello, Mary, it's been a long time since we met. How are you? Missing the House?' He held out a hand, which Ming shook.

He was very tall with smooth dark hair and startling blue eyes. Ming had only ever seen him at work or at Flixe's parties, when he had always worn impeccably cut dark suits, but on that Sunday he was dressed as informally as Julia, in baggy flannel trousers and a soft-looking lovat tweed jacket so old that it was fraying at the cuffs and buttonholes.

'I'm very well, thank you,' she said, thinking how much more approachable than usual they both looked. 'Escape from Westminster has proved marvellously good for me.'

'I can see that. You never looked so blooming in the old days. Tell me about this magazine of yours,' said David. 'Julia's accounts of it sound most intriguing.'

'Not yet,' said his wife firmly. 'You two have all afternoon to deal with the magazine and the interview. We need to get lunch over first. David, can you chase up those children while Ming and I dish up?'

The two women went into the kitchen, where Ming was amused to watch Julia's almost clumsy handling of her pots and pans. She had always seemed so unassailably competent that her lack of domestic skills was rather touching. Eventually she had all the vegetables in dishes, the chicken on a warmed charger and the gravy bubbling ferociously in its enamelled roasting tin.

'Shall I take these in?' asked Ming, gesturing to the vegetable dishes.

'Oh, would you? Marvellous. Where's that spoon?' muttered Julia, pushing some escaping hair behind her left ear. She looked over her shoulder at Ming and winced as a bubble of gravy exploded and splashed her hand. 'There's a spare oven cloth somewhere on the table.'

Ming found it without difficulty and, having picked up the dishes, asked where she should take them.

'I'll show you,' said Amanda importantly, stressing the pronoun. She was standing in the kitchen doorway, watching her mother with a supercilious expression in her blue eyes. 'Come on. It's through here.'

She led the way into a formal dining room, papered with a Regency striped wallpaper in cherry and white. The furniture looked as though it were genuinely from the Regency, although the portraits were modern. There seemed to be a lot of silver, both on the sideboard and on the long mahogany table.

'I've already laid the table,' said Amanda, pointing to the mats where Ming was to deposit her burden. Then she giggled and admitted: 'Well, Mummy did most of it, but I helped.'

She went on talking, telling Ming about her school, her friends, her young brother, the books she was reading, the clothes she had in her wardrobe and her Hungarian godfather. Ming was not sure whether to believe all she heard about him until Amanda turned and pointed to a portrait of herself that hung in an alcove to the right of the fireplace.

'He's a painter. He did that.'

'It's very good,' said Ming, moving closer to get a better view.

The small painting was luminous with a kind of amused delight, as though the artist had enjoyed his sitter's conversation as he worked. In the portrait Amanda looked both attractive and real, almost as though she had just stopped playing for a moment. There was no formality about it at all.

'It's very good,' she repeated. 'He must like you a lot.'

'Why?' Amanda demanded, looking pleased.

'Because no one could paint such a happy picture if he didn't like the subject of it.'

'What about that?' The question sounded almost truculent as Amanda gestured with her round arm to a much bigger painting that hung on the wall behind Ming. She turned.

'That one, too,' she said after she had looked at a portrait of Julia for a few moments.

Simply dressed and with her hair looking as though it were about to escape its pins, Julia smiled down from the canvas. All her strength of character was there, but there was something else as well; something that Ming had not yet seen in the real woman and which surprised her: an uncertain, almost bemused, tenderness.

'He's a superb painter,' Ming said. 'What's his name?'

'Tibor Smith.'

The voice was David's and Ming swung round in surprise.

'Isn't it stunning?' he said. 'Julia doesn't like it much, but I love it.'

'I'm not surprised.'

Ming saw Amanda standing with her bottom lip jutting out and a hard look in her eyes.

'He's done Amanda beautifully, too,' she said to distract the child.

Amanda immediately rushed into a staccato description of his studio and what had happened during their sittings.

'Pipe down, Amanda. You'll give Ming parliamentary earache in a minute!' David put his son down on the floor and hugged his daughter.

'What's that?' she asked, obviously fascinated by a new piece of information.

'It's what we get in the House of Commons when we have to listen to too much nonsense when we ought to be eating or going home or reading a book,' he said in mock seriousness. Both Ming and Amanda laughed. 'Jonathan, say hello to Miss Alderbrook.'

The child, who looked quite different from Amanda, took his thumb out of his mouth and smiled at Ming. He seemed to be not nearly as robust as his sister and much shyer. He leaned against his father's legs and put his thumb back in his mouth. His hair was a soft brown that looked almost fair where the sun fell on it and his face was more delicately modelled than hers.

'He's just four,' Amanda informed her, 'and . . .'

'Pipe down!'

'Sorry, Daddy.' For a second she looked chastened and then her plump face creased into an infectious grin: 'How are your ears?'

'Aching horribly!' he said. Ming laughed again, enjoying their ease together. But she remembered her own difficulties with her strong-charactered elder sisters and wondered how Jonathan would cope as he struggled to catch up with the dominating Amanda.

Julia appeared in the doorway, carrying the chicken and the gravy and looking as though something was about to spill at any moment. David leaned forward to relieve her of the chicken and Ming took the gravy boat.

'Thank you. Did you wash, Jonathan?' she asked.

'Yes, Mummy,' he said.

'And poured what looks like a bathful of water on the floor,' commented David. 'Don't worry, I mopped it up.

That's why we were all so long up there. Breast or leg,
Ming?'

As lunch got under way, Julia began to relax again. She
seemed quite happy to leave the disciplining of the two
children to her husband, who cajoled them into eating,
stopped Amanda talking with her mouth full, and mopped
the gleaming mahogany when Jonathan spilled his orange
squash.

'He's so much better at it than I,' said Julia quietly at one
moment as she saw Ming watching him.

Ming looked up and saw in Julia's face some of the wistfulness her portrait showed. It made her look years younger
than usual and peculiarly vulnerable.

'He seems very efficient – quite different from Peter,
who's the only other man I've ever really watched with his
children,' said Ming, smiling at her hostess.

'They're very different sorts of men,' Julia answered,
adding even more quietly, 'thank heavens. I think Flixe is
positively saintly with what she puts up with.'

'I don't think she minds,' said Ming, who had been
thinking about it a lot. 'You can see how happy she is just
by looking, let alone listening to her. He does cherish her –
and they get on so well.'

'I know. It's often hard to see why those one really values
love the people they do.'

'Who do you love?' A sharply interested voice from the
other side of the table made Ming look round.

'Never mind, Amanda. Eat up,' said David, looking
warningly at his wife.

When lunch was over, he took Ming into his study and
sat her down in a deep armchair by a window overlooking
the garden.

'Now, what can I tell you?' he asked, sitting opposite her
and taking out his pipe. 'Do you mind this? It helps me feel
at ease.'

'I don't mind in the least,' said Ming, remembering some
of the things that the advertising psychiatrist had told her
about the reasons why men smoke. Somehow she did not
think David Wallington was either seeking a substitute

breast or trying to make breathing difficult for her because she frightened him. 'This is your territory, after all.'

'True. So?'

Ming began to ask him all the obvious questions about his political beliefs, his passionate wish for the remains of the Empire to be dismantled and the colonies to be ruled by their own people, his fears of the effects of unrestrained immigration into the British Isles, his determination that the five-year moratorium on capital punishment should be infinitely extended, and all the rest of his particular interests in Parliament. He gave her answers that were fluent and always interesting, but little different from what she had read of him in all the cuttings Max had given her to study. After a while she laid down her notebook and started to talk to him about his children.

He took his pipe right out of his mouth then and settled back more deeply into his chair. They talked for the rest of the afternoon, with Ming making notes every so often, occasionally checking with him when he said something unexpected, and in the end she was left with a picture of a rather remarkable man. He had not been afraid to diverge from strictly socialist principles when expounding his ambitions for the country, or even to admit to uncertainties, and he showed himself to be not only philosophical but also practical.

His vision was realistic but compassionate, and his personal philosophy immensely attractive with its insistence that rights imply obligations, that endowments necessitate the giving of as much in return as it is possible to give, and that every human being, regardless of sex, class, race or age, should be educated and encouraged to fulfil every scrap of potential.

'Of course I'm glad that Julia works and is so successful,' he burst out at one moment when Ming had asked one of her prepared questions.

'And the effect on your children?' asked Ming with her pencil hovering just above the page.

'Of having a working mother?' he asked, his voice a little less certain. Ming nodded. David ran both his hands through his dark hair, ruffling it into an attractive confusion.

'God knows! And we'll never know, because whatever they do or become we'll never know how they would have turned out with Julia at home all day. All I can say is that I could not bring myself to ignore the stifling of Julia's ambitions and intelligence that would be involved in her staying at home with them.'

'It's difficult, isn't it?' said Ming with real sympathy and was rewarded with an admission.

'Almost impossibly so. When I look at Amanda and the way she behaves to Julia, I do wonder ... and the way Jonathan sometimes clings to her when she leaves for chambers in the mornings. But the price would be too high and since it's a price that I would not have to pay myself, I can't even think of imposing it on her,' he said, staring at the foaming roses just outside the window.

Ming sat, looking at his averted head and thinking that she had rarely met a man for whom she had such instant respect. He turned and, noticing her expression, smiled ruefully and shrugged.

'You can't imagine,' she said, slowly picking the right words, 'what it is like to meet someone who is reluctant to lay burdens on other people.'

'I'm not certain I know what you mean.'

'So many people are quite happy to lay down laws for other people that they themselves would not dream of bothering with. That's not very elegantly put, I'm afraid.' Ming grinned at him, looking suddenly mischievous and very pretty. 'You don't seem to be like that at all and, quite frankly, it gives me hope.'

David's face relaxed and he settled back into his chair.

'I'm glad.' He caught sight of the notebook open on Ming's knee and hastily added: 'But you're not going to print any of my anxieties about Julia's work, are you?' For the first time that afternoon there was an edge to his deep voice.

'It's interesting,' said Ming neutrally. Her burgeoning identification with her job fought with her urge to comfort.

'I don't have to put it in the context of you and your wife, but as a general point about wives with careers? Please?'

'If you don't talk about my wife or children, yes, of course. I'm sorry to have impugned your scruples,' he said with a smile. 'You're very ... very sensitive, Ming.'

'It's got me into an awful lot of trouble in the past,' she said, folding up her notebook. 'Look at the time! And I've hardly asked half the things I wanted to know.'

'We can squeeze a few more minutes together. What else is there?'

'Well, where do you stand on the equal pay issue, for instance?' Ming asked.

David picked up his pipe again and went through the performance of scraping out the half-burned residue of tobacco, refilling it, tamping down the new tobacco and laboriously lighting it. When it was smouldering to his satisfaction, he held the bowl in his right hand, sucking at the end now and again.

'It's difficult,' he said by way of a preamble.

'I know,' answered Ming, a gleam of amusement brightening her eyes. It seemed to her that David's pipe was used defensively rather than aggressively.

'I have to agree with the principle of equal pay for equal work. I don't really see how anyone who really thinks about it could not. Equal pay for work of "equal value" is more difficult, because, after all, who can judge the value of someone's work except in the baldest commercial terms? And even then it's difficult in any but the most clear-cut cases.'

'And the question of paying a single woman the same as a man who has to support a wife and three small children?' asked Ming, intrigued that David allowed her to see the real struggle he was having with his ideas. 'What about those schoolmasters who get so hot under the collar about spinster teachers being paid so much that they can go off on holidays to Italy and so on.'

He said nothing for so long that she applied a prod.

'Do you accept the maxim of "From each according to his means, to each according to his needs"?'

David managed to smile.

'Bakunin,' he said. 'In fact it translates more accurately as "From each according to his faculties".'

Ming brushed aside his quibble.

'Again in theory, yes, I accept it. But it does seem very unjust to pay someone less merely because of her sex. You might as well say, why pay a single man the same as a married man? Or why pay a childless married man the same as one with ten children? I would support any move towards equal pay, provided there were a corollary of increased welfare benefits for those whose needs were greater.'

'Thus neatly having it both ways,' said Ming, with a smile to take away any sense of criticism. 'Don't you believe that people are responsible for their own destiny? That if they choose to have a greater number of children than their neighbour, they can't demand that their neighbour ought not to be allowed more income to spend on holidays, boats, what-have-you?'

David carefully balanced his hot pipe in a large pottery ashtray on the table at his side and then put his head in his hands.

'You're asking me impossible questions,' he muttered.

'Impossible or painful?'

'The latter,' he said, looking up with a smile that seemed to strip off layers of self-protection. 'Yes, people must take responsibility for their own surroundings and destinies. But,' he paused, obviously trying to gather his faculties, 'but you cannot extend that principle infinitely. You could never, for example, say that only the well-off may repro-duce.'

'Almost any principle becomes absurd when taken as far as that, doesn't it?' said Ming with deceptive gentleness.

'Absolutely,' said David. Ming laughed.

'What I was going to ask next was: and so would you say there are no absolutely right or wrong propositions? What a very difficult line for a politician to hold.'

'It is, but compromise is essential.'

'On that admission, I'd better leave you,' said Ming, once

more looking down at her watch. 'I've absorbed almost half your one free day. I'm sorry.'

'Painful though some of your questions are, I've enjoyed it,' said David with truth. 'And that's as rare as hens' teeth, I can tell you. I'll drive you home.'

'Oh, no, I can get a taxi.'

'Nonsense,' he said, getting up. He went out into the hall and called, 'Julia, darling?'

'Yes, what is it?' she asked, emerging from the kitchen, where she had been giving the children their tea. She was very tired, her stock of patience had been badly tried by Amanda's antics, and she still had several hours' reading for the case she would be defending the following day.

David's voice sounded crisper than it had done for weeks. When Julia saw his face she noticed that his eyes were clearer than usual and had lost the weariness that seemed to drag them downwards. Her own fatigue left her for a moment as she walked towards him, her face as openly happy as he had ever seen it.

'I'm just going to run Ming home. She'll never get a taxi. All right?'

'Yes, of course,' she said after a moment.

Ming emerged from David's study into the hall, looking radiant.

'Thank you, Julia, for a wonderful lunch,' she said, holding out her hand. 'You've been very kind to me and David's given me some wonderful material.'

Julia felt a sudden sense of exclusion that shook her. Ignoring it, she took Ming's hand and said truthfully that she, too, had enjoyed their lunch.

She watched them leave the house, David tall and broad-shouldered in his old grey-green tweed jacket and Ming slight and elegant in a tightly belted navy-blue linen dress with a big white collar. Remembering that the ancient gods were said to listen to the prayers of mortals and maliciously grant them, Julia shivered. The words she had spoken in Flixe's conservatory threatened to haunt her.

CHAPTER 8

A week later Ming was sitting at her kitchen table in her dressing-gown, eating breakfast and reading a letter from Jack Hazeldene, who had gone back to Cyprus alone:

Your sanity and your kindness helped enormously and got me through a bad time. I'm afraid that I poured out a lot of misery on you and never even thanked you for listening. You gave me a kind of peace then that's still with me. I feel as though I could say anything to you now.

If there's anything I can ever do for you, Ming, I hope you'll tell me. I owe you a lot.

It's pretty frightful here, really just policing the island, but having to put the men at far more risk than they ever would be if they were ordinary police. But I find that I don't much care any more — about anything. I'm beginning to think that Caroline used to do the caring for both of us.

I've done as you said and let myself think about her without trying to stop what it does to me. God knows it's painful, but you say it helped you after Annie died and I'll try. Send me a line when you've time. Now I know I can talk to you, it's not so bad. Bless you, Ming. Jack.

PS The memsahib's latest plan is someone's unmarriageable niece who's doing a governess job for some Americans in Athens, God help us. It's thought that she could be persuaded to pop over to Cyprus for a holiday. I'm being kind but firm. It's wonderful to be able to laugh about it all, however wryly. You've done that for me, too.

Ming smiled at the post-script just as the telephone began
to ring. She tilted her red-painted chair on to its back legs
so that she could reach the telephone on the dresser.

'You're early,' she said gaily when Max had wished her a
brisk good morning. She realised that she was feeling
particularly cheerful.

'The proofs of next month's issue are supposed to be
passed for printing this morning, and we can't possibly
bring out the next edition without some mention of this
Suez business.' Max continued to be brisk.

'What business?' asked Ming, who had been so absorbed
in Jack's letter that she had not even opened her newspaper.

'President Nasser nationalised the Canal last night and
that is a little too dramatic for us to ignore, even though
you've subverted the magazine from its worthy aims to the
vulgarity of money and worldly success.'

'Well, even if he has I don't see what we can write about
it,' said Ming, laughing at Max's mock sneer. 'After all,' she
added, mimicking his precise and donnish articulation,
'you know perfectly well that whatever we write now will be
out of date by the time the magazine reaches the
subscribers.'

'You're having a bit of trouble with my vowel sounds,'
said Max, 'but it's not a bad impression.'

'Thanks a lot.'

'Not at all. But do be serious for a moment. The seizure
by the president of Egypt of our most important international asset is something we cannot ignore without
looking ludicrously parochial.'

Max had never sounded more derisory and Ming
grimaced, but she was determined to stand her ground.

'But anything we write now *will* be out of date by the
time the magazine comes out.'

'Not if we simply record the views of a representative
range of people. That's all I want you to do this morning.
There's just time. I can hold the printers off until tomorrow
and if you work hard you'll do it.'

'Max, I . . .'

'It's important, Ming. If you're going to be a journalist

you've got to behave like one. If you don't like it, you can go off and organise bazaars like a lady.'

'Damn you, Max.' Ming's smile made her voice warm and Max realised that she was about to yield.

'By the way,' he said, sweetening coercion with a compliment, 'I think your interview with David Wallington is excellent – and I suspect he'll like it, too, which should help us a lot. Well done.'

'All right, you old manipulator. I must be feeling peculiarly benevolent today: I'll do it.'

'Glad to hear it. You can either bring the article down first thing in the morning or dictate it to me this evening if you'd rather. That'll take time since I've no shorthand, but it might be more convenient for you.'

'I'll see,' said Ming, her voice softening in response to his. 'Thanks, Max. By the way, are you all right?'

'Certainly. Why not?'

There was enough frostiness in his answer to choke off any more expression of Ming's sympathy for his loneliness and so she merely said goodbye.

Having finished her cooling coffee, she pushed both hands through her unkempt hair, leaned her elbows on the formica table and tried to decide which of her friends and acquaintances could provide useful opinions. After a while she stood up, tightened the sash of her *eau-de-Nil* dressing-gown and went to her desk for a pad and pencil. She was still jotting down and crossing out names when her charlady arrived.

'Well, and are you ill then, Miss?'

Ming shook her untidy head and smiled.

'No. I just forgot to dress before I started work. Tell me, what do you think about this nationalising of the Suez Canal?'

'It's not right,' said Mrs Crook, exchanging her tightly buttoned overcoat for a mauve-flowered overall. She tied a clean duster over her hair and then added: 'It's ours like. We built it; we own it.'

'Well, actually the French designed it and the Egyptians built it; we just bought a lot of shares in the Company that runs it,' said Ming, remembering everything she had learned from the elderly vicar in Egypt.

'Comes to the same, I'd say. It's ours. And that Nasser didn't ought to have taken it. Never. Are you going to dress, Miss, or shall I do your bedroom first?'

'I'll dress,' said Ming with a laugh. 'Sorry to put you out.'

She gathered up her notes and went to put on an old pair of dark blue trousers and a loose jersey, before sitting down at her desk and pulling the telephone towards her.

By the end of the morning she had spoken to almost everyone on her list and had pages and pages of neat short-hand to transcribe. Most of the views she heard were as simple as Mrs Crook's, even when they were expressed in a more sophisticated fashion. But there were a few who stood out.

David Wallington believed that Nasser had behaved high-handedly but almost within his rights. To David the nationalisation of the Canal Company was little different from his own party's nationalising the coal mines, some of which had been owned by French companies. But he stressed that he was not a spokesman for the party. Its leader, Hugh Gaitskell, was calling for retaliatory action to be taken as soon as possible.

So, Ming discovered, were her father and Roger Sill-horne. Both of them believed that Nasser's action was comparable with Hitler's invasion of Czechoslovakia and that Nasser must be stopped just as Hitler should have been. When she first heard this, Ming felt herself growing cold.

'This would never have happened if that ass Eden hadn't agreed to withdraw our troops from the Canal Zone,' said her father. 'It's all very well to have said that with thermo-nuclear weapons ground forces are unimportant, but he can hardly drop a nuclear bomb on Egypt.'

'God forbid!' said Ming at once.

Her father laughed gruffly. When he had given Ming his forthright opinion of the intelligence of members of the British Cabinet, he went on to say:

'There's only one consolation, m'dear. The wretched Gyppos won't be able to run the Canal or pilot the ships through without running 'em aground. This great triumph of Nasser's will turn pretty sour, mark my words.'

'I see. Thank you,' said Ming, scribbling busily. 'That's very helpful. I've got to finish my article by this evening so I'd better get on.'

'When are we going to see you? Your mother misses you,' he said gruffly. Ming felt a sudden squeezing in her guts.

'I'm sorry,' she said. 'But it's not very long since I came down. And we've been so busy on the magazine, and ...'

'I know, I know,' said her father. 'We've agreed not to talk about that. But don't forget us, will you?'

'Of course not. I'll ...'

'You get on with your work now. Seen anything of your sisters?'

'Yes,' she said, pleased to be able to report that both Flixe and Gerry were well.

'Good, good. Well, goodbye now, m'dear. Don't let things get on top of you, will you? You looked pretty peaky when you were here.'

'I'll be all right. That was just such a hot, stuffy week. 'Bye,' she said and then sat looking at the black telephone, wishing that she could divide herself like some primitive organism, so that part of her could entertain her parents and write only things that would never offend them, while another part worked on the magazine with Connie and Max, a third fell in love with Mark and perhaps a fourth was the sister her sisters so obviously wanted.

The telephone rang under her hand, making her jump.

'Hello?' she said inadequately as she picked it up.

'Ming? Mark here. I was ringing to find out what time you'd like me to pick you up tomorrow.'

'Tomorrow?' said Ming, who had no idea what he was talking about. 'I've got to finish a piece on this Suez business for Max by this evening. I'm all over the place.'

'I just thought I'd find out where you'd like to dine and what time. The dance isn't supposed to start until ten,' said Mark's voice, sounding wary.

'The dance,' said Ming blankly. She had completely forgotten it, which was absurd since her invitation was propped up on the chimney-piece to her left. 'Oh, yes, the dance. Well, what about eight o'clock?'

'Perfect. I'll pick you up. 'Bye.'

'Before you go, Mark,' said Ming in a hurry.

'Yes?'

'What do you think about what Nasser's done?'

'Ming,' he said, his voice sounding as though he were holding on to his patience with difficulty. 'I'm a civil servant and you're a journalist. I couldn't possibly say anything. Try your political friends. See you tomorrow.'

Ming was left holding the buzzing receiver in her hand, thinking of all she had to do for Max. She pushed her free hand through her tangled hair again and realised in irritation that she would have to have it washed and set before the dance. Having made an appointment with her hairdresser for late the following afternoon, she turned back to the ruthless use of her friends.

The call that gave her the most pleasure was to one of Peter Suvarov's sisters, who lived in Paris.

'Ah, Ming,' said Natalie Bernardone, 'what does it all matter? Politics! They all make a terrible noise and nothing is really changed by what they do.'

'War changes quite a lot,' said Ming, having to concentrate quite hard on what Natalie was saying. Ming's French was fluent, but it always took her time to adjust to hearing it spoken.

'No one is going to be stupid enough to go to war over this.' Natalie, who had not only lived under German occupation in Paris but as a child had also suffered through the Russian revolution, shared all Ming's passionate hatred of war.

'Even the politicians know too much now to do that. Besides, in thirteen years the Company's lease of the Canal expires. Nasser would have had it then in any case. It's a fuss about nothing.'

Ming tried to believe that, but some of the things Roger and her father had said made her add:

'People over here seem to be getting very bellicose.'

'Some people always do. In Paris they are saying that

Nasser has stolen our property — as though he had not promised to pay in full the value of all the shares. And they are saying that it is all you could expect from a man who has been inciting the Algerians to rise up against us in North Africa.'

'And Bertrand?'

'My husband is, as always, reserving his judgment until he knows more,' said Natalie, sounding as affectionate and loyal as she always did. 'But all this is too boring. When do we see you? You haven't been in Paris for ages. Come and stay.'

'I'd love to,' said Ming genuinely as she thought of the Bernardones' wonderful flat on the Ile de Saint Louis and the gaiety that Natalie had always managed to create around herself.

'We go away for August, but we'll be back in September. Come then. I will write when we come back. Good-bye, Ming.'

By the end of the day she had interviewed fourteen people over the telephone and set about trying to create a coherent article from her pages of notes. She herself believed that it would be both unnecessary and dangerous to risk a fight over the Canal and she was determined to make the point without sounding either hysterical or unpatriotic.

By the time she drove back into London the following day after delivering the finished piece to Max, Ming felt a sudden and quite unexpected satisfaction. She had done a piece of urgent work in time and reasonably well, and Max seemed pleased with her. Her assumption that Connie had involved her in the magazine only out of altruism had begun to dwindle long ago, but that day it actually disappeared.

Parking the car near her hairdresser, Ming wished that she had not agreed to spend her time at anything so absurd as the Attingers' dance. Unlike her sisters, who had each done the appropriate Season before the war, Ming had never officially come out. Fifteen at the beginning of the war, she was twenty-one when it ended and far too old in her own estimation to give up three months or more to a husband-hunting season.

Later, with her blonde hair newly set, she went home to make up her face carefully and put on the dress she had bought. As she stood in front of the long mirror in her bedroom, Ming lifted her chin, squared her shoulders and looked at herself with a measure of approval.

She had searched shop after shop until she found the dress she wanted. In each one assistants had brought her frocks they considered suitable to her slight figure and delicate fairness: pink or white or pale blue, with closely fitting waists and large skirts, they had all made her look absurdly young. In the end, in a small shop in Belgravia, she had been offered a slim, straight dress made of black grosgrain silk. Strapless, it had a low, heart-shaped neckline and was deceptively simple, but it made Ming look much taller and much older than any of the others she had seen. With its short, matching jacket it would be very useful, she had told herself, as she noticed the shocking price.

Her long kid gloves, a diamond necklace that Connie had lent her and her own diamond earrings added a necessary lightness to the glamorous dress. Ming knew that she would never look as magnificent as Flixe – she simply was not built for magnificence – but that evening she felt that she looked like a sophisticated and intelligent woman. For once there was nothing fragile about her appearance and nothing of the young girl.

Heartened, she answered the door to Mark's ring and saw from his expression that he had noticed the efforts she had made. He stepped across the threshold and kissed her cheek.

'You're looking wonderful, Ming,' he said.

'And so are you,' she answered truthfully, looking him up and down. 'I've never seen you in white tie before. It suits you.'

Mark grinned as he thanked her. He took her to dine at the Ivy, which was relatively empty at that hour, while the theatres were playing, and they spent a comfortable two hours together, eating good food and talking easily in the familiar dining room.

'Did you get your article finished?' asked Mark just as one of the waiters brought their pudding plates.

'Yes,' said Ming. 'I'm sorry I asked you what you thought. I wasn't trying to force you into indiscretion. It simply hadn't occurred to me that you wouldn't be allowed to say.'

'It didn't matter,' he answered, shaking his head slightly. 'I just hope that I didn't sound too brusque.'

'Only brisk, which is perfectly all right.' Ming smiled. 'What do you suppose is going to happen? It's only me asking, not the magazine,' she added hurriedly as he raised an eyebrow.

'God knows.' Mark shrugged. 'That's not official discretion. I simply have no idea. But it'll be interesting.'

'This is wonderful,' said Ming, changing the subject abruptly. For some reason she could not bear the thought that Mark might echo her father's belligerence. 'Do eat some.'

Mark smashed his silver teaspoon through the glassy burnt-sugar surface of his *crème brulée* and ate some of the smooth, dense, slightly sweetened cream underneath.

'Isn't it just?' he said when he had swallowed. 'One of my favourites.'

They talked about food then and, later, about places they had been abroad and Ming relaxed. Mark had planned to spend his summer fortnight's holiday with friends in Ischia, but was not sure whether the crisis would mean that leave had to be cancelled. Ming said that she had had all the holiday she could reasonably take in one year and was planning to work right through August.

'Although,' she added, remembering Natalie's invitation, 'I might go to Paris for a few days in September.'

'I haven't been to Paris for years,' said Mark with a slightly wistful expression in his eyes. 'It should be lovely then. Lucky old you.'

'Yes,' agreed Ming, 'but the magazine takes up so much of my time now that I might have to combine holiday with work of some kind to salve my conscience. I say,' she added, looking down at her watch. 'Talking of consciences, I suppose we ought to get going.'

'Pity,' said Mark with a rueful grin. 'I'd much rather stay here with just you and talk about Paris – or anything else, for that matter.'

Ming looked at him in silence for a disconcertingly long moment and then veiled her remarkable eyes. Mark looked thoughtfully back at her before turning to signal to a waiter.

When they were sitting side by side in his car, Ming said: 'I would too.'

'Would you?' he asked with a return to the wistfulness that seemed so odd in someone as direct and strong as he. 'I'm glad.'

He drove slowly to Belgrave Square, where the Attingers had borrowed a huge house with a first-floor ballroom. From the moment the car turned into the square, Ming could hear the thin, sweet sound of a Strauss waltz floating out across the trees in the middle of the square. The house itself was obvious, with all its windows open wide and light and music pouring out of them between the looped curtains. Ming felt a light tickle of anticipation that surprised her.

'Doesn't it look romantic?' said Mark, echoing her silent thoughts as he parked the car.

Ming nodded her silvery-fair head in a movement of great grace, but when she spoke she surprised him.

'Perhaps it's the sort of thing one should enjoy from outside, instead of having to admit that the reality is boredom, sweaty bodies, smoke and a longing for one's bed,' she said with a laugh in her voice.

'I'd never realised you were so cynical.' Mark swung his legs out of the car and walked round it to open Ming's door.

'D'you mind?' asked Ming without getting out of the car.

'The cynicism? No. It's just surprising – but I like it. In fact you're turning out to be surprising in lots of ways. Come along: into the fray!'

Ming left her jacket in the ground-floor cloakroom and together they walked up to the ballroom, where they stood in a queue waiting to shake hands with their hosts. Ming congratulated them when it was her turn and was duly kissed.

'Both your sisters are here,' said Mrs Attinger over her shoulder as she turned to greet the next arrival.

Mark took Ming's arm and they walked together into the ballroom, where the young were twirling cheerfully in each other's arms and the older guests were standing or sitting in groups chatting with glasses in their hands.

Realising that she was not at all sure in which camp she belonged, Ming stopped at the edge of the floor to watch. She felt excluded from both. It was an odd sensation, which disappeared only when Mark touched her bare arm to urge her forward.

The first people Ming saw whom she knew were the two Suvarovs and Julia Wallington and she took Mark to meet them.

Flixe was looking noticeably pregnant by then but superb in low-cut ivory silk embroidered with gold. Her huge sapphire and diamond brooch was pinned to the deep neckline of her tactfully spreading dress and echoed the colour of her eyes. There was a wall sconce just above her head, shedding its light on to her luxuriantly piled fair hair. At her side Peter Suvarov, looking slim and dark in his evening clothes, was chatting to Julia Wallington. Flixe caught sight of her sister and waved.

'You look pretty well,' said Ming as she kissed her sister. 'Hello, Peter. Julia, how are you? That was a wonderful lunch you gave me.'

'Well, thank you. And you?' said Julia with a full smile.

She was wearing a severely cut dress the colour of new horse chestnuts, which added warmth to her skin and emphasised her tall, straight figure. Her gold jewellery was simple and unobtrusive, but there was a big ruby above the wedding ring she always wore. She looked thoroughly distinguished, completely in control again, and quite unlike Amanda's harassed mother in Kennington.

'I'll get you a drink, Ming,' said Peter, blowing her a kiss as he wandered off. Ming nodded and then turned to answer Julia's question.

'Oh, I'm fine. But I had some dull news today. I'm awfully sorry, but this wretched crisis in the Middle East has meant that my editor has postponed my piece about you until the autumn.'

'That doesn't matter in the least,' said Julia, with a self-mocking grimace. 'In some ways it's rather a relief.'

Ming laughed and asked whether David was at the party. Julia shook her head.

'Not yet. He'll be here after the Division,' she said and then she turned to Mark, who was talking to Flixe.

Ming remembered her manners and introduced him to Julia.

'Gerry's right. He's nice, Ming, and intelligent, and attractive too,' whispered Flixe, as soon as the others were distracted.

'I know,' answered Ming with some asperity. 'But I do wish that you and Gerry would stop matchmaking – and mother.'

'Oh, who's she picked on?' asked Flixe, her blue eyes alight with amusement. 'She can't really have thought she could do anything with that man who bought Church Hall Farm last year, can she?'

Ming burst out laughing at the thought of the fifty-year-old bachelor who had four cats and an unrivalled collection of antique church vestments.

'No,' she said. 'Not even mother has thought him suitable. I don't think she likes him much.'

'Then who? I wouldn't have thought that there was anyone else available down there.'

'She thought I'd do nicely for Jack Hazeldene,' said Ming forgetting her amusement.

'That's not really decent, is it?' said Flixe at once. 'No wonder you're angry. Did you see him when he brought the children back?'

'Yes. Mother asked him to lunch, but he and I met on our own first. It'll be a long, long time before he's in any state to think about anyone else. Poor man, he is still completely devastated.'

'I can imagine,' said Flixe, adding by way of distraction:

'Have you seen Gerry and Mike yet?'

'No. Are they here?'

'Somewhere about. Gerry's dressed in the oddest frock – rather like a gym-slip. Shall we go and sit down? My back's beginning to go.'

Ming nodded, touched Mark's elbow and told him that she was escorting Flixe to a chair and would see him later. As they sat down on gilt chairs at the edge of the dance floor, Ming saw Gerry dancing with her husband. They looked completely absorbed in each other, moving in perfect time.

'I don't know how poor Charlie Bederley is going to recover from your savaging,' said Flixe, still trying to distract Ming.

She smiled dutifully just as they saw Peter coming back towards them with three glasses of champagne in his hands. Before he was more than half-way, he was stopped by a ravishing young woman with a fashionably tousled mop of red hair. Her stunning figure was clothed in a clinging grass-green frock and she looked both beautiful and fun. Peter bent towards her with a smile that Ming remembered well. Flixe sighed.

'Do you mind?' Ming asked her for the first time. She did not look at Flixe as she spoke.

'That Peter's a rake, and an irresistible one? Yes, I mind,' answered Flixe truthfully. She tipped her head back, partly to ease her aching neck and partly so that she did not have to look at her husband exercising his devastating charm. 'But I try to keep it under control.'

She brought her head back to its normal position and made herself watch Peter. He looked almost boyishly eager and very happy as he talked to the red-haired beauty.

'He always was, and he always will be. When it gets a bit much for me, I remind myself that it's me he always comes home to, that he seems to want me more – or at least more permanently – than any of the others.'

'Is it worth it?' Ming asked gently. Flixe not only looked at her sister then, but she also touched her hand.

'Yes, Mingie, it is well worth it,' she said. 'Even after all these years I'm potty about him. It is simply not rational to mind that an awful lot of other women are potty about him too. It's a fact of life.'

'I suppose so,' Ming was beginning when they were interrupted.

'Champagne?' Peter Suvarov's voice, which still had a faint, attractive Russian accent, stopped Ming from saying anything else. Both sisters accepted.

'Sorry it's a bit warm, but I got waylaid. You look lovely, Ming. I don't think you need have any fears about being a cabbage white. How's the work?'

Before Ming could do much more than tell him which articles of hers Max had accepted for publication, they were interrupted yet again.

'Ming?' The familiar voice of Roger Sillhorne surprised her. She stood up, shook his hand, and introduced him to the others.

He was fair-haired and had a strong-featured, if pale, face. He would have been quite attractive had he not been rather portly and full of self-consequence. Flixe smiled to herself as she listened to his pompous greeting. He looked as though he ought to have a rich, deep voice, and when he spoke the light, drawling sound was almost shocking.

'Will you dance with me, Ming?' he asked and then added as she obviously tried to think of an excuse to refuse: 'And give me a chance to tell you I'm sorry?'

At that she had to smile, and she tucked her hand in the crook of his arm.

'You don't have to do that, Roger,' she said. 'I'll see you later, Flixe. Peter.'

Roger held her stiffly and danced as though he were afraid that he might slip and fall on to the floor in an undig-nified heap. His constraint made Ming feel uncomfortable, but she did her best to look as though she were enjoying himself.

'I meant it, you know,' he said after a while. 'I owe you an apology.'

'For what?' asked Ming lightly, suppressing a sudden

fear that he was about to admit to having written the anonymous letters.

'Driving you into the arms of that wretched pervert,' he said, not sounding apologetic at all.

'I beg your pardon?'

'You were ill when you left and it really wasn't fair of me to try to make you come back then.'

'That sounds better, Roger.'

'Your judgement was obviously affected,' he said, swinging her round and forcing her out of step with the music.

'Wait a minute, we've lost it,' she said and persuaded him to moderate his steps.

They danced in silence for a while and she tried to forget what he had said, but eventually she realised that she could not.

'What did you mean by pervert?' she asked. Roger gave a short laugh.

'What do you think? You can't really believe that simply by changing his name he was going to mislead people into believing that he's a decent man.'

Ming stopped and moved off the floor.

'What are you talking about?'

'The so-called Mr Hillary,' said Roger, laughing at her distress. 'Typical to choose a girl's name for his surname.'

'You're as bad as my father. What are you talking about?'

'For God's sake, stop playing the little innocent. You must know as well as I do that he spent eighteen months in Wormwood Scrubs after the police caught him.'

'Poor Max,' said Ming, understanding at last all the things that had puzzled her about him and the life he was leading sequestered in the country.

The music stopped and she knew that she had to get away from Roger, who was watching her with a kind of satisfaction that disturbed her.

'You really didn't know, did you? Poor little Ming. How wretched for you. Did you have romantic feelings for him? Dear, dear.'

Ming wrenched her arm away from him.

'Don't be ridiculous,' she said. 'He's old enough to be my father.'

Over his shoulder she caught sight of her eldest sister and left Roger to stand alone at the edge of the dance floor.

Gerry, seeing the tension in her sister's face, walked across the floor at once.

'What's up? Are you feeling faint? It is horribly hot.'

Ming shook her blonde head and in spite of her muddled feelings tried to concentrate on Gerry's blue dress, which she saw did look rather like a long version of a gym-slip, comfortable but not at all elegant.

'Then what is it?' asked Gerry, pointing to two gilt chairs behind them. They sat down.

'Roger has just told me ...' Ming found that she could not repeat his exact words. 'That Max served a sentence in prison.'

She took a tiny lace handkerchief from the gold bag that hung over her wrist and blotted the sweat carefully from her upper lip.

'Of course. Didn't you know? Why did you think Connie set up the magazine if not to give him a job when no one else would?'

'I feel so stupid. I never realised he's a ... you know, a ...'

'Oh, grow up, Ming.' Gerry sounded thoroughly impatient. 'You must have been talking to Father – or Flixe. It's one of her most incomprehensible blind spots.'

'Flixe?' Ming ought to have been used to Gerry's impatience but she found it almost as daunting as she had done in childhood.

'Yes,' said Gerry, still angry. 'She believes they suffer from an illness that should be cured by the nearest doctor or psychiatrist.'

'I feel ... It's difficult to absorb the fact that a man one's liked – and trusted – could be ... well, something like that. No wonder Father was so put out at my championing the magazine.'

'That's absurd, Ming. Max hasn't changed just because you've heard about his past. You can still like and trust him as you always have done.'

'Do you really not think that they are dangerous? What about the Russian spies?'

Gerry raised her eyes to the ceiling and tried to control her irritation. After a moment she looked back at her youngest sister and understood that she was grappling with a concept that was quite new to her.

'That's like saying that promiscuous heterosexuals are wonderful painters simply because a few geniuses have been rakes. If the law didn't make criminals out of the homosexuals no one could blackmail them and they would not be subject to that sort of pressure.'

The tension was leaving Ming's face under Gerry's bracing treatment.

'Sorry. I don't think I've ever thought about it before. It's not something I've ever come across. You're probably right, Gerry.'

'Don't worry about it. Just concentrate on what you've always known and liked about Max.'

'Gerry! How good to see you.'

Both sisters looked round to see Mark and Julia walking towards them. Gerry smiled at Julia and kissed Mark. Julia turned to Ming, who was still sitting down.

'I've just been trying to persuade Mark to bring you on a picnic we've planned on the river at Oxford. Will you come? Next Sunday. David and I thought we'd drive down in the morning with the children, take a punt up the river and picnic on the bank somewhere.'

'It sounds lovely,' said Ming vaguely, still taking in what Gerry had just said.

'I thought so, too,' said Mark from Gerry's side.

'Good,' said Julia. 'Now, I'm sure you're pining to dance with each other, so I'll leave you to it. See you both on Sunday.'

When she had gone, looking self-contained and impressive in her austere dress, Mark offered Ming his hand.

'How about it? Will you waltz with me?'

Ming looked quickly at Gerry to see whether she would mind being left on her own.

'I'm going to find Mike,' she said with a smile. 'Off with

you, and forget all about your erstwhile boss and his idiotic ideas.'

Ming stood up and Mark swung her into his arms and led her into the dance.

He was completely at ease with the music and the steps and Ming lost both her shock and her distress as they danced. After a while she gave herself up to his lead. He felt her relax and tightened his hand very slightly on hers. She could feel the strength that he usually disguised and she suddenly admired the confidence that let him keep so many attributes and talents out of sight.

'You dance beautifully, Mark,' she said. 'It's very unexpected.'

'Like you, I'm an unexpected sort of person,' he replied with a cheerful smile.

'I'm beginning to think that you are,' said Ming more seriously. 'And a very kind one.'

They were passing one of the three immense open windows that led to a balcony overlooking the garden. Mark looked down at her sleek head.

'I'm awfully hot. Shall we?'

'Let's,' said Ming and preceded him through the swagged, gold silk curtains.

The air was almost as warm outside, but the sky was clear for once and the stars in their indigo background gave an impression of coolness. Ming breathed deeply and looked up, wishing that she recognised more of the constellations.

'I'm beginning to think that I should have waited to ask you to marry me until now,' said Mark, sounding more amused than anything else. 'This is a positive cliché of romance.'

'Ah, but we were always told as girls never to believe a man who told us he loved us in a ballroom,' said Ming, growing more cheerful with every minute in his company. 'Over bacon and eggs is much more romantic really.'

Mark was silent for so long that Ming regretted her instinctive teasing. He put his right hand lightly on her bare shoulder.

'You will tell me if you change your mind, won't you?'

'Mark, I ...' Ming broke off, biting her lip. Her eyes were huge and worried when she looked up at him. 'I'm so bad at this. It's just that I'm not ...'

'Not quite sure? Don't worry, darling. I shouldn't have said anything, but I have been getting the feeling that you might be moving towards me a bit and I couldn't resist asking.' Mark's face looked pale in the moonlight and his eyes seemed very dark.

'I am,' she said with an effort. 'But ...'

'Don't spoil it, Ming,' said Mark as a smile broke the seriousness of his face. He leaned forward and let his lips touch hers for a moment and cling.

Ming felt a sudden surge of pleasure so intense that it almost frightened her. Amazed that anything so ordinary and familiar as a kiss could affect her so much, she put her hand on his shoulder as much to steady herself as to respond to his caress. He drew back and looked down at her seriously. She could see that he was shaken too and seemed at a loss for words.

'We'd better go back inside or I might lose my head,' he said at last.

Just then an erect, arrogant figure appeared silhouetted against the lighted window. Ming hissed slightly as she breathed in. Mark took her hand and led her forward. Not recognising Roger, Mark merely nodded to him as they walked past.

'Who was that?' he asked as they moved out of earshot.

'My late employer,' she said.

'Ah.' Mark's monosyllable seemed full of comprehension. 'D'you know, I think I'm actually enjoying myself after all,' he said. 'Come and have a drink.'

CHAPTER 9

The next Tuesday Ming drove down to Etchingham for her weekly meeting at Max's cottage. Despite Gerry's exhortations and her own determination to cope sensibly with what she had learned about Max, Ming was nervous of meeting him again.

He felt her tension as soon as she came through the oak door into his long blue-and-white room and for a while he could not understand it. But when she flinched as he handed her a cup of coffee and touched her, he thought he knew what had happened. He tried to concentrate on his surprise that Ming had taken so long to discover what must have been common knowledge, but her distaste for him was obvious and hurt too much.

Connie saw it, too, and it made her angry. At the end of the meeting, which she kept much shorter than usual, she insisted that Ming walk back to the Dower House with her.

'Just what do you think you were doing?' Connie asked as soon as they left the cottage. At the fury in her voice, Ming flinched.

'I'm sorry. I wasn't doing anything except trying to conceal my ... shock, I suppose.'

'You didn't do a very good job, I'm afraid.'

Ming stopped on the gravel drive up to Connie's house.

'Did Max know?'

'Of course he knew. He's morbidly sensitive in any case. Even though your face was politely blank you showed exactly what you thought of him every time you moved away from him.'

'I'm sorry,' said Ming again, sounding helpless. 'I never meant to upset him. It's just so difficult. Don't you find it difficult?'

'Not any more,' answered Connie more gently. 'Come on up to the house and I'll try to explain. How did you find out? I was sure you knew nothing.'

'Roger Sillhorne was at the Attingers' last week and he told me. I might not have believed him because he was in a beastly mood, but Gerry confirmed it – and told me to brace up,' said Ming with a faint smile.

'I'll bet she did. She's always been sensible, that sister of yours, if a little intense.' Connie pushed open the unlocked door.

Ming preceded her into the hall, a double-height cube with a black-and-white marble floor and pale walls covered in family portraits.

'Would you like a drink?' she asked, pointing to a laden table to the left of the front door.

'I think not. I ought to get back to London pretty soon. Connie, will you say something to Max for me?'

'Certainly not.' Connie poured herself a glass of sherry and went to perch on the edge of the fender. 'Sit down, Ming.'

Obediently she sat in one of the blue wing chairs beside the empty fireplace.

'I don't know how much you've been told, but you have to understand that all Max ever did was to have a love affair with another man, a painter. He has never seduced a boy, just as he has never pursued guardsmen in the park or any of the other things you've read about in sensational newspapers. He is the civilised, intelligent man you've always known.'

'That's what Gerry said, and I understand it intellectually, but I can't help feeling peculiar with him.' Ming paused and tried to explain, 'I suppose it's just the way I've been brought up. Gerry's different.'

'Indeed she is.'

'But if Max is all those things, how could he have done it? I thought he once told me he was married.'

'He was.' Connie's strong face seemed to shrink. 'He was married to a very old friend of mine, who treated him really badly. Max was completely faithful to her for years – until he fell in love with his painter.'

'I understand,' said Ming gently, not because she did but because Connie seemed so distressed.

Her answer was a look of exasperation.

'I don't think you do. Gerry seems to have been remarkably discreet. Max's wife was staying here with me one weekend and she started to taunt me for my single state.' Connie's voice held none of its usual confidence. 'She often did that but for some reason that day she caught me on the raw. She went on and on about how wonderful it was to have a man's love, and how Max was so devoted to her that he didn't mind what she did so long as he could live with her.'

'She sounds quite mad.' The outrage in Ming's voice made Connie laugh for a moment.

'Not really; just stupid and incorrigibly vain.' Connie drank some sherry and sighed. 'But I was just as stupid. I got so angry with her that I told her about Max.'

'Ah.' Ming did begin to understand the real story then.

'Yes,' said Connie, her dark eyes bleak and her mouth stiff. 'And because of what I said, she put private detectives to watch Max and then denounced him to the police. Because of what I said out of outraged vanity he spent eighteen months in Wormwood Scrubs.'

Ming could not think of anything comforting to say to that and so she stayed silent. After a while, Connie looked at her with eyes that seemed darker and harder than ever.

'Can you imagine a man like Max locked up with thieves and murderers? One shower a week; no more than three books out of the library in a week; rationed letters; rationed visits; nothing to write on or with; petty-minded warders. And it was my fault.'

'It doesn't bear thinking about. Connie, I am sorry if I've hurt you – either of you. I just didn't understand.'

'Will you let me lend you a book?'

'Book? Why? I mean ...'

'Don't look so scared, Ming,' said Connie, sounding just as exasperated as Gerry had done at the dance. 'I'm not proposing to introduce you to pornography. It's a French novel. You read French, don't you?'

Ming nodded. Connie got up off the fender and disappeared for five minutes. When she came back she held a thick, buff-coloured paperback in her hand. Ming took it.

'I'll read it, Connie. Thank you. I must go.'

'Drive carefully.'

'I always do.'

Ming decided to take the book to bed with her that evening so that she could make a start on it. She expected to find it distasteful if not actually difficult to read, but after the first chapter or two she found herself gripped.

The novel, *Story of a Lost Love*, turned out to be an exquisitely written account of a love affair between two young men who had met in the war. Ming read fast, hardly noticing the time, murmuring at intervals, 'I see,' and, 'now I understand.'

By the time she reached the end she had tears in her eyes. Completely caught up in the delicately revealed love between the two men, she was desolated when one fell ill and died. Her own emotions were so near the surface of her mind just then that the mental and physical intimacy described in the book seemed idyllic.

The following morning she posted the book back to Connie with a short note:

You were right, Connie. I do understand more now, and I am bitterly sorry that I upset you and Max. You and Gerry have both said that there are too many people who are too ignorant of the subject. Do you think that we might print an excerpt from the novel in the magazine?

It is so beautifully put – and so illuminating – that it might change a lot of people's attitudes.

Love, Ming

She took the parcel round to the Post Office, enjoying the warmth of the July day. When she returned to the flat her charlady told her that Mr Sudley had telephoned and wanted her to ring him back to make arrangements for Sunday's picnic. Ming was smiling as she dialled the number of his office.

They agreed to meet at Ming's flat and drive down to Oxford in her car.

'Unless it's raining,' said Mark. 'I draw the line at a river picnic in the rain.'

'I can't imagine Julia wanting that either. If it is wet, perhaps you and I could do something together in London.'

There was a short pause until Mark said quietly:

'Perhaps I should pray for rain. Either way, I'll see you on Sunday.'

Ming was rather relieved when she woke on Sunday morning to see bright sunlight pouring through the pale green curtains of her bedroom. The temperature rose steadily throughout the morning as they drove to the appointed boat house, where the Wallingtons were waiting with two punts. Julia sat in the first punt with her children on either side of her and David took the lead up the river.

After an hour's gentle progress, he turned his head towards the second punt and signalled towards a break in the willows on the bank.

'Let's stop for lunch,' he called.

Ming, who was punting at the time, nodded. She felt as though she were encased in a thin, hot, transparent shell, and she put up a dripping hand to cool her forehead. Carefully manoeuvring her unwieldy boat, she laid it beside David's at the bank, where Mark tied it up to the roots of a willow.

'Hot?' he asked, amused, as he watched Ming lay the long, heavy pole along the bottom of the punt.

'Boiling. I'm glad I'm such a clumsy punter that I seem to get half the river trickling down my arm each time I bring up the pole,' she said. 'At least it's cooling!'

Mark laughed and held out a strong arm to help her out

of the punt. The neck of his shirt was open and he had rolled up the sleeves. As he reached for her, Ming saw his muscles moving under the tanned skin of his forearm and the sunlight glinting on the fine gold hairs. He looked happy and very masculine in a way that his London clothes seemed to disguise.

She took his hand, which felt cool and firm as he pulled her up the bank into the field above. David and Julia were already unpacking their large wicker hamper and the children arranging paper plates and plastic beakers.

Ming went at once to help David spread out the rugs and groundsheets they had brought, while Mark returned to the punt for a basket in which he had packed a bottle of Anjou rosé wine swathed in damp newspaper. Julia laid a thick white cotton cloth over the groundsheet on the grass and began to set out the food.

There were soft bridge rolls for the children, stuffed with ham and chicken, while for the adults Julia had brought a selection of smoked salmon, pâté and game pie. Fruit, slabs of dark Belgian chocolate, Bath Oliver biscuits and cheese, and a heavy, dark plum cake followed.

As she lay on the grass, propped up on one elbow, Ming became increasingly aware of Mark, who was sitting with his back against one of the smooth-barked willows. They were at least four feet apart and yet whenever he breathed or swallowed she was aware of it. Watching a pulse beating in his strong neck, she even felt as though she could feel the blood beating through his veins. Her own breathing became difficult. She caught his eye and knew suddenly that he was having to exercise enormous self-control to stay leaning negligently against the tree. Something in her insisted that she lean forward and touch him.

Pushing herself upright instead, she turned away to pick up her glass and swallowed a mouthful of the fresh pink wine.

'Cake, Ming?' asked Julia, who had been watching them both with a faint smile.

'Thank you.' Ming reached for the paper plate Julia was holding out to her and took a mouthful of the dark, heavy cake. Her teeth bit through the hard-baked almonds on the top and sank into the sweetness of the sultanas and crystallised cherries.

'It's wonderful,' she said when she had swallowed. 'Did you bake it?'

'Janice made it,' said Amanda quickly and Julia exchanged a rueful smile with Ming.

Her breathing had returned to normal and she found herself able to turn back to Mark again. He looked at her almost sternly for a while and then his face relaxed into the same friendly, unthreatening smile he had always used. He, too, accepted some cake from Julia and added a thin slice of sharp white Wensleydale cheese to it just as David said abruptly:

'Is it true that there's already a complete battle plan for a possible invasion of Egypt, Mark?'

The cheese slipped off the cake as Mark jumped, and it crumbled into irretrievable pieces as it hit the grass. Ming moved at once to pick them up, wondering why David had decided to bring up such a depressing subject. Julia cut another slice of cheese and silently handed it to Mark.

'I've really no idea,' he said with a careful lack of emphasis. 'You politicians always know far more than any of us in Whitehall.'

David grimaced a little self-consciously and then nodded.

'I don't believe that's true, but you're right. I shouldn't have tried to pump you.'

'They can't go to war over something as unimportant as this,' said Ming with a depth of feeling that rather surprised Mark.

She carried her handful of cheese fragments to the river and flung them in, standing for a moment to watch the ripples spread out and distort each other as they met. Staring down at the dark green, midge-speckled water all she could think of were the torn bodies and broken minds, the betrayals and the torments that the last war had brought.

When she came back, she stretched out her legs and lay back in the cool grass, staring up at the bright patterns of sunlight and green leaves above her head, trying to bury her memories and ignore her sympathy for the regiments serving in Cyprus, who would be in the front line of any attack on Egypt.

'They can't put us through all that again,' she said when her feelings were under control. 'Not just for the Canal and the price of oil.'

Amanda, bored with sitting still and listening to the adults' incomprehensible conversation, scrambled up from her place at David's side and stood with a hand on his shoulder.

'Can me and Jonathan go and play, Daddy?'

'Julia?' said David, lifting an eyebrow.

'Good idea,' she said, smiling at them both. 'Take care of Jonathan. And no paddling.'

'All right,' said Amanda with an enormous sigh.

She heaved Jonathan up from the rug and ran off with him to explore the edge of the river. Ming could hear them pointing out to each other holes they were convinced must conceal moles and water rats and toads and felt some of the tension begin to seep out of her body. If she could only concentrate on the children and their games, she would stop thinking of what might happen in the Middle East. The children's shrieks of delight grew less shrill as they wandered further and further from the others.

'Even if some kind of military action were undertaken it wouldn't spread beyond Egypt,' said Julia carefully, remembering the little that Flixe had told her of Ming's war work.

Ming turned to smile gratefully at her and between them they turned to talk of less important matters. Gradually the conversation slowed over the debris of the picnic into a desultory murmur as they all gave themselves up to the languor induced by the wine and the heat.

The sun poured down on them through the dappling leaves and a faint wind rustled the willow branches that overhung the river. Birds sang and an occasional tractor could be heard chuntering over distant fields.

'This is heaven,' said Ming, waking up at last. She lay

back with her arms under her head, staring up through the leaves.

She was wearing the white clothes she had bought for Egypt and she looked utterly at peace as she lay with her face tilted towards the sun, smiling slightly. The other three watched her as they smoked, Mark with an expression of hopeless tenderness on his face and David with un-concealed admiration. Ming tilted her head to look at him and he smiled at her.

'I'm glad you're enjoying it,' Julia said, slapping away a horse fly that had settled dangerously on her bare leg.

'It was a brilliant idea of yours. Don't you think, Mark?'

'A wonderful break in the dusty routines of meetings and minutes, arguments and reasoned syntheses! It's hard to think we're only an hour or so from London. Why do we let ourselves be shut in offices all day, worrying about what's happening on the other side of the world when we could lie about like this?' he said, gesturing to the green-and-gold landscape of fields and trees and sluggish water.

An iridescent dragonfly, like a miniature helicopter, circled the small group, hovering just above Ming's face, and then darted away to settle on the surface of the river for a moment, before skimming off again.

'It does seem mad, doesn't it?' agreed David, through his teeth as he chewed the succulent white root of a long piece of grass. He looked at his watch and pulled the grass out of his mouth. 'But we have to do it, even if we let ourselves forget for a while. And we can't forget for much longer, Julia.'

'Oh, not yet,' she wailed, thinking of the long, hot drive back into London and the struggle to get her children bathed and into bed. In theory she enjoyed the rare treat of looking after them herself at weekends, but in practice she found it remarkably difficult. 'As Ming says, it's heaven here; don't let's waste it.'

'Well, if we leave it much later the traffic will be horrible getting back into London,' said David. 'And Jonathan is bound to be sick. Better get it over with.'

Julia pushed herself up from the tree against which she

had been leaning and brushed some leaves out of her hair.

'I suppose you're right. I'll go and round up the young,' she said, sounding tired. 'It's astonishing how energetic they can be in all this heat.'

'You stay put,' said Mark cheerfully. 'I'll get them. I'd like to stretch my legs a bit in any case.'

He strode off, leaving the others to shake crumbs off the plates and rugs and pack everything up into Julia's hamper.

'Thank goodness for Scotland!' she said as she buckled its leather straps. 'Are you going away this summer, Ming?'

'I don't think so. If London gets too horribly stuffy I'll probably spend a few days down with my parents, and perhaps extend my weekly visits to Connie Wroughton. When do you go?'

'Julia and the children are off next week,' said David, putting out a hand to help her up off the grass. 'I'll follow as soon as I can. We always try to spend the whole of August in Scotland, recharging our batteries for the first two weeks and then shooting. It's glorious up there, Ming, even if you don't shoot. She ought to come for a bit, shouldn't she, Julia?'

'Yes, indeed,' she said after an appreciable pause. 'Do come and stay, Ming, if you'd like to. It's wonderfully relaxing after the rush and worry of being in London. Peter and Flixe brought the children up last year and seemed to enjoy themselves.'

'That's awfully sweet of you,' said Ming, who had noticed the pause and wondered about it, 'but I really don't think I can this year while we're still fighting for the magazine's very existence. I can't help thinking that if I stop my battle to boost the circulation I'll lose what little ground we've gained.'

'Well, we'll have to make a plan for next summer then,' said Julia, smiling more easily. 'You and Mark both, perhaps.'

'Perhaps,' said Ming, thinking that they might none of them be in a position to take any kind of holiday if the politicians really plunged them into war. 'You are kind.'

Mark hove into sight then, with Jonathan riding in

triumph on his shoulders and Amanda dancing along at his side chattering in excitement. David went to meet them.

'And good with children, too,' murmured Julia, smiling so that her brown eyes narrowed and gleamed.

'I know, I know,' said Ming, almost snapping. 'He's positively too good to be true. Has Flixe been trying to make you egg me on?'

'She did mention how much she wants to see you happily established,' admitted Julia, wishing that she had said nothing, 'and it is hard not to think how well the pair of you get on together. But it is absolutely none of my business.'

'No,' said Ming frankly. 'It isn't really. If Flixe asks you about today, perhaps you ought just to tell her that I'm not the marrying kind.'

There was a sharpness in her voice that surprised Julia, as well as a hardness in her eyes and a determined look about her mouth.

'I've made you angry,' said Julia quickly. 'I'm sorry about that. It's just that we're all so fond of you, we'd like you to be happy.'

'Is marriage really so wonderful?' asked Ming, remembering all her various friends' tribulations.

'I think it's the most important thing there is,' said Julia at last. Her eyes were fixed on the tall figure of her husband, who had just relieved Mark of his burden. In a rush of honesty, she felt compelled to add, 'And there are times when it's quite hellishly difficult.'

As Julia turned to Ming and looked straight at her, Ming saw real unhappiness in her eyes and a kind of terror. Much of Ming's anger dissolved and her need to offer comfort persuaded her to smile.

'I'm sorry. I didn't mean to sound ungrateful. It's charming of you to mind about me. I just have terrible difficulty in letting myself believe in any kind of permanence.'

Julia winced noticeably, but she recognised Ming's sincerity and knew that she was completely unaware of David's state of mind. It was not Ming's fault that she had come into his life at a time when he was facing disillusion

and a sense of failure, or that her open admiration of him
had somehow given him back his faith in himself. Julia had
been trying to make herself believe that that was all there
was to it, but she found it hard.

Whenever David was anywhere near Ming, his face
changed from bleak depression to eager interest. Julia had
to watch that, just as she had to listen to his innumerable
accounts of how intelligent Ming was, how sweet and how
sensitive.

The very openness of David's delight told Julia that there
was no question of a love affair in his mind, and yet she
could not avoid the knowledge that he was to some extent
falling in love with Ming. If she had not been so vulnerable
she would have seemed less dangerous, and if she had not
presented such a threat then Julia could have watched her
reawakening of David's zest for life with undiluted pleasure.
That she could not was the hardest aspect of it all to bear.

'There can never be any guarantees of permanence,'
Julia said as gently as she could, 'but if anyone has loyalty
stamped on them, I'd have thought it was your young man.'

'Yes, I know,' answered Ming readily. 'He's like David in
that.'

They said no more, but stowed the rugs and baskets in
their respective boats and waited in the brindled shade for
the two men.

Ming said very little on the slow, hot drive back into
London. Mark was not sure whether it was contentment or
boredom or even a headache that kept her silent and had
begun to worry by the time they reached the suburbs. As
they rounded Shepherd's Bush Green and were held up at
a red traffic light, Ming turned to him.

'Mark, it's been such a lovely day that it seems a pity to
end it so soon. Would you like to come back with me to
Cheyne Walk and have some supper?'

The lights changed before he had framed his answer and
it was not until they were driving down towards Kensington
that he said slowly:

'I'd love to, if you really mean it.'

She turned briefly to smile at him. The traffic miraculously cleared and Ming put her foot down, changing up to fourth.

When they got to the flat she took him into the drawing room and asked what he wanted to drink.

'Oh, anything,' he said, looking at her as she stood, slim and relaxed, beside the marquetry tray on which she kept a selection of bottles.

'Really?' she said, smiling mockingly over her shoulder.

She looked so happy, so certain of herself and him, that he believed he had managed to cross a barrier that had been keeping them apart. He moved closer and put a hand on her fair hair. The wind on their drive back into London had whipped it into tangles and he began to smooth it, stroking her head over and over again. Ming turned to face him and he put his other hand on her head.

'I'm sorry about the tangles,' she said with a humility that touched him almost unbearably. She seemed so trusting that he wanted to build defences all round her so that she should never be hurt again. It had always been obvious to him that someone had once hurt her badly.

'Don't worry about the tangles, my love,' he said, putting both arms around her and laying his cheek against her head. 'You look adorable when you're untidy. When you were lying there in the grass with twigs in your hair it was almost impossible not to come and kiss you despite our formidable chaperones.'

He slid his smooth cool hands on either side of her face and turned it up towards him. She was smiling faintly, remembering the last time he had kissed her and waiting for him. Her wonderful dark blue eyes were clear and seemed to be full of love.

Mark bent his head and kissed each of them in turn, then her slightly tilted nose and finally her parted lips.

Ming moved a little closer and reached up towards him, her hands on his arms. For a moment she felt utterly at peace. His gentleness and the warmth of his affection seemed to be everything that she had ever wanted.

As he felt her responding to him, Mark's hands moved to her neck and his thumbs stroked the smooth skin, reaching

down between the lapels of her linen shirt to her breast-
bone. His breathing changed and quickened.

Ming drew back a little and saw in his face an urgency of
need that warned her of what she was doing to him.

'Mark, no,' she said, suddenly realising that he had
misunderstood her invitation to supper.

'Ming?' he said, puzzled and rather worried. 'Did I hurt
you?'

She managed to smile as she shook her head, unable to
explain why she had to stop him from touching her in case
she in turn had misunderstood him.

'Then what? What's the matter?' His voice had been
sharpened by anxiety but to her it sounded like anger.

'I can't ...' she began and then shook her head again.
'I'm sorry.'

Mark dropped his hands to his sides. Ming saw his
mouth twist and his eyes grow cold and she moved away to
stare out of the window. With one hand clinging to the
curtain, she said:

'I'm sorry, Mark. I didn't mean to let you do that.'

'What do you mean by "let"?' he asked. His voice was
quiet but she could still hear anger in it and her hand tightened on the chintz.

'You spent half the picnic looking at me as though you
loved me,' he added in a voice that sounded distant. 'You
invited me back here. When you stood in my arms just now
I could feel that you wanted me.' He stopped, took a deep
breath and then went on more quietly: 'And then you talk
about letting me kiss you, as though you thought I wanted
something you found hateful. But you didn't hate it. I
couldn't have misunderstood the way you moved towards
me, the sweet way you kissed me. What are you trying to
do, Ming?'

At that she did turn and as he saw her face he closed his
eyes.

'Don't look like that,' he said in a voice of aching despair.
'God knows, I don't want to make you unhappy.'

'Or I you,' she managed to say, despite the tears that
seeped from her eyes. She tried to stop them.

'Then what the hell is going on? If I could even understand what it is that you want, I could cope better.'

'Oh, don't,' she said instinctively. 'Mark, please don't be
angry.'

'Ming,' he said in a voice of determined reason. 'I'm not
angry. But I am worried and ... and lost. You know that I
love you and I would do anything in my power to protect
you from anything in the world. But I don't understand
what you are after, what it is that you want from me.'

He waited, but she found she could not answer since she
herself did not know what she wanted.

'If you want me to get out of your way, all you have to do
is say so,' he said. When she still said nothing, he added in
a harder voice: 'Well?'

'I don't understand it either,' she said with difficulty. 'All
I know is that I am very fond of you and I should hate it if
... if I didn't see you sometimes.'

'But that's all. I see. I can't blame you, I suppose,
because it's pretty much what you told me when I first
asked you to marry me – even if you seemed to have
changed your mind last week.' He shrugged. 'But I really
don't think that I am capable of going on like this.'

The sight of her white, unhappy face wrenched at him
but he was having a fierce enough battle to keep himself in
control and at that moment there was nothing he could
have done for her.

'I suppose,' he added in a voice of such bitterness that she
felt unbearably guilty, 'that just because I'm half suffocated
by desire for you, there's no law that says you have to reciprocate. I'll go.'

'Mark, don't ...' she began, but he had gone before she
could finish her sentence.

CHAPTER 10

Ming spent the days before she expected her next anonymous letter in dread that it would say something about
Mark. Her sisters had figured in earlier letters, as had
Connie and Max. Ming's work, her character, her looks,
even the black dress she had bought for the Attingers'
dance had aroused her nameless correspondent's malice.
Only Mark had never been mentioned.

When the letter came on the expected day in the usual
style, it informed Ming only that she was lazy, exploitative,
unfair and greedy, and that the false charm she exercised
over people so destructively would lead to her humiliating
downfall. Relieved, she even managed a grim smile at the
irony. Mark was the only person she had actually exploited
and he had never been mentioned as one of her victims.

Her excitement over the magazine and her attempts to
lighten its tone and content were overtaken by her muddled
feelings for Mark, and she lost most of her ability to inject
fun into the articles she wrote. She continued doing what
she could to expand the circulation and for most of the rest
of her time simply followed Max's orders, one of which was
to monitor the Suez crisis.

As far as they could discover diplomatic negotiations
were being carried on as discreetly as possible with all the
countries who used the Canal regularly. The two most
important were the French and the Americans.

The French, who had as much or more interest in the

Canal as the British, were pressing for military action against Egypt. The Americans, richer and infinitely more powerful, were urging negotiation rather than war. Nasser had for some time been playing them off against the Russians, which had made them withdraw their offer to help finance an immense dam at Aswan just before he nationalised the Canal; but they disliked British and French imperialism, did not themselves make much use of the Canal and disapproved in principle of military intervention in the affairs of other countries.

They proposed first an eighteen-power conference on the Canal, which led to a doomed attempt by the Prime Minister of Australia to negotiate with Nasser, and then the Suez Canal Users' Association, which was to organise the operation of the Canal, collect the fees for its use and pay a proportion of the proceeds to the Egyptian Government.

Ming, reading the little information that reached the newspapers, hoped that the Americans would prevail and that some kind of negotiated settlement would be reached. But there were plenty of others who preferred the French view.

While the negotiators' efforts continued and the international lawyers produced arguments for and against the acceptability of military intervention, Anthony Eden was preparing for it in case Nasser failed to yield to diplomatic pressure. Elite forces were withdrawn from their policing duties in Cyprus for retraining in Malta, reservists were called up, and the Chiefs of Staff drew up plans first for a landing to the north of Alexandria, then a land assault from the south and finally a sea-borne assault on Port Said. The Treasury were working out how a war might be financed and what consequences it could have for the value of sterling.

The members of Eden's Cabinet were divided, in increasing but secret bitterness, between those who shared his view that force must be used to destroy the Egyptian army and bring down Nasser, those who were prepared for war only if the Security Council of the United Nations sanctioned it, and the others who believed that armed intervention was not only inappropriate but also morally and legally unjustifiable.

The Cabinet disunity was not publicised but many people suspected it, and it was mirrored in the country as a whole. Half the press and its readers were furious that nothing had been done to teach Nasser a lesson and the rest were equally angry with the obvious military preparations.

Jack Hazeldene's occasional letters to Ming were appropriately discreet, but since they came from Malta, she knew that he would be one of the first into Egypt if the government did decide on war.

Increasingly afraid of the prospect, she badly wanted to discuss what she had heard with Mark, but she knew that she had cut herself off from him. Throughout that summer she saw nothing more of him until one Sunday morning in October, when she was on her way to lunch with Gerry and Mike.

Ming had taken the lift and arrived at the door of their flat at a quarter to one, just as Mark reached the top of the stairs. He said her name and she whirled round, almost overbalancing.

She was so astonished to see him that she lost all her self-control and reached out for him with both hands.

'Mark,' she said, her face eager. 'I had no idea Gerry had asked you. Are you all right?'

Evidently surprised by the warmth of her welcome, he hugged her lightly and then drew back to smile at her, but his eyes were dull. He looked so ill and so worried that she said at once:

'Mark, please don't be so angry. I know I deserve it, but I ...'

'I'm not angry with you, Ming. Things are awfully sticky just now in the office, that's all.'

'I can imagine.'

As Ming smiled at him, the happiness died out of her eyes and her mouth looked vulnerable. He longed to be able to tell her just how hard the civil servants and politicians who hated the thought of war as much as she did were working to prevent it, and how frustrated they were by the almost furtive secrecy of Eden's supporters on the Egypt Committee. Even members of the Cabinet who had shown themselves hostile to the idea of military intervention were denied information and many senior civil servants knew that they were being kept in the dark if not actually told lies.

'It may blow over,' he said unconvincingly.

'Really?'

'No one knows what's going to happen, but you mustn't be afraid. Even if the worst happens, it'll be a local affair. It won't touch you.'

Ming shuddered.

'It's not that,' she said with some difficulty, 'so much as what might happen if it all escalates. Don't you think the Russians might come in on Egypt's side? If that happened it could be even worse than last time.'

'No. I don't think so. We're in no position to fight another major war, the French certainly aren't, I doubt if the Russians are, and even the Americans would find it difficult. Whatever happens it won't be that. Besides we've got the bomb. No one's going to risk it.'

'I hope you're right,' said Ming, turning to knock on Gerry's door.

Almost before they were inside the flat Mike insisted on taking Mark round to the local pub for a drink before lunch, leaving Ming to help Gerry cook.

'What's that about?' Ming asked as soon as they reached the kitchen.

Gerry, who was dressed in a pair of navy slacks and a clinging pale blue sweater that showed off her slim figure, looked up from the batter she was making for Yorkshire pudding and grinned. She looked young and free, and her resemblance to Ming was much clearer than usual. There was flour in her hair and a spot of milk on her nose.

Ming realised that she had not seen Gerry look happy in so uncomplicated a way for a long time.

'Mike's up for promotion to Assistant Secretary at last,' she said. 'We'd got rather worried, because it's been held up a lot. I think he wants to ask Mark's advice on what to do next.'

'Ah,' said Ming, smiling both in pleasure at the news and in relief that she had not been left alone with Gerry for an interrogation. 'I am glad. He really deserves it – you both do.'

'Nothing to do with me, ducky,' said Gerry, taking the whisk out of her batter and carrying it, dripping, to the sink. 'That needs to stand for a while. Would you like a drink?'

'Why not?' After a pause, Ming, who had been remembering what her anonymous correspondent had written about Gerry's hard-working life and her own lazy extravagance, added: 'Gerry?'

'Mm?'

'Do you mind about Anna's money?'

'Coming to you?' Gerry turned with the sherry bottle in her hand. Her face was innocent and still looked happy. 'Ming, of course I don't mind. I've always thought it was wonderful. Why should I mind?'

'It just seems rather unfair that you and Mike work so hard and I was presented with all that just because I had the luck to be her godchild.'

Gerry brought her sister a drink.

'Listen, ducky, of course I'd have loved to have it myself, but if anyone deserved a windfall like that it was you. I am really glad you've got it. You've had some very bad luck in your life and it was more than your turn for something good.'

Gerry poured herself a drink and went to sit at one end of the pale wood Scandinavian sofa. She patted the yellow cushion beside her. Ming obediently came to sit down.

'It makes you free of all the things that were causing you such trouble,' Gerry said, watching the concern in Ming's eyes. 'It means that when you do decide to marry Mark you'll be able to live with him on your own terms. Whatever happens to you, you'll at least be able to feed and house yourself – and your children.'

'But I'm not going to marry Mark,' said Ming blankly.

The wide smile on her sister's face faded.

'Why on earth not?' Gerry had never sounded so impatient with her sister. 'He's besotted with you, and it's been perfectly clear almost since the beginning that you care for him.'

'Not like that.'

'Ming, think. He'd be ideal for you: intelligent, kind, patient, gentle, interesting. What are you messing about for?'

'God knows,' said Ming hopelessly. 'You're right in a way: I do like him enormously and since I made him so angry that he's stopped seeing me, I've missed him a lot. But, Gerry, I can't marry him just because he's suitable and because he wants me and because I like him.'

'I can think of a great many worse reasons.' Gerry was half amused but also still exasperated. 'I hadn't realised that you weren't seeing each other any more. But listen: he can't be that angry. I told him that you were coming today when I invited him. He could easily have refused to come.' She smiled at Ming in spite of her impatience. 'Since he didn't refuse, he must have wanted to see you.'

Ming's face relaxed. Gerry shook her blonde head so that a small cloud of flour flew round it like a halo in the sunlight.

'After Mike, Mark is the best person I know,' she said more gently. 'Don't throw him away unless you're really sure you don't want him. They don't come much better than Mark Sudley.'

Before Ming could say anything the two men returned with bottles of cider from the pub. Mike looked so cheerful that Ming and Gerry buried their various anxieties and allowed themselves to share in his celebration.

The beef was perfect, the Yorkshire pudding crisp and the apple pie that followed them a wonderful combination of tastes and textures. Mike, who was always good company, was positively ebullient that day, although Mark was obviously not at ease.

Gerry could not help looking from him to Ming as they talked and wishing that she could force her sister into making the right decision before it was too late. Mark was undoubtedly in love with her, and his patience and loyalty were beyond question, but it was asking a great deal of a man to tease him as Ming was doing, particularly at a time when his work was causing him such strain. Gerry hoped that Mark knew as well as she did that the teasing was involuntary and that Ming had no idea of how much pain she was causing him.

Mark caught Gerry's eye and, noticing how anxious she looked, blew her a kiss.

'You're a wonderful cook,' he said, 'and the best of friends.'

Gerry's affection for him overtook all her worries and she deliberately started to talk to him about a new film she had read about and hoped to see. He listened, commented and then suggested that they go and wash up while Mike and Ming finished the cider.

Laughing, Gerry agreed and later the two of them came back with a big pot of coffee. It was well after five before their enthusiasm for each other's company waned at all. At last Ming smiled across at Mark with the old unshadowed friendliness. Then she turned to her sister.

'I think I ought to be off.'

'I'll come with you on the tube,' said Mark. 'Gerry, thank you for a wonderful lunch – the perfect way to celebrate Mike's news. Well done, old man.'

They left and walked down to Tottenham Court Road in peaceful silence. At the top of the steps Mark turned, suddenly remembering that there was no tube station at Chelsea.

'Isn't it easier for you to catch the bus?' he asked.

'Well, yes,' admitted Ming. 'Much.'

'Shall I come with you?'

Ming shook her head.

'There's no need and it's miles out of your way,' she said. 'I'll be perfectly all right.' She slipped off her right glove and held out her hand. Mark took it and held it.

'I really like your sister,' he said, looking down at her hand.

'So do I,' answered Ming with feeling. 'And Mike, too. They're very lucky with each other.'

'I think it has to do with good judgement and carefulness as much as luck,' said Mark, beginning to play with her fingers.

Ming felt a surge of emotion that seemed to be neither fear nor love but some impossible amalgam of the two. Staring straight ahead and seeing nothing, she said his name. There was both pleading and a warning in her voice.

'It's all right,' he said. 'I didn't mean to sound nagging. I know you don't want the same things as I do. There's no reason why you should. I don't know whether – or for how long – I'd be able to be like an ordinary friend, but if you'd like it, I will try again.'

'Mark,' said Ming, a wonderful smile breaking over her face, 'if it wouldn't make you miserable I'd like it so much.'

He looked down at her bright face.

'That's something, I suppose. You do look happy.' There was a bitterness in his voice that made her smile fade. 'It is almost unbearable to know that I can only make you look like that with a promise to pretend I don't love you.'

He set off down the steps to the underground before she could say anything, turned back half-way down as though to come back, but then went on his way. Ming walked slowly to the bus stop, wishing passionately that she had been able to love him properly and wondering why she could not.

It was a long time before she could sleep that night, and she spent the next day trying to ignore her exhaustion and do some useful work. She ate almost nothing all day and felt so tired by the evening that she went to bed as soon as the last of the daylight had gone. She was still asleep when Mrs Crook arrived to clean the flat the following morning.

'Well I never!' she said as she pushed open the door to Ming's bedroom, Hoover in one hand and duster in the other. 'Seeing as how it's Tuesday, I thought you must have gone to your meeting early. I never thought you'd be laying in bed.'

'What's the time?' asked Ming, having hardly understood anything she had heard. She rubbed both eyes vigorously and pushed her tangled hair away from her forehead, feeling stupid and rather ill.

'Half-past nine,' said Mrs Crook. 'Shall I make you a nice cup of tea?'

'That would be lovely,' said Ming, flinging back the bedclothes and stumbling across to the chair where her dressing gown lay. 'I'll have a quick bath and then I must run or I'll be dreadfully late.'

'Well, that's what I thought,' said the charwoman. She leaned the Hoover against the bedroom wall, tucked the duster into the string of her apron and hurried off to put on the kettle, muttering to herself.

Fifteen minutes later Ming had forgotten her malaise in the rush of getting dressed. Wearing a pair of thin jersey trousers and a loose white silk sweater, she sipped the tea and brushed her hair at the same time. She found her bag, car keys and sunglasses, said goodbye to Mrs Crook and ran out of the flat to where she had parked her car.

The traffic was fairly light and she made good time down to Etchingham, but when she pushed open the heavy oak door of Max's cottage there was no sign of him. The windows in the long drawing room were all wide open, which suggested that he could not have gone far, and the room was cool after the heat of the drive. Ming dumped her files on the gate-legged table and went to sit down on one of the sofas and catch her breath.

There were white autumn roses, faintly flushed with pink, in the Delft bowls and they added freshness to the familiar scents of the room: Max's tobacco, the old wood, the leather and cloth bindings of the books, and the cold ashes in the twin fireplaces.

Ming lay back against the padded sofa back, thinking how odd it was that of all the houses she knew and the places she had loved all her life, it was only in Max's rooms that she felt truly herself. The horror she had felt when she had first heard about his past seemed almost incredible in retrospect. She let her eyelids close and tried to ignore the headache that was biting behind her eyes.

Max, coming into the room a few minutes later with a pot of coffee and a plate of spiced biscuits, saw her from the

doorway and knew at once that something had happened
to her. Despite the relaxation of her pose, her mouth looked
pinched and there were huge half-moon shadows under her
eyes. He laid the coffee pot down in the hearth, put the
biscuits on one of his oak coffers and went to sit on a stool at
her feet. She opened her eyes at the clink of the plate as it
touched a pewter bowl of pot-pourri.

'What's up?' Max's question was casual, but his tone
invited confidence.

'I'm in a terrible muddle,' Ming said, her voice quivering
slightly. It seemed odd that a man like Max should be the
recipient of confidences like hers, but despite everything she
knew that she trusted him.

'That happens to all of us sometimes,' he said. 'What
form has yours taken?'

He did not sound particularly sympathetic, but Ming
desperately needed to talk to someone who was a little
detached from her.

'I've badly hurt someone I care about and made him . . .'
Her voice faltered. Deliberately she stopped, recovered and
went on: 'I've made him angry with me.'

She looked Max full in the face. 'And there's nothing I
can do about it.'

'Tell me,' he said, taking her hands and shifting from the
stool so that he could sit beside her. She told him everything that had happened, letting all her instinctive privacy
go as she never had before, even with her sisters. She told
him of Gerry's and Flixe's campaign to make her marry or
at least have an affair, adding:

'You see, they both think it's unhealthy for women of my
age to have no sex life. But I can't just launch into it as
though it were no more than a game of tennis, to do me
good and give me a bit of exercise.'

Max laughed wryly, but Ming ignored it and went on to
tell him of Flixe's dinner parties and direct advice, of
Gerry's more subtle persuasions, and of Mark's niceness and
great suitability, of the fact that she liked him.

'I understand all that,' said Max when she finished, 'but
there's more, isn't there? There's something you haven't

told me. Has he been horrible to you?'

Ming bit her lips and looked at him with eyes that seemed guilty. 'No. He lost his temper once, but he was quite justified.'

Max said nothing and so Ming felt that she had to tell him more.

'Some time ago I made him think that I wanted to go to bed with him. I never meant to mislead him, and it hadn't occurred to me that he would assume I wanted to make love. I couldn't unless I loved him. He didn't understand me when I said I wouldn't and he clearly thought I'd been teasing him.'

The irony of the situation was not lost on Max and privately made him smile.

'I think you're probably making a pretty good stab at it, Ming,' he said in a voice of surprising gentleness. His arched eyebrows pushed the skin of his forehead into neat wrinkles as he smiled at her.

'Stab at what?' she asked, stunned by his accusation. 'Teasing him?'

'Loving him, you idiot,' said Max kindly. 'Isn't that why you're so upset? If you felt nothing for him, why should you worry? It doesn't seem to be what he thinks of you that's bothering you, but your own feelings.'

Ming got up and went to stand in one of the windows, her right knee propped on the blue cushion, her arms on the window sill, staring out at the heavy, hot, golden-green countryside.

'I feel plenty, alas, but it isn't love. I'd do almost anything to be able to love him, but I can't. I don't know why not. He's everything my sisters say, but I can't do it. Oh no! Here's Connie. Max, don't tell her, please.'

'All right. She's quite trustworthy, though.'

Suddenly remembering the little Connie had confided of Max's history, Ming turned to look at him. He nodded.

'She is, whatever you may have heard to the contrary,' he said.

By the time Connie had walked round to the front door, Max had poured out three cups of coffee and Ming had taken hers to the table, where she had left her files. Connie grinned at them both in something like triumph and announced that the circulation of their magazine had passed the break-even point. The last issue had even made a little money.

'Hurrah!' said Max with enough enthusiasm to cover Ming's slower response.

'I'm so glad, Connie,' she said at last.

'It's no wonder you're looking so tired,' said Connie. 'You've been working like a slave all through this horrible weather.'

'I think she needs a holiday,' said Max, smiling comfortably across the table at Ming. 'How about it?'

Her eyes misted with emotion all over again as she felt the warmth of their liking and approval.

'I had been thinking of nipping over to Paris for a few days,' she admitted. The thought of escaping from England for a while suddenly seemed inviting. 'Peter's sister has asked me to stay, but I'd have to do some work while I was there.'

The other two laughed.

'I knew we were on to a gold mine when we managed to snare Ming,' Max said, ostensibly to Connie. 'I've never known anyone so conscientious.'

'Well, you could do something actually,' was Connie's contribution. 'We haven't had a travel piece in the last two issues, and Paris is always popular. Three thousand words or so of enticing descriptions would do a treat.'

'I feel a little as you did after the stoning on the Nile,' said Ming with a faint smile. 'What was it you said? "I'm not sure I'll find the right lyrical touch." '

The other two looked at each other and Connie slightly shook her head.

'I'm sure you will. You're becoming relatively professional,' said Max.

'All right, I'll try.'

'That's agreed then,' said Connie briskly. 'Oh, and by the way, Ming, Max and I have decided to do as you suggested and print a short excerpt from *Story of a Lost Love* in the October issue. I've had it translated.'

Ming smiled shyly at Max and he nodded at her. Although he could not have told her so, he was grateful that she had made an effort to understand him and that she wanted their readers to do the same.

'I think you ought to take at least ten days in Paris, Ming,' he said. 'Or more if you want. You need time away from London and all your friendly advisers so that you can work things out. Understood?'

Ming agreed to go. She also renewed her request to put some money into the magazine as she walked back to her car with Connie after the meeting. Connie let her pleasure show in a broad smile.

'I'd love it now that we're making money, if you really still want to,' she said. 'I can't imagine having a better, more sympathetic or knowledgeable partner.'

'Thank you,' said Ming. 'I'll talk to my solicitor about the best way of going about it.'

'Ming, I am so glad that you're with us.'

CHAPTER 11

When Ming arrived at the airport outside Paris soon after five o'clock on Friday 12 October, her nerves were still jangling, and the prospect of getting herself across the city by Métro seemed almost too daunting. While she was still putting her passport back into her bag, she heard someone call her name and looked round, surprised. She could see no one whom she recognised and was just thinking that she must have imagined it when a slim dark-haired girl with a short fringe and a swinging ponytail came forward.

'It is Ming Alderbrook is it not?' she said in French, smiling.

'Why yes,' said Ming as her sluggish memory began to stir. 'Can you possibly be Danielle?'

'They call me Dannie now,' she said, leaning down to pick up Ming's case. 'Maman would have come with me, but she was caught by a friend and we didn't want to be late. We thought you might have forgotten the way home.'

'Dannie, you are kind,' said Ming, feeling herself relax. 'And you look wonderful,' she added, noticing the skin-tight trousers, the black polo-necked sweater, the sootily made-up eyelashes and the flat shoes. 'An existentialist, perhaps?'

'But of course,' she said cheerfully. 'We all are in my class at the Sorbonne. This way.'

By the time they had reached the Métro, punched their tickets and forced their way on to a crowded train, Ming's ear had begun to adjust to French, and she no longer had to struggle to understand what Dannie was saying to her. The last time she had been in Paris, Danielle had seemed no more than a child, but now she was full of talk about her philosophy classes and the man she loved. Ming listened amused and yet regretful that so few years should have brought about such an immense change.

When they emerged from the Métro and set off across the bridge into the pale grey quietness of the Ile de Saint Louis, Danielle took a packet of Gauloises out of her pocket with her free hand, and offered it to Ming, who shook her head. Dannie shook one out, took it between her lips, stuffed the packet into the back pocket of her trousers and flicked open her lighter. Ming was amused at her display of sophistication.

'Here,' she said, 'let me carry the case for a bit.'

Dannie gave it up without a struggle and casually picked a piece of loose tobacco from her bottom lip. When they reached the door of her parents' house, she dropped the remains of the cigarette and ground it out under her shoe.

'Don't tell,' she said with an engaging grin.

Ming promised and only a few moments later was being hugged by Natalie.

Anyone would have known her for a younger sister of Peter Suvarov, Ming thought, for she had the same intriguingly slanted eyebrows and long dark eyes, but where his glittered hers were calm and much kinder. Her face was differently shaped, too. With its wide cheekbones and small chin, it looked almost cat-like, which seemed to give her a cheerfully sensual air that was at odds with the extreme elegance of her clothes and hair. Her simply cut dark red dress showed that she had kept her slim figure, and her hair was as dark as it had been in her girlhood.

She and her husband lived in a huge flat on the first and second floors of a house on the unfashionable side of the secretive island that lies in the middle of the Seine. Facing north, the house was always in the shade and the big rooms were dark.

The flat was the antithesis of everything that Ming

admired and was trying to achieve in her own. Where her rooms were coolly pale and filled with light on all but the dullest days, the Bernardones' were decorated in rich, dark colours that seemed to accentuate the heavy gloom of the sunless house by day. At night, with the light of lamps and candles reflecting off vast looking glasses, silken fringes, gilt picture frames, and the dully gleaming bronzes, the great rooms came into their own with a magnificence to which even Ming found herself responding.

Natalie's husband, Bertrand, had some political function to attend that evening and Dannie was going out with friends, leaving Ming and Natalie to dine alone, exchanging family news and catching up on their old friendship. They ate simply and as the meal progressed towards the cheese, Ming began to feel very much at home.

Although Natalie was a good fifteen years older than Ming, she had never taken advantage of her seniority as both Ming's sisters and Connie were apt to do. Natalie had never given unsolicited advice, brought suitable young men to her guest's notice, or asked questions about her private affairs, and that evening was no exception.

For once Ming felt tempted to confide, but ironically she found that she could not begin without some encouragement. Her reticence had been developed over the years since her twin's death. At first she had hardly been able to say Annie's name without breaking down and so she had stopped even trying to talk about her. Combined with their elder sisters' tendency to pass anything Ming told either of them to the other and on to their parents, that early experience had convinced her that it was better and safer to tell no one anything. What had started as a defence had become a habit that was so ingrown it was hard to break.

Instead of telling Natalie about Mark, Ming talked about the magazine and about the disaster that had overtaken Max Hillary. Natalie had never met him, but as she heard his story, she became almost as indignant as she would about a close friend.

'It is barbarous,' she said at one moment, her face wrinkling in disgust. 'Everyone knows that the English are monsters of hypocrisy, but that ... How is it that Peter says it? Yes, that takes the biscuit. To convict a man who prefers to make love with men rather than women and lock him up in a prison full of men with no woman to be seen! It is idiotic as well as cruel.'

Ming smiled at Natalie's mixture of outrage and common sense, but they helped to reinforce her own still-shaky agreement. Then she grew more serious.

'It has ruined Max. He skulks in one of Connie's cottages, hiding under his false name, and won't ever go to London in case he's recognised.'

'He should move here and live freely,' said Natalie. 'We have not persecuted men like that since the Revolution. Perhaps he could become your "Paris Correspondent".'

'I'm not sure that we're big enough for a Paris Correspondent yet,' said Ming with a rueful smile, thinking it time to change the subject. 'As it is we only just manage to cover our costs; I know that Connie draws no salary at all – and mine is derisory. Besides,' she added with a grandly theatrical gesture, 'for the next issue at least, I am doing the Paris pieces.'

Natalie mockingly congratulated her, got up to pour them some more Armagnac and asked what aspect of the city interested Connie.

'Oh, the romance of beautiful Paris, I suppose; it's to be a moody travel piece,' said Ming accepting the glass. 'You know the sort of thing: the turning leaves on the chestnut trees, the mist over the Seine, the smell of baguettes as they leave the oven, the elegance, the glamour.'

'Ah yes,' said Natalie, wrinkling her nose. 'I know. And even more tourists will come to disturb our peace. Don't tell them about the Ile de Saint Louis!'

'All right; I promise that. Perhaps I should ask Dannie to take me to her jazz club, and write about the life of a young Parisian existentialist. We don't seem to have anything like them at all in London: just scruffy undergraduates in duffle coats drinking coffee in expresso bars. It's terrible when even your students are more glamorous than ours.'

Natalie looked at Ming from under her lowered

eyelashes and wondered why she sounded so disillusioned; there was amusement in her face and in her voice, but beneath it seemed to be real distress. Sitting with the light of a silk-shaded lamp falling across her face, Ming looked much older than when she had last been in Paris. There were lines around her eyes and lips, and the eyes them- selves were infinitely more knowing than they had been in the old days. To Natalie those were signs of character rather than disintegration.

She thought that Ming was more attractive than she used to be and better dressed, although without the elegance she could so easily have achieved. Having heard from Flixe all about Ming's inheritance, Natalie thought of suggesting a visit to one of the big couturiers. Just before she could think of a polite way of doing it, Ming looked up, caught Natalie's eye and blushed.

'You look as though you were about to be particularly tactful,' she said, laughing a little self-consciously.

Natalie, taken by surprise, dropped the idea of new clothes and instead shrugged.

'Not really, I was just wondering what had happened to make you so unhappy with life in London.'

After a long silence Ming tried to answer.

'It's not really London, it's a combination of things. Partly the hypocrisy that seems to have got worse and worse since the war.' She sighed. 'And the horrible prospect of another one. I try not to be a bore,' she added with a vivid memory of the elderly parson who had talked to her in Egypt, 'but I can't stop thinking about it.'

'I can imagine,' said Natalie slowly. 'Bertrand thinks that some military action is inevitable now that the Canal Users' Association has failed.'

'I suppose I could always write about that, too,' said Ming, rather depressed at the prospect. 'Do you think he might help me find out what is really going on over here?'

Natalie shrugged her shoulders. She looked remarkably pretty and surprisingly young as she sat with one leg tucked under her in a white-and-gold Louis XIV chair.

'Who can say? I expect so. Like you, he thinks it is stupid

to risk a war, but not many people here agree. You must ask him at breakfast.'

'Thank you. Natalie, I'm already rather tired. Would you mind if I went to bed?'

'Of course not. I'll take you up. A few days here and you will feel better. You can walk and look at lovely things and perhaps even buy some new clothes.'

Natalie escorted her guest to a grand and gloomy bedroom which was hung with old claret-coloured curtains. She turned down the bed and made certain that the hot-water bottle she had put there earlier had not grown tepid. She kissed Ming's cheek and told her not to get up in the morning until she had rested as long as she needed.

Ming returned the kiss, feeling fully relaxed for the first time since Julia's picnic, and that night she slept better than she had for months.

The next morning, after an enticingly French breakfast of bitter coffee and croissants during which Bertrand promised to collect as much information for her as he could, Ming set out on a conscientious search for material for her article on the sights of Paris.

Natalie had said apologetically that she had unbreakable commitments for most of the day and that Dannie had to attend her classes at the Sorbonne. Ming had told them both truthfully that she was not averse to having a private day in which to rediscover the parts of Paris she had loved and the three of them had gone their separate ways.

Ming went, as she had done ever since her first childhood trip to the city, to the towers of Notre-Dame. There, alone amid the gargoyles, she looked out over Paris, reminding herself of it and of her own freedom. Most of the landmarks were familiar and easily identifiable, particularly Sacré Cœur, dazzlingly white and unlikely against a thunderous sky. Turning her back on Montmartre at last, she gazed down across the river towards the lovely gilded dome of the Invalides and tried to put a name to the buildings in front of it.

Footsteps and cheerful American voices disturbed her silent contemplation of the beige-and-grey roofscape and she moved on to look down towards the Ile de Saint Louis. From the informed conversation she could not help over-hearing, she learned that on the top of a neighbouring department store there was a panorama that identified all the important landmarks that could be seen.

Taking advantage of the tip, she left the tower and made her way instead to the more prosaic vantage point. There was a woman already there, standing quite still with her back to the precipitous staircase. She seemed unaware that there was anyone else on the roof and so Ming was as quiet as possible as she looked down at the painted representa-tion of the view.

Signed and dated 1922, the panorama named every land-mark she could distinguish. Delighted with it, she walked slowly round the circular terrace, discovering exactly which building was which and making notes for her article.

Just as she was looking back at Notre-Dame and ident-ifying the spire of the Sainte-Chapelle, which she was deter-mined to include in her list of sights, the other woman moved.

'Ming!'

She looked up at the sound of Natalie's voice.

'Hello,' she said, trying not to sound surprised. 'Are you all right?'

'Yes,' answered Natalie, rather embarrassed to be found apparently sightseeing when she had told Ming that she would be busy all day. 'I always come up here at this time every week.'

'But why?'

Natalie pointed her with her gloved hand to a section of the panorama. Ming leaned forward to read: 'Direction de St Petersbourg'.

'Oh, Natalie.' Ming wished that she had chosen any other time of day for her sightseeing. 'I'm sorry I disturbed you.'

Natalie shook her head.

'There's no need. It's very sentimental of me, but it's the only contact I have with home. I can't go there. We can't get letters back from any of the family. We don't know who is alive and who is dead. It is ... difficult.'

The restraint of the word Natalie had chosen moved Ming.

'Do you remember much about Russia?' she asked gently.

'Very little detail really, just impressions and vague memories.' Natalie brushed some dust off the edge of the panorama and leaned against it in her fur coat. 'We had to leave when I was seven, but it was home and I've never managed to stop feeling ... deprived. If our parents had been able to come too it might have been easier. But it's a long, long time ago now. I must not keep you from your itinerary.'

'You're not. Do you suppose Peter misses Russia as badly as you?'

Natalie's dark head nodded.

'I'm sure of it: and not just Russia and the family, but all his idealism about the revolution; all the things he wanted for everyone. It must be worse for him, because he was part of it all and he must look at Russia – and East Europe – and hate what he did.'

'I always forget that,' said Ming, finding it hard to imagine the attractive, cynical, civilised man she knew so well as a fiery student revolutionary.

Natalie watched her face.

'I sometimes think that that is why he has always behaved so badly to people he loves,' she said slowly, 'as though having lost so much he can't ever let himself believe that he won't lose everything again. I think he protects himself against that fear by pretending not to care for anything.'

Ming stood, quite still, staring at Natalie for so long that eventually she said:

'Are you all right, Ming?'

'Yes. It's just that I had never thought of that. It makes such sense.'

'I must go,' said the other woman, 'if you are really all right. I'll see you at dinner.'

'Yes, thank you, Natalie. Don't worry about me. I was

just surprised,' answered Ming.

For the rest of the day, Ming kept thinking of Natalie's insight into her brother's state of mind. As Ming sat in the dark, gilded cosiness of the Sainte-Chapelle, idly noticing that the pillars looked just like rolls of Christmas wrapping paper, she wondered whether her own predicament might owe as much to a fear of losing what she badly wanted as Peter's did. The idea certainly made sense of the apparent contradiction that in a world where people were as hostile as her anonymous letter writer, the thing that seemed to frighten her most was Mark's love.

As she walked about the streets, noticing the elegant ironwork of balconies and railings here, the perfect carving over a doorway there, Ming began to look back at the events of the summer with more rationality than she had achieved in London. Gradually she began to think she had been absurd to refuse Mark what he had so badly wanted after Julia's picnic. She had refused because she could not bring herself to marry him, but the two were not inextricably linked. Looking back she seemed idiotically naïve.

What harm, she asked herself, would it have done anyone for her to make love with Mark?

That afternoon, after she had eaten an omelette and *frites* in a tiny brasserie in the Marais, she ordered a cup of coffee and pulled her big notebook out of her bag.

Instead of making notes for her article on the shabbily beautiful Place des Vosges and the Marais hotels as she had originally intended, she wrote to him:

My dearest friend,

What a mess I have made of things between us! I am sorry for it. If I had not been so muddled about it all, I might have been better able to understand my own feelings. The measure of them is the misery I have felt since we left each other after Gerry's lunch.

The whole idea of marriage still seems tricky, but I can't bear the thought of your being angry with me — or unhappy. I have realised how silly I was that day we picnicked on the river with the Wallingtons. Perhaps it was just my conven-

tional upbringing that made me deny us both what we wanted. I have begun to understand more and I would so much like to see you when I get back.

I shall be here for another ten days or so, staying with Peter Suvarov's sister. Their telephone number is the one at the top of this letter. It would be lovely to hear from you.

Ming

The days passed and there was no telephone call from Mark and no letter. While Ming waited, she worked hard on her travel piece on the city and wrote chattily to her parents and to Jack Hazeldene, who was still training with his men on Malta and waiting for the government to make up its mind.

Dannie did her best to help Ming see every different aspect of Paris, taking her to the jazz club in St Germain-des-Prés, to Jean-Louis Barrault's theatre and even to see Roger Vadim's new film *Et Dieu créa la femme,* which surprised Ming with its frankly erotic shots of the naked figure of Brigitte Bardot, including one of her lying on a beach with the waves foaming up under her.

With Dannie, Ming drank onion soup at dawn in Les Halles one day and ate *crêpes Suzettes* at a tiny restaurant in Montmartre the next. On sunny days they walked in the various Paris parks and listened to Edith Piaf from what sounded like a hundred wireless sets.

Occasionally as she was wandering alone around Paris, thinking and collecting material, Ming would imagine that she might suddenly see Mark emerge from a Métro station or a restaurant. She hardly ever ordered a cup of coffee without looking at the occupants of the other tables in case he was there, and when she prowled about the churches and art galleries of the city, she looked behind her every so often.

On her last day in Paris she thought that she actually saw him. A man of similar height and broad shoulders was walking ahead of her across the short bridge from the Ile de Saint Louis towards Notre-Dame. He had Mark's floppy brown hair, and Mark's way of walking: an apparently

casual stroll that covered a lot of ground very fast. Suddenly
breathless and happy, Ming called out to him.

When he did not look around, she ran after him to the
bridge and then saw that he was someone completely
different. Stricken with disappointment, she apologised and
turned to walk back the way she had come. A tiny muscle
under her right eye fluttered uncontrollably and her legs
ached. She felt thwarted and foolish.

Leaning against the hard stone parapet of the embankment on the south of the island, looking across the slow,
grey-green river, Ming told herself that Mark might not
have received her letter, that he might be waiting until she
was back in her own flat before he telephoned her, and even
that he might have been so surprised by what she had
written that he wanted to see her before he wrote anything
back. She also told herself with an attempt at detachment
that he might well have had enough of her uncertainties
and vacillation.

On that thought Ming stood up, squared her shoulders
and walked on to Notre-Dame. By the time she got there
she could not remember why she had come and instead
crossed the Petit Pont to the Left Bank in order to browse
among the second-hand bookstalls that ran in a dark green
line along the embankment.

Looking at the batches of prints hung on clothes-pegs,
picking up a book here and there, Ming gradually banished
Mark to the back of her mind. She found a charming illus-
trated edition of some Russian fairy tales, which she bought
for Gerry, and leafed through the collections of nineteenth-
century fashion plates until she found a set that might
please Flixe.

That evening Natalie and Bertrand took her to see two
short ballets by Manuel de Falla. She had never heard his
music in London and sat in amused delight watching *Le
Tricorne* danced against the wonderful set designed by
Picasso. At the end she emerged into the red-and-gold foyer
more cheerful than she had been for some time.

Bertrand had ordered some wine for them, and it was
standing there with a glass in his hand, surrounded by well-

dressed men and women in frocks from the great couturiers, that he asked Ming quite casually whether she knew what representatives of her government had been doing in Paris.

She shook her head, still smiling in amusement at the cheerful debunking ballet she had just seen. She was not really interested in anything her government might have been doing until Bertrand told her what he had heard. According to his informants, various Englishmen had attended two secret meetings at a house in Sèvres, where they had discussed the possibility of a joint attack on Egypt to be carried out by the British, the French and the Israelis. After much negotiation a protocol had been signed that day setting out what had been discussed.

Ming's delight in the ballet was overtaken first by surprise and then revulsion as Bertrand told her what the three governments had agreed. Apparently on a certain date the Israelis would launch an attack on Egypt through the Sinai desert. In order to stop the Egyptians from destroying Tel Aviv with their Russian-made bombers, the British air force would bomb the Egyptian airfields as soon as possible after the attack.

When the Israeli army had reached striking distance of the Suez Canal the French and British Governments would issue an ultimatum to the Israelis and the Egyptians demanding that they cease fighting and withdraw to positions ten miles from the Canal. If they did not, and it was considered most unlikely that the Egyptians would withdraw, then the French and British armies would launch an assault on the pretext that they were fighting to protect the Canal.

'I do not believe it,' said Ming, standing white-faced in front of Bertrand.

'Careful of your wine, Ming,' he said, pointing to her glass, which she had quite forgotten. It was tilting so much that as she started some of the wine spilled over the edge.

She licked it off her hand as simply as a child, which made him smile.

'What don't you believe?'

'I do not believe that the British Government would behave in so underhand a fashion.'

'But it's very sensible,' said Bertrand, looking as cynically amused as she had ever seen him. 'They want to fight Nasser. Without the Americans, France and Britain do not have enough strength to be certain of winning. We need the Israelis. This way your government does not need to let its people know of the alliance.'

'It's not that,' said Ming, biting all the lipstick off her bottom lip. 'Are you sure?'

Bertrand shrugged, looking like every Frenchman in an English play.

'No. It is what I have been told. My source is usually reliable. If you put anything in your magazine, you must not say where you got it.'

'Of course not,' said Ming.

A bell rang and they went back to the auditorium for the second of the short ballets, *L'amour sorcier*. Even de Falla's thrilling music could not make much of an impression on Ming as she thought over and over what Bertrand had said. She was vaguely aware of the heroine battling to release herself from the ghost of an old lover so that she could give herself to a new one, but it seemed quite unimportant. The colourful figures of the dancers moved in their intricate patterns on the stage but all Ming could think about were the patterns that would be made by the dead in the pale pinkish-buff sand of the Egyptian deserts she had seen encroaching at the edge of the fertile strip beside the Nile.

She remembered her moment of instant identification with the furious young men who had flung stones at the cruise boat and felt uncontrollably angry all over again.

CHAPTER 12

Ming went miserably back to London with her mind almost equally full of the apparently inevitable war and the fact that Mark had not even tried to get in touch with her. Her transparent offer of herself seemed ridiculous in retrospect and his silence was humiliating. To cap it all, she knew that there would be an anonymous letter waiting for her at home and loathed the thought of it.

Throughout the short flight back to Heathrow, she tried to read the newspapers she was offered by the stewardesses. There seemed to be a lot of articles about the Russians misbehaving in Hungary, but she found she could not concentrate on them.

When she reached her flat and saw the pile of letters on the hall table, she dropped her suitcases and seized it. On top of the heap was the plain white envelope from SW1 that she had expected. Feeling coldly angry, she ignored it and shuffled through the rest of the pile. Right at the bottom was a letter addressed to her in Mark's firm writing. Ripping it open with shaking fingers, Ming read the salutation and closed her eyes in relief. Then she read on:

Dearest Ming,
This is just to let you know that I am taking my belated leave at last. I'm off for a couple of weeks or more to stay with a friend from university. I'll give you a ring when I get back.

I'm sorry for being so difficult after Gerry's lunch party. It was hardly fair.

Mark

Ming looked quickly back at the date and realised that he had probably left London before he could have received her letter. Released from the conviction that she had ruined everything that Mark had tried so patiently to build, Ming felt strong enough to deal with the other expected letter and went to fetch her paper knife.

Over the months during which she had been getting the anonymous letters she had found herself quite unable to stick her fingers under the flap to open the envelopes. The thought of touching paper that her hateful correspondent had licked made her feel sick. She had gone out to Woolworth's and bought a plastic paper knife, which she kept for that one task alone.

Well, Ming, did you think you could escape by going to Paris? Fool! You'll never be rid of me. I'll always know what you are doing and who you are seeing.

And I know that you are causing your usual trouble wherever you go. People are being hurt because of you, just as they always are. Take care you don't go too far.

With fingers that felt as sticky, swollen and boneless as a bunch of sausages, Ming thrust the single sheet of paper back into its envelope and put it into the overflowing shoebox where she kept all the evidence of the nameless writer's hatred. She told herself that a few lines of typed words could do her no harm; that anyone could have found out that she was going to Paris; that the letter did not betray any real knowledge of her character or life; and that there was no reason to think that the writer knew anything of the way she had hurt Mark.

Considering the hurt, Ming became more determined than ever to make up for it, but until Mark answered the letter she had written from Paris there was nothing more she could do.

Instead she turned to work, sitting down at her desk to write notes of the allegations that Bertrand Bernardone had made and sketch out a plan for an article based on them. When she had finished she rang Connie at Etchingham.

'I couldn't wait until next Tuesday,' Ming began, 'because I've got so much to tell you.'

'All right.' Connie had hoped to hear a real change in Ming's voice, but she sounded just as tired and worried as she had before she left for Paris. 'How was Paris?'

'Beautiful, and rather sad ... no, not exactly sad. Hard to describe. I've done a piece. I thought I'd bring it down on Tuesday. But that's not why I was ringing.'

'I don't understand.'

Ming repeated everything Bertrand had told her. Connie kept absolutely silent until Ming had finished.

'And I think we ought to do a story, don't you?' she said when she had finished relaying her information. 'After all the notion of parts of our government making that sort of secret agreement is pretty shocking.'

'I don't think it can possibly be true,' said Connie slowly. 'And we could never print allegations like that without some kind of corroboration. The unverifiable information from an interested French source? Much too dangerous.'

Ming felt as useless as an inflatable boat with a large gash in its side.

'I suppose you're right.'

Hearing the depression in Ming's voice, Connie could have kicked herself.

'Why not try to find some proof of the story in London? If it is true it would be a wonderful scoop, but in our position we can't risk being wrong. All right?'

'Yes.' Ming sounded slightly more energetic. 'I'll see what I can find before I come down on Tuesday. How are you and Max?'

'Fine. But we've missed you these last two meetings. The excerpt from *Story of a Lost Love* has drawn a mixed bag of letters,' Connie said. 'Quite a lot are favourable luckily.'

'I'm glad. Will you give my love to Max?'

'Yes. He'll be pleased. Goodbye, Ming. Don't work too hard.' Connie put down her telephone.

Leaving the rest of the post untouched on her desk,

Ming went to unpack and have a bath to soak the remains of the tiredness and unhappiness out of her bones. She was still there when the telephone rang.

Pulling herself out of the bath, she wrapped a thick towel around her dripping body and padded to the nearest telephone, which was on the kitchen dresser.

'Ming, is that you?' Mark's voice was wonderfully familiar and desperately welcome.

'Yes. Mark, how kind of you to ring.' He laughed and Ming's lips curved in pleasure at the sound of it.

'And how kind of you to write. Ming, darling, it was wonderful to get your letter. Did you mean what you said about regretting that we never . . .?'

'Yes,' she said, flushing slightly. 'I realise I've been most awfully selfish all summer. I wasn't deliberately teasing you, Mark. I do hope you understand that I was just muddled.'

'I do understand. Can I see you?'

'Of course. Now?'

'Really? Can I come to the flat?'

'Why not? I'll be here,' said Ming.

She went back to her bath, washed and dressed in a comfortable blue woollen dress. Pinning a pearl brooch to her left shoulder, she thought about what she was going to do and tried to ignore her last few doubts.

When she had done her hair and clipped on a pair of pearl earrings, Ming looked around the bedroom to check that it was tidy. The last thing she wanted was any kind of avoidable embarrassment for either of them. Drawing the curtains and switching on the silk-shaded porcelain lamps at either side of the bed, she began to feel as though she were arranging a stage set.

As she tried to get rid of that uncomfortable sensation, she checked that Mrs Crook had made up the bed with clean sheets and noticed how cold they were. It crossed Ming's mind to fill two hot-water bottles and she found herself laughing at the incongruity of red rubber bottles and a night of illicit passion.

She was still amused as she took her dirty stockings into the bathroom to thrust them into the laundry basket. The front-door bell rang and she went out to meet Mark with a smile on her lips.

'You look heavenly,' he said as he came through the door and took her in his arms.

His face was thinner than it had been when they last met and much less tanned. She reached up to lay her hand on his hard cheek and when he smiled at her she could feel the tightening muscles of his face. The sensation reminded her vividly of Julia's picnic and she was almost sure that she was right to do what he wanted.

'How are you, Mark?' she asked gently.

'I'm fine now.' He took her hand away from his face and held it between both of his. 'Although I wasn't before. Are you sure about this?'

Ming smiled. A nerve started bumping in her throat and she put up her hand to still it.

'I promise I won't run out on you again,' she said, adding with difficulty: 'I want you, too, you know. I think I probably always have. I simply didn't realise it. You must think I'm a complete fool.'

'Never that,' he said, thinking that she looked like herself for the first time in months. Or perhaps it was just that he could see her properly again. He pulled her close to him again and stroked her hair with his lips, smelling the clean scent of her shampoo.

'You're shaking,' he said, sounding worried. 'Ming darling, making love now isn't a price that has to be paid. We can wait.'

'I know it isn't a price,' she answered, raising her head. 'It's just been a very long time since I was in a situation like this and I'm not certain ... I don't know ...'

'It's all right,' he said again, suddenly confident that he could carry them both over the last few obstacles that stood in the way of his heart's desire. 'You'll see. Don't be frightened.' He took his arms away from her, and went to open her bedroom door.

Ming walked past him and he followed her into the pretty, warmly lit room and put his hands on her shoulders.

'Look at me,' he said. She raised her dark blue eyes and

very deliberately smiled. 'That's better, my darling. This is supposed to be a pleasure; if it isn't for you, then it can't be for me, and I don't want it. Understood?'

'Understood,' she said and suddenly everything seemed all right. They lay down together and he began to talk, telling her why he loved her and what he wanted for her, keeping his almost overwhelming desire within rigid bounds until he felt her begin to relax.

He made her feel cherished and soon she found the confidence to turn to him. Very gently he took off her earrings and unpinned her brooch, laying them all carefully on the bedside table. He turned back and took her face between his hands.

Later, after she had given him everything for which he had longed and he had given her pleasure undreamed of, they lay at peace, holding hands and sometimes turning their heads on her pillow so that they could talk. It struck her at one moment that it was absurd of novelists to talk about women surrendering to men; there could be no greater physical surrender than the one Mark had just made as he lay, spent and defenceless, in her arms. She felt protective and touched by his vulnerability, and she was glad that she had at last been able to give him something.

'Ming,' he said as the old French clock on the chimney-piece struck eleven, 'tonight you have given me more than any man has a right to. Thank you, my love.'

'Oh, Mark,' she said, turning to lay her hot cheek on his shoulder and tucking her head under his chin. 'I'm sorry I held out for so long. I never wanted to make you unhappy.'

'No,' he said, holding her to him. 'You have made me complete.'

They slept and then woke, very hungry, an hour later. Ming got out of bed and suggested cooking bacon and eggs and Mark laughed.

'That would be splendid, darling.'

'What's so funny?' asked Ming, tying the cord of her thick velvet dressing-gown around her waist. She was so relieved to see his grey eyes clear and happy that she smiled affectionately at him despite his obvious mockery.

'The extent of your culinary repertoire,' he said at last. 'Perhaps when we're married we'll both have to go and learn to cook.'

Ming's delicate lips straightened as she looked at him, trying to decide whether he was making a joke. It worried her that she could not be sure. He noticed her stillness and got quickly out of bed to stand in front of her.

'What is it? What have I said? You look stricken, Ming. Darling, tell me.'

'Mark,' she said, and it sounded inside her head as though her voice was coming from a long way away. 'I thought you got my letter. The one I wrote from Paris.'

'Yes, I did. That's why I'm here.'

'But I told you in that I couldn't marry you.'

He stood looking at her in a silence as puzzled as her own until he became aware of his nakedness. Turning away from her, he found his clothes and quickly dressed. When he turned back with his shirtsleeves flapping, she was still standing where he had left her, with the same, beaten expression on her face.

His eyes narrowed as though he were trying to see through acrid smoke that was making them smart.

'You let me make love to you,' he said slowly as though his brain was still not working property. 'You ... I thought you'd changed your mind at last and were saying "yes".'

He sat down abruptly on the bed. His voice and the bleakness in his grey eyes forced Ming out of her shock. She walked forward and sat down beside him, not touching him.

'I thought that you wanted to make love to me,' she said slowly, trying to ward off the trouble that at last, too late, she could see coming. After all it seemed that her first instincts had been right. If she had not been prepared to marry him she should have kept out of his way, however much she missed him.

'Ever since that dreadful evening when you told me you were half-suffocated with desire and then again after Gerry's lunch. Wasn't that what you meant?'

'In a way,' he said and the despair in his voice cut into her. 'Yes, it was, but ...'

'I don't understand,' Ming said sadly. 'We seem always to be at cross purposes. I'd begun to realise how unfair I've been all these months, letting you take me out, give me things, make me really extraordinarily happy, and yet not giving you what you seemed to want so much. Was I wrong about that too?'

Mark shook his head, but he also covered his face with his hands. After a moment he breathed deeply and took his hands away again. Looking straight ahead of him at the drawing of her father that she had hung on the pale green wall, he took a grip on his emotions and said in a voice of almost official calm:

'I suppose it must be my fault; I must have confused you. I wanted you terribly, but in a different context, Ming. I wanted you for ... life. I wanted to share with you; to make a commitment to you that would override every other in my life and to know that you had done the same.' He turned to face her and she was horrified by the look in his face. 'God knows, if I'd just wanted someone to sleep with, I could have ...' He broke off, making her feel despicably cheap.

'What a mess!' said Ming, getting up off the bed and standing with her back to him. 'I was trying to be fair to you. Since I knew that I couldn't say I'd marry you, I wanted at least to give you something you seemed to want and I could give.'

The hurt that she had inflicted on him was mirrored by her own. 'I'd hate you to think that it is something I gave lightly – or that I have given anyone else.'

Mark stood up and went to find his tie. He stared at his reflection in a pier-glass and knotted the tie round his neck.

'You did say that "it was a long time" since you had been to bed with anyone. That sounds as though ...'

'Just after the war,' she said in a detached voice, as though she were talking about someone else, 'I was in a rather bad state, very unsure about how to cope with things that had happened to me and things I'd done. A man I'd known for some time seemed to offer a new way. We were

... I had agreed to marry him, but it was not until he had taken me to bed and made love to me that I realised that I could not, and so I ended it. That was all.'

Mark swung round. A bitter question suggested itself to him, but even as the words formed in his mind he knew that they were inappropriate. He and Ming might have misunderstood each other over their needs and feelings, but she was still the woman with whom he had fallen in love. It would be a pretty poor love, he told himself, if it could not stand a blow or two, if it could answer hurt with hurt.

'Was this evening just a test then, a test that I failed, just as he did, whoever the poor beggar was?' he said coldly in spite of all his good intentions.

Ming looked stricken. She tried to speak, failed and simply shook her head.

'I'd better go.'

'Yes,' Ming managed to say. 'That might be best. Oh, Mark, I've hurt you all over again,' she added, feeling hot tears welling under her eyelids. 'I never meant to do that.'

'I suppose not,' he answered. 'Goodbye.'

'Yes, I see. Mark?'

'Yes?'

'Please do not think too badly of me.'

He made himself smile at her, but it was not a particularly successful effort.

'I'll telephone you,' he said as he left the flat.

Ming woke the next morning trying to tell herself that she had no reason to feel so miserable. She might have sacrificed Mark's friendly company, but at the same time she had been released at last from all responsibility for his feelings. He had gone and that was that. She was free to get on with her life. She ought to have felt relieved.

It took considerable resolution to face the life for which she had freed herself and which seemed infinitely less important than the man she was certain she did not love. Eventually she got out of bed and dressed, deciding to fill her days with so much that she had no time to think about her tiresome and contradictory emotions.

Eating breakfast at the kitchen table, she planned her programme. The first thing was obviously to follow Connie's instruction to find some incontrovertible evidence of Bertrand's allegations. After that, Ming thought, she might concentrate on arranging to have the rest of her flat decorated and furnished.

The post brought a letter from Miss Roseheath, congratulating Ming on one of her articles about women and money, which helped to keep her mind on her work. It had so impressed her, the teacher wrote, that she wondered whether Ming would consider going to the school one Saturday and giving a lecture to the senior girls.

Apparently there were no suitable dates for it during the current term, but Miss Roseheath suggested a Saturday at the end of January. Ming wrote it into her diary and scribbled a letter of acceptance.

By the time she had decided who to approach first in her search for proof of what Bertrand had said it was well after eleven o'clock. Ming picked up the telephone to talk to the most intelligent of the secretaries she had known in the House of Commons.

'Diana?' she said when the call was answered. 'Mary Alderbrook here. How are you?'

'I'm very well. How is life when you're released from the grindstone?'

'Pretty good in most ways. I'm just back from Paris.'

'Lucky old you!'

'But there are other ways in which it's not so good. I miss all the chums for one thing. I was wondering: would you care to have lunch one day?'

'I'd love to,' said Diana. Ming thought that she could hear real enthusiasm in Diana's voice. 'James is away today, and so I'm relatively free. Would that be too soon? It seems a pity to miss the opportunity.'

'Today would be perfect,' said Ming and suggested a small Italian restaurant where they had occasionally lunched in the past. They agreed to meet there at half-past twelve.

Before she changed out of her trousers, Ming went to the small boxroom beside the kitchen to see whether she might be able to convert it into a study. It was beginning to annoy her that her drawing room looked so like an office, and that the piles of paper she had accumulated were threatening to overwhelm everything else in the room. The boxroom was dull and dark, with only a small window looking out over the back of a row of undistinguished buildings. Remembering the way Natalie had decorated her flat and almost made a virtue out of its gloominess, Ming decided that she might be able to make something of the little room in a similar style.

It would be impossible ever to make it look as light as the rest of the flat, but if it were done up in a rich, dark colour it could at least be cosy. Then she thought of the pillars in the Sainte-Chapelle and wondered whether she could find anyone who made wallpapers decorated with small gold fleur-de-lis or castles on rich, dark blue or red backgrounds, and if not whether it would be feasible to paste gilded wrapping paper on to the boxroom walls.

Having telephoned four shops to describe what she wanted and ask for samples of their most suitable wallpapers, Ming went into her bedroom to change out of her trousers. As she was pulling on a girdle and unwrapping a new pair of stockings, she tried to decide how to phrase the questions she had to ask Diana.

CHAPTER 13

Ming arrived early at the restaurant, chose a table that was separated from its nearest neighbour by a large potted palm, and settled down to wait for her friend.

Diana Frontwell was a few years younger than Ming but much taller and more fully built. Her hair was a pale, carroty red and her face strikingly pale. Her big nose had a pronounced bump and when she wore her hair piled up she looked remarkably like portraits of Elizabeth I, which had caused some amusement when she had first appeared at Westminster three years earlier. Intelligent and hard-working, she had always impressed Ming, although some of the other old hands had found her lack of deference irritating.

Watching her walk into the little restaurant, Ming recognised some of the impatience Connie had expressed in Egypt. It seemed absurd that anyone with Diana's gifts should be working as a secretary to a dull, second-rate Tory back-bencher. If she had only been a man as interested in politics as she was, she would have been fighting her way up the ladder to a safe parliamentary seat of her own. If she had had money of her own or a rich and complaisant husband, she might have been doing it despite her sex. As it was, the nearest she was likely to get to representing a constituency would be as the wife of its Member of Parliament.

Over a plate of lasagne and a glass of red wine, Ming

suppressed her instinct to urge Diana to strike out on her own and instead encouraged her to relay all the gossip of the Palace of Westminster: who had resigned and who had taken their places; which secretaries were in love with the Members for whom they worked and which Members' marriages were in trouble; what Ming's replacement was like, and how much she resented the eulogies she kept hearing about her predecessor.

'I rather doubt those,' said Ming, amused at the distance she had travelled since her own resignation. 'When I saw Roger Sillhorne in the summer, he seemed positively to loathe me. Perhaps I ought to drop in and try to make friends with her. I don't like the thought of people hating me for something that's not my fault.'

Diana drank a little of the sour, thin wine, pulled a face that made her look even more like Gloriana than usual, and then said:

'I don't suppose it could do any harm, and it might help; particularly if you wore some of your older clothes. I think the Paris glamour might put her nose out of joint even more badly than Sillhorne's unending nostalgia for the days when you ran his office.'

Ming looked down at the plain dark suit she was wearing. It had not in fact come from Paris, but from a small shop in Knightsbridge, which Flixe had recommended. Cut with a short jacket that ballooned below the shoulders and a narrow skirt ending about four inches below the knee, the suit's very simplicity marked it as far more expensive than the pleasant, decently cut grey-green dress and jacket that Diana was wearing.

'I see what you mean,' said Ming, rather embarrassed. 'But let's forget about me. What is Roger making of all this Suez business? I'd have thought it was right up his street.'

Diana laughed and told Ming a little about the government's handling of the crisis and a lot about its effect on the individual Members of Parliament she knew well.

'Veronica says Roger's been beside himself ever since Nasser stole the Canal. He's outraged that the United Nations is forbidding any intervention in Egypt. She says it's even overtaken you as his chief topic of conversation, although now, of course, there's Hungary, too.'

Ming vaguely remembered reading about trouble in Hungary, but there were no details in her mind.

'Yes, that puzzles me,' she said carefully. 'I can't quite work out from the papers what is really happening there. Do you know?'

'No more than what I've read. Students have been rioting, one lot of Communists is fighting another lot, and the Russians are killing both sorts: nearly eight hundred yesterday according to one report I saw.'

'I read that, too. Women and children and students, almost none of them armed.' She remembered the newspaper stories she had read on the aeroplane. 'It's frightful, isn't it?'

'Awful, but what can you expect of the Russians?' Diana looked down at her watch. 'I'm going to have to go. I've got a pile of letters to type even though James is away. It was good to see you.'

'Hasn't it been fun? Although it's peculiar hearing about the old place as an outsider,' said Ming, bending down to pick up her gloves and handbag. 'I hadn't expected to feel so ... excluded. It was so marvellous to be free of it all in the beginning that I hadn't known how much I might miss it. We must keep in touch.'

'That would be nice. And I'm sure you were right to go: you look so much better than in the old days – and not just better dressed. It can't only be that you've inherited a fortune,' said Diana with a friendly smile.

At that reminder of their unequal resources, Ming signalled to the waitress for a bill, which she paid. When they left the restaurant, Ming decided to walk home. It seemed mad to walk all over Paris to look at beautiful buildings and then to ignore London. Besides, she thought that if she were physically tired out, she might be able to stop her mind from turning over and over the way she ought to have handled her friendship with Mark. She set off to walk slowly back to her flat along the river.

It was a glorious day, bright and clear but cold, with a

crisp, wintry tang in the air. Only a few leaves still hung on the naked trees, and Ming revelled in the smell of drying vegetation, bonfires, dust, petrol and something that seemed to belong peculiarly to London. Once she had passed the comforting, squat familiarity of the Tate Gallery there was not much to see except for the acres of dilapidated once-cream houses of Pimlico until she reached the Royal Hospital, which she knew well.

With her feet aching badly, she walked the last hundred yards to her flat and wished that she felt invigorated by the exercise. She changed her shoes for a pair of slippers and her suit and savage underclothes for the morning's comfortable trousers and jersey and settled down at her desk.

Before she had done more than unscrew the cap of her pen the telephone rang. Ming was constitutionally incapable of leaving a telephone ringing without answering it, however much she resented the interruption, and so she picked up the receiver.

'Ming?' She immediately recognised Peter Suvarov's voice even though its usual charming languor had been transmuted into hoarse urgency.

'What's the matter?' she asked quickly, wondering if he could be in a state about the rising in Hungary. After what Natalie had told her about his loathing of the revolution in which he had participated she would not have been surprised.

'It's Flixe. She started about two hours ago, but there are complications. An ambulance is on its way to take us to the hospital. There's not much time. Could you bear to come and oversee the girls?'

'Of course,' said Ming, betraying none of the sudden terror that made her head swim. 'I'll come at once. How long have I got?'

'It's not that urgent. We've got Flixe's midwife and Brigitte to look after them, but they're a bit weepy and I think it would help to have an aunt.'

'Don't worry about them or me, Peter,' said Ming, putting all the comfort of which she was capable into her voice. 'Give Flixe my love, and tell me ...' Her voice trembled. 'And tell me how it goes,' she went on more steadily.

'Will do. Here's the ambulance. 'Bye.'

He cut the connection and all Ming heard was the electric buzz on the line. She put down her receiver and tried to think clearly. With no idea of how long Flixe would be in hospital or when she herself would be able to return to the flat, Ming thought that she ought to pack plenty of clothes and take some work too.

Twenty-five minutes after Peter's call, she had fetched the car from its garage and was loading a suitcase into the boot. She had a bag full of notes and her portable typewriter. Trying not to think of all the horror stories about fatal confinements and damaged babies she had heard over the years, she drove carefully towards Kensington and found a parking space just outside Flixe's house.

Her two daughters, six-year-old Fiona and the baby Sophie, were playing listlessly in the brightly painted attic nursery with Brigitte, their German *au pair* girl, while the midwife was busy making tea in the kitchen. She was much slimmer and younger than the nurse who had overseen Flixe's first three confinements, and in her starched white uniform she looked out of place in the cosy kitchen, which was designed to look as much like a romanticised farmhouse as possible.

There was a huge, scrubbed wooden table in the centre, dark red quarry tiles on the floor, and brightly polished copper saucepans in a rack above the cooker. Bunches of herbs, strings of onions, dried mushrooms and garlic hung from hooks in the ceiling. Ming had often told Flixe that she expected to see hams and sausages there too, but so far there had been nothing but vegetables.

Ming introduced herself to the nurse and sat down at the kitchen table before asking as calmly as possible what had happened to Flixe.

'Nothing so far,' said Nurse Jenkins with a quick smile. She warmed the kitchen tea pot, threw away the water and measured three spoonfuls of tea into the pot. 'But the baby span round just as labour was beginning and I could not turn it back. A breach delivery is safer in hospital in any case, and I think she might have to have a caesarian section.'

'Is that serious?' Ming asked, feeling very ignorant. 'It doesn't sound too bad.'

'No, it isn't, but her condition might have become serious if we had kept her here. Would you like a cup of tea, Miss Alderbrook?' she asked, pouring boiling water on to the tea leaves.

'Thank you, yes. That would be splendid. Is there anything wrong with the child?'

'Nothing as far as I could tell, but they'll be able to check that, too, at St Mary's. I'll call the girls for their tea.'

As the nurse left the room, looking capable and reassuring, Ming wondered whether she had heard the whole truth about her sister's condition. But there was nothing she could do except wait for a call from Peter and do her best to amuse the children.

That proved simplicity itself. After tea Ming read stories to Fiona while Brigitte helped Sophie with a simple jigsaw puzzle. The only difficult moment was when Fiona looked up at the end of one book to say:

'When Mummy comes back will she be able to stand up straight again?'

'I expect so,' said Ming, ruffling the child's dark hair.

'And she'll have a baby, won't she?' said Fiona, giving Ming a piercingly interrogatory stare. At that moment she looked very like her father.

'Yes,' said Ming firmly, deciding that Fiona was far too young to have to cope with any equivocation, however truthful. 'Won't that be nice?'

'It depends,' said the child.

'On what?' asked Ming, oblivious to danger.

'If it's a boy,' came the brisk answer. 'We don't want any more baby girls. Sophie is very . . .'

'Bathtime, Fiona,' said Brigitte from the opposite end of the nursery. 'Go and show Auntie Ming your bathroom.'

To Ming's relief, Fiona did as she was asked and made no further reference to the new baby or to her existing sister. When both children were in bed, Brigitte apologised for the interruption, adding:

'She finds Sophie very frustrating just now; the little one can talk about everything, but she still can't understand Fiona's games and often spoils them. She gets very upset when Fiona criticises her.'

'I'm not surprised,' said Ming, remembering all too vividly the sense of humiliated panic engendered by her elder sisters' mystifying games and incomprehensible jokes and teasing.

Brigitte smiled, explained that her day's work ended after the children's bedtime and disappeared to her own bed-sitting room. Ming went downstairs again, discovered that the nurse wanted to watch a programme on television, and took her bagful of work into Peter's study.

She was still sitting there staring at the wall when Peter telephoned to say that there was very little change in Flixe's condition. The doctors had decided that a caesarian was not necessary and Flixe had been in increasingly violent labour ever since.

'It's so odd,' he said and Ming could hear the suppressed terror in his voice. 'She's had all the others so easily. Sophie only took about an hour and a half.'

'She's that much older, Peter, but she is in good hands there. They'd be doing a caesar already if it was going to be necessary.'

'You are a rock, Ming,' he said. 'How are my girls?'

'They seem fine. They've been in bed a couple of hours now and all is well here. You will tell me how things go, won't you?'

'Yes, but I'll have to go now. They're calling me, Ming.'

He rang back half an hour later to say that Flixe's son had been safely delivered.

'Are they all right?' asked Ming baldly.

'Apparently everything's in working order. And Flixe is fine. Tired and badly torn, but all right. I'll be back eventually.'

'All right. But stay as long as she needs you.'

As soon as he had rung off, Ming rang the operator, asked for a trunk call to her parents' house to give them the news, telephoned Gerry, and then went to tell the nurse. The expression on her face told Ming how worried she had been, but all she said was:

'I am glad. Mrs Suvarov can rest now. She must have had a very tough time. I think I'll go to bed. Good night.'

'I'll stay up for my brother-in-law,' said Ming. 'Sleep well.'

She sat up until half-past one, finding her eyes closing and her head nodding at increasingly frequent intervals. Eventually she decided to go to bed, but she slept only fitfully and soon after four heard the sound of a key in the front door. She got out of bed and pulled her dressing-gown round her shoulders. There were no lights on in the hall, but the moon shone in through the fanlight over the front door and its light was reflected in a huge mirror that hung on the right-hand wall. From the stairs Ming saw the reflection of a man standing just inside the door.

'Peter,' she called softly. 'Is that you?'

'Yes,' he said and switched on the hall light. Ming gasped as she saw his face. It was grey and dragged with fatigue and his eyes were red. She ran down the rest of the stairs, stumbled over the hem of her long dressing-gown, steadied herself against the bannister and went on.

'What's happened?' she asked when she was close to him.

Peter swallowed. Ming caught the smell of brandy on his breath.

'She had a terrible haemorrhage. Just after they said everything was all right and let me in to see her, she started gushing blood. Never trusted doctors; don't ever trust them, Ming.'

He stumbled forward and leaned his full weight on Ming. Her arms went round him automatically, while she stared unseeingly ahead of her. Flixe, she said to herself, Flixe, as though the repetition of her name could make the story untrue. Every minor irritation Flixe had ever caused was wiped away from Ming's memory and all she could remember was how important Flixe was to her.

'She lost pints and pints before they managed to stop it,'

said Peter into her hair. A sudden wave of relief surged through Ming's body, making her knees feel as though they could hardly support her, let alone him as well.

'Have they stopped it?' she asked, just to make certain.

'Yes, and given her a transfusion. They swear she'll be all right now.' Ming held him for a moment longer and then took her arms away from him.

'Come into the kitchen, Peter. I'll make you something hot. You look as though you need it,' she said, urging him forward. She wondered how much brandy he had had to drink.

He obeyed her as docilely as a good child, sat at the table, and waited while she heated up a tin of tomato soup, poured some of it into a bowl and gave it to him. Ming made herself a cup of tea and sat opposite him, watching the colour come back into his face and the fiery red in his eyes dwindle to a less terrifying flush.

'That's better,' he said when he pushed away the empty bowl. His voice was almost back to normal and he even managed to smile. 'I'm sorry. Did I frighten you?'

'A little,' answered Ming. 'Are you all right?'

Peter nodded, rubbing his hands vigorously over his face and through his thick, grey-streaked hair.

'I am now. I'm ashamed to say I fainted at the hospital when she started bleeding and came round on the floor with about six of them stepping over me, trying to help her.'

'I'm not surprised. It must have been a terrifying sight,' said Ming.

'It wasn't that.' Peter shut his eyes. 'I was just visited by an unshakeable conviction that she was going to die.' He propped his elbows on the table and buried his face in his hands. 'Oh, God! Ming, I really thought she was going to die.'

Ming leaned across the table so that she could put one slim hand on his rough hair and stroke it. He wrenched away, pushed back his chair and stumbled round the table to kneel at her feet and bury his face in her lap. After a while she could feel his tears soaking through her thin dressing-gown and her heart ached with pity for him. She went on stroking his hair, waiting for the storm of tears to end.

When at last it did he looked up through swollen eyelids. 'Thank you, Ming.'

'Oh, Peter,' she answered, reaching to pick up a clean drying-up cloth with one hand, while she kept her other on his shoulder. 'Here, blow!'

'That's what Flixe always says to the children,' he said with a hint of his familiar, sardonic smile.

He got up from the floor and went to wash his face at the big, stainless-steel sink.

'Thank you for being here. I couldn't have done that with anybody else,' he said after a while, standing with his back to her. 'I don't think I'd have dared show anyone but you how much I ... how much I love her.'

After a long pause, Ming gathered her disordered senses together and tried to respond adequately.

'I'm glad you do,' she said at last with considerable emphasis on the last word.

'Did you doubt it?' Peter turned back from the sink and went to sit down in his own chair.

'Just occasionally I have wondered,' said Ming with a faint smile. 'But then I know so little about "love" that I'm still not sure I'd recognise it if I saw it.'

It was Peter's turn to try to offer comfort. He reached across the table for her hands.

'That's strange,' he said, looking into her tired face. 'You've made so many people love you; I'd have thought you were a bit of an expert on the subject.'

Ming's lips thinned as she tried to control a suddenly frighteningly powerful urge to tell Peter everything.

'Me?' she said sadly. 'Alas no. I'd need someone like you to tell me about it. Could you?'

'Love?' Peter looked up at the ceiling and then down at his orange-smeared soup bowl, trying to order his thoughts. 'I suppose it boils down to minding more about someone else's happiness than one's own. It makes you want to protect that other person and know – passionately, desperately want to know – how the other's mind works.'

'I used to think that,' said Ming so quietly that her voice
hardly impinged at all on Peter's thoughts.

'If you love her, you feel that she makes life whole. . . . To
such an extent that you become brave enough to lay yourself open to really swingeing hurt. Darling Ming, I can only
describe the symptoms, but I think that is probably the
crucial one: being prepared to be hurt and putting down all
the defences you've erected against it.' He looked at her
then and saw that her face was sad but more open than it
had been for some time.

'I don't think there are words for the thing itself,' he said
gently. 'If there are, you'd need a poet, not an inarticulate,
superannuated revolutionary like me. That list of symptoms
is the best I can do.'

There were tears on Ming's darkened eyelashes as she
said:

'Superannuated revolutionary or not, you've confirmed
most of what I used to think.' She took her hands away from
his clasp, folded them in her lap and sat looking down at
them.

'What happened to change it?' he asked. Ming achieved
a small smile.

'The man I thought I loved didn't love me,' she said
simply, 'and as I watched him with someone else most of
those feelings seemed to die. So I doubted that they constituted love after all.'

'Seemed?' he said gently but with all the acuity she had
once known so well.

'I've just discovered that they still exist,' she said with the
frankness that only comes in the cool aftermath of drama.
Through the tears that she would not allow to fall, she
watched his lined face. Once more it was lit by the affection
she used to believe could never fail her.

'Ah, Ming,' he said. There seemed to be regret in his
voice, infinite kindness, and compassion, too. 'I have always
loved you, you know.'

She made an almost irritable gesture with her hands, as
though to brush away what he had said. It seemed crass
and unlike him to use that moment to exercise his charm.

He took her hands again and held them firmly in his.

'I have, Ming. Not as I love Flixe.' Ming relaxed again. 'There is something in her that calls to something in me as no one else ever has or could. But you are very dear to me; your happiness matters terribly. And in every way except that one indescribable way I love you.'

CHAPTER 14

Throughout the weekend, as Ming tried to work, she kept thinking of what Peter had revealed to her both of his feelings and of her own. Once or twice it occurred to her to wonder whether she would have so messed up her dealings with Mark if she and Peter had talked sooner and whether she might yet retrieve something from the trouble she had made. It was a tantalising idea and she could not prevent herself from dreaming of the happy ending that she knew was unlikely.

She was still thinking about it as she ate her lunch on Monday, half-listening to the wireless in her kitchen. Peeling the top off her second boiled egg, she heard that the Israeli army had invaded Egypt through the Sinai desert, and her attention sharpened.

The telephone began to ring just as the announcer came to the end of the news bulletin. Swallowing her mouthful of egg and toast and turning down the volume of her wireless, Ming picked up the receiver.

'Ming? Peter here.'

'Hello,' she said, startled to hear his voice after her long mental deliberation about him. 'You sound better. How is Flixe? And the baby?'

'Both fine. That's why I'm ringing. She's allowed visitors now and is longing to see you. Might you be able to go this afternoon?'

'Yes, of course. I've been waiting for a summons. She's really all right?'

'Really. They're absolutely sure there's no more risk of haemorrhage, and she's looking better too. By the way, she and I wonder whether you'd like to be the boy's godmother?'

For a moment Ming was so moved that she could not speak.

'You were very much part of his birth, and we'd both like it so much if you'd take him on,' Peter went on, wondering why she had not answered.

'I'd love it,' she said at last. 'And ... I'd love it. Thank you.'

'If you hadn't been there on Friday night, I don't know what I'd have done. You've been so good to us all – always.'

'Thank you, Peter. I haven't done anything that Gerry wouldn't have done in my place, but I ... I'm glad if I helped. And I'm glad it was me.' She paused for a moment and then said more easily: 'When can I go to the hospital?'

'Any time. I may run into you there, but if not we'll see each other soon. 'Bye.'

When he had rung off, Ming went straight to her bedroom to change and then walked round to the nearest florist to choose a big, mixed bunch of unseasonable and very expensive roses before hailing a taxi.

She reached the hospital soon after two o'clock to find Flixe lying against banked-up pillows and surrounded by flowers. She looked pale and much thinner than usual. There were deep hollows under her eyes and her skin looked blotchy, but there was a serenity in her face, too, which reassured Ming. She kissed Flixe and was introduced to her godson, who was lying in his mother's arms.

Tiny, wrinkled, and black-haired, he was tightly wrapped in a shawl and Ming could not think of anything flattering to say about his appearance.

'Thank God you're all right,' she said instead.

Flixe smiled slowly and pushed her dulled hair off her face.

'I'm fine. Peter says he frightened you badly last week. I'm sorry about that.'

'It's hardly your fault, old thing. And it sounds as though it was all very dramatic. He was desperate, you know.'

'I know,' answered Flixe, looking down at her son and then up again at Ming. 'He told me all about it, and I'm very grateful that you were there with him. He needed you badly.'

Ming looked at her sister and realised from her expression of mingled sympathy and affection that Peter had told her everything that had been said in their dawn conversation. A year earlier she would have felt humiliated that either of her sisters should know she had confessed to loving Peter, but for some reason it no longer seemed to matter. In a curious way Ming felt as though her confession and his reception of it had freed her from something she had not understood.

'He's been awfully good to me, Flixe.'

Before her sister could reply the door opened and Gerry appeared, also bearing a huge bunch of flowers.

'Golly! You've more here than there were in the shop where I bought these,' she said cheerfully. 'Hello, Ming. You look stunning and much tougher than the time you came to Sunday lunch. What's happened?'

'I thought there was something, too,' said Flixe, watching her sisters as they stood at the end of her white bed, which was bathed in cold, autumn sunshine.

Ming, who had been thinking that Gerry was looking particularly tired and not nearly as cheerful as her voice would have suggested, said easily enough:

'Nothing. If I look different I suppose it must be because I'm busy.'

'That always makes me look particularly fragile,' said Gerry with a laugh.

'Nonsense, old thing,' said Flixe, looking carefully at her elder sister, 'you're never fragile. Will you take him for a bit? My arms need stretching.'

'Oh, let Ming. I'm no good with babies.'

'He might sick up all over her elegant suit. Come on, Gerry.'

Ming could not understand why Flixe was so determined

to push the knowledge of her fertility on to Gerry, who could never share it.

With obvious reluctance, Gerry walked forward and picked up the shawled bundle. The others watched as she gazed down into the baby's crumpled face, her own a cold mask of detachment. After she had held him for a while, and even tried to croon appropriate endearments to him, she handed him back to his mother.

When she had passed on the burden, Gerry said with her old teasing smile:

'It's not just the busyness that's making Ming look tougher, Flixe. What with you in your nightie and me in my old coat, her suit shines out like a beacon. Very glamorous, Ming. Anna would have been pleased.'

'D'you think so, really?' asked Ming, squinting down at her tight skirt. She sometimes had to battle with both her ingrained puritanism and her sympathy for Gerry's comparative lack of money when she was spending what still seemed to be enormous sums on clothes as well as on furniture and pictures for the flat.

'Definitely,' said Gerry. 'Anna was always so elegant herself. I'm sure you're doing the right thing. I'm very glad you're toughening up, Ming. Mike will be, too, and Mark as well I expect.'

She looked teasingly at Ming and was disconcerted to meet only a cool stare in return.

Ming turned at once to Flixe, as though she was forcing herself to remember why they were all there. 'What are you going to call your boy?' she asked.

Flixe pushed herself gingerly up the bed to sit higher against the pillows and brushed her lips against the flat dark wisps of his hair.

'I wanted Rupert, but Peter thought Rooo Soovarov would be too much,' said Flixe, pulling out the vowel until it sounded ridiculous. She smiled her familiar smile. 'And so I think we've nearly settled on Sylvester.'

'You can't!' shrieked Gerry, waking the baby who began to howl. 'See, he can't bear it.'

'She's pulling your leg, Gerry,' said Ming, watching Flixe

in an amusement that was beginning to relax her.

'I'm not so sure,' said Gerry, sounding almost tart. 'She always loved that Georgette Heyer novel with the tyrannical old grandfather in it and I wouldn't put it past her.'

'D'you know I'd forgotten that he was called Sylvester,' said Ming, 'but it was Ludovic that Flixe adored. In any case you're not going to call him Sylvester, are you, Flixe?'

'Actually, no,' she said, 'but I can never resist teasing Gerry. She rises so easily.'

'If you weren't still delicate, I'd pay you back for that one,' said Gerry, still sounding deliberately cheerful.

She well remembered the fights she and Flixe used to have when they were children. In the past Flixe had been able to drive her into paroxysms of frustrated rage, but by now she could usually control her feelings.

'Come on, what's the real decision?'

'Nicholas,' said Flixe. 'It sounds perfectly all right in all three relevant languages, we both like it, and Peter's favourite relation was called Nikolai, so it seemed to fit. Ming, could you take him for a moment?'

Ming obediently accepted the child. Holding him in her arms, she had a sudden vision of Mark after they had made love. He had laid his head against her breasts then. She had held him and murmured his name and felt as full of tenderness as she did with the child. How could she have been so sure that she did not love him?

'That's better,' said Gerry. 'I'm going to have to go. I've got a lecture to give in three-quarters of an hour, but I couldn't resist popping in for a minute. You're an absolute monster, Flixe, but I'm glad you're recovering – and that Nicholas is all that he should be.'

'Thank you. I must say that's about the most touching compliment you've ever paid me,' said Flixe, laughing at her. Gerry bent down to kiss her. 'And thank you for the chrysanths; they're lovely.'

'I knew you'd have a lot,' said Gerry, standing up and surveying them, 'but I hadn't expected quite such a display. Who produced those dramatic bunches?'

She was pointing to a matching pair of bouquets of wired

white and red carnations, stiffly arranged against a band of
dark green leaves.

'Tibor Smith,' said Flixe, her tired face softening. 'He
came this morning, overjoyed about the news from
Hungary and said the baby ought to be properly
welcomed. They're the Hungarian national colours apparently. We've asked him to be one of the godfathers and
David Wallington the other.'

'So they are,' said Gerry. 'But is the news so good? What
about the massacres and all the fighting? It sounds quite
grisly to me.'

'Haven't you heard? Tibor said that the Russians are
withdrawing from Hungary altogether.'

'It sounds too good to be true,' said Gerry. 'I can't see the
Sovs allowing a satellite so much independence.'

'And poor Tibor was so happy,' said Flixe, convinced at
once by her sister's caution. She might tease Gerry, but she
had complete faith in her political judgement. 'I believed
him.'

'Don't sound so sad,' said Ming, banishing thoughts of
Mark with difficulty and rejoining the conversation.
'Gerry's always been a bit of a pessimist. Perhaps Hungary
really will free itself from Russia.'

'One thing you can say of us is that, as pessimists, we are
never disappointed. I must go or I'll be badly late,' said
Gerry. 'I'll come again as soon as I can. 'Bye, both of you,'
she added and left the room.

'Isn't it extraordinary how things change?' said Flixe as
the door closed behind her sister. 'When we were growing
up it was always Gerry who seemed to have everything.'

'She still has a fair bit,' said Ming. She pulled a chair
close to the bed with one hand and sat down. 'What with
Mike and all her work successes. Do you want your infant
back or shall I put him in his basket? He's getting a bit
restive.'

'I'll have him. You're partly right about Gerry, but she
can't ever have this,' said Flixe, holding out her arms to take
the child.

She stroked his face and held him close to her breast.

After a few moments he stopped whimpering. Flixe looked up again.

'Gerry's never got over the fact that she can't have children. She tries really hard not to be jealous, because we've learned how to be friends with each other now, but she can't quite manage it.'

'I know,' said Ming, who had noticed that for herself. 'I wondered why you were so determined to make her hold Nicholas.'

'Because I want her to be involved with him. She's avoided having anything to do with the others until they were past the blissful baby stage and I wanted her to have a chance to know it.'

'I'm not sure it's altogether wise,' said Ming, feeling again the visceral sensation of longing that holding the child had produced in her. 'I think it might hurt too much.'

'Well, I'd have to defer to you on that one,' said Flixe. 'You must know . . .'

'Golly, Flixe, I must go too,' said Ming quickly, determined to forestall any attempt to remind her that she probably could – and definitely should – have children of her own. With her emotions so near the surface she knew that she was incapable of listening politely to anything so painful. She had got to the door of the small hospital room before Flixe's voice stopped her.

'Thank you for being so good to Peter the night Nicholas was born.'

Ming turned and smiled. Flixe thought that she looked particularly ravishing in her dark blue suit, with her fine blonde hair sculpted away from her face under a neat hat.

'It was a pleasure to do anything I could. I'm very fond of you both,' said Ming, blowing a kiss from the doorway. 'And I'm so touched that you've given me a share in Nicholas like this. Thank you, Flixe.'

Ming shut the door behind her and breathed a sigh of relief. At least she had kept her miseries to herself and not spoiled Flixe's triumph.

Flixe watched her leave and then, feeling suddenly bereft and almost lonely, fished among the cards and letters on her bedside table for the telegram that her elder son had sent her:

'Well done we could do with more men in the family but he'll never love you more than I do Andrew.'

It seemed to her to be remarkably sophisticated for an eight-year-old and to her already unbounded love for her favourite child was added a huge measure of pride. There was relief, too, because if he could send a telegram like that he could not be too miserable at his spartan boarding school. She held her new child more firmly and bent to kiss his crumpled forehead.

The following day saw Ming driving down to Max's cottage. On the passenger seat of the car was not only her Paris piece but also a list of ideas that had been sparked off by the things she had seen and heard while she was staying with Natalie.

When she reached the cottage Max insisted on reading the article at once, which left Connie and Ming free to discuss Flixe's child and all the drama of his birth. They sat in front of one of Max's fires, while Ming's chilled feet warmed up, drinking his excellent coffee and talking about what she might give her nephew as a christening present.

'When's it to be?' asked Connie when the rival merits of a silver mug, gold cufflinks or a case of port had been weighed.

'Not until November the thirtieth. There's no particular urgency, and Peter wants Flixe to have plenty of time to build up her strength again. Besides, my parents ...' Before she could finish her sentence, Max had swung round in his chair to call down the long room to her.

'Ming, this Suez stuff is terrific – quite chilling. Are you sure of your facts?'

'What? You're supposed to be reading about Paris,' said Ming in surprise.

'I've done that. It's fine, but these notes were clipped to the last page and they're much more interesting. Shocking, too.'

'Ah,' said Ming, 'I hadn't meant to bring them until I'd got more corroboration for Connie. If you're shocked, she can't have told you what I heard in Paris.'

'The subject didn't arise,' said Connie drily.

'I see. Max, most of those notes are a mixture of speculation and reported gossip.'

'Yes, I can see that. Who is this minister who was seen emerging from Cabinet in tears?'

'What?' demanded Connie, following Ming to Max's work table. She put out a hand for the typescript.

'According to our fearless reporter's sources,' he said, 'a certain minister, who had been excluded from the cabal's discussions, insisted on knowing what was going on. Eden allowed him in to a particular meeting and he was so appalled that he emerged in tears,' he said, handing her the article.

'Leaning back in his chair Max lit a cigarette and watched Ming intently.

'I don't really want to give you a name, since it is only hearsay,' she said. 'I heard about it quite by chance and it's unsupported.'

'All right. Who told you about it? Perhaps we could check with him.' Ming shook her blonde head.

'Not a hope, Max. I promised everyone I talked to that I wouldn't reveal my sources, and I think it's easier and better all round if I don't even tell you,' she said.

Max acknowledged her firm stand with quirkily raised eyebrows and an exaggeratedly pursed mouth. Ming smiled, but she was not dissuaded by his implied mockery. She lifted her chin. He grinned at her.

'Ming, do you really think that our government would do any of this?' Connie's doubting voice brought the others' pantomime to a close.

'Which of their actions particularly bothers you?' asked Ming with a touch of sarcasm. 'Taking care not to appoint new ambassadors to the vacant posts in Canada and the United States so that they could stop news reaching those governments? Excluding selected ministers and officials from their deliberations? Or is it . . .?'

'I'm still bothered by the story you brought back from Paris. Despite the Israeli attack, I just can't believe it.'

'I think we ought to publish this stuff, corroboration or no.'

'We must have more evidence,' said Connie doggedly. 'It's too dangerous to print anti-government stuff without evidence.'

'All right. I'll try and get more, but I'm not optimistic.' Ming had a sudden memory of her elder sister and thought of the benefits of pessimism. She sat even more firmly on her fantasies about Mark.

'People are playing their cards very close to their chests,' she went on.

'You could at least pump that dreadful little man you used to work for,' said Max. 'Will you?'

'If I must.' Ming could not help thinking of the last time she had spoken to Roger Sillhorne and the things he had said of Max.

'I think you must,' said Max. Reluctantly Ming agreed to do what she could.

When they had settled the rest of the decisions on the next issue, Connie got up to go, saying:

'See you next week, Ming. Max, are you coming to the Dower House this evening?'

'Absolutely. I wouldn't miss your glamorous dinner party for the world,' he said.

But when Connie had left the cottage he did confess to Ming that he felt nervous of it.

'But, Max, why? No one Connie has to her house is going to be crass enough to say things that ... might worry you.'

'You're probably right. I just don't know how I'll react. Still, I can't stay in purdah for ever. How's the love life coming on?'

Ming went to sit down in front of the fire, holding out her thin hands to the flames.

'Disastrously,' she said, watching the yellow and orange patterns the fire threw over a Portuguese needlework hearth-rug. 'I've completely mucked it up and the whole thing seems to be over.' She was about to say that the ending of the affair was a relief but the words would not come out.

'Are you sure?'

'Nearly,' Ming went on more realistically, 'although I have been beginning to wonder if I couldn't somehow pick up some of the pieces and put them together again. I just can't quite see ...' Her voice faded into silence.

'Like Humpty Dumpty,' said Max as he drained his sherry glass. He got up from the table. 'Or perhaps not. I'd better go and see about lunch before I make any more ill-advised remarks. There's nothing ready. Would you be insulted if I offered you bread and cheese? It's quite nice cheese, Connie got it for me from Soho and I made the bread.'

'Bread and cheese would be fine,' said Ming, turning to smile at him, grateful that he had not pressed her for details about Mark and trying not to think about all the king's horses and all the king's men.

'Something's made you less gloomy than you were.' Max stood, looking down at Ming as she knelt on the rug. 'If it's not the love life, what is it?'

The easy casualness of his question seemed to make it possible for Ming to answer simply.

'I didn't realise that it showed,' she said, 'but I do seem to have rewritten a bit of the past that used to bother me. In fact that's what's made me think I might be able to sort out what you call the love life.'

Max waited for more. His eyebrows arched high above his blue eyes and he looked so like a caricature of himself that Ming gave him the rest of the story.

'That bloody man!' Max sounded thoroughly irritated. 'He's completely destructive.'

'It's hardly his fault that I fell in love with him.'

'I think it probably is,' said Max, watching her carefully. 'There are people who arouse devotion without apparently wanting it or doing anything to achieve it, but I've often thought that they must be so desperate to prove themselves lovable that they do everything they can to make everyone they meet worship at their shrines. I'll go and get the cheese.'

He left the room abruptly. Ming realised that she had pins-and-needles in both legs and hobbled to one of the sofas. Sitting on it, massaging her knees, she began to think about what Max had said. It was possible that he had not been talking solely about Peter Suvarov. She started to feel acutely uncomfortable and to ask herself just what her motives were in wanting to bring Mark Sudley back into her life.

Ming was almost grateful the following day when the Suez crisis blew up into melodrama, because it distracted her completely. That night waves of RAF planes from Cyprus bombed the Egyptian airfields. Everything that Bertrand had described was happening.

As he had warned Ming, the French and British Governments delivered an ultimatum ostensibly to divide the battling Israelis and Egyptians and safeguard the Canal for international shipping. It was not particularly convincing as the Israelis were still some ninety miles away from the Canal when the demands were made.

Radio Cyprus broadcast statements warning the people of Egypt to stay away from military targets in order to avoid being killed, and there were apparently very few civilian casualties. It was only later that Ming discovered that at the same time leaflets in Arabic, which had been printed weeks in advance, had been dropped to explain that the bombardment was a punishment for the Egyptians' having supported Nasser.

Convinced by the bombing that Allied warships would try to shoot their way through the Canal, Nasser had it blocked with sunken ships, preventing all the traffic that the ultimatum had been designed to protect.

CHAPTER 15

Obediently if pessimistically following Max's instructions, Ming decided to drop into Roger Sillhorne's office at Westminster and, if he was there, talk to him as though they had met often in the past few months. As she walked through the gates to the great arched doorway, it occurred to Ming that at the same time she could have a friendly word with his new secretary and perhaps defuse some of the anger that Diana Frontwell had described.

When Ming put her head round the door the first person she saw was Roger himself.

'Hello!' she said. 'How good to see you, Roger.'

He looked up from the letter he was reading and saw Ming's face framed in a small mink hat. Dropping the letter on his secretary's desk, he beamed at Ming and held out his hand.

'What a charming surprise.'

There was enough sarcasm in his voice to make her say quickly:

'What a debate that must have been yesterday! Did you speak?'

'Weren't you in the gallery?' he asked, diverted at once by the thought of his own triumph. 'You ought to have let me know if you were having trouble getting a place. I'd have seen you got a seat.'

'Alas, I missed it. I was in Sussex. But I've been reading

the reports. I'd love to know what you think of it all.'

'I'd be delighted to tell you,' he said with the familiar self-satisfied smile. 'Why don't you come and have a cup of tea with me now? We've just time before this afternoon's debate.'

'You really ought to get these letters done.' The secretary's voice was slightly harsh and had overtones of complaint that made it unattractive. Roger turned to Ming and raised his eyebrows in an expression of theatrically exaggerated patience, then he looked back at his secretary and shook his head.

Ming turned deliberately and smiled at her replacement.

'I'm awfully sorry for coming to distract him,' she said. 'I remember how infuriating it always was. My name's Mary Alderbrook,' she added and walked over to the desk with her hand outstretched.

'I know,' said the woman shortly and gave Ming's hand a brief, limp squeeze. Ming saw that she was quite pretty with a rosy complexion and softly curling brown hair. Her plain grey jacket and skirt looked thoroughly appropriate for the office and fitted well enough, although something about her made Ming feel uncomfortable.

'Come on, Ming,' said Roger, grabbing her arm. 'Veronica can manage. She always does.'

Ming looked at the girl with what she hoped was a friendly, commiserating smile and allowed Roger to usher her out of the office. His willingness to talk seemed to present an opportunity that she would be silly to ignore, even if it increased his secretary's animosity. As they were walking down the long, dark corridors towards the tea room, Ming asked why he had disliked Veronica so much when she first went to work for him.

'She seems perfectly clean and tidy, polite, good-looking, efficient, even if her voice grates a bit. What made you so cross with her?'

'It's true that she's getting a bit better, but she's still got a lot of rough edges and she stares at me in a most peculiar manner. Perhaps I was just spoiled having got used to your brilliance,' he said, nodding to a colleague who passed them and looked curiously at Ming.

'Brilliance nothing,' she said, laughing. 'I just let you exploit me till kingdom come.'

'Your godmother's money is going to your pretty little head,' said Roger, tucking his chin into his neck as he smiled.

Ming wondered whether he knew how pendulous his double chin had become and decided from his satisfied expression that he did not.

'Perhaps it is just as well that you left. I'm not sure I'd have enjoyed such uppitiness in my office.'

When they stopped at the tea-room door, Roger looked her up and down. Ming had a sudden impulse to smooth her straight skirt lower over her knees and pull the lapels of her jacket together. He put his left hand under her elbow and urged her forward. She was amused to notice a tiny, involuntary resistance in herself that made him push even harder.

'But as it's made you look so gorgeous as well, I'll allow that it's probably a good thing, despite its deleterious effect on your character. I like the hat; it's a great improvement on your old blue felt.'

'I hope that was a joke, Roger,' said Ming with more than a hint of caustic in her voice as she yielded to the increasing pressure on her arm.

'Of course, my dear,' he answered smoothly, pushing open one of the double doors for her with his free hand. Ming disengaged herself and walked forward out of his reach.

As they were drinking their tea, Roger gave Ming the benefit of his opinions on Egypt and the spinelessness of the countries he felt ought to have supported Britain and France in their attempts to regain the Canal and so preclude the necessity for any bombing. He told her, too, about the equal cowardice and disloyalty of members of his own party who had objected to the government's necessary actions.

'I'm surprised that you're not part of the Suez Group,' said Ming as she listened, trying to pick out from his diatribe any facts that she could use.

'They don't like me and I don't find them particularly appealing,' he said shortly and went on to talk about the Americans' reluctance to support their British allies in the attempt to get the Canal back in their own control.

'It's only partly their so-called hatred of colonialism,' he said, 'and infinitely more that they've a presidential election coming up. If it weren't for that, Eisenhower would have supported Eden; we'd have shot our way through the Canal months ago and Nasser would already be discredited and out of the way. I'm sure of it. As it is, Dulles, who's always loathed us, has won and we're getting no help from the United States at all.'

'Is it as personal as that?' asked Ming.

'Oh, I think so. Politics is usually pretty personal when you come down to it. Although there's always economics, too.'

While he was talking, David Wallington appeared in the tea-room doorway. Recognising Ming at once, even though she had her back to him, he made his way between the tables, nodding to colleagues, exchanging a word here and there, but moving steadily nearer to Sillhorne's table. When he reached it, he smiled at Roger and laid a hand on Ming's shoulder.

'Hello, Ming. I haven't seen you for far too long. How are you?'

She leaned back in her chair and tilted back her head so that she could look up at him. He closed his hand lightly on her shoulder for a moment.

'I'm all right myself, but horrified by what's going on in the world,' said Ming, surprised by his touch.

David stood looking down at her, thinking how much he hated seeing her with anyone as crass and bullying as Roger Sillhorne. Disconcerted by his reaction to her presence, David tried to concentrate on what Ming had said.

'As well you might be. It's all pretty hideous, isn't it? May I join you both?'

Roger agreed reluctantly and behaved so sullenly for the next twenty minutes that it was impossible for any of them to discuss anything that mattered. Ming took the first opportunity of a break in the meaningless conversation to suggest that they all go to the chamber. Both men stood up and she smiled impartially at them as she escaped.

She found a place in the crowded gallery and looked down into the chamber, noticing how full it was. The Secretary of State for the Colonies was answering a question about British officials in Haud, but very few people seemed to be paying him any attention. Ignoring him herself, Ming took out her notebook. Sitting surrounded by the familiar sounds and smells of the Palace of Westminster, where she had spent so many years of her adult life, she hated the thought of the little plots and conspiracies that took place all the time as people manoeuvred for power and advantage.

From her seat she could see David Wallington when he edged into a place in the back row of the Opposition benches. Suddenly he raised his head, almost as though someone had called his name, and looked straight at her. For a moment some of the colour left his distinguished face, but then he smiled and lifted a hand. Ming smiled back, and waited for the real business of the afternoon to begin.

As soon as the questions had all been answered the Chief Whip proposed the motion to adjourn the House and the Prime Minister came forward to the Dispatch Box. It was just after half-past three. Ming leaned forward to see him more clearly.

He was as elegant as ever, standing apparently at ease with one hand in the pocket of his superbly cut double-breasted suit, but she noticed heavy bags under his eyes and thought he looked not only exhausted but ill. It was almost impossible for her to believe that anyone who looked and sounded as he did, anyone who had always been as honourable as he, could have sanctioned a secret agreement of the kind she suspected. She wondered whether the rumours about his health might be true and whether it might have affected his judgement.

As soon as the Prime Minister started his speech he was interrupted by shouts from both sides of the House. From the Opposition benches there were catcalls, insults, and demands for straight answers to their questions, the most frequently reiterated of which was whether or not the United States had been warned about British plans to bomb the Egyptian airfields.

Later, listening to the Leader of the Opposition's criticisms of the Prime Minister, Ming could not help remembering how Gaitskell himself had demanded that the government take retaliatory action back in July when Nasser had made his first move, and once again she thought what an unpleasant business politics could become.

She had seen the House in many moods: tremendous excitement, the depressing torpor of a dreary debate with only a handful of members in the chamber, genuinely furious anger, or the well-rehearsed antagonism of Budget Day; but she had never seen it in such ferment.

After hours of sound and fury that signified very little, the leaders of the respective parties left the chamber, soon followed by most of their front-bench colleagues and gradually in descending order of importance the majority of Members of the House, until the only ones left were ministers with questions to answer and a few long-winded MPs with questions to ask or points to make.

For Ming the most interesting moment of the entire debate came quite late in the evening when a young Conservative MP rose to announce that he had recently been in France, where he had come to the conclusion that the government had been involved in an international conspiracy.

The Speaker interrupted the young Member and refused to let him continue. He changed tack, and asked the Speaker on a point of order whether, believing that the action the government had taken to be wrong, he would be considered 'right and patriotic' if he tried to bring that government down.

Ming felt that at last she had all the confirmation that Max and Connie could expect, but she waited with considerable interest for what the Speaker was going to say. When it came it was an anticlimax: he announced that the MP's question did not constitute a point of order, that there were many Members in the House who were clearly trying to bring the government down and that they were quite entitled to do so. He then called on the Lord Privy Seal and the young Member was silenced.

When it became clear that he would not be allowed to speak again, Ming left the chamber and went to visit Flixe and the baby. Horrible and worrying though the crisis might be, the reality of Nicholas's arrival seemed much more genuinely interesting.

Flixe was warmly welcoming and Nicholas increasingly attractive, if rather sleepy, and Ming spent a happy hour with them. When she got up to go, Flixe reached into the small cupboard by her bedside and took out a clutch of gaily wrapped parcels.

'I probably won't see you on Saturday,' she said, 'and so here are your birthday presents. Don't open them until the day. I hope it's a happy one for you.'

'Flixe, you are sweet.' Ming took the packages and bent down to kiss her sister. 'Thank you. I'll see you soon.'

On the day itself Ming's postman delivered a big bundle of letters and packages. There were cards and presents not only from her parents and her sisters but also from various friends. But first Ming opened the ones Flixe had given her. Two of them were from her nieces.

Each of the girls had painted a card and Fiona had made her a penwiper of circles of dark red felt sewn together at the centre with huge, clumsy stitches. Sitting looking at it, Ming felt entranced by the child's apparent affection and determined to keep the little object prominently on her desk, even if she never actually used it.

There was nothing from Mark, but while she was sensibly telling herself that she could hardly have expected him to contact her after what had happened he telephoned to wish her a happy birthday.

'Thank you, Mark,' she said, having recognised his voice immediately although it was tentative and rather cold. Hearing it made her slightly breathless and she gripped the telephone receiver hard, as though afraid that she might drop it.

'I've got a small present for you, and I wondered if we could meet.'

Trying to control her instinctive relief so that she did not sound threateningly eager, Ming said calmly:

'That would be nice. When were you thinking?'

'What about this afternoon if you're not doing anything better? It's a lovely day. We could go for a walk as soon as I get away from the office.'

'What a good idea. How about Richmond? It's ages since I was there and it's much nicer than the ordinary parks.'

'Perfect. I'll come and pick you up at two. Or is that too early?'

'No. Two's fine. I'll see you then.'

As she replaced the receiver, Ming thought about his voice. It had been worryingly formal. He obviously wanted to see her, or he would never have telephoned, but he sounded quite different from the old days, almost like someone with bad news to deliver.

By the time he rang her front-door bell, Ming had dressed in warm, comfortable clothes that were suitable for a muddy walk, and she had made up her face with scrupulous care. Part disguise, part convention, the cosmetics helped her to present a calm face to Mark. As he stood there in the doorway of her flat, she felt a moment's impulse to lean against him and tell him everything she thought and felt about him, but the memory of what Max had suggested about her motives held her back.

It was not long before she noticed that Mark was both angry and extraordinarily tired. When she asked if he was all right, he almost snapped at her and so she changed the subject.

He drove to Richmond Park, saying so little that Ming felt compelled to make conversation in a way that she had not done with him since the weeks just after they had first met. She asked about his holiday and after he had answered in monosyllables, she searched for an impersonal subject and led him to tell her what he thought about the horrible events in Budapest.

'I know very little of Hungary,' he said more easily, 'except that their prime minister has appealed to the U.N. for help protecting Hungarian neutrality. The Russians are apparently streaming back over the border in force. But there's not a lot anyone in the West can do to stop them invading any of their satellites short of starting World War Three. No one, not even the Americans, is in a position to take on that. How was Paris?'

Since he clearly wanted to talk about anything that did not directly concern them, Ming obediently chattered away about Paris and the article she had written. By the time she ran out of things to say, they had reached Richmond.

Mark drove slowly round the park until they reached the Pen Ponds car park. He switched off the engine and, with the keys in his hand, said:

'Is this all right?'

'Fine,' said Ming, puzzled but willing to accommodate him. 'Shall we walk around the ponds or up to the top of the hill?'

'Whichever you prefer.' Mark got out and came round to open her door.

'Let's go up the hill,' she said. 'With the trees bare, it'll be light as well as a more interesting walk.'

Mark acquiesced and they walked side by side up the gradual, grassy incline towards the wood. At the edge of the trees, Ming stopped and turned back. Part of the deer herd was grazing quite close by, apparently unconcerned by the presence of humans. The stag was a magnificent animal with a wonderful spread of antlers. A car backfired far away and he threw up his head to stand, almost black against the sunlit blue sky. At his feet was rough, country grass quite different from the ordered lawns and raked gravel of the Parisian parks she had been describing. Behind them rose the wood, its floor carpeted with years of decaying leaves, soft underfoot and wonderfully comforting.

'I do like this place,' she said, sounding more natural than she had since Mark had collected her.

'I'm glad.'

At the faint warmth in his voice she turned and saw a

more familiar expression in his grey eyes. His mouth, too, looked less pinched.

'It's so completely English,' she said, suddenly hopeful again. 'Paris is wonderful, but it's not until you come to somewhere like this that you remember the point of England.'

Mark's tight face relaxed a little more.

'What is the point?'

'Uncontrived, free, with a kind of natural generosity ... It's hard to put into words. And it's sentimental in any case. Ignore me.'

'And you a journalist.' The mockery in his voice was warm and kind and Ming turned to smile at him.

'I know; absurd, isn't it? I suppose it's just that somewhere like this makes one remember that whatever the bloody politicians do, whatever the fashions in this or that, whatever the mistakes and the horrors, there's a kind of core to the place – and to all of us – that ... means more than what's going on at any particular time. A bit like that day on the river at Oxford.' She hoped that he would understand what she was really saying to him.

'Ah, yes,' said Mark blankly, 'that day.' He turned his back on the view and on her.

Disappointed, Ming followed him and they walked up between the old, naked trees, smelling the dying leaves, the fungus and the damp logs they stepped over. Since it was clear that he was not going to follow any of her leads, she wished that he would tell her whatever it was that he had to say and get it over.

'Ming, I know that I have upset you,' he began abruptly, 'and I can only plead that I wasn't exactly happy myself when I did it.'

'I know that. It seems extraordinary that we should be so good at making each other miserable when we used to be so easy together before we tried to ...' Ming broke off, aware that whatever she said would sound critical.

'I can't quite think why I teased you for finding words difficult just now,' Mark went on as though she had not spoken. 'I'm finding it almost impossible to say what I

mean at the moment – or even to be perfectly certain what
it is that I do mean.'

'That is definitely something we share.' Ming's voice was
breathless again and she hoped that he would put it down
to the effort of the walk.

'This is a hellishly difficult conversation, isn't it?' He
stopped again and looked down at her.

As the sun fell on his face, Ming saw just how exhausted
he looked. It was quite clear that he had almost no energy
left for their muddled romance.

'I rather expected that it would be hard,' Mark went on
after a moment, 'but I couldn't let you go on waiting for me
to do something. Ming, I'm sorry that I haven't been what
you wanted. I did try, but it's all been too much for me.
What I came to say is that I think we would both find
things easier if we didn't see each other for a while.'

'I see.' Ming tried to think of some way of persuading
him that they should try again but until she could be
certain of herself she could not possibly expect him to go on
when he wanted to stop.

'I'd have written to you but that seemed very cowardly.'

'Thank you.' Ming was keeping a tight grip on her feelings. 'It does sound sensible, particularly at such a time, but a
little sad.'

'Does it?' There was a difficult pause until he added
coolly: 'Shall we stretch our legs a bit or would you rather
go straight back?'

'Since we're here, shall we go on?' Ming tried to emulate
his detachment, and was grateful that it was the sharp wind
that was making her eyes water. 'Unless you have to get
back soon. We could go down the other side of the hill,
round the first pond and back over the causeway. Would
that suit you?'

'Fine.'

They walked their circuit in almost complete silence,
occasionally pointing out a bird, or a particularly interesting tree, and drove back to Ming's flat, tired, muddy and
drained of all expressible emotion. At her door he handed her
a hard, wrapped package and said goodbye.

Ming waited until he had driven off before she let herself in to the flat. Then she made a pot of tea and opened the parcel to discover that he had given her a copy of Olivia Manning's new novel. It was definitely something that she wanted to read, but it seemed a slightly impersonal present after everything they had shared.

The knowledge that she had brought that sharing to an end by her own stupidity and selfishness suddenly overwhelmed her and she leaned over the kitchen table, burying her face in her hands, and tried to stop the sound of her dreadful, howling sobs from reaching the neighbours.

She spent the next day entirely alone, battling to regain her serenity. Peter telephoned and asked whether she would join him and the girls for lunch, but she said that she had too much work. Her voice still did not work properly and it seemed to her quite impossible to face anyone when she felt she might burst into tears at any moment.

When she had finished reading the Sunday papers, there did not seem to be anything else to do except work and so she got out the notes she had written and tried to put them into a coherent article about Suez. Even that seemed unimportant and she had to struggle to concentrate.

By half-past seven she was worn out and bored, and she went into her red-and-grey kitchen to make herself some scrambled eggs. She ate them listening to the news and heard reports of a series of pathetic appeals from Budapest. The Russians had returned in ever-increasing numbers and were steadily taking over the country again. Hungary's few short days of freedom were coming to an end, and the people who had won them for the rest knew that they had very little time left.

Listening to the pleas for help, for food, medicine, and armed protection against the ferocity of the Russian Red Army, Ming remembered Gerry's pessimism. The wireless crackled again.

'We ask every Western station which receives our message to transmit it in English, German and French. We need help! The people of Budapest have no food. We need food and arms. Only military help can save us. The whole nation is asking for help.'

'Attention, attention! We ask you to forward our call to President Eisenhower. We ask for immediate intervention, immediate intervention.'

Then there was nothing. At exactly seven minutes past eight the newsreader announced that the radio stations all over Hungary had been silenced. When she was certain that there would be no more, Ming switched off the wireless and took her supper dishes to the sink.

As she washed up like an automaton, she felt a passionate, furious rage against the world's bullies that drove her own unhappiness away for a moment.

CHAPTER 16

Jack died attack Port Said stop letter follows stop Helen Hazeldene.
Ming held the telegram in her hand and felt her teeth
grinding together. All the anger she had ever felt about
anything seemed to gather and swell inside her. At that
moment it seemed quite monstrous that men like Jack
Hazeldene should have been sent to die in such a way for
such a cause by the men to whom she had listened in the
House of Commons.

The memory of Jack clinging to her as he talked about
Caroline was so vivid that Ming could almost feel her hands
contract as they had done under the force of his grip. Her
teeth ached.

She had to do something to release her fury and went
straight to her desk, where she tore up the measured article
she had been writing and sat down at her typewriter to
compose a ferocious attack on the government. It then took
her hours to tone down what she had written into something that Max and Connie might be prepared to print.
Whatever their reservations, Ming was at last determined to
force them to publish what Bertrand had told her.

During the afternoon, while she was still struggling with
her article and her rage, Ming was interrupted by the telephone.

'Ming? Connie here. How are you?'

'Not so bad,' she said, not wanting to have to talk about
Jack's death. 'By the way, have you and Max decided

whether you dare print an anti-government story?'

'That's what I'm ringing about,' said Connie, surprised by Ming's hostility. 'We do think so now, particularly if we cover ourselves by setting out all your Paris information as speculation and putting in the received view as well. We ought to get away with it.'

'It's not we who are getting away with anything,' said Ming more coldly than Connie had ever heard her speak. 'It's them.'

'I don't know that they are getting away with it.' Connie tried to talk calmly. 'Stories about collusion with Israel are beginning to seep out.'

'That's not really the point any more, is it?'

'Isn't it?' said Connie, puzzled by the bitterness in Ming's voice. 'I must go in a minute. When will you have the piece finished?'

'A couple of days, perhaps. Why? There's no particular rush, is there? We ought to wait and see what happens in the end and how many more people get killed for the bloody Canal.'

'I'd quite like to get the new issue out on the streets a little earlier than usual, and everything else is ready except for Suez and Max's piece on Hungary. By the way, we were counting up the approving and the angry letters about *Story of a Lost Love* last night and they come out about even.'

To Ming just then any subject other than the war seemed irrelevant and trivial, but she did her best, saying:

'Oh, Connie, I am pleased. Perhaps there really will be a change in the law when the Wolfenden Committee eventually reports.'

'Perhaps.' Connie did not sound sanguine. 'Anyway, we can hope. Goodbye, Ming.' She cut the connection.

Ming sat holding her receiver and looking out of her window across the muddy-coloured river to the bare trees of Battersea Park. To her right the sun hung low and blood-red in a white sky underlined by the black triangles of warehouse roofs and patterned with a few spiky trees.

She felt as though she had travelled an immense distance since Roger had enlightened her about Max's past. It was

quite hard to remember what she had felt then, the odd
mixture of distaste for Max and the increasingly secure
happiness with Mark. She had thrown the happiness away
as though it were no more important than an old newspaper.

The buzzing in her ear reminded her that she was still
holding the telephone receiver and she put it gently back in
its cradle. She told herself that it was silly to feel as though
nothing mattered any more. Jack's life might have been
destroyed and she might have lost any chance of happiness
with Mark, but there must be other things that were
important even if she could not think just what they were.

Ming watched the red ball of the sun begin to sink
behind the roofs and when it had gone, leaving only a faint,
pinkish glow, she looked down at the messy page in front of
her. It seemed as though every line she had written was
contradicted by another. Arrows shot in all directions over
the page, extra comments in balloons were planted here
and there amid the mess of crossed-out words and ink blots.
She tried to make herself go on with it and could not. In the
end she had to admit to herself that her anger over Jack's
death was stopping her from thinking clearly.

The next day she was bitterly amused to read in the
newspapers that the Russians had announced that they
intended to restore peace in the Middle East and were
threatening rocket attacks against Britain and France.
Considering the mercilessly violent revenge they were
wreaking on Budapest it seemed the height of hypocrisy.
Krushchev went so far as to propose to President Eisenhower a joint Russian and American force to stop the
fighting over the Canal.

The Americans, not surprisingly, were strongly opposed
to any such initiative, but took their own by engineering a
run on sterling. The British Government bought furiously
to support the pound, spending some eighty-five million
dollars. The Chancellor of the Exchequer, who had been
among the most fervent advocates of military action against
Nasser, knew that such buying could not go on and advised
Eden to stop the war.

With their unchallenged economic power the Americans

had succeeded where all the committed opponents of war
in Britain had failed and forced the Prime Minister to
abandon his obsession and withdraw his troops from
Egypt.

All he had achieved was the deaths of hundreds of Allied
soldiers, an enormous increase in President Nasser's
prestige in the Arab world and the destruction of years of
patient diplomacy. The Americans would obviously look
askance at any British initiatives for a long time, while the
French believed that their British allies had betrayed them
and would obviously not trust them again.

Mrs Hazeldene's promised letter arrived before Ming
was satisfied that what she had written expressed enough of
her disgust and yet remained publishable. She turned away
from her typewriter to open the letter:

> *My dear Ming,*
>
> *It is hard to write about what has happened but Jack's
> affection for you gives you the right to know as much as we do.
> His CO's letter says that he was killed, quite quickly, soon
> after the beginning of the assault on Port Said. He was shot in
> the head and did not suffer, they say. I hope it's true.*
>
> *They will be letting us have his things back and I want
> you to have his watch. He cared so much for you, Ming, and
> you helped him so when you were here, at a time when the rest
> of us simply could not reach him at all.*
>
> *I am at my wits' end about his children. I am seventy and
> Jack's father is seventy-three and very frail. Caroline's parents
> are in no position to care for them. What will happen to them?
> If only . . . No; it's not fair to you to write that. They are very
> bewildered and unhappy and cannot really understand what
> has happened to them.*
>
> *Come and see us when you are next in Gloucestershire.*
>
> *Helen Hazeldene*

Ming sat with the letter in her hands saying over and over
again to herself: I am not responsible for those children. I
did not infect their mother with polio and I did not kill their
father. Even if his parents and mine wanted us to marry, he
disliked the idea as much as I did. It is not my fault.

* * *

The December issue of the magazine was distributed to the usual booksellers and posted to subscribers on November the twenty-fifth. There was no reaction to it for four days, but on the fifth Ming woke to the sound of a shower of envelopes falling through her letter box. Bundled into a rug-like dressing-gown, for it was very cold, she carried her letters into the kitchen, where she lit the gas and filled the kettle. While it boiled she picked up the first envelope and ripped it open, recognising her father's angular writing as she did so.

He had written in restrained but obvious anger at her 'disloyalty' and her 'pandering to the Communists and weaklings'. Ming had winced at his first criticisms but that one made her smile wryly to herself: it was after all the Russians who had proposed a joint action with the Americans to stop the Suez expedition. She finished the page and then turned it over. As she read the second side, she stopped smiling.

It's people like you who destroyed any possibility of success. If your journalistic colleagues hadn't sapped the Prime Minister's strength with your carping, he'd have listened and given the services enough time to prepare properly. As it was we didn't have anything like adequate reserves and the Navy were stymied too. Even so we would have succeeded if we'd been allowed to fight through to the end. If people like you hadn't been so treacherous after the attack was launched we'd never have been pulled out. Betrayed. It appalls me that you could have written such things while men like Jack Hazeldene were dying for our country.

I've always hated your being associated with a magazine that prints the kind of filth that appeared while you were away in Paris. It's some comfort to know you could not have had anything to do with that issue, but other people may not realise it. Can't you get out? I'd like you to find some other work and protect what's left of your reputation. There must be something else you could do to amuse yourself.

What with one thing and another your mother and I will not be coming up for the christening of Flixe's child.

Ming let the crisp sheets of writing paper drop into her lap as she sat heavily on a chair in the kitchen. Unlike both her sisters she had never found herself in serious opposition to her father until his outburst about her working for Connie the previous summer, and she hated it.

The telephone rang, startling her. She dropped the letter as she got up to answer it and was relieved to hear Flixe at the other end of the line.

'You sound awful, Ming. I take it the old buzzard's written to you as well,' she said cheerfully. 'He is absurd, and you mustn't take him too seriously.'

'He's not absurd. He's only ...'

'Well, perhaps not, but he's never been able to accept the fact that we all had minds of our own. I suppose with mother endlessly telling him how disappointed he had made her, he hoped we'd think him marvellous and hang on his every word. Don't let him upset you, Ming. Both Peter and I thought your article was superb, very clear and perfectly justified.'

'Did you?' A slight smile lifted the corners of Ming's mouth.

'Definitely. Don't worry about things, Ming. All will be well. Now, about tomorrow. Would you like to lunch with us first? Then we could all go ceremoniously to the church together and meet the other godparents there.'

'Flixe, that would be lovely,' said Ming, feeling cheered by her sister's approval. 'I'm sorry about the parents, though. I know you wanted them there.'

'You know,' said Flixe in such a meditative voice that Ming was surprised, 'he really is a monster. You sound as though he told you they weren't coming because of your article.'

'He didn't actually put it in so many words, but ...'

'I thought so,' said Flixe with some energy. 'Mother has sprained her ankle badly and has been confined to bed. That's why they're not coming. Don't you worry. He will get over his rage. We'll all have a splendid time tomorrow and Nicholas isn't going to know the difference either way. Half-past twelve, then; don't be late.'

Ming promised and went back to her post. When she had read it all, she discovered that about half her friends and relations agreed with her father and the other half was divided between those who were grateful for her exposition of the political background to the aborted invasion, and those who thought she ought to have supported the government.

Roger Sillhorne's letter was the angriest of all. He wrote that Ming had abused their friendship by including in her article things he had told her in confidence. Neither Helen Hazeldene nor her husband wrote at all.

Not surprisingly Ming's anonymous correspondent had not been able to resist such a good opportunity, and wrote to tell Ming that she was an evil-minded source of filthy disloyalty who would reap her just rewards in due course.

Sighing, she slid the unsigned piece of spite back into its envelope and added it to the brimming box in the bottom drawer of her desk, telling herself that one day the writer of the letters would become bored and leave her alone. As she shut the drawer and straightened up, Ming suddenly smiled and immediately felt better. The letters were vile and she hated their writer, but that hatred was a completely legitimate feeling. No one in the world could have expected her to feel anything but loathing and anger. There was a kind of freedom in accepting her hatred.

Mrs Crook's arrival to clean the flat provided a welcome respite from the weight of disapproval that had descended on Ming, and after they had drunk a cup of tea together and the daily had settled down to 'do' Ming's drawing room, she went to have a belated bath and dress.

While she was thinking about what to put on, she looked at the suit she planned to wear for the christening and decided to go out and buy herself a new hat to wear with it.

Wearing her new hat the next day, Ming stood at the font with Nicholas Suvarov in her arms. David Wallington stood on one side of her and on the other was a short, untidy but extraordinarily attractive man whom she had never met before. Flixe had introduced him to Ming as Tibor Smith and he had shaken her hand in a warm, firm grip.

It was not until she looked down at his hands and noticed some paint caught under one fingernail that she remembered Amanda Wallington's chatter in the dining room at Kennington. Ming was almost certain that Amanda had said that the artist who painted the two masterly portraits was called Tibor Smith.

Beside David, who was very tall, Mr Smith looked almost squat and Ming wished that she had not worn such exaggeratedly high-heeled shoes and that her new hat had a less immense brim. She edged a little further away from him so that she did not dwarf him.

David felt the movement at his side and looked down at her, but all he could see of her was the crown and vast brim of her elegant hat. He shivered. Whatever heating there was in the big church was quite inadequate to cope with the icy draughts that poured through the doors and ill-fitting windows and crept up under his trousers. Any warmth there had been must by then have been high up under the beautiful stone ribs of the vaulted ceiling.

Ming looked across to her sisters standing on either side of Peter Suvarov. Flixe had completely recovered her health and looked superb in a new coat of thick cream wool trimmed with bands of dark fur around the hem and sleeves. Her bright blonde hair was piled up at the back of her head and a small fur cap was perched on the top, accentuating the shine and colour of her hair.

Gerry looked both less elegant and less blooming. She had on a scarlet suit that made her look almost sallow and although her hair was quite as clean and well-brushed as Flixe's it had none of the bounce or the brightness, and her hat was not becoming. But Gerry looked almost as happy as her sister, as she leaned slightly to her right so that her arm brushed that of her tall husband. Ming watched him look down at Gerry and give her a conspiratorial wink.

The child in her arms moved suddenly and Ming was distracted from everything else. Flixe had wrapped a warm shawl over the white lace christening robe he wore. As Ming smoothed the shawl away from his face with one gloved finger and smiled at him, he opened his bright brown eyes and stared up at her. Her smile shrank as he moved within her arms and turned his face towards her, opening and shutting his mouth in a plaintive rhythm as though he were searching for her breast. An extraordinary sensation shot through her, part pleasure and part pain.

Disappointed in his search for sustenance and comfort, Nicholas let out a cry of rage. Ming looked up guiltily and across the grey stone font she caught Flixe's eye. Her smile seemed to express such immediate understanding that Ming felt almost afraid of what she might have betrayed.

'Dear me.' The vicar, who had just emerged from the vestry, had a light voice that managed to be audible even through the child's increasingly violent screaming. He was a pleasant but ordinary-looking man, and not even the ecclesiastical splendour of his gold-embroidered stole and long white surplice could lend him presence.

'I am sorry,' whispered Ming. 'I can't stop him yelling.'

The vicar smiled reassuringly and told her that he was quite used to it. He explained what she was to do at each stage of the service and told her to hold Nicholas the other way so that when she handed him over, his head would rest against the vicar's left arm. Obediently Ming turned the baby around and was unutterably relieved when he became quieter.

The priest began his prayers as the congregation shivered and tried not to think of the cups of hot tea that awaited them at Flixe's house. At the appointed moment Ming undertook to renounce the devil and all his works on behalf of the child in her arms and handed him to the priest.

The baby yelled again as the cold but holy water was dripped on to his forehead and he was baptised Nicholas David Alexander.

As soon as his mother rescued him from the arms of the church's representative he stopped crying again, and along with everyone else Ming smiled at the sight of Flixe making faces at her baby, apparently quite oblivious to her surroundings or the other people who filled them.

Flixe's house seemed a paradise of warmth, colour and

scent after the monotonous grey stone and the damp chill of the church. There were large vases of informally arranged cream- and flame-coloured flowers all round the big, pale drawing room, and it smelled deliciously of them and of the woodsmoke of the fire in the Adam fireplace. Flixe's friends and relations soon lost their pinched expressions as they drank whisky or China tea, nibbled savoury sandwiches and ignored the vicar, who stood in a corner of Flixe's elegant room looking lost and hungry.

Ming took pity on him and collected two cups of tea from a laden table by the window.

'Would you like one?' she asked when she reached him and was rewarded with a grateful smile.

'I don't know how Mrs Suvarov manages to keep this house so warm,' he said. 'We can never do anything with either the vicarage or the church.'

'It is nice, isn't it? Sometimes I think she overdoes it, but on a day like today it really comes into its own. That was a lovely service.'

After that she could not think of anything more to say and, since the vicar could not either, Ming was relieved to see David Wallington strolling casually towards her, cup in hand.

'Hello!' she said cheerfully. 'We were just talking about central heating and the weather.'

'How very English!' said David with a cheerful smile. 'May I remove my fellow-godparent, Mr Hackinster?'

'Oh, my goodness! Yes, by all means. So nice to have had a chance to chat to you.'

Ming smiled at him, and let David take her to the opposite side of the big room.

'Oughtn't we to talk to our other fellow-godparent?' she said. 'It seems a bit mean ...'

'He's busy just now,' said David with a nod towards the fire. Ming looked and saw that the Hungarian was talking seriously to Julia Wallington. She was leaning towards him and neither of them paid any attention at all to the people who passed by.

'So he is Amanda's godfather and the painter of those

wonderful portraits at your house,' said Ming. 'I thought he must be.'

'That's right. I'd forgotten that you didn't know him. He was Julia's main prop and stay here in London after the war, while I was still stuck in Italy. They're devoted to one another.'

'Don't you mind?' asked Ming curiously. There was something extraordinarily intimate about the way in which they were so absorbed in each other. David shook his head.

'Julia and I are much too solidly rooted together to fear each other's friendships. Tibor is part of the family. And he needs her very badly just now.'

'Why?' asked Ming, too surprised to conceal her curiosity. She was about to retract her rude question when David raised his eyebrows.

'Coming as he does from Hungary, he's not unnaturally ... distressed.' There was enough surprise in his voice to make Ming say quickly:

'I haven't forgotten them, David, all those young men and women who tried to stop the Russian tanks with little more than their bare hands and who died so horribly. I haven't forgotten, but there isn't anything I can do about it. And there's far too much that I should be doing something about and can't.'

'I know you'd never forget. Ming, please don't think I was criticising you. I ... couldn't. I'm sorry you've so much to worry about just now. You look tired too. You'd better sit down.' David pointed to one of Flixe's sofas.

Ming sank down into the yielding softness and sighed, still concerned that David should have thought her indifferent to the suffering of the Hungarians. Whenever she thought about it, she was full of useless sympathy, but it was inevitable that her distress over Jack's death, the loss of Mark and her father's fury should seem more immediate.

'I hadn't realised how wearing it would all be,' she said, smiling gratefully up at David. 'Being so tired makes me concentrate on all the wrong things.'

'You need to take more care of yourself – or let other people take care of you.'

Ming thought of Mark and clamped her lips together. David watched her anxiously, thinking that she looked almost ill.

'Would you like some more tea?'

'That would be heaven.' Ming smiled up at him. 'Perhaps a sandwich too, if you've got enough hands.'

David nodded. He was back in a few minutes with a plate of sandwiches and biscuits and her refilled cup. Having put them on a small table he sat down beside her and stretched his arm along the sofa back. Ming ate and drank and began to recover.

'You look better,' said David after a while. 'At least as much of you as I can see under that hat.'

'It's a very elegant hat, and quite the latest thing.'

'Oh, I'm sure it is,' said David quickly, 'although the sight of your face unshadowed would rival any hat.'

'I do feel much better,' said Ming, rather taken aback. Max's warning about the people who are so unsure of themselves that they try to make everyone else fall in love with them echoed in her mind.

'Thank you, David. You've been very kind,' she added formally in an attempt to counteract any subconscious flirting.

'For feeding you or rescuing you from the vicar?' he asked with a smile, but then he did not wait for her answer. 'How are you generally? Apart from being tired, I mean. I don't seem to have seen you for ages – not since that day we had tea together in the House.'

'Oh, I'm all right.'

'Really? You don't look it,' he said, studying her tired, beautiful face. 'In fact you look as though you've been badly hurt. Have you been having a hard time over your article?'

Ming let her head droop, so that he could no longer see anything of her face, and closed her eyes for a moment. His sympathy was almost more than she could take.

'It's not so much that, as that a friend of mine was killed at Port Said,' she said after a moment.

'I am so sorry,' said David quietly. 'I didn't know.'

'No. It's hard to talk about. I really don't resent the fury of people who disagree with what I wrote,' she said, diverting them both from the subject of Jack Hazeldene. 'After all if one is publishing one's opinions, one must expect people to criticise them. It isn't fair to take up a platform and then whine about disagreement or criticism.'

'I don't think you'd ever whine,' said David quietly. 'You're far too brave and generous for that.'

A shadow fell across the white-and-gold plate Ming was holding and she looked up to see Julia Wallington standing watching them both. She was dressed as simply as usual but with a certain understated magnificence that Ming had not noticed in her before. On the left shoulder of Julia's short, belted crimson jacket was a superb diamond sunburst, and both her face and her hair were more elaborately arranged than usual.

'Julia!' said Ming in welcome as David got to his feet. 'How lovely to see you. Come and sit down. David has just shown me how blissful it is to take the weight off one's feet.'

Julia smiled as she recognised the unaffected pleasure in Ming's face, and took David's place. He fetched his wife a cup of tea and then left them alone.

'Christenings are rather depressing, aren't they?' she said to Ming. 'I disliked both of ours. I'm not quite sure why.'

'Perhaps it's because there are no hymns,' suggested Ming, 'or perhaps just because there's such a tiny huddle of people at the back of a great, echoing grey barn of a church.'

'Could be,' said Julia. 'Or it may be all those portentous announcements about sin and the devil and punishment.'

Ming was interested and considered the point.

'I'd have thought that you'd have known all about that anyway,' she said and, as soon as she noticed Julia's peculiar expression, hurried to add, 'in your job.'

Julia relaxed and nodded.

'By the way,' she said, 'I was impressed with the latest issue of your magazine.'

'Were you?' Ming's face lit up as it had not for either David's compliments or his kindness. 'Thank you very much. I've been a bit worried about it ever since I handed it over. I was so angry that I didn't really think about the Official Secrets Act and so on.'

'I think you'd be very unlucky to be prosecuted,' said Julia kindly. 'I shouldn't worry too much. And as far as I can tell you were entirely justified.'

CHAPTER 17

Two more letters reached Ming at the beginning of the following week and she began to feel like a boxer who has taken so many punches that his will to fight begins to go. It seemed to her that life had been much simpler when she had spent her energies merely trying to fulfil what everyone wanted of her. Then she had never had to worry about what she was doing. She had simply followed orders. It might have made her angry, but a little suppressed rage seemed a small price to pay when consequences and responsibilities could be handled by those who had ordained her actions. She felt sick whenever she remembered Connie's light-hearted instruction to cause trouble.

Ming decided to shut down completely. She would read no more of the anonymous letters when they arrived but simply add them unopened to the boxful in her desk. She would not think about Mark or Jack Hazeldene. She would not let herself hope or dream or want anything at all. Instead she would do whatever was necessary for the magazine and try to think as little as possible about anything else.

At the first editorial meeting after the December issue of the magazine had been published both Max and Connie noticed the change in her. Ming was much quieter than she had been, purple-grey shadows lay under her eyes, and the corners of her mouth drooped. It was obvious that her recently acquired confidence had already been shaken and they thought she looked ill as well.

Connie put the change down to Ming's distress over her father's disapproval of her article, of which Flixe had passed on a detailed and angry account. Max assumed that Ming's abstraction had been caused by troubles with her young man.

Both of them were right. Ming's unhappiness over her father and Mark had grown, and damaged her in growing, but there were other things troubling her, too, of which the worst was Jack's death. Of the rest, the most recurrent was a fear of legal action over her article. Julia's reassurance at the christening did not seem to help much.

Ming had decided to say nothing to Connie or Max, because there was nothing either of them could do to contain the damage that might in any case not happen, but it was hard. After the meeting Max made Ming stay behind when Connie left, on the pretext that he had cooked a special lunch and did not want to waste it.

'I'm not very good company just now,' Ming said. 'But if you'd rather be bored than waste your cooking, then so be it.'

Max made no comment, but he cleared the papers off his gate-legged table, took some cutlery out of a drawer in the oak cupboard, told Ming to lay the table, and went out to the kitchen to fetch lunch.

It proved to be a salmi of woodcock, cooked according to the recipe in *The Gentle Art of Cookery*, a book which entranced Max with its eccentric elegance. Ming ate her share with more real pleasure than she had felt for days, drank the wine he had poured and complimented him as she laid her knife and fork tidily on her empty plate.

'I'm glad you liked it,' said Max. 'Now tell me, what is it? The young man?'

'Partly,' said Ming. 'He told me some weeks ago that he thought we ought not to meet for a bit, and now he's written to say that he's been offered a job outside London that seems more interesting than the Civil Service and he's going to accept it. He suggests that we might see each other some time next year.'

'That sounds fine. Why haven't you rung him at once and suggested meeting him on the first of January? I assume from your face that you haven't.'

'No,' said Ming. She got up from the table and went to fetch her bag. 'There are two reasons. One is that he once told me there was no job he could imagine that would be more important and satisfying than what he was doing in the Ministry of Defence.'

Max watched her, thinking that she looked as though she had lost weight. Her well-cut blue tweed skirt was so loose that it had swivelled round and the back pleat was six inches to the right of its proper place, and the clinging paler-blue twin-set showed off the sharpness of her shoulders and elbows.

'What is the other reason?' he asked when it became clear that she was not going to volunteer it. She came back to the table, but obviously found it difficult to answer.

'Tell me something else,' said Max with a mischievous smile. 'Do you always dress to go with this room or is it pure chance?'

A faint smile twitched at Ming's dry lips and she began to look more like herself. She glanced around the room at Max's carefully orchestrated blues, creams and whites and nodded.

'I'd never thought of it like that, but I suppose I have nearly always worn blue-and-white when I've come down here. It's not that surprising, because a lot of my clothes are blue.'

'And a good thing, too, with your eyes. Now come on, tell me what's really worrying you.'

Instead of answering, Ming offered him the piece of paper she had taken out of her bag. Surprised, Max accepted it and unfolded it to read the few, typed lines:

Well, well, Ming, you've done it now, haven't you? Where will your destructiveness end? Not content with driving the poor man mad with frustration, now you've got him the sack. Didn't you think of what the Ministry of Defence would do to a civil servant known to be 'friendly' with a journalist who criticised the government like that? I think you did. I think

*you were punishing him. One day you will get your just
rewards and I for one will laugh and laugh and laugh.*

'Have you had many of these?' asked Max, folding it up
again and laying it on the table. He wiped his fingers fasti-
diously on his white damask napkin.

'Yes,' said Ming. 'One a fortnight ever since Connie and I
got back from Egypt. Just recently I found a kind of satisfaction in feeling furious about them, but now that's gone
again, and I don't think I can bear it much longer. Not if
they're going to tell me things like that.'

She put her elbows on the table and propped her head
up on her hands. When she looked at Max again he saw
that her darkened eyelashes were wet, but she was not actually crying and her face was under control.

'Why haven't you said anything before?'

Ming shrugged and tried to think up rational excuses to
explain her wholly irrational conviction that she had to
keep the letters to herself.

'I did ring the police at the beginning, but they said they
couldn't do anything unless the letters contained physical
threats. They never have.'

'But still, you must have needed sympathy at least.'

Ming felt a sudden pain in her bottom lip and she
realised that she was biting it. Having released it, she
looked at Max, but she said nothing.

'I've had my share of that sort of letter,' he said gently. 'I
do understand.'

'I suppose,' said Ming slowly, 'that I was afraid I couldn't
cope with sympathy. Sometimes it's easier to keep things at
a bearable level if you don't have to thank people for being
kind and find appropriate things to say to their reassurances. I suppose I thought if I could just put them away
and not think about them that would be best since no one
could do anything to stop them coming.'

'Except the person who was writing them,' said Max,
watching her carefully. When she shivered, he went on:
'Isn't that really the trouble? That you were afraid to find
out who it is who thinks like that about you?'

He was shocked by the thought of what she had been

enduring for so long and hiding so successfully and he wanted to try to help, but when he saw her face crumple he wished that he had kept his mouth shut.

Ming turned away and walked down the long room to the fireplace. Max's kindness – and his perspicacity – had got right under her guard. She knelt down and held out her shaking hands to the flames until she was sure of herself. The fierce heat against her skin helped. After a long time, she came back. Her face was completely controlled again.

'I think you're probably right, Max,' she said.

'I'm sure it isn't him,' he said in a very quiet voice.

Ming put out both hands as though to try to silence him physically.

'Most anonymous letter writers are women,' he went on, knowing that she needed to hear what he had to say, even if she did not want to listen. 'The one humane policeman I ever talked to told me that. It's known to be a particularly female vice.'

Ming sighed.

'I don't actually believe it's Mark. I simply can't imagine him doing something underhand like that. Why should he, after all? And he is the straightest and most honest man I think I've ever met.'

'Lucky man,' said Max, 'to have someone to say that of him.'

Ming hardly heard him and went straight on:

'But whoever it is knows a terrible lot about me – and clearly about him too. For months the letters never mentioned him but now ... He is leaving the Civil Service. Perhaps I have driven him to do that; perhaps I've ... No. But I do know that I have made him very unhappy.'

'Come on, Ming,' said Max, allowing a little exasperation into his deep voice. 'You love the man. You keep telling me that you don't, but it's always been perfectly obvious that you do, and I can't believe that you knew him so little that you would have fallen for someone who could possibly write a letter like that.'

'But does love depend on knowledge?' Ming's eyes looked very dark. 'Couldn't ...'

'Yes, it does,' said Max firmly, not even allowing her to qualify her question. 'You can lust after people you don't know, and that can confuse you into thinking that you love them; but you've known this Mark for too long for that to be the case.'

'How do you know?' She felt as though she kept asking people impossible questions and paying no attention to their answers.

'Oh, Ming! Lust is a very simple thing; it can be combined with love and therefore last, in which case I suppose you should call it desire. Or it can be lust on its own, which is terrifically exciting for a short while; it is then either satisfied and ended or it is frustrated, in which case it reaches a peak and then quite quickly dies.'

'But how do you know, Max?' asked Ming again, putting the emphasis on the pronoun. She was too beaten to care about tact any longer. Max gave a short laugh, and Ming winced.

'Even you can ask things like that,' he said sadly. Then he remembered the corrosive misery and self-loathing that made it easy to forget everyone else's sensibilities and added: 'Because the emotional mechanics are just the same for me.'

Ming nodded. 'I see. Sorry. Well, what do you think I ought to do?'

'Only you can decide,' said Max, getting up. 'I'm going to make you some coffee. From my own experience, the only thing to do with anonymous letters is to refuse to read them and ignore their existence.'

'That makes sense, and I've tried it. But I've come to the conclusion that I'd rather know what it is this person thinks of me. Besides,' Ming added with a spark of resistance hardening her lips and bringing some colour back into her cheeks, 'I keep hoping that he'll slip into a real physical threat one day and then the police will do something about him.'

'You have got guts,' said Max with real admiration.

That compliment stayed with Ming through the next few days. It helped her to write to her father, setting out why she had taken the line she had over the Suez affair and asking whether she was still invited to Gloucestershire for Christmas. It also gave her the courage to write straightforwardly to Mark, telling him that she would very much like to see him when he next came to London. She added:

I've never forgotten what you said to me about your work that evening when you came to the flat after I got back from Egypt. It would be good to know that you are doing something that means a great deal to you. I should love to know about the job and to hear that you are well – and happy.

Answers to both letters came a few days later. Her parents were, it seemed, still expecting her for Christmas and suggested that she should take a lift with Gerry and Mike, pooling her petrol ration with theirs. Mark wrote to say that his job was to be in Oxford and would be involved with the production of computer components, but that he did not want to bore her with details. He would be in London for the day on the second of January and suggested that they meet for tea at Searcy's in Sloane Street at half-past four. His mother would forward any letters.

Remembering the white-clothed tables, silver tea pots and little rectangular iced cakes, Ming thought that Searcy's seemed a surprising place for a man to choose to meet a woman with whom he had once made love, but she picked up her pen at once to accept. Before she could write any more than his name, Ming heard her door-bell ring. A tall, thickset policeman was standing there when she opened the door.

'Miss Mary Inge Alderbrook?' he said in a south London accent.

'Yes,' answered Ming, surprised but politely smiling. Her upbringing and inclinations had given her implicit trust in the police, and his dark blue uniform and silver buttons reminded her satisfyingly of her childhood.

He held out a stiff buff envelope embossed with the official stamp of all government communications. Ming looked down at it and then up at the impassive pink-and-white face of the policeman and fear poured into her mind.

'Julia was wrong,' she whispered and wished that her rage over Jack's death had never made her write so violently against the government.

Her hands were sweating as she raised them to take the envelope from the policeman. Then her mother's early training took over and she thanked him.

'What do I have to do?' she asked and was annoyed to hear the tremor in her voice. Forcefully reminding herself that even if she were to be prosecuted for contravening the Official Secrets Act, she was at least in no physical danger, Ming managed to collect enough courage to add in a firmer voice: 'Do I have to sign something?'

When she had shut the front door behind the policeman, she took the envelope back to her desk, where she sat and looked at it for some time before she could bring herself to open it. When she did she had to read it twice before she understood it.

It proved to be a summons to appear before the magistrates to answer a charge of publishing an obscene libel in respect of the excerpt from *Story of a Lost Love* printed in the October issue of *The World Beyond*. Also named in the action was Constance Wroughton as joint-proprietor of the magazine.

Ming felt a disgusting tingling down the inside of her legs, combined with a terrible emptiness in her stomach. It was a sensation that she remembered with sudden, agonising vividness from her short mission in occupied France during the war and from a particular night of the London Blitz, when she had lain in the bombed basement of her godmother's house and heard her twin sister die beside her. She knew that it was born of terror, shame at the terror, and an irrational idea that she would always bring trouble on herself and on all the people for whom she most cared.

If she had not been so silly about her discovery of Max's homosexuality, Connie would never have had to lend her the novel. If she had not been so ignorant and prejudiced before she read it she would never have been so struck with it and would not have suggested to Connie that they print an extract from it in the magazine.

It was some time before Ming could make any rational assessment of her real responsibility for what had happened. As soon as she could exercise some control over her emotions and the physical sensations of shock, she forced herself to go into the kitchen to make some toast and tea. She knew from experience that the effect of eating something sweet and drinking tea would help control the panic.

Swallowing the hot buttered toast and honey proved difficult, but she managed to suppress her nausea, and the tea had an immediate effect. Before it wore off, she read the summons once more and noticed for the first time that the name of the person who had brought the complaint of obscenity to the magistrates was Roger Sillhorne.

Hot fury pushed the shock out of her mind. That Roger, who had known her for so long and had once professed to love her, could do such a thing seemed utterly monstrous. Her earlier decision to shut down all her feelings and all her hopes could not survive in the face of what had happened. She was going to need all the faculties Connie had once urged her to use.

When she was sure that she had controlled her fury enough to speak evenly, Ming went to the telephone and rang her up.

'You've had one, too,' said Connie as soon as Ming had announced herself. Connie's voice was shaking. 'I am so angry I could spit.'

Ming's legs started to tingle again.

'I am most dreadfully sorry,' she said, separating each syllable of each word to get them out clearly.

'Not with you.' Connie's voice sounded firmer and warmer. 'Or even with that unspeakable Sillhorne. Ming, hold on. I'm furious with my lawyer. I asked him whether we would be safe to publish and he said all we risked was a magistrate's destruction order, which would hardly have mattered at all. He never even warned me of this – and he sent me a swingeing account for his professional services.'

'Adding insult to injury,' said Ming breathlessly. She steadied her voice to say: 'I think we ought to meet, don't you?'

'Absolutely,' said Connie. 'And there's no point in your coming down here, since all the professional advice we're going to need is in London. I think Max and I had better come to your flat, if that's all right?'

'Yes, of course it is. We're going to need a solicitor at once. Have you got a good one?'

'No,' said Connie with emphasis. 'It was he who produced the useless advice. You?'

'Mine's marvellous at death duties and so on, but I can't imagine he'd know much about obscene libels. Look, I think I'd better get on to Julia Wallington and ask her advice. Is that all right with you?'

'Certainly. It's a bit cockeyed going to a barrister for an introduction to a solicitor, but ...'

'But at least she'll be knowledgeable,' said Ming grimly, 'and we know she's trustworthy. I'll see you and Max later. Unless you think we ought to keep him out of this. After all, he's not named in the summons. Shouldn't we let him off?'

'Yes,' said Connie slowly. 'I think perhaps you're right. I have told him what's happened, but there's no need for him to go through the whole business of lawyers' conferences and appearances in court again.'

'No,' agreed Ming. 'When do you suppose you'll get here?'

There was a pause while Connie obviously looked at her watch and did some calculations.

'Say, half-past twelve. Then we can talk as long as we need and if I have to stay in London for any reason, Flixe will give me a bed I'm sure.'

'Yes, I'm sure she will,' said Ming, adding a little dryly: 'Both my sisters are wonderful in a crisis. I'll ring Julia now.'

Julia's clerk announced that she was in court and not expected back in chambers until late that afternoon. Ming, feeling desperate, put her question to him instead. There was a peculiar sound down the telephone, rather like a stifled snort.

'I'm sure I couldn't say, madam. I could not give advice of that kind,' said Tomkins.

'No indeed,' said Ming, brushing her damp forehead with her free hand. 'Will you ask Mrs Wallington to telephone me as soon as she has a moment?'

'Certainly, madam.'

Ming put down her receiver and then picked it up again to dial Connie's number. When they were connected, Ming explained what had happened.

'I'm not sure it's worth your coming up until we've heard what Julia has to say. All you and I could do would be talk about what's happened and work ourselves into a worse panic.'

'That makes sense, Ming, although it'll be damned frustrating to have to sit here and do nothing.'

That was the first time Ming had ever heard Connie swear.

'Better than sitting here doing nothing but make each other miserable,' said Ming. 'I'll ring you as soon as I've any news.'

Later in the day Ming did manage to speak to Julia Wallington, who asked for time to consider which solicitor would be best. Ming, who was determined to have the most suitable, most knowledgeable, most skilful lawyer she could find, agreed at once. Julia rang back just before five o'clock to say that a man called Terence Ratterley was probably Ming's 'best bet'.

'I've talked to several colleagues and he's their unanimous choice. If you can get him you should be in good hands,' she said.

'Thank you,' said Ming seriously, adding: 'You can't imagine how much I wish we had not relied on Connie Wroughton's man and had come to you in the first place.'

'Ming,' said Julia and then stopped. After a long pause, Ming asked what she had wanted to say.

'I am very sorry this has happened. But it's not necessarily the catastrophe it must seem. Don't give up hope. Opinion on these obscenity trials is changing. Even two years ago when there was a spate of trials, two of the four most important ones ended in acquittals.'

'Julia, thank you. It's comforting to know that. May I ring you again if we need you?'

'Yes,' said Julia firmly.

Mr Ratterley listened to Ming in such complete silence that she wondered from time to time whether he had simply put the telephone receiver on his blotter and gone away, but when she had finished her account, he said at once:

'How horrible for you! But it's not a disaster, and I shall certainly do my best to help. You say that your partner wants a meeting and I think that would be a good idea. Would you like to come here . . .' he paused, 'at ten o'clock tomorrow morning?'

'Could it be a little later? Miss Wroughton is based in Sussex and will have to drive up. If we were to meet at eleven or even half-past, she'd have to make a less frenzied start.'

'That's more difficult. I shall be tied up all the rest of the morning. Would half-past three suit you? Splendid! I look forward to it, Miss Alderbrook.'

Ming felt considerably better for having taken some definite action. There was less panic in her mind and her physical symptoms had dwindled to a quite bearable ache in the pit of her stomach. But she was left with a passionate need to talk about what had happened to a disinterested audience. She was tempted to ring one of her sisters, but she knew that they would both be instantly partisan and she needed reasoned not instinctive sympathy. After a while she pulled forward her big address book, lifted the telephone receiver and asked the operator for the number of her old school.

When the secretary answered Ming asked to speak to the headmistress. A moment later an efficient voice that she would not have recognised said:

'Janet Roseheath here.'

'Hello, Miss Roseheath, this is Ming Alderbrook.'

'No! What a lovely surprise. How are you?' The crispness of the voice had softened.

'Oh, I'm all right really. Is this an inconvenient time for you?'

'Not at all; what can I do for you?'

Ming explained what had happened and then said: 'In the circumstances I don't think it would be terribly appropriate for me to come and address your girls. You might well get complaints from parents and I'd hate to do that to you.'

There was a pause, during which the pips went. Both women ignored them.

'Normally I would say "stuff and nonsense",' said Miss Roseheath, 'but as things are at the moment, you might be right. I myself thought that you were both brave and very sensible to print that excerpt, but I can imagine some of our less imaginative parents could take a different view.'

'I am glad you approved. Ever since the summons came I've been thinking that it was the most idiotic thing I could possibly have suggested.'

'You always did worry too much about what other people would think of you.'

There was great affection in the headmistress's voice and Ming felt a tiny, much-needed surge of confidence.

'Thank you for that,' she said.

'No need for gratitude. I meant it. You need to do what you think is right and hold on to it, whatever they tell you and whatever it does to you. It is better to make mistakes than never to do anything for fear of them. And I've always thought that you needed to stop yourself from feeling responsible for the whole world.'

At that wholly relevant admonition, Ming managed a small laugh.

'You have done me good, Miss Roseheath. Perhaps we can reorganise the talk when all this is over.'

'I'll hold you to that, my dear. Goodbye.'

CHAPTER 18

The following morning's post brought Ming a letter from
Jack Hazeldene. She stood beside her front door, staring
down at his familiar writing with a mixture of horror and
pity. After a while she pushed aside the superstitious fear,
ripped open the envelope and took out the letter. He had
written it ten days before he was killed:

My dear Ming,

*Your letters have really kept me going here. It's wonderful
of you to have written so often and so well. Thank you.*

*At last I have decided what to do and I thought you should
be the first to know. I will be leaving the army as soon as this
shindig is over. All that's left of Caroline is the children and it
would be idiotic as well as cruel to leave them thinking that
they've lost both parents instead of only her.*

*It's funny (peculiar) how selfish misery makes you and how
irrational. I seem to remember telling you that I wished I'd
never even met Caroline and if I did, I hope you refused to
believe it. There has never been anything in my life as
important as she was and what I felt for her. We had it for
only a few years, but we had it, and that's more than most
people could say. To have denied that would have been . . .
criminal.*

*All this sound pretty high-flown, I know, and there is still
a lot of time when I feel ground-down by it all and terrified
that my being with the children won't help them a jot. But I*

*must try. I've got a job with a stockbroker, which ought to
leave me plenty of time for them, and I'll have to find a good
nanny.*

*Will you help us, Ming? Me and the babies? We're going
to need our friends and you're the best of those.*

Love, Jack

Ming sat down at her kitchen table with the letter still in
her hand and nothing in her mind except desperate pity for
the man who had written the letter and for his children.

'Of course I'd have helped,' she said aloud and then tried
to force her mind into thinking of something that she could
do. Her mental efforts seemed to drive out of her mind all
thought of the afternoon's meeting with Connie and the
solicitor Julia had recommended to them and it was two
o'clock before she remembered it.

That gave her only just enough time to change into a
dark blue suit and telephone Gerry to ask whether she
could drop in at tea-time.

'It would be lovely to see you,' said her sister at once and
Ming set off for her meeting with a faint sense of optimism.

She and Connie met in the hall of the solicitor's stately
building in Lincoln's Inn Fields and were quickly shown up
to his office. It was a gracious room with an elegantly
moulded ceiling. All but one of the walls were lined with
soberly bound legal books and on the fourth, over the
chimney-piece, hung an early eighteenth-century painting
of the square outside.

Mr Ratterley himself proved to be younger than Ming
had expected from his voice, perhaps forty-one or -two. He
greeted them as friends and invited them to tell him everything about the magazine and their decision to publish the
'article in question'. He grinned privately then, as though
he had enjoyed his own pun.

Connie, who was less amused, gave him a brief description of the magazine and its expected readership and
described the opinion her own solicitor had given her of the
probable consequences of publishing the article.

Mr Ratterley sat, once more in absolute silence, until she

had finished speaking. Then, laying both hands on his impeccably clean blotter, he looked across at the two women on the far side of his desk.

'And have either of you any idea why Mr Sillhorne should have taken this step? It's pretty unusual and I've never heard that he was particularly obsessed with the subject of homosexuality.' He watched Ming flush. 'Miss Alderbrook?'

'I used to work for him in the House of Commons,' she said. 'He was angry when I left and when he heard that I was writing for the magazine he accused me of working with "a filthy pervert".'

'That sounds as though he has some pretty strong feelings,' said Connie, tapping a long cigarette on her gold case. Mr Ratterley got out of his chair to light it for her.

'How long would it have taken him to arrange this prosecution?' asked Ming, shaking her head when he offered her a cigarette.

'It varies,' said the solicitor, shrugging his shoulders. 'I suspect that he will have tried to persuade the police or the Director of Public Prosecutions to pursue the case and then resorted to a private prosecution when they would not take it up. Why do you ask?'

Ming crossed her slim legs at the ankle. She looked composed and at ease, giving no clue to the mixture of anger and fear that was swirling around inside her.

'He was furious with what I wrote about the Suez fiasco. I wondered whether this might have been a punishment for that.'

'Hmmm. It seems a bit tortuous. Pity.' Catching a glimpse of Connie's narrowed eyes, he laughed slightly. 'Otherwise we might have suggested that this was a malicious prosecution and tried to persuade the DPP to stop the case.'

Ming sat in silence, wondering whether she ought to tell the solicitor about her anonymous letters.

'Mr Ratterley.' Connie's cool voice interrupted her thoughts.

He raised his eyebrows and smiled.

'Can you tell me precisely what is involved in all this? I know so little of the courts.'

'Certainly. You will appear at the magistrates' court as summoned, and you have three options then: to plead guilty, to defend the action or to request a trial by jury. If you plead guilty, you are likely to get off with a fine.'

'How much?'

'That depends. Two years ago, a novel called *Julia* was prosecuted; its publisher pleaded guilty at Clerkenwell Magistrates' Court and was fined thirty pounds with ten pounds costs.'

Ming uncrossed her legs and leaned forward in her chair. The terror that had been consuming her seemed absurd. Forty pounds was nothing in comparison with her nightmares.

Watching the intentness of her lovely face, Mr Ratterley thought that with her comparative youth, her prettiness, vulnerability and gentle voice she would be a considerable asset in the witness box. Constance Wroughton, on the other hand, might well antagonise both judge and jury with her commanding presence and intimidating black-browed elegance.

'And if we opted for trial by jury?' said Ming.

'Then the trial would probably be held at the Old Bailey. The fine, in the event that you were convicted, could be ten or even fifteen times that sum and the costs could add up to thousands.' As Mr Ratterley spoke he watched their faces. Connie's could have been that of a statue for all the emotion it showed; Ming's was thoughtful and a little stubborn.

'Who would pay the costs if we won?' she asked.

'You, I suspect,' said Ratterley. 'There is no point in hiding unpalatable facts now that you have been faced with this.'

'I see.' Connie opened her bag, took out a slim, black leather notebook and wrote down the sums he had mentioned. 'And what do you think our chances are? Of winning, I mean?'

'It is impossible to say. This is one of the most difficult cases to assess, because until the jury has pronounced, no one knows whether a crime had been committed or not. If it were virtually any other case, there would be a crime and a victim, and your lawyers' business would be to ensure that the prosecution could not prove that you had done it. Here, we have to prove that what you have done is no crime. Dicey.'

'Yes, I see that,' said Ming, 'but isn't it worth fighting?'

'That depends. There's not a great deal that can be used to defend that sort of action.'

'Presumably in that case we need Counsel's opinion as to our chances,' said Connie crisply, 'before we can take any decision.'

'Yes, indeed. I must think who would be most suitable.'

'What about Julia?'

Mr Ratterley's forehead twitched. Ming was not sure whether it was because he was irritated by her suggestion or amused by her informality.

'Mrs Wallington has no particular experience in trials of this nature, and she is not yet a Queen's Counsel,' he said dispassionately. 'She is of course a most able junior, and I suppose in some respects it could be an advantage to have a female advocate, but experience would be more valuable.'

'Would she take the case?' asked Connie, ignoring his caveat.

'I should have to make enquiries.'

'Please do so. I know so little of legal etiquette, but it seems to me that we haven't much time to decide whether to plead guilty or not. Shall we wait while you telephone her?'

'It can't be done quite like that, I'm afraid,' said Mr Ratterley with a laugh. 'We have to go through channels.'

'Very well,' Connie stood up. 'In that case we ought not to take up any more of your time. I shall be staying in town for the next few days in any case. This is my telephone number. You already have Miss Alderbrook's. Thank you for seeing us.'

Ming stood too and said:

'If we were to plead guilty, would there be any risk of prison?'

Connie looked at her in horror.

'Technically yes,' said the solicitor quietly. 'Otherwise you wouldn't have a right to trial by jury, but I find it hard to imagine any magistrate imposing a custodial sentence in this case. A fine is much more likely, although there are booksellers in prison now for selling pornography.'

Connie's face registered her disgust, but Ming merely looked as though she were concentrating.

'And there was a case some years ago,' said Mr Ratterley slowly, 'of a poet, who was prosecuted for showing some of his work to a printer – translations of Rabelais and parodies of Verlaine, I think it was. He served six months in prison.'

'When was that?' asked Ming at once.

'1932 I think. I'd have to look it up to be certain.'

Connie lit another cigarette, as she always did in moments of stress.

'That's twenty-five years ago. Things must have changed since then,' said Ming. She looked at Connie and then turned back to say: 'Thank you, Mr Ratterley. Will you let us know when you've spoken to Julia Wallington?'

Mr Ratterley nodded and shook hands with both of them before summoning his clerk to show them out of the office. Then he went back to his desk, re-read the few lines of tidy notes he had written and sent for his clerk.

Outside in the square, Connie asked whether Ming would return to Flixe's house with her.

'I've got to nip to Gerry's flat. I promised to have tea with her today,' said Ming, still seething inwardly with rage at what Roger Sillhorne was doing to them.

'I see. Well, give her my love. I'll telephone you if I have any news.'

'Thanks, Connie. There's a taxi.' Ming hailed it and gave Flixe's address to the driver.

'Don't you want it?' asked Connie, switching her gloves and umbrella to her left hand preparatory to getting in.

'No. I'll walk. It's not far. Goodbye, Connie.'

Ming set off towards the Tottenham Court Road, trying not to remember the Sunday in the summer when she and Mark had lunched with Gerry.

Gerry answered the door only a minute after Ming had rung the bell.

'Come on in. You were quite right to come. Flixe has told me all about it.'

Gerry's face, framed in newly washed but unset hair, looked intent and alert as well as affectionate.

'But Flixe doesn't know anything about it,' Ming protested as she took off her coat in the small white hall.

'Leave your hat, too. You might as well be comfortable. I'll make the tea. There's a cake from that French patisserie you like. I won't be a minute.'

'Gerry, wait a minute,' said Ming, obediently removing her hat. 'You're talking as thought I were a child facing the dentist.'

'Sorry. Perhaps Julia is right and we do try to mother you. It's not intentional; I just can't bear the way foul things keep happening to you and I suppose it brings out all my maternal frustrations.'

'Oh, I see. Flixe has told you all about the summons. That's not actually why I came. Let's go and make the tea and then I can tell you all about it.'

Looking puzzled, Gerry led the way into her narrow, galley-like kitchen, pushed her new liquidiser out of the way and switched on the electric kettle.

'Will you take the tray?' she said. 'I'll bring the pot in a minute.'

Ming picked up the heat-proof tray and was touched to see the care with which Gerry had laid it and the lavish cream-and-nut confection that formed its centrepiece. She carried it through to the living room and put it down on a low table in front of the yellow sofa. Besides the piles of journals, there was a wide bowl of unseasonable red tulips, which surprised Ming. Gerry and Mike rarely splashed out on unnecessary extravagances and relied on their potted ivy plants for botanical decoration.

They were still there in their white wrought-iron *cache-pots*, looking as though they had grown yards since she had last seen them.

'Milk or lemon, Ming?' said Gerry, as she put the teapot

down on the tray. 'And for heaven's sake sit down.'

'I was admiring the plants,' said Ming with a laugh. 'Aren't you afraid that they'll take you over?'

'No. We snip bits off whenever that threatens. Help yourself to cake.'

'I'm not sure that I could eat anything,' Ming said as she tried to think of a way of broaching the subject of Jack's children.

'You mustn't worry too much,' said Gerry, pouring out two cups of tea. 'Even if the verdict goes against you, no one who matters is going to think any the worse of you – and the fine ought not to be too bad. Besides, presumably Connie will pay. She's much richer than you.'

'Gerry, it wasn't that I came to talk about.'

'So you said. But why not?' Gerry handed her a cup and pushed forward the milk jug. Ming took it.

'Until Connie and I have decided whether or not to defend – and we can't do that until we've got Counsel's opinion – there's really nothing to talk about.'

Gerry frowned and added milk to her own tea.

'I wish you trusted us,' she said after a while.

Ming, upset by the implications of that, put down her cup and said she trusted her sisters implicitly.

'Not really. You can't bring yourself to be completely open with either of us. I know that we can never make up for Annie. But we could help a bit if you'd only let us.'

Ming choked on a mouthful of scalding tea.

'Don't look so worried, Gerry,' she said when she could speak again. 'Annie died half a lifetime ago; it's not a present tragedy for me, and I'm not the same person as that fifteen-year-old girl.'

'I know.' Gerry went on stirring her tea needlessly. 'I only meant that we could give you the sort of support she would have given you if she'd still been alive – the sort Flixe and I give each other all the time: listening, talking, comforting.'

About to say that there was no comfort she needed, Ming knew that that was a lie; she had gone to Max for it often enough. For some reason it was easier to talk to him than to either of her sisters.

'We do sometimes feel shut out, you know,' said Gerry sadly. 'Drink your tea.'

Ming looked down at her hands. Then, obediently, she drank.

'I'm sorry,' she said helplessly. 'I never thought of it like that. I do just find it difficult to involve other people in my affairs, particularly when there's nothing they can do about them.'

'I know. It's all right. Don't look so anguished. Just remember when − if − they get on top of you, we're here and wanting to help.'

Ming put down her cup and got out of her chair. She crossed the room, hearing her high heels echoing on the parquet floor. Standing with her back to the windows and looking at the back of Gerry's head, she said:

'I did come for help today, but not that sort at all.'

Gerry turned at once, her face lit with a smile as vivid and generous as any Flixe could produce. Ming thought of the two children and how good Gerry would be to them, how much she had to offer them.

'I'm glad you came, Ming. I'll do anything I can.'

Taking a deep breath, Ming explained everything that Jack had said to her and what his mother had written about her grandchildren. As she spoke she saw Gerry's face harden into a mask of detachment before she turned away. Pushing on through a growing conviction that she should never have broached the subject, Ming added:

'Those poor children most desperately need someone like you who could mother them. It's not money, you see. There's some of that − if not an enormous amount − but that isn't what they need.'

Gerry leaned against the cushions behind her, letting her head tilt right over the back of the sofa and staring up at the ceiling. Ming walked back to her chair.

'We are not going to adopt any children,' said Gerry, slowly bringing her head upright again. 'We decided against it years ago for all sorts of reasons that still hold good.'

'But . . .'

'Ming, don't.' Gerry's voice was suddenly harsh. 'We took our decision and nothing has changed.'

Ming started at the sound of Gerry's anger and sat dumbly, trying to think of some way to deflect it.

'But I saw the way you looked at Flixe's baby and I know the way I felt when I held him,' she said at last, attempting to explain why she had made her suggestion rather than trying to persuade her sister. 'You need a child, Gerry; and there are two who most desperately need a mother. I know that it would be difficult taking on someone else's children, but they're still so young.'

Gerry's temper snapped as it had not done for years.

'I wish to God that you and Flixe would stop interfering. It's bloody painful to know that we can't ever have children, but Mike and I have managed to get used to it. It's like a deep cut: once the scar's formed it doesn't hurt any more unless people start picking at it. If people would only leave us alone we'd be fine.'

Gerry got up off the sofa. Ming saw that her eyes were fiery and her mouth had thinned to a tight line.

'Mike and I went through hell when we were making up our minds. I don't want him ... Neither of us can go through all that again,' she said a little more calmly.

'I'm so sorry, Gerry.' Ming could hardly speak through her bitter regret, but she had to mend things with her sister. 'It does no good to say that I was only trying to help, but I never meant to make you unhappy.'

'No, I know.' Gerry drank her tea. 'There's no one less malicious or trouble-making than you. It's all right. Just don't raise the subject again. I can't cope with it.'

Ming sat in unhappy silence. Phrases from the anonymous letters surged through her mind and yet again she wondered how close their writer actually was to her.

The whiteness of Ming's face surprised Gerry out of her own distress and she forced herself to explain the reasons why she and Mike had decided against adopting a child.

'We have a good life together,' she ended up, 'and we're happy, which is more than you can say for a lot of parents.'

Ming said nothing.

'Look at Julia Wallington,' Gerry went on, trying to get some reaction from her suddenly unresponsive sister. 'She has awful trouble with that daughter of hers and I suspect positively dislikes her sometimes.'

'I don't think so,' said Ming, pushed into speech by Gerry's injustice. 'I'm sure Julia loves Amanda.'

'Oh, she probably does, but liking is a different matter. Think of our mother: she would say that she loves all three of us, but she's no idea what we're like. I'd hate to bring up a child like that: wanting so much from her that I couldn't even see what sort of person she was, let alone like her for being it. And if it were not my own it would be even more difficult.'

Ming got up to pour herself another cup of tea.

'I don't think that's quite fair, Gerry. Mother wanted things for us, not from us.'

Ming took a gulp of tea, but it was cool and tasted bitter. She put down the cup.

'Mother wanted a lot more.' Gerry's voice held none of the bitterness of her past quarrels. Instead it sounded tolerant and a little regretful.

'Haven't you understood how much she wanted us to make up for all the things she resented? Giving up her old life as her father's hostess for one thing and exchanging it for the dreariness of married quarters and the duties of an army wife?'

'I know she's often bored and she can be quite savage, but ...'

'That's because she feels as though she sacrificed all that glamour and importance for us and we've done nothing to pay for it. She wanted us to do things or marry men who would give her back her sense of being someone important. Instead Flixe caused a scandal when she took up with Peter and there were all those suggestions in the press that he might have spied for the Russians in the war. Mike makes me wonderfully happy but he has no ambition to change the world; and you ...'

'But she must be pleased with your success, Gerry.' At that moment Ming thought she could not bear to hear of the ways in which she had disappointed her mother.

'Why? Well-reviewed translations of Russian novels and a growing reputation within the university world are not achievements that mean anything to her.'

There was the sound of a key in the lock and Mike's voice, light with happiness and welcome, called out:

'I hope you two girls haven't finished the cake.'

'No, we haven't,' said Ming quietly as he came in, his bowler hat and neatly rolled umbrella still in one hand. He looked at his wife and his sister-in-law, and then at the untouched cake.

'What's happened?' he said quietly.

Ming opened her mouth to try to produce an answer, but Gerry got there first. In a voice brittle with self-control she said:

'Jack Hazeldene, who was killed at Port Said, left two orphans. Ming thought we should adopt them.'

There was a clatter as Mike dumped his umbrella with his hat on the floor. He stood behind his wife and wrapped her in his arms, stroking her fair hair over and over again.

Over her head he looked at Ming. She had expected to see anger there, but there was only regret. She tried to show him how much she, too, regretted what she had done.

After a while he sat down on the sofa beside Gerry and cut the luxurious cake into three enormous slices.

'What about a fresh pot of tea, Gerry?'

'I'll make it,' said Ming, pleased to be able to do something for them.

When she returned with the hot tea, the other two were discussing Christmas plans and Ming joined in. They ate the cake and when she got up to go Gerry managed to smile at her. Ming did not risk any reference to the children.

Later that evening she rang up and when Mike answered she apologised for upsetting them both.

'That's all right,' he said. 'Gerry minds much more than I do, and I've learned not to raise the subject any more. You weren't to know.'

'But it was insensitive of me.'

'Don't beat yourself, Ming. You're having a beastly time

yourself, aren't you? I wish I could help.'

Ming was about to say bitterly that it looked as though no human being could ever help another without causing worse trouble when she remembered something that Mike might be able to do.

'You can, actually. I've heard a suggestion that Mark Sudley was sacked from the Ministry of Defence because of what I wrote about Suez. Could that be true?'

'Absolutely not. Who on earth told you anything so malicious and stupid?'

When Ming did not answer, Mike went on: 'Mark has been restive ever since the Suez business began; the reason he went on that long holiday was because he couldn't bear it but didn't think it fair to resign in the middle of the crisis. Once it was over, he did resign and left as soon as they'd let him go. I'm surprised he didn't tell you.'

'Mike, this is too important for you to tell me comforting lies.'

'I know, and I'm not,' he said seriously. Then his voice lightened: 'Don't worry about it, Ming. They say that you're never sacked for indiscretion – just sent to the Min. of Ag. and Fish.'

Ming laughed dutifully.

'Thanks, Mike. Let me know if there's anything I can do for Gerry.'

'I will. Goodbye.'

Ming buried all thoughts of the children and of the misery she had caused Gerry under her concerns about the magistrate's summons. With Connie and Mr Ratterley she went a few days later to Julia's chambers to hear her advice about their chances of acquittal.

Unlike Ratterley's offices, Julia's room in the Temple was small and dingy, overlooking a dusty light-well, although from the front the building looked charming and beautifully proportioned. As they climbed the stone stairs Ming and Connie saw various large, elegant rooms, but Julia's was different, almost completely filled by her big masculine desk and the three cramped visitor's chairs.

On the shelves behind her head were stacked innumerable dusty briefs tied in pink tape and there were even more piles of typescript and books in lopsided heaps on the floor than in Max Hillary's cottage. Julia's long black gown hung on a hook on the back of the door and there was a battered black tin wig box perched on a pile of new-looking briefs on her desk.

Julia laid out for them what they faced if they were to plead guilty before the magistrate, if they were to defend the action there, and if they were to opt for trial by jury as was their right. She told them that she thought their chances of an acquittal in the High Court were good, but that for safety she would advise them to plead guilty in the magistrates' court and pay their fine.

'Only you can decide what to do now,' she said at the end. 'If you do decide to defend in the High Court, I'll do everything I can to fight the case, but there is no guarantee that I shall be able to win. You would be risking a great deal of money – not to speak of your reputations and your liberty.'

'Is the risk of that much greater than in a magistrates' court?' Ming hoped that her voice was businesslike.

'The sentence would be longer,' said her Counsel dryly.

CHAPTER 19

Flixe Suvarov gave a dinner party for her two sisters on Christmas Eve, the day before they were due to drive down to their parents' house. Connie Wroughton had already left London, telling Ming that they should wait until after Christmas to decide on their strategy about the case, and the only other guests were Mike, the Wallingtons and Tibor Smith.

Flixe and her children had spent most of the day decorating the house and wrapping up Christmas presents, so that by the time the first guests came the drawing room sparkled with baubles, beribboned presents and the dancing light of dozens of candles. A huge, dark green tree had been dressed with red and gold glass balls, iridescent birds with spun-glass tails and tiny white lights. It filled the entire room with a resinous, nostalgia-evoking scent.

While Ming was putting on a new evening dress of wonderfully gleaming dark green velvet, she wondered how Gerry would greet her and whether she should make any kind of direct apology. Eventually, as she was stroking a little mascara on her eyelashes, she decided that the best thing to do would be to ignore the misery she had caused Gerry and try to be as normally cheerful as she could.

Ming collected up the presents she had bought for Flixe and the family, which were wrapped in gold paper and tied with green ribbons, and drove round to Kensington. Flixe opened the front door herself and admired the dress.

'You're all so Christmassy. Gerry's wearing pillar-box red.'

Her own lavender silk dress was the one she had worn for the ill-fated dinner party when she had introduced Ming to Charles Bederley. Flixe had still not quite got back her figure and she had decided to buy no new clothes until she was slimmer.

'The children are all agog. I couldn't bear to send them to bed,' she said, taking Ming's fur.

'I should hope not. The whole point of Christmas is that it's for children,' said Ming, with a smile.

When she walked into the drawing room, her hands full of glittering packages, the two elder children shrieked with delight and bounded across the pale carpet towards her. They were bundled into matching red dressing-gowns and their faces were almost the same colour with excitement.

Ming handed them the presents, which they took to add to the vast heap under the tree, and then went straight across the room to where Gerry was standing.

She was looking well and there were no signs in her face of resentment or sadness. As Ming leaned forward to kiss her, Gerry put an arm round her sister's shoulders.

'You're not angry with me, are you?' Gerry said. 'I was a bit upset and said things that I regret.'

Ming did not trust herself to speak and so she merely shook her head. Gerry gave her shoulders a slight squeeze and then let her go. 'That's a wonderful dress,' she said on a lighter note.

'So's yours,' answered Ming sincerely. She thought that Flixe's slight sneer was unjustified. Unlike the coat and skirt she had worn for the christening, the dress suited Gerry and made her look much less serious than usual, and younger, too.

'I bought it a couple of years ago.' Gerry smoothed the heavy red silk down over her slim thighs. 'But I've only worn it once. It seemed a suitably cheerful colour for Christmas.'

Behind her Mike, looking particularly handsome in his barathea dinner jacket, grinned at Ming and sketched a victory sign.

'Will you have one, Auntie Gerry?'

Andrew Suvarov held out a big silver tray. Gerry obediently took one of the squares of brown bread and smoked salmon.

'Fiona's being very lazy,' said Andrew crossly as he lifted the tray towards Ming.

She looked over her shoulder to see Fiona earnestly talking to Tibor Smith who was perched on the edge of the club fender. Ming smiled at Gerry and moved a little closer to find out what they were discussing.

'Yes, it was difficult, because I'm not very good at blanket stitch yet and for needlebooks you have to sew the back and front together with blanket stitch as well as doing lazy-daisy on the front.'

'And these daisies, they are easier?' Tibor's voice with its plummy Hungarian accent sounded quite as serious as Fiona's.

'Oh, yes, lazy-daisy's lovely.'

'I wish I could see the book, but I expect you've already wrapped it up. What colours have you used?' Tibor might easily have been talking to another adult about some subject of considerable importance.

Fiona looked hastily round to make sure that her mother could not overhear and then said:

'The felt is purple, because that's one of Mummy's favourites, and Mrs Irons lets us have three colours for the embroidery. I've used green for the blanket stitch and the stalks and leaves of the daisies, and pink and orange for the petals.'

'That sounds like an exciting mixture.'

'Yes, it is, but I wish it was painting, because sewing takes so long,' said Fiona. Suddenly remembering her duties, she offered Tibor the plate of smoked salmon. He took a piece.

'Painting takes a very long time, too, if you're doing it properly. Perhaps one day your mother will bring you to see my studio and I can show you how long it takes. Amanda Wallington often comes. You could come together. Would you like to do that?'

'Yes,' said Fiona definitely. 'But Amanda's older than me.'

'Yes, thank you, Uncle Tibor,' prompted Flixe, who passed the little group just in time to hear her daughter. 'And have you said hello to Auntie Ming?'

A mulish expression banished the eagerness from Fiona's face, and Ming did what she could to retrieve the situation.

'I'm sorry to interrupt your conversation, Fiona,' she said formally, 'but I hardly know Mr Smith. Will you introduce us?'

Smiling once more, the child performed a creditable introduction, chose a piece of smoked salmon for Ming and went on her way, leaving the Hungarian to say:

'That was clever – and kind.'

'Not really,' said Ming. 'I just have such vivid memories of the frustration I used to feel when adults – and my sisters – refused to take me seriously at that age that I wanted to help. And she's such a nice child.'

'Better than "nice" I think,' said Tibor, his face creasing around his smile. 'But with such parents, she would be.'

'Have you known them long?' asked Ming, thinking that it was odd that she had never met him before the christening.

'Some time, yes. Julia introduced us at her wedding, I think. I've heard about you from all of them, but Felicity seemed determined to keep us apart until the other day.'

Thinking of all the dull, suitable young men Flixe had invited to meet her over the years, Ming could not help smiling. Flixe might not think Tibor a suitable candidate for her younger sister's affections, but she would have been much happier talking to him than to the others.

'And we only just managed to meet then,' she said. 'I've had a conscience about that.'

Tibor smiled faintly, but he said nothing and so Ming plunged on: 'I wanted to say something about Budapest, but I was afraid of being clumsy. You must be very sad. I know so little ... Do you still have family in Hungary?'

'Some, but I haven't seen them for many years, not since I left in the war and letters are difficult. I know that one of my nephews was killed in the fighting, but I haven't heard about any of the others. Life for them all will be even worse now than it was before the revolution.'

Tibor's lined expressive face seemed to say so much more than his words that Ming was at a loss.

'But we cannot help them,' he said, spreading his hands in a gesture that seemed to accept fate and disclaim responsibility for it at the same time, 'and it is Christmas, and Flixe has taken very great trouble for us.'

'And so we should enjoy ourselves,' said Ming. 'That's very sensible.' It seemed to her that if Tibor could banish thoughts of Russian tanks rolling through Budapest, destroying both the city and its inhabitants, and the relentless punishment of doctrinaire Communism being imposed on the survivors, she ought to be able to forget her own anxieties. 'Where are you spending Christmas itself?'

'With Julia and David,' he said, reaching out to take a champagne bottle from Peter Suvarov and refilling Ming's glass and his own. 'Thanks, Peter. They are very good to me, always.'

'They are wonderful, aren't they? I don't know what I'd have done without Julia these last few weeks.' Ming's voice was heartfelt enough for Tibor to look curiously at her.

Hers was a prettiness that he found rather uninteresting, but he could see why it frightened Julia. Many men would respond to that mixture of fragility and sparkle. What he had not expected from Julia's descriptions was the sensitivity Ming had displayed towards her niece or her gentleness towards himself, who after all had no claim on her.

'How ...?' he was beginning when he caught sight of Julia's tall figure in the doorway. 'Here they are,' he said instead and waved.

Julia walked across the room towards them, looking magnificent in a straight, low-cut frock of wine-coloured velvet. She kissed Tibor. Keeping an arm around her, he said:

'Ming here has just been telling me how much she depends on you, Julia.'

'That's sweet of you, Ming,' she said, holding out her hand. Ming shook it. 'She's been having a horrible time, Tibor,' she added.

He raised his shaggy eyebrows and Julia hastily added one word, 'professionally'.

Thinking that he must be puzzled, Ming explained about the magazine and Roger Sillhorne's action, and the difficulty she and Connie were having in deciding whether or not to defend it. As she described the article to which Roger had taken such exception, she was relieved to see a flash of real anger in Tibor's eyes.

'Oh, the English!' he said. 'Such terrible hypocrites.'

'We probably are,' said Flixe from the other end of the room, 'but we're brought up to it, Tibor. You will have to forgive us. Shall we dine?'

They followed her into the dining room, where Ming almost gasped as she took in the magnificence of the long mahogany table. Not only had Flixe got out and polished all the silver that was usually kept swathed in plastic bags out of sight in the basement, but in front of each place was a pile of small parcels wrapped in silver paper and tied with red ribbons. There were scarlet candles in the silver sticks and in the centre of the table, between a pair of antique silver pheasants quite ten inches high, was a large silver bowl of luxuriantly-berried holly.

'Flixe, it looks glorious,' said Gerry. 'You are a dear to have gone to so much trouble.'

'Well, since we can't all be here for Christmas itself, I thought we'd have a sort of dress rehearsal,' she said. 'The children and I got every last piece of silver out of the strong-room last night and spent most of the afternoon polishing it.'

'And Sophie got herself blacker than all the other rags we used,' said Andrew with a smile that showed a great resemblance to his sardonic father.

'Now chicks,' said his mother when everyone had finished laughing, 'you've seen all there is to see, so off to bed. Andrew, make sure that Fiona gets upstairs safely.'

The children went reluctantly and the adults settled down to a sumptuous dinner of unexpected dishes. The *pièce de résistance* was a whole carp, stuffed with chestnuts and raisins. It tasted rather odd, but it was stylish and entirely different from any of the traditional Christmas dishes that the others planned to cook.

Ming had been placed between Peter and Tibor and opposite Gerry, who had David on her right. They talked easily about all sorts of important subjects that did not matter personally to any one of them, ignoring the various emotional conduits that connected them and yet held them rigidly apart.

Once Flixe had served the pudding, an impressive confection of small spherical eclairs filled with orange cream and topped with caramel, she began to relax and the conversation, which had been fragmented, became general. By some unspoken agreement they dropped politics and the latest moves in the international situation, and instead talked about past Christmases. Between them they managed to remember plenty of old disasters that were funny in retrospect and slowly the formality around the table warmed into real laughter.

'You are lucky,' said Julia at one moment after Gerry and Flixe had been telling Ming of early Christmases in India before she could remember much. Flixe smiled at Julia, but Gerry looked interested and alert.

'Lucky?' she said.

'Having each other, I mean. I never had any siblings and I envy you horribly,' said Julia.

David looked across the table at his wife, surprised by the feeling in her voice. She sounded lonely. His eyebrows touched over his nose as he frowned. For months he had been so preoccupied with hiding his own depression and then with the exhilaration of its departure that it had not occurred to him that Julia might not be happy either. She always seemed so equable and content.

'I suspect we all envy each other for things we can never have,' said Gerry bitterly, breaking off David's thoughts and making everyone look at her. 'You at least need never know what it is to watch mothers and small children and to know you can never be one of them.'

No one said anything for a moment. Gerry pulled a small lace handkerchief from the sleeve of her cheerful red dress and blew her nose.

'I'm so sorry, Julia, Flixe. I don't know what came over me.'

Ming longed to help. She was sure that Gerry's renewed sensitivity to the subject of babies was her fault and there was nothing she could do about it. She glanced quickly across at Mike and saw that he was looking helpless and miserable. Ming knew that she had to distract everyone's attention and give Gerry time to recover.

'Oh, I don't know, Julia,' Ming said with spurious cheerfulness. 'It's all very well to wish for siblings but you don't know what you'd be letting yourself in for. They might be elder sisters after all.'

Tibor laughed at the theatrical stress Ming gave to her warning. Her eyes sparkled as she answered his smile.

'When they're not telling you what to do, they're bullying you into running their errands and generally exploiting you. D'you know, Julia, Flixe even used to make me muck out her pony.'

'Really? Flixe, you never told me that,' said Peter, looking down the long table at his wife. He was amused to see a very slight blush on her cheekbones.

'Once, Ming, you must admit it was only once,' she said, looking guilty. Everyone's attention was diverted from Gerry and Mike.

'True,' said Ming, 'but you tricked me into it by promising to give me that ravishing pink party dress of yours.'

'Do you know that's been on my conscience almost ever since,' said Flixe. She knew what Ming was trying to do and would have admitted to anything to help her do it. 'I can't remember what excuse I gave you for reneging on the deal.'

'You didn't, you simply took advantage of the power bestowed by your great age. You were a rotter sometimes.'

Everyone laughed, even Gerry.

'Christmas is a terrible time for families,' said David with a quiet smile in his eyes. He, too, had been watching Ming as she spoke and thinking how much he admired her care for other people and her intelligence. 'We always used to quarrel – and get very emotional. My mother positively hates it.'

'So do I, sometimes,' said Gerry with a heavy sigh. She turned quickly towards Flixe. 'Not this, this is lovely. How does your mother cope, David?'

'She always stays firmly in Scotland, where they don't make much fuss over it, and pretends that it isn't really happening. Then when they go in for all that whisky and grim good cheer at Hogmanay, she comes south.'

'Mike, shall we go to Scotland next year?' said Gerry. 'It sounds an excellent solution.'

'Good idea, darling,' he called from the foot of the table. 'Unless, of course, we were to get snowed in. That could be dull. May I open my packages, Flixe? They look so enticing.'

'I'm glad you think so, Mike,' she said, touching his hand. 'They're nothing special, but I always think that Christmas without presents would be like ... oh, a salad without dressing.'

Mike laughed. 'Or a kiss without a cuddle, eh Flixe?'

He picked up a silver package so that he could untie the red ribbons. The others did the same, discovering small but useful presents such as handkerchiefs, shaving soap, bath salts and pen-knives. While they were busy unwrapping, Peter got up from his chair and walked down the room to the other end of the long table. He put both hands on his wife's firm shoulders and kissed her neck. As he straightened up, he put a hand into his waistcoat pocket and took out a ring.

'I've got one for you,' he said as he slid it onto her finger to join her engagement and wedding rings.

'It's lovely, Peter,' she said, turning her hand this way and that so that the sapphires and diamonds caught the candle light. 'Thank you. Yours is under the tree. Do you want it now?'

Peter shook his dark head. The candles threw shadows across his saturnine face, making him look even more intriguing than usual.

'That's not your Christmas present; it's your combined pre-Christmas and baby present.'

Flixe kissed him.

'Now be off with you, my love,' he said, helping her up from her chair. 'I can see that Mike wants his port.'

'And a little peace from all these chattering women.'

They all laughed except for Tibor, whose full lips took on a sardonic twist. He enjoyed the company of women and had always disliked the enforced segregation of the sexes after dinner. At least in the Suvarovs' house he had no need to fear either ponderous ill-informed political chit-chat or the laboured salacity he had come across at some London dinners.

Flixe led the women upstairs towards her bedroom. Ming was immediately behind her sisters when she heard Gerry whispering an apology to Flixe for making a scene at dinner. Flixe put an arm around Gerry's shoulders and leant her blonde head towards her sister's. Ming was visited by a sudden bitter pang of regret for her dead twin.

She turned her head so that she need not see so clear a demonstration of what Gerry had been trying to tell her that she lacked and saw Julia directly behind her.

'That's what I miss. Aren't they lucky?' Julia said.

Ming nodded.

'In that respect, yes: immensely lucky. How are your children? I liked them so much when I came to lunch last summer.'

Julia answered politely and they followed the other two into Flixe's comfortable, flower-scented bedroom.

Christmas at the Alderbrook parents' house seemed rather an anticlimax after Flixe's luxurious party, but for most of the time it was a lot less emotional. Ming was relieved that her father greeted her just as he always had done and seemed to have overcome his fury about her Suez article. He said nothing at all about the *Story of a Lost Love*, and in gratitude, Ming slipped back into the role of dutiful daughter that she had played so well for so long.

The small party ate a great deal, drove to various neigh-bouring houses for drinks, went twice to church, walked off their meals in the fields and woods around the house, and played innumerable hands of bridge. Ming, who was not very good, and Mike, who was not very interested, took it in turns to make up the table.

On the afternoon of Boxing Day it was Mike's turn to play, and so Ming took herself to the kitchen to tackle the mountain of washing-up that had been left after lunch. Gerry came to join her whenever she was dummy, and between them they washed and dried nearly everything but the saucepans, trying to keep each other amused enough not to exchange notes about how dreary Christmas was in a house without children. At one moment Gerry did say:

'Doesn't it make you feel second-best to Flixe?'

Ming longed to say something serious, something that might comfort Gerry, but she was afraid that there was nothing that would do that.

'I've always felt a long way second-best to both of you,' she said with a clear smile. 'Being the youngest, I suppose that's inevitable. You grow up knowing that your sisters will always be cleverer, more grown-up, more sophisticated, more at ease with other people than you.'

Gerry laughed and Ming thought that she had done something to help after all.

'But you caught up long ago, Ming,' she said, reaching for the water jug. Before she could dry it, she had to obey a call from the drawing room to take up her next hand, leaving Ming to run a new bowlful of hot water and begin to tackle the greasy pans.

She had dealt with the first when her mother appeared, looking as neat as she had when she had come down to breakfast that morning. Her tweed skirt and moss-green twin-set were as conventional as all her clothes and suited her better than usual. She wore the pearls her father had once given her and suitably discreet make-up. Her hair had become so thin that she had taken to having a light pink rinse put in to disguise the amount of scalp that showed through.

As she walked nearer the sink the light fell directly over her and Ming noticed the device for the first time and felt sorry for her mother. Mrs Alderbrook had always been impeccably dressed and had taken infinite pains to make certain that no one could ever laugh at her or criticise anything she wore. The indignity of losing her hair must have hurt.

'I'm dummy this time, darling,' she said. 'Let me take a turn. You've done far more than your fair share.'

Ming smiled over her shoulder at her mother. It was pleasant to have her wholehearted approval for once.

'I'm perfectly happy doing the washing-up,' said Ming, 'and you look jolly tired. How's the ankle? It must have been an awful sprain to stop you coming to the christening.'

'Fairly awful,' said her mother, pulling the moss-green cardigan down over her hips. She went to feel the damp cloths Gerry had hung in front of the cream-coloured Aga and then reached into a cupboard to fetch a pile of dry ones. Shaking one of them out, she looked down at her slender ankles above the heavy brown country shoes.

'I was rather afraid the swelling would be permanent, but I think it's gone now.' She picked the water jug off the splintered wooden draining board and started to dry it. 'But it wasn't really the ankle that stopped us.'

'Oh,' said Ming inadequately, dreading the signs of an impending reprimand.

Long experience had shown her that she could do nothing to stop it and she focused all her efforts on not minding whatever her mother might say. Ming had tried all her life to avoid offending or disappointing her, but she had never succeeded and had usually blamed herself for it. Since her conversation at Gerry's flat she had begun to look at the past differently, but even Gerry's insights did not stop her feeling cold and hollow as she waited.

'No,' said Fanny Alderbrook, looking at Ming over the top of the spectacles she had forgotten to remove, 'your father was so upset by what you wrote that he really wasn't up to seeing you just then.'

'Well, he seems to have got over it all right now,' said Ming, brightly.

She did not look at her mother, apparently concentrating on removing the stain from the bottom of a pale blue enamelled pan. She had heard a defensive note in her voice and hated it.

'I can't believe he should have minded that much. A lot of people have written far more controversially about Suez than I did.'

'But none of them was his daughter.'

Mrs Alderbrook put a hand on Ming's thin wrist, around which clung a high-water mark of half-dissolved fat. Ming turned to face her, teeth clenched behind her smiling lips.

'Didn't you think about what you were doing to him, Ming?'

'Oh, Mother! Why must you make it so personal?' Ming turned back to the washing-up. 'I wasn't doing anything to him – or to you. I was just doing my job.'

'But you must have known how much we would feel it. After all, you went to the trouble of finding out what we thought about the whole business way back in the summer. It was pathetic, you know,' she added, her voice softening slightly. 'Your father sat in his chair in the morning room and kept saying: "Of all of them, why Ming?"'

Ming rinsed another pan under the hot tap, trying not to see how the fresh hot water splashing into the bowl drove ripples of fat globules across the grey water already there.

'You see, darling, he's always believed that you were going to make up for all the other disappointments: for Annie's death, for all Flixe's scandals and the insinuations about her husband, for Gerry's childlessness ...'

'Mummy, don't,' said Ming like a six-year-old having a splinter extracted from under her fingernail. She had not called her mother that for years. Mrs Alderbrook paid no attention and dug a little further into Ming's defences.

'He was so proud of what you did in the war and of the way you managed to stay the same, despite what you went through then, and the decoration and everything. He's had you on a pedestal ever since, and assumed that all the best young men would feel the same. And yet in spite of Anna's money, you're still unmarried.'

Mrs Alderbrook paused, as though waiting for Ming to confide in her. There was enough hardness behind the interest in her blue eyes to make Ming feel wary. Some of Gerry's explanations of their mother's tendency to verbal brutality began to seem less fantastic. When Ming said nothing, Mrs Alderbrook went on:

'And since almost the beginning of this magazine business, he's been afraid – we've both been afraid – that you'll drive them off. You're showing yourself to be so aggressive, darling, so unfeminine, that men will simply not understand what you're really like.'

'What am I like?' asked Ming, cut to the quick. The misery of her last meeting with Mark was underlined by a fear that she had driven him away by coarseness or brazenness.

'Fanny!' The general's voice called from the drawing room. Ming's mother put down her drying-up cloth.

'He's always loved you best, you see. And when he hears about scenes like the one at Flixe's dinner party when you were so horrible to that young man from the Stock Exchange he can hardly bear it. Just as he can't bear the thought that it's you who've made him into a laughing stock.'

'But I haven't,' said Ming, furious with Flixe for telling tales and with her mother for exaggerating so much.

'What do you think the regiment must have thought when they saw his name on an article like that?'

'No one in the regiment is going to read anything like *The World Beyond*,' said Ming with more crispness than she had ever used when speaking to either of her parents.

It dawned on Ming that her mother was not only her husband's mouthpiece but was speaking for herself as well. Anger and resentment that she was using Ming's affection for him to make her own dissatisfaction hurt more, pushed Ming to add:

'And if they did, all they would have seen is an attempt by someone who loathes the basis on which they run their lives to show up the foolishness of killing people to settle a political point and the deviousness of the means by which the war was started.'

'And what do you think that all our old friends are saying now?' Fanny paid as little attention to the content of Ming's outburst as she had to childhood protests of unfairness. 'Can't you imagine them raking over the old scandals and saying, "Well, what can you expect of one of the Alderbrook girls?" Do you think it's pleasant to know that we're being pitied for the things you do?'

'What can it possibly matter what other people think?'

'Of course it matters. I've had a hard enough life without being pitied and despised because of what you do for a living. Why couldn't any of you have behaved like other people's daughters?'

Ming did not answer.

'Fanny!'

'Coming,' she called. 'Try to make it up with him before you go back to London,' she added more kindly to her youngest daughter. Then, as though something long repressed were being forced out of her, she added with less apparent sweetness:

'You know, sometimes I wish you three would remember me when you take it into your heads to punish him for whatever it is you imagine he did to you or didn't do.'

'Fanny!' The general's voice sounded exasperated.

Without waiting for a reply, Fanny Alderbrook went to answer her husband's call and Ming turned doggedly back to the saucepans and roasting tins. Her anger helped to control all the guilt that her mother had managed to stir up in her. She felt infinitely relieved that she had said nothing to her parents about her summons to the magistrates' court and that they had been too embarrassed to talk about the *Story of a Lost Love*.

Ming slept badly that night and was awake soon after seven, when she heard her father letting the dogs out into the garden. Knowing that she had very little time to find out what he really felt and repair the damage her mother had talked about, Ming dressed quickly in her warmest trousers and jersey. Downstairs she picked a coat at random from the rack by the back door, stuffed her feet into a pair of wellingtons and followed her father outside.

There had been a hard frost that night and the short grass felt crunchy under her boots as she walked across the small lawn to the ha-ha. The dogs were careering up the field beyond and her father was walking slowly after them, leaning on his stick. He looked much older than when she had been there in the summer and she felt the sharp tug of all the hooks that joined her to him.

'Daddy!' she called, when she was near enough to do it without waking the rest of the family.

He turned and his face lit up as he saw her. Ming hurried to the edge of the ha-ha and he came across the field to help her down.

'Morning, Ming,' he said, raising his hat.

'Good morning. Golly, it's cold, isn't it?'

'You're getting soft with all that London central heating,' he said with a short, sharp laugh. Ming smiled obediently. 'It's jolly invigorating really.'

'At least the frost makes everything look gorgeous,' said Ming, pointing to the prickly hedge, whose branches seemed to be coated in sparkling white powder. 'One forgets in London quite how beautiful winter can be.'

'Wish you spent more time here,' her father muttered. 'Do your bridge a power of good, too. Gone to seed a bit, old girl, what? Not playing much these days?'

'Hardly at all,' she said. 'I'm not that interested, I'm afraid, and I've been awfully busy this last year.'

'Yes,' he said so drily that she knew she had to tackle what was between them.

'Mother says you were upset by what I wrote about Suez.'

'A bit,' he said shortly. 'Seemed rather uncalled-for, and disloyal. I'd never expected that of you. Loyalty's always been one of your strong suits; loyalty and sweetness. That wretched Wroughton woman's been a bad influence. You've changed since you started seeing so much of her. Got rather hard.'

'Oh, no,' said Ming sadly, 'it's not Connie changing me; it's me waking up to who and what I am. I'm not sweet. I've always agreed with everyone, because I've been too afraid of what would happen if I didn't. I've always tried to please people, because it's the only way I've known of stopping them being angry with me. But I've slowly discovered that it's been killing me.'

'Don't exaggerate, Ming. That's new, too. Piglet!' he roared to one of the labradors, who was wriggling under the fence that divided the empty field from one full of sheep. 'Damn dog. Piglet!'

The animal obeyed its master and slunk back to his side. Something in Ming said, I won't, I won't, I won't.

'Daddy,' she said quietly, 'it's hard to explain when you're so cross with me. Perhaps "killing" was too emphatic. "Stifling" might be better. But whatever the word, I was very unhappy. I've realised that for years and years I've done what was expected of me without giving any thought to what I wanted. I've suppressed every thought that seemed at all dangerous, and any opinion that might upset people. Then in the end I realised that if I went on trying to be what everyone else wanted of me, I'd never grow up into my own self.'

They walked on in silence through the scrubby field grass, and Ming tried again.

'I realised that if I never did that, I'd always be miserable and probably go rather potty too. I'm sorry that you're hurt to find out that I'm not the sweet child you always thought, but I'm thirty-two for heaven's sake!'

'Sweetness needn't be childish, Ming,' said the general, keeping his voice level and his eyes on the horizon. 'Some of the best – and most successful – women have been that: kind, gentle, good. It's not to be despised even nowadays. All this modern stuff about – what do they call it? – individuality is just a new name for bad, old-fashioned selfishness. What?'

Ming felt as though the hooks were being dragged out of her and she knew that they had barbs on them. They hurt too much to be simple hooks.

'I'm sorry,' she said as calmly as she could. 'I think I'll go back and help mother get breakfast.'

'Ever read Dr Johnson, Ming?'

'What?' she said, surprised and bemused. 'Sorry, no, hardly at all. Why?'

'"Want of tenderness is want of parts, and is no less a proof of stupidity than depravity",' he quoted unexpectedly. 'Always seemed like good sense to me.'

'And to me, too,' admitted Ming when she had thought about it, 'but tenderness can't be used to hide behind – and I used to do that. I'll see you at breakfast.'

The general strode off, leaving Ming to watch him in silence. She tried to look at him as a stranger might, a knowledgeable stranger, perhaps, but one who had no emotional hooks in her. She saw a man of little education and less imagination, of almost limitless physical endurance and unquestioning obedience to a code he believed was immutable. He would have died, she realised, to protect her, but would hate the thought of her acquiring the toughness that would make his protection unnecessary.

The army had been his life and he missed it badly now that he was retired. He mistrusted foreigners, he believed in the rightness of his country and, in a faintly embarrassed fashion, in the existence of God. He had been born, educated and trained to stand firm against the enemies of his country and its Empire. But he knew nothing of the talents of peace, nothing of the delicate building up of relationships between people who were not divided by a hierarchy, and nothing at all of the need to behave to the women of his family as though they were independent human beings. Ming felt very sorry for him.

'Piglet! Roo!' The general shouted at his dogs, who would never answer back and could be beaten when they disobeyed.

CHAPTER 20

It was a relief for Ming to be travelling down to Etchingham on the Tuesday immediately after Christmas, even though she had used all her petrol ration and was sitting in a chilly train compartment. Her physical state was as nothing compared with the pleasure of being back in her own world. Connie Wroughton met her at the station and drove her to Max's cottage for the editorial meeting. Connie seemed to be abstracted and rather worried. Ming sat in silence until they were within the gates of Connie's estate.

'How's the market garden doing in this beastly weather?' Ming asked as they passed the manager's cottage.

Connie turned to glance quickly at her passenger. It was almost the first time she had ever mentioned the garden.

'Not too bad. Bill is very good at coping with things like expected frosts. All the cloches have been out for weeks. But the greenhouses had to be shut down with the fuel crisis. We're certainly going to lose a lot of money on them this year.'

'I'm sorry. You've got an unfair number of worries on your plate.'

'I suppose one benefit of that is that one can't get too worked up over any particular one,' said Connie wryly. 'Have you decided what you think we ought to do about the summons?'

'Yes. I think we've got to defend, because ...' Ming was beginning just as they turned on to the gravel in front of Max's cottage.

'No, tell me why later,' said Connie decisively. 'I'm following your lead in keeping Max right away from it all. Will you come and have lunch with me after the meeting? We can talk about it then.'

'All right. Thank you,' said Ming, getting out of the car.

Max welcomed them with his usual pleasure and pot of good strong coffee. The three of them took their accustomed places at his gate-legged table and discussed the articles for the next month's magazine. Max asked for several changes to Ming's major retrospective piece on 1956.

'Must I?' she asked, rather depressed. 'I thought it was so good.'

'That's a real danger signal,' Max said, laughing. 'Wasn't it Dr Johnson who said that if you were particularly pleased with anything you had written you ought to cut it at once?'

Ming's eyebrows twitched.

'Probably. You are extraordinary, Max, the way you produce echoes of all the disagreeable things people have said without being the least disagreeable yourself. I'll have a bash at it. May I come back after lunch and use your typewriter?'

Max looked from one woman to the other, realised that they must have decided to discuss the case without him, and simply nodded.

'I do particularly like your tying up the final closure of the *Boy's Own Paper* with the ending of the Imperial Dream in the blockage of the Suez Canal, but we've had an awful lot of Suez recently and I think you need to emphasise some of the other things that happened in 1956, not least the events in Hungary. After all we've joined the rest of the press in criticising the British Government for bombing Egypt, but the Russians have done far worse.'

'Did anyone ever expect them to behave decently?' Ming asked coldly.

'Perhaps not, but that's a point that should be made too. Suez may have been (what did you call it?) "our greatest national disgrace" but it is not uniquely frightful.'

'But—' said Ming. Before she could complete her protest, Connie intervened.

'What did you write?' she asked.

Max shuffled his heap of articles and picked out Ming's. He turned to the last page.

'"Perhaps at the end of this, the year the *Boy's Own Paper* ceased to exist,"' he read out, '"we can look forward to a time when our government is no longer obsessed with its imperial past. People in England have come to understand that powerful countries have no right to impose their will on the rest of the world. The arrogance that has been displayed so nakedly in both Budapest and Cairo is as out of date as the belief that the State should ordain what its adult citizens may read in the privacy of their own homes."'

'No, Ming,' said Connie forthrightly. 'We've annoyed enough people. I really don't think that we ought to be so provocative. To tie up Suez with the obscenity case like that is ... well, it's unwise to put it mildly.'

'All right,' said Ming at once. 'I'll take all allusion to the case right out if you like.'

'But ...' Max began.

'You can talk about it all after lunch. I'd like to get on with the meeting now.'

'You're the boss, Connie. On to the next issue,' said Max, pulling a sheet of paper towards him. 'Any views?'

'I did wonder whether we ought not to have a sequel to Ming's women and money article last year.'

'I'd like to do that. I got some splendidly approving letters after it. What angle, though? I doubt if I'd find many more high-earning women,' said Ming, looking happier.

'I was thinking more on the lines of some of those sadder letters we got just after it was published,' said Connie. 'Max, did we ever show them to Ming?'

'It seemed inappropriate just then,' he said, turning away to reach into the oak coffer behind his chair where he kept the most interesting readers' letters. 'Here, Ming.' He held out a bundle attached at one corner with a long, green Treasury tag.

'Why inappropriate?' Ming did not take the bundle.

'You were a bit preoccupied in October,' he said, 'and they're not very happy letters.'

'Quite angry, too,' murmured Connie. 'Now, apart from women and money, what else have we?'

'I've been wondering whether we ought not to do something on the Morton Commission Report on Marriage and Divorce,' said Ming.

'Could be tricky. With the moral crusaders already arming against us, we don't want to get our names up for being anti-marriage.'

'It wouldn't be anti-marriage, Connie.' Ming was adamant about that. 'But I've been talking to lots of people recently and hardly any women seem to know what their legal rights and obligations are once they marry and have children. Surely we could do a purely informative piece without being tarred as destroyers of family life ... but I really do think that we ought to show some of the reality behind this myth of the happiness of housework and babies.'

'She's right you know. After all, showing truth behind myths and pouring a bit of light into housebound women's lives are what the magazine is supposed to be doing,' said Max quietly. 'We can't let them beat us, Connie.'

'Beat us? Who?' It was clear from her voice that Connie knew she was fighting a rearguard action.

'The mythmakers, the paternalists, the chaps who ignore their own foibles, miseries and knowledge and impose the results of their fantasies and neuroses on the rest of us.'

'Look here,' said Ming, tackling Connie's anxieties as best she could. 'Why don't we describe the findings of the Commission and as a tailpiece add something about juvenile delinquency and the problems of broken homes? That way it will be clear that we're hardly advocating divorce, just laying out the facts.'

'All right. Can you do that as well as the financial piece? Max, you'll oversee to make sure it all fits?'

'Yes, Connie,' he said and then went on to hand out books for review and discuss the articles they ought to commission from their growing stable of freelance writers.

When they had agreed what they wanted for the cover design and which artist should be asked to submit sketches,

Connie took Ming back to her Dower House for lunch.

'Food first or talk?' said Connie, letting them both in through the front door. 'I haven't prepared anything.'

'Why not both at once?'

Connie smiled at Ming's suggestion.

'All right. I'll go and load up a tray and take it into my study,' she said. 'There's the remains of Sunday's joint: would sandwiches do you?'

'Perfectly. Let me help, please?'

They went together to the kitchen, made themselves thick sandwiches of cold lamb, redcurrant jelly, and cold potatoes that had been grown in Connie's garden, and carried them with a jug of water to the room that Connie's sister had always used as her private drawing room.

Ming had not been in it since Diana's death, for Connie always entertained guests in the much bigger room on the opposite side of the hall. In the old days the smaller one had been a place of great peace and gentleness, with a rose-coloured carpet, silver-grey walls studded with French drawings of cosy domestic scenes, and delicate eighteenth-century furniture made of various golden woods.

When Connie opened the door and urged Ming to precede her, Ming was so astonished that she almost dropped the tray she was carrying. Never had there been such a transformation in any room. Where once there had been quietness, now there was drama.

After a while she realised that the silver-grey walls were the same and so were the eighteenth-century tables and bureau. The new carpet was dark green and the curtains green trellised with gold, but it was not they that had made the change. The delicate drawings of cats and washer-women, children and sunny rooms had gone and the only picture in the room was an immense Old Master hanging on the wall opposite the fireplace.

'I'll stoke up the fire,' said Connie, as Ming stood trans-fixed by the painting. 'Put the tray down on that table and pull up a couple of chairs.'

'Connie, the picture.' Ming's voice held awe as well as shock.

Connie turned from the fire and smiled.

'I couldn't think what the matter was. I'd forgotten that you wouldn't have been in here recently. It's marvellous, isn't it? Max helped me buy it during the war, but I didn't hang it until after Diana died. It didn't seem appropriate.'

'It's staggering. It must be Jael and Sisera, but who on earth painted it?'

'We're not absolutely certain, but the theory is that it might have been Artemisia Gentileschi. No one but she produced such powerful women at the right sort of date, and she did specialise in Old Testament heroines.'

'But how can you live with it? It's shocking ... wonderful, but quite overpowering,' said Ming.

'I find the rage in it helps,' said Connie frankly. 'Remember what this room was like when Diana was still alive?'

'Indeed yes.' Ming had a moment's pang for the gentleness of the French drawings.

'Diana accepted things; a contented resignation was more important to her than almost anything else. Well, I don't accept things and I won't use my energies for suppression and rationalisation. I won't pretend and force myself to believe in pretence. If things are horrible, I'd rather know and cope with them.'

Turning her back on the painting, Ming sat down and took a bite of her sandwich.

'And yet,' said Ming when she had swallowed her mouthful, 'you want to accept what Roger's done and plead guilty, don't you?'

'How do you know that?' asked Connie with a sidelong look at Ming.

'Because if you agreed with me you'd have said so in the car before the meeting. Come on, Connie, why?'

Connie shrugged and ate some more of her sandwich, reaching out for a napkin as a piece of jelly-covered potato slid out from between the two thick pieces of bread.

'If we fight, we will probably lose the magazine,' she said when she could speak again. 'Ratterley has made it clear that even if we win, we'll have to pay our own costs. The operating profit is slender at the best of times and hardly pays the bank's interest on their loan. We've lost some advertisers – and some subscribers – who disapprove of our stand over Suez. We can't afford pride. Much as I want to smash Sillhorne's face in a not-guilty verdict from an Old Bailey jury, I know that it would be more sensible to get the whole thing over with as quickly and cheaply as possible.'

'That does make sense,' said Ming. Her reluctance was very obvious to Connie.

'But?'

'But I can't help thinking that we ought to fight, for all the same reasons as we published the piece in the first place. And I loathe the idea of giving way to Roger without even a protest. Besides, Gerry thinks we ought to push for the principle of the thing.'

'Gerry would.' There was a caustic note in Connie's voice.

For the first time it occurred to Ming that Connie might find Gerry's independent mind and success in her work more of a source of jealousy than Flixe's luxurious maternity.

'What does Flixe think?'

'Flixe thinks we should let him get away with it and feel morally superior,' said Ming with a shrug. 'She's never been as interested in principles as Gerry.'

'No,' agreed Connie, 'and yet she loves the Gentileschi. Odd that. It seems rather foreign to her comfortable, sensible, sybaritic character.'

Ming swivelled in her chair and looked again at the fair, ferocious woman hammering a tent peg into the head of her sleeping enemy.

'I'm not surprised,' she said, 'after what happened in the war.'

'What did happen?' Connie put down the sandwich and looked so puzzled that Ming understood her indiscretion. She was rather surprised that Flixe, who loathed secrets and considered that they caused inordinate trouble, had never told Connie about the night when she had been set on and half-strangled in the blackout.

'Oh, just the general violence and beastliness. She knew quite a lot of people who went into occupied Europe and had ... had a bad time. Don't let's talk about it, Connie.'

Knowing a little of what Ming herself had done, Connie dropped the topic at once.

'We're going to have to decide about the case today,' she said. 'Julia wanted to know straight after Christmas. What do we do?'

'It's mainly your magazine, Connie, and I do see your point of view. It would be a very expensive way of showing Roger Sillhorne what we think of him. I admit I'd like to put him through the wringer but there's not much point. I'm not going to force you to change your mind and risk it all. I'll plead guilty if you think it's better.'

'Thank you. I'll ring Ratterley now.' Connie dusted the crumbs off her black-and-white tweed skirt and stood up. With a hand on the telephone receiver she added: 'I know I've said it before, but I'm very glad you're with us.'

Ming smiled while Connie dialled the number of Mr Ratterley's office to give him the news.

'Very wise, Miss Wroughton,' he said drily. 'I'll tell Mrs Wallington. There's no need to have Counsel in the magistrates' court. I can act for you there if you'd like. We can brief Mrs Wallington, but it seems hardly worth it.'

'No, I agree. Will you tell her and thank her for her advice?'

'Yes, of course. Goodbye.'

'That's that then,' said Connie, turning back to Ming.

'Yes. I'd better go back to Max's and deal with the corrections you both want to the retrospective.'

'I'll drive you, Ming.'

'Don't bother, Connie. A walk will do me a lot of good. I can work off some of my rage.'

'All right. Give me a ring when you want to go back to the station.'

When Ming let herself into her flat that evening, much more tired than she usually was after one of Max's Tuesday meetings, she heard the telephone bell ringing.

'Hello?' she said breathlessly when she had picked it up,

hoping to hear Mark's deep voice.

'Ming? Julia Wallington here. Ratterley has just been on the telephone and I wanted to say that I think you're very sensible. It sticks in the craw a bit to let Sillhorne get away with it, but taking the case to trial could have ruined you and Connie Wroughton.'

'It sticks in my craw too,' said Ming frankly, 'but Connie's persuaded me that it's only sensible. You sound very worried. Is it about this?'

'Do I? No. Your case should be easy now. I'm just a bit bothered about one I'm prosecuting at the moment.'

'I'm sorry,' said Ming, answering the almost despairing tone rather than the unemotional words. 'Is it particularly difficult?'

'No. Very straightforward, but I hate them. It's a young man who tried to commit suicide. He slit his wrists in the bath and – unfortunately for him – his landlady found him before he'd bled to death. Now he faces life imprisonment if I do my job properly.'

'Julia, I am so sorry.'

The warmth in Ming's voice and her obvious sincerity got right under Julia's guard. She found that she couldn't speak.

'How long will it take?' Ming asked.

'Not long. It will probably be finished by the end of tomorrow.'

'It's hard to know what to say: I can hardly wish you luck. The poor man.'

'I know. Thank you.'

'We must meet soon, Julia.'

'I'd like that. Goodbye now.'

Ming spent the next morning reading the bundle of letters Max had given her and trying to think of an angle for her new article. She quite understood why he had wanted to keep the letters from her when she was so newly unhappy, but she found herself getting passionately angry as she learned about the letter-writers' lives. Remembering the arguments she had had with Flixe's stockbroker about the rights of married women to work and earn their own money, she wished that she had had some of the letters with her then.

Of all of them, the admiring, the angry and the sad, the one that seemed the most heartbreaking to Ming was from a young mother living in Hampstead:

> *I was going to be a doctor when we met, but I gave it up when we got married. My husband wanted me at home and I was so ignorant that I wanted it too. I spent a few blissfully happy months.*
>
> *But it didn't last. Now I spend all my days mending, cooking, cleaning, taking the children to and from school. My whole life is taken up with work that bores me so much I've come to hate it. My husband gives me generous housekeeping, but disapproves of what I spend. He has no idea how much food costs, and whatever I do, he criticises as extravagance. It's got to the stage when I feel that I have to wear my clothes to rags before I buy anything new, and then he accuses me of looking 'drab'. I don't think he has any idea how his antagonism buries me, or how hard I struggle to keep going.*
>
> *I can hardly bear to think that now I might be a doctor in my own right, with my own money to spend as I chose. I wouldn't be without the children or my husband for anything, but the cost in my own happiness has been very high. I wish it had been possible for me to have both family and work like the woman in your article. Does she know how lucky she is?*

Remembering Julia's depressed voice on the telephone the day before, Ming managed to smile. Her own telephone rang and she picked it up.

'Ming, is that you?' said Mark, making her heart begin to bump.

'Yes. How are you? Did you have a good Christmas?'

'It was fine, thank you. But I've a problem today. I haven't been able to come to London after all and so I can't meet you at Searcy's. I am sorry.'

'Not at all,' said Ming automatically while her mind shrieked protests and regrets and frustrated emotion.

'Perhaps we could do it some other time. Have you any plans to come up?'

'Nothing fixed. But I'm sure I will be able to find a day soon. May I telephone you?'

'I should like that, Mark.'

'Good. Well, goodbye, Ming. I am sorry.'

'Mark,' she said, but it was too late. He had already cut the connection.

Admitting that it was all too late, Ming tried to think who else she might see so that she could keep her mind away from Mark and remembered what Julia had told her. It occurred to her that she could go to the Old Bailey, meet Julia as she emerged from her unhappy trial and take her out to tea. Quickly looking at her watch, Ming saw that she had at least three-quarters of an hour before the court was likely to be adjourned and she hurried to change and call a taxi.

Walking up the front steps of the Old Bailey half an hour later, Ming was slightly breathless. When she could speak, she asked a uniformed man where she should go to meet Julia.

'If you just wait here, madam, you'll be able to catch her when she comes out,' said the man.

Ming thanked him and sat down to wait on a leather-covered seat in the round, multi-coloured hall. Five minutes later a crowd of people streamed down the central staircase. In the middle of them Ming saw Julia, black-robed and wigged, talking to a man dressed in striped trousers and a black coat, and so she merely stood up, hoping that Julia would recognise her without her having to interrupt.

The little group swept right past Ming, but she caught Julia's eye. Looking a little startled, Julia disentangled herself from her colleagues and the instructing solicitor and walked over to Ming's bench.

'Are you all right?'

'Definitely. I just remembered what you said about this case and thought I'd come and see if I couldn't whisk you away to somewhere like the Ritz for tea to cheer you up. Has it ended?'

'Yes. Badly for the young man.'

'I'm so sorry.'

'Thank you. It's horrible to know what my professional success means for him.' Julia shook her head and before Ming could say anything more added politely: 'And thank you for coming. I'd have loved to have tea with you, but I promised the children I'd be home to have it with them today.'

Ming suddenly realised how peculiar her approach must have seemed. After all, she and Julia could hardly be said to be friends. She felt as though she had been both impertinent and intrusive, and she tried to think of a graceful way to extricate them both from the situation she had created.

When she saw Ming's face fall, Julia made herself remember that Ming had just as much to worry about as she herself did.

'But why don't you come, too? The children would love it, and so would I. Will you?'

'Well, that would be nice, if you're sure,' said Ming, the doubts in her face chased away by a smile.

'Give me a minute to get rid of these,' said Julia, gesturing to her legal fancy dress, 'and get my hat and coat, and I'll join you.'

They discussed Julia's case as they went back to the Kennington house by tube and then spent a happy couple of hours in her kitchen, having tea with the two children and the housekeeper. Ming watched with amusement as Julia ate just as many honey sandwiches, chocolate biscuits and slices of fruit cake as her children.

Afterwards, since it was the nanny's half-day, they all played pelmanism on the drawing-room floor. Amanda was already past the stage of having a perfect memory for the cards and it was interesting to watch her struggle to come to terms with the fact that her younger brother was able to beat her easily. She obviously hated it, but had enough will-power to stop herself protesting and, to Ming's admiration, actually managed to congratulate him.

Julia dropped a kiss on Amanda's dark head at that.

'Well done,' she said. 'And now it's bathtime.'

'I'd better go,' said Ming, conscious that she might have outstayed her welcome. As a shadow crossed Julia's face, she added: 'Unless you'd like a hand? I'm quite used to bathing Flixe's brood.'

'I'd be eternally grateful,' said Julia above her children's heads, 'if you really mean it.'

All four of them trooped up to the children's bathroom at the top of the house, where Julia watched in admiration as Ming turned bathtime into an extension of the games. Amanda clearly loved it, behaved beautifully and sat happily on her mother's lap to be dried. As soon as the two children were safely in bed Ming said that she ought to go. Julia offered her both drinks and supper, but Ming stuck to her guns and left the house.

As soon as she had gone, Julia poured herself a glass of sherry and dialled the number of the Suvarovs' house.

'Flixe?' she said when the telephone was answered. 'Julia here.'

'My dear! How are you? How was Christmas?'

'Fine. Lovely. And I was ringing to say that the more I see of your little sister the more I like her.'

There was the sound of warm laughter down the telephone and Julia smiled instinctively. Despite their very different lives and their continuing argument about the upbringing of their children, they were the best of friends.

'I always thought you would,' said Flixe cheerfully. 'Has she managed to cast out all your doubts?'

'No,' answered Julia with all her characteristic honesty and self-knowledge. 'Because it was never her that I doubted. I know that she's not been in love with David.'

'And he?'

'He still thinks she's marvellous and he's terribly worried about the effect the case will have on her and ...'

'I'm not surprised.' Fixe's voice was dry.

'No. And he's started having nightmares of her in prison. He knows a bit too much of what Holloway is like. But don't worry, Flixe,' Julia added, quickly remembering that they were talking about her sister. 'It's most unlikely to come to that.'

'I hope to God you're right.'

'Even if it does, Flixe, she'll pull through. She's much tougher than you think.'

'You've said that before,' said Flixe. 'But I'm not sure you're right. I thought she was looking particularly vulnerable at Christmas. But I am glad you like her – and that you're defending her.'

'I wanted to say something to her,' said Julia, 'to make up for my less than charitable thoughts in the summer, but we're not on the sort of terms that would let me be frank.'

'Don't worry, Julia. I'll convey something to her. We must meet.'

'Yes, indeed. Things are horribly busy in chambers. May I ring you when I've a gap so that we could have lunch or something?'

'Lovely. Thanks for calling. 'Bye.'

Flixe smiled as she replaced the white telephone. She was in the process of changing to go out to dinner with Peter and had too much to do in too short a time to telephone Ming then, but she made a mental note to do it soon. With her husband and children in as good a state as they had ever been, Gerry reasonably happy again after Ming's unfortunate suggestion that she adopt Jack Hazeldene's children, and Julia back to her accustomed sanity, there was really only Ming left to sort out. Flixe thought that might be difficult but she was determined to try.

CHAPTER 21

It was not until the day before the magistrate's hearing that Flixe decided what to do about Ming. Abandoning all subtlety, she had come to the conclusion that a direct attack was the only way of breaking through her sister's reserve. As soon as she had dealt with her household, given her husband and children their breakfast, and handed the children to Brigitte, Flixe put on a hat and her fur coat and walked down to Kensington High Street to flag down a taxi. Having given the driver her sister's address, Flixe sat back on the creaking leather seat and tried to decide exactly what to say.

Ming's charlady opened the door to Flixe's ring.

'Ah, good morning,' said Flixe, a trifle disconcerted. 'Would it be possible to see Miss Alderbrook?'

'Well, I don't know. She's working. Shall I go and see?'

'Yes, please. I'm her sister.'

'Flixe, is that you?' Ming's voice called from the back of the flat. 'Come on in.'

There was the sound of footsteps and Flixe saw her sister, looking distracted and uncharacteristically messy, with a large smear of ink down one porcelain cheek. Mrs Crook disappeared and Ming came forward to kiss Flixe. Ming was still cross with her for tattling to their parents, but as usual the sight of Flixe herself made her sister smile as pleasure overtook her anger.

'I'm obviously disturbing you. I'm sorry.'

'Don't be silly, Flixe. It's lovely to have another distraction. I'm only working this hard to try to take my mind off what's going to happen in the magistrates' court tomorrow.'

'Poor you. But surely there isn't anything to worry about. It'll just be a formality now you've decided to plead guilty.'

'Probably. But I can't help worrying a bit, and so I've been wrestling with a piece for the magazine about female finances as a distraction. Would you like something? Coffee or sherry?'

'Coffee would be lovely. Breakfast feels as though it was hours ago.'

'How impressive! Come into my writing room and ignore the mess. I'm trying to persuade poor Mrs Crook to leave it like this just for today, but she hates the thought.'

Flixe sat down on the one comfortable chair in the tiny room, looking at its wrapping-paper decoration with amusement. It had still been full of old boxes and cobwebs when she had last seen it. Since then Ming had put her flat-topped desk under the small window. At one side of it she had hung a glass-fronted corner cupboard to house a collection of ruby-coloured Hull glass, and diagonally opposite that was the deeply-cushioned armchair in which Flixe was sitting. Bookshelves covered the wall opposite the window and a simple swivel chair stood in front of the desk.

There were no pictures or looking glasses on the walls, only the glowing chestnut-coloured wallpaper that was patterned with gold fleur-de-lis.

Flixe herself would have used the decorations to make the room lighter or at least prettier, but she could see the attraction of the gilded richness of the walls. She was impressed by the fact that her sister was taking her writing work seriously enough to devote a room to it.

'Max Hillary is trying to teach me to make coffee as he does, but mine never seems to come out as rich-tasting,' said Ming as she carried in a tray.

'Now, what can I do for you, Flixe?' she asked, putting it precariously down on top of a pile of paper. She poured the coffee and handed a cup to her sister.

'Nothing at all,' Flixe said, watching Ming over the rim of

the flowered porcelain cup. 'I was in Knightsbridge first thing this morning, trying to find something for Fiona to wear at parties now that she's grown out of her velvet, and I was so disheartened by the selection that I thought I'd drop in and see you.'

'How very nice!' Hiding her surprise, for Flixe had never dropped in on her before, Ming sipped some coffee. 'I saw Julia a few days ago.'

'Yes, I know; she rang me after she'd seen you and said among other things how much she likes you,' said Flixe, delighted to have the subject introduced. 'How was she? Last time I saw her she seemed to have got over her anxieties about David.'

'She seemed to be depressed about her case, but otherwise all right. I never could imagine why she ever had doubts about him. There was never the remotest breath of gossip about him in the House in all the years I was there. He's always seemed devoted to her.'

'I know, but she's one of those women who finds it difficult to believe in her own attractions,' said Flixe, leaning forward to put her empty cup down on the tray. 'And what about you, Mingie? Are you all right? I thought you seemed rather under the weather before Christmas.'

Ming abruptly pushed her swivel chair nearer to her desk and stared down at the muddle of papers on it. The cup she was holding rattled slightly in its saucer and she put them down on the desk.

'I'm quite functional,' she said firmly. 'Various things have gone wrong recently, but there's nothing I can't survive. The flat is turning out just as I want it, I'm exceedingly busy, and I enjoy my work – and that's the most important thing.'

There was a clatter in the hall and the fluttering sound of envelopes falling. Ming winced involuntarily.

'What is it?' Flixe's voice was very kind. 'I'm not trying to prise secrets out of you, I just want to help.'

Ming sighed. She had always found it difficult to share her deepest feelings, but Flixe was offering the kind of maternal support neither of them had ever had from their mother and for once she needed it too badly to resist.

'If my correspondent is as punctual as usual, one of those letters will be an anonymous one, telling me how frightful I am. That's one of the things that's been going wrong.'

Flixe got up to go and stand beside her sister.

'How beastly! Why haven't you said anything?'

Ming just shook her head.

'And what about the other things that have been going wrong? What are they?'

'Oh, my upsetting poor Gerry with the idea that she should adopt Jack's children; this business of Roger trying to get Connie and me into court; the parents being so angry about what I wrote about Suez; having messed things up so badly with Mark Sudley; being ... wishing ... That's really it.' She faltered in her stoicism. 'Oh, Flixe, I have messed things up.'

'I doubt it. You're going through a bad patch, that's all. It happens to us all. And if you look back, isn't even this better than life before you were freed by Anna's money?'

Ming smiled and she laid her head briefly on Flixe's shoulder.

'You're right, of course. And while I keep working I'm perfectly all right. It's only thinking about it all that makes me quaggly. I'd better go and see the post.'

'Who's writing the letters?' Flixe asked with little enough surprise in her voice to suggest that she already knew about the first one. It seemed as though Gerry, too, had been indiscreet. Ming shrugged.

'I've no idea. There are times when I've passionately wanted to know and others when the thought of identifying him makes me ill.'

'What do they look like?'

Ming shrugged. 'The paper is perfectly ordinary, the sort anyone could buy at Smith's. The typing is efficient, but the typewriter an ordinary one. The only way presumably of identifying the writer would be fingerprints and that's hardly practical.'

'What do they smell of?' asked Flixe. Ming halted on her way to the door and looked back.

'I've no idea,' she said. 'Nothing really. I've never even thought about it.'

'Most letters smell at the instant when you open them: smoke, scent, petrol, curry sometimes. Haven't you noticed? I always do.'

Ming shook her head, watching her sister in amazement.

'How practical you are, Flixe!' she said. 'I never notice anything like that and I don't think I could distinguish it if I did. No, that's not actually true. I could identify the mixture of flowers and woodsmoke and beeswax polish in your house, but that's peculiarly strong – and delectable. I don't think I could identify any particular smell in Gerry's flat or here.'

Flixe laughed.

'What about the paper at Gerry's? Piles of dusty paper smell very characteristic. And then there's usually something foody, because of the dining room being part of the drawing room. And Gerry's bath salts: they've a powdery kind of eau-de-Cologne smell. And there's the polish: it's that faintly cherry-smelling one. They use it on the parquet floor.'

'You amaze me,' said Ming in genuine admiration. 'Look here, if there is an anonymous letter, will you sniff it for me? I'd never pick any of that out.'

Flixe agreed with enthusiasm. In a moment Ming was back, holding out a white envelope with a typewritten address.

'It's the first time I've ever been remotely pleased to see one of these,' she said, handing it to Flixe.

'May I open it?'

When Ming nodded, Flixe put a finger under the flap of the envelope, ripped it open and held it up under her nose.

'There's a faint violet scent,' she said at once. 'Artificial, I mean, not the flowers, and something else, faintly chemical ... sharp, no ...'

Ming waited.

'Acetone: nail-varnish remover, of course!' said Flixe. 'But that's all I can recognise, and even that's fading,' she added, taking one last deep sniff. 'No; gone now. But I'd say these are written, or at any rate stuck up, by a female who wears violet scent, or violet-scented cosmetics, and had just done her nails. A bit low, probably, which would be likely, wouldn't it? I'm afraid it doesn't get you much further, though.'

There was a smile on Ming's face that reminded Flixe of the way she had sometimes looked in childhood when some particular terror had been removed.

'A bit, though,' she said. 'What a Sherlock you are, Flixe! Thank you.'

'I haven't done much. Aren't you going to read it?'

Ming took the envelope, pulled out the letter, read the five lines, frowned and then handed it to her sister.

'It's much like all the others. Nothing new.'

Flixe read it with a grimace of disgust.

'It's ridiculous,' she said, adding more gently: 'But I can understand why they've been getting you down. Try not to worry about them.'

'Quite frankly, I don't think I will now. What bothered me so much was that it must be someone I knew. It was impossible not to try to think who. But I can't think of a single soul who wears violet scent. I wish I'd told you sooner.'

'That ghastly governess Annie and you had the year Gerry was presented wore violet scent, but that was ages ago.'

'I wouldn't have thought she knew anything about me now, but if it is her, I really don't care. She can be as malicious as she likes. Flixe, goodness how you've helped!'

'Good. Well, I suppose I ought to go on to Peter Jones in case they've got anything Fiona might be prepared to wear. I hadn't really noticed how big she's getting, but she actually split her cherry-coloured velvet the other day, playing "sardines". It's been lovely to see you, Ming. And I think you're making the flat quite gorgeous.'

Ming escorted her sister to the front door of the flat and was about to open it when Flixe stopped.

'What did you mean when you said you'd mucked it up with that nice Mark?' she asked, unable to suppress her curiosity any longer.

'It's not something I want discussed round and round the family,' Ming said with a small sigh as she thought of everything that did get passed from one of her relations to the others.

'Would I?'

'Yes, Flixe. Be realistic, you know you would.'

'Not if you specially asked me not to,' said Flixe with her head on one side.

'Even Gerry?' Ming was amused by her sister's wheedling, but it was the seductive and almost unknown pleasure of confiding that was making her want to talk.

'If you say so. I won't tell even Gerry.'

Not really believing her, Ming smiled and gave her sister a brief account of the last unhappy time she had seen Mark and his cancellation of their tea at Searcy's.

'Well, for heaven's sake! Why haven't you protested and written to him again?'

'It's not so easy, Flixe. I have made one overture, which he turned down. I can't go nagging him to see me if he doesn't want to.'

'Haven't lots of men nagged you?' Flixe's deep blue eyes, so like Ming's own, were amused as well as sympathetic and forced Ming to tell her the truth.

'That's really why,' she said. 'I couldn't bear Mark to think of me as I have thought of . . . well, of any of them.'

Flixe kissed her then, wished her good luck at Bow Street the next day and left. Ming shut the door behind her and returned to smell the box of anonymous letters, wondering why she had never noticed the violet scent before. But the more she sniffed, the less she could smell. Even so, Flixe's diagnosis had taken much of the sting out of the letters, and Ming went back to her typewriter feeling happier.

The idea of writing to Mark again kept presenting itself to her as she battled with her work, but each time she pushed it back. He had avoided meeting her and that was that. It might be consoling to daydream about his changing his mind, but she knew that if she were ever to achieve serenity she would have to learn to live in reality, however lonely it might be.

The following day, feeling sick with nerves, she went with Connie and Mr Ratterley to the Bow Street Magistrates' Court. Mr Ratterley tried to comfort her by saying that the whole thing would be a formality.

So it was, but not quite the kind he meant. As soon as the charge was read out the magistrate announced that the case was too complicated for his court and sent it for trial at the Old Bailey.

There was a part of Ming that responded almost jubilantly to the news, but once they were out in the street again anxiety began to bite.

'Did you see how sick Mr Sillhorne looked?' Connie asked.

'Yes,' said the solicitor. 'If you and Miss Alderbrook were not facing huge costs and a possibly enormous fine, I'd say that today had provided an excellent lesson for him and that he was well served.'

'But surely he won't have to pay the costs of an Old Bailey prosecution,' said Ming.

'It all depends. There's no certainty that they'll be paid out of official funds. He might find that as well as trying to ruin you, he's ruining himself.'

The word 'ruin' quelled Ming's rebellious pleasure at once. She looked around the bustling street, thought of the small writing room she had made, and tried to imagine losing it. Anna Kingsley's legacy had set her on the road to freedom and she hated the thought of turning back.

Ming had a sudden vision of what her life might be like if she and Connie lost their case. She could never live on what her articles earned; she would probably have to go back to being a secretary. Already thirty-two, she might never have another chance to break out of that depressing, menial state. Prison would be almost preferable.

'Miss Alderbrook?'

'Sorry, Mr Ratterley,' she said, quickly jerked out of her miserable introspection. 'What now?'

'The case is unlikely to reach the top of the lists for another two months, but we'll have to brief Counsel as soon as possible. Do I take it that you would still like Mrs Wallington?'

'Definitely, I'd say. Connie?'

'Yes. If she'll do it. I have a lot of faith in her.'

'I'll make the arrangements,' said Ratterley, 'and then it's really all up to her and me. There'll be lots of questions for you to answer, but there won't be anything for you to initiate.'

'I see. Well, I suppose it may give me the material for an article on the workings of the law.' Ming was determined not to be beaten into surrender by the case.

Connie said nothing.

When Ming reached the cottage at Etchingham for the next weekly meeting, she found both her colleagues in a state of acute depression, discussing whether or not to shut the magazine down at once. Despite having been woken by her own terrors in the small hours of each morning since their visit to the court, Ming did her best to rouse them.

'You mustn't even think about doing that. Now's the time to pull out all the stops,' she said, surprising herself almost as much as the others. 'The case is going to cost us a fortune: well, we must just make a fortune between now and when it comes to court.'

'What a lovely fantasy!' Max's exclamation had enough of a bite in it to bring a rueful smile to Ming's lips.

'I know, I know. But this is definitely not the moment to be defeatist. We've a chance now to become far more widely known and read. We ought to write to all the people who have ever given evidence or been prepared to give evidence for the defence in this sort of trial.'

'Why?' asked Connie.

'Most of them will be writers; we can get them to produce stuff for us. So far we've either written it ourselves or got it from friends, relations, inexpensive unknown journalists and so on. We ought to cash in on this to get some people with famous names. That would make it even harder for a court to convict us.'

'We won't be able to pay them anything like the going rate.'

'Constance Wroughton, where are your ...' Ming broke off and recast her sentence: 'Where is your fighting spirit? If ever there was a time to dig it up, this is it. Grit your teeth. It's time we raised the advertising rates, in any case.'

'That really will ruin us. We've lost so many advertisers over the Suez article.'

Ming turned away from Connie's stubborn face at the sound of Max's laughter. His eyebrows were arched higher than ever above his eyes and his whole face was suffused with amusement.

'Fragile, little Ming,' he said. 'Who'd have thought it? In a way she's right, though, Connie. We'll never make a fortune, but at least we'll go down fighting.'

He looked at his old friend and his face sobered as he saw the doubt in hers.

'I know that I'm in no position to say it, because I've no money to lose, but ...'

'Nonsense, Max. That's not the point,' said Connie, adding in a sarcastic voice: 'I thrill to your battle cry, Ming, but there are complications. How many booksellers do you suppose will stock the magazine now? How many of them are going to risk being prosecuted for being in possession of obscene literature? Remember what Julia Wallington said: there are booksellers in prison at this moment for doing that.'

'There won't be anything obscene.'

'Don't be naïve, Ming; they're not to know that. And certain police forces will undoubtedly scrutinise each issue as they've never done before.'

'Coffee,' said Max, getting up. 'I was too low to make any before, but I think we need it now. Give me a hand, Ming?'

She nodded and went with him to the neat kitchen, where he put a kettle to boil on the ancient solid-fuel range. Ming collected cups and saucers, found a tray and a milk jug and set them out on the kitchen table.

'Give Connie a minute or two to herself. She hates publicly changing her mind,' said Max, warming his back against the range.

'You're very fond of her, aren't you, Max?'

He looked at Ming as she stood in front of the sink and thought of the mess he had made of his life, of Connie's unstintingly generous rescue, of what might have happened if he had understood what she was really like at the beginning instead of marrying her pretty, selfish best friend. Then he shrugged. It would not have made a material difference.

'Yes, I am. Very fond. It took me a long time to discover what she's really like: that commanding manner used to be very offputting when she was a girl. But she's grown into it.' He smiled suddenly. 'And into her face. It used to look very odd above the frills her mother thought suitable for her. And Diana was so pretty always. It's no wonder they disliked each other then.'

Ming was a little chilled by his analysis and was about to protest just as the kettle lid started to bounce up and down on the rising steam. Max turned and made the coffee.

'It's only since my disaster that I've discovered how much genuine concern there is at the bottom of her manipulations,' he said as he was stirring the grounds. 'She wants us all to do as she has planned because she really thinks we'll be better off.'

'She's done a lot for both of us, Max,' said Ming.

'And we for her.' Max read Ming's obstinate expression with ease and half-smiled again. 'It's silly not to recognise that. She put so much of herself into caring for Diana that when she died there was a big hole in Connie's life. She was lonely, living out here on her own. She's got plenty of friends, but they're all busy with their own affairs. We've allowed her to organise us into becoming her family.'

'Max, you are beginning to sound horribly cruel. This isn't the moment to start digging holes in each other.'

At that protest his eyebrows arched and the eyes themselves looked very cold.

'Cruel? Surely not. It's important to be realistic about one's friends. Otherwise you risk awful disillusionment. We'd better go back; she's had time to cope with having her opinion overturned.'

Chilled but willing, Ming picked up the coffee tray.

When they walked into the sitting room, Connie was lying back along one of the sofas, peacefully smoking. Ming put the tray down in front of the fire and brought Connie a cup of coffee.

'All right,' she said, accepting it and stirring in a spoonful of brown sugar. 'I'll go this far: if each issue continues to make enough money to cover its costs, we'll go on; but if one – just one – fails, then I'll pull the plug.'

'That seems fair.' Ming took a deep swallow of coffee and savoured the rich bitterness of it. The taste seemed highly appropriate. She watched Max's face over the rim of her cup.

'Up to standard?' he asked in a derisive voice as he noticed her looking at him.

'As always.'

He inclined his grey head in gracious thanks, fetched a notebook and said:

'I think we ought to draft a letter to possible supporters. Ming, can you find out who did speak at the four big obscenity trials in 1954 or who wrote about them?'

'I expect so.'

'And I suppose,' said Connie, 'that we ought to mobilise all our friends and acquaintances and get opinion moving our way as fast as possible.'

'That makes sense,' said Max.

They got down to work and slowly their pessimism began to dissipate as they discussed future articles. Ideas began to spin between the three of them, sparking off arguments, new ideas, resolutions and at least some of the old excitement.

Ming suffered the obvious anticlimax as she was sitting in a slow train back to Charing Cross. Her compartment was not a smoker, but it smelled stale and dirty, and was cold as well. Condensation streamed down the windows although by then she was the only person in it. She turned on the heater switch, but it had little effect. Bundling her soft, dark fur coat more closely together, she sat, shivering and working on her courage. She wished that she had asked Max what prison had been like so that she knew exactly what she faced.

The train pulled in to Charing Cross at last, and Ming collected her belongings and went to try to find a taxi to take her to Chelsea. One day, she thought, there might be a tube line that would make life there a great deal easier.

The flat seemed warm and colourful after the dreary, frustrating journey and, as she flopped down on the drawing-room sofa, Ming realised that she had come to think of it as 'home' in a way that none of the rooms she had ever rented had been, or even her parents' house. It seemed bitterly ironic that she should have achieved a home only just in time to lose it.

CHAPTER 22

While Max was left to run the magazine on his own and Connie was grimly mobilising all her friends and acquaintances to take her about London so that she could be seen by everyone who might have any useful influence, Ming relied on her sisters and their husbands. She knew that she was being wet, but she could not bring herself to court any rejections from people who might share her parents' views.

Connie understood Ming's fears. To a certain extent she shared them, but she had a thicker skin than Ming and a wider social circle. Having taken up Ming's challenge, Connie determined to do her best. She packed her smartest clothes, borrowed one of Flixe's spare bedrooms and shamelessly raided her address book for anyone she had ever met who might be useful.

The results were impressive. A few people pretended they could not remember who she was; and a few others were frank enough to tell her that they disapproved of what she had done; but the rest seemed happy to be seen with her. She went to the opera or the theatre almost every evening; she lunched out every day before going with friends to an exhibition or an afternoon concert. She held her head high. Even Flixe, who knew her well, could not tell whether Connie was really as confident as she seemed.

Ming watched her campaign in slightly shocked admiration and did the best she could to emulate it, ignoring, as far as she was able, the prospects of both prison and finan-

cial ruin. Flixe took her to a dress show at Hartnell and
introduced her to dozens of useful women. Ming accepted
all the invitations that she was sent, instead of refusing most
on the grounds that she had too much work to do as usual,
she dressed well and did her best to impress her hosts and
fellow guests wherever she went.

Evenings with Gerry and Mike were like half-term treats
in comparison with the rest. Everyone Ming met at the big,
Bloomsbury flat seemed to share Gerry's opinion that Ming
and Connie were fighting for a worthwhile cause. Ming
spent hours sitting with Gerry's university friends, drinking
cold Italian wine and eating olives and sharp, dry cheese,
and talking. Sometimes they were joined by civil service
colleagues of Mike's, who participated in the easy discussions and gave Ming a feeling of reassurance that she badly
needed.

Conferences with Julia and Mr Ratterley helped too, as
did the work that still had to be done for the magazine. Ming
understood quite well that as long as she kept herself busy
she could manage to stay adequately calm. Only when she
woke in the early mornings did her fears threaten to overwhelm her. She would wake from nightmares of bars and
rats and weevily food in a primitive prison to the more realistic, if just as frightening, anxieties of debt and ostracism.

In the end she went to her doctor and demanded
sleeping pills, because she was afraid of what might happen
to her if tiredness destroyed her remaining resistance. He
wrote out a prescription for a hundred powerful pills.
They proved strong enough to knock her out for at least
eight hours and, even though they left her feeling dull and
stupid, the rest they gave her was a boon.

Occasionally, as she sat in her gold and chestnut-
coloured writing room trying to work, she would think
through everything that had happened in the last year and
try to find some meaning in it, much as she had searched
the hieroglyphs and bas-reliefs of the Egyptian temples. But
like the warm, dead stone, memories of things she had done
and said and things that had been done and said to her
carried no meaning. There seemed to be no pattern or

reason, unless it was simply that she was being tested for some great challenge.

When she arrived at that fatalistic conclusion she told herself to stop being sentimental and vain. It was absurd to think that her mismanagement and misfortunes could be part of a cosmic plot. She had had some bad luck and she had done some silly things. That, she told herself briskly, was all that there was to it.

By March even Connie's resolution was beginning to flag and both of them were very tired. The case was not due to be heard until April and occasionally they would look at each other and wonder whether they could keep going. Peter and Flixe started to take them both out to dinner in fashionable restaurants once or twice each week, and Ming forced herself to go to the House of Commons to listen to Prime Minister's questions whenever she had no other engagements.

David Wallington saw her there about half-way through the month and kept an eye on the gallery so that he could leave the chamber as soon as she got up to go. They met in the lobby as she was hurrying away. It was one thing to allow herself to be seen, but quite another to have to talk to people who might well believe in what Roger was trying to do to her.

When she felt a hand on her arm and heard a man saying her name, she whirled round in a mixture of shock and irritation. Seeing David, her face relaxed.

'It's you,' she said, the relief evident in her voice. 'How are you, David?'

'I'm fine. What about you? Julia's very discreet, but I know you're going through hell.'

'She's being wonderful. Connie and I are both madly impressed and very relieved that she's on our side.' Ming managed to laugh. 'It was good to run into you.'

'Don't go,' said David, almost unwillingly. 'Won't you come and have tea with me?'

'Here? No, I don't think so. There are rather too many interested people, I think.'

'Then come for a walk?'

'All right. But let's get out of here quickly. There's Roger.'

David understood the urgency and, putting a steady hand under her elbow, walked her down the long, cold corridor and out of the building.

Parliament Square was bathed in sun, even though the air felt very cold on their faces. Ming noticed for the first time that her upper lip was chapped and becoming sore under the bright lipstick. White clouds were being bowled across the bright blue sky by a ferocious wind that picked up the sharp dust and flung it in their faces. They had walked half-way round the square, waiting for several minutes to cross the road, before Ming realised that David had no overcoat.

'I'm sorry,' she said. 'I've got horribly thoughtless with all this on my mind. You must be freezing. Let's go back. I'm dreary company in any case.'

'No. I couldn't leave you in this state, Ming. Why don't we just go and sit quietly in the Abbey? It'll be warmer there.'

He pointed at the open door of the great, grey church and after a moment's hesitation, Ming let him take her inside. They walked slowly up the long nave, around the grave of the Unknown Soldier and then turned right. Ming, who did not know the building well, was puzzled, but David led her competently past the high altar, on past a huge, dark tomb and into a chapel decked with multi-coloured banners.

Distracted for a moment from her preoccupations, she looked around in delight.

'I never knew this was here,' she said, as she took in the glorious vaulting of the ceiling and the contrasts between the cool black-and-white floor and the silken gaudiness of the flags.

'It's nice, isn't it?' said David, pleased to see the drawn tightness of her face relax. 'I occasionally drop in here to think when things begin to get on top of me. Come and sit down in one of these stalls. We can be private here. No one will disturb us.'

They sat down side by side in the curved stalls at the left

of the doorway, opposite the altar. The silence of the place as much as its incongruous colour soothed Ming and she let her shoulders drop and her mind go blank for a while. David sat, quiet and still, waiting until she needed him.

At last she pulled off her gloves and wiped her bare hands over her face.

'Thank you.'

'There's nothing to thank me for,' answered David. 'I owe you so much, you know.'

'Me?' Ming was surprised into looking into his face. He smiled down at her.

'Yes. Before you came to see us last summer I'd got very disheartened with my work and with myself. What you wrote about me and the way you brought out of me the things in which I really believe, gave me back my ... my pleasure in both. I'd like to do something much more useful in return than just giving you a few minutes' peace and quiet.'

'I don't know that there's anything else I needed more just then,' she answered as she leaned against the carved back of the stall. Her conviction that she must have been trying to make him fond of her to bolster her fading confidence disappeared at last. 'You're a very kind man, and Julia is enormously lucky.'

'How's Mark?'

At that obviously sequential question, Ming turned her head away from him.

'I don't know. I haven't heard from him since just after Christmas. We were to have had tea together then, but he had to cancel it and I haven't heard anything from him since.'

'What happened, Ming?' David asked gently. She looked very young and forlorn as she sat at his side in her black overcoat and little fur cap. 'He adored you.'

With her voice quaking every so often, Ming told David most of the story, breaking off at one moment to add:

'I seem to spend all my time at the moment complaining to my friends about the things that go wrong. It's a nasty habit I shall have to break pretty quickly.'

'Nonsense!' There was nothing gentle about David's voice then and Ming looked at him in surprise. 'Come on: you're in the middle of a bad time; your friends want to help. It's unfair to bottle everything up.'

'All right,' she said, startled but acquiescent, and told him the rest.

David listened patiently and when she had finished his advice was simple.

'You must write to him. You can't simply wait for him to come back for more punishment, Ming. No man is going to go on laying himself open to what you've handed out to the poor beggar. If he really doesn't want to see you, he'll tell you so and then you'll know where you are. But my bet is that he's pining just as much as you are.'

Despite her determination not to fantasise about a happy ending with Mark, Ming could not help letting some hope into her mind. Then she remembered Roger's letters and the fury they had aroused in her. She shook her head.

'I can't. I just can't force myself on him. He was absolutely clear that he didn't want us to meet yet and would let me know when he did. After making such a mess of everything for him, I can't make him see me when he doesn't want to.'

After a while David took one of her hands in a warm clasp. Not looking at her, he said:

'I know it's not considered ladylike to show a man that you care for him unless he's made the first move, but Mark has made about the first twenty moves. Ming, it simply isn't fair for a woman with your brains to . . .'

'Don't, David, please,' she said, closing her eyes. He heard the desperation behind the simple words. 'You can't imagine how much I want to, and I mustn't. Perhaps after the case I could.'

'What's the case got to do with it?'

A little of her dormant sense of humour woke as she said: 'A great deal. After all I might be in prison in a month's time.'

'Don't be ridiculous,' said David with an anger that his wife would have recognised. Ming, who had no idea about his nightmares, was both surprised and rather hurt. He saw that and moderated his voice as he went on:

'I know that's technically possible, but it's absurd to think like that about it.'

'I'd rather think about the worst that could happen to us,' Ming answered honestly, 'and then nothing will be a shock.'

She found that she could not tell even David about the more likely fears that tormented her each morning when she woke before dawn. He watched her face and noticed the way the skin around her lips was roughened, as though she had been biting her lips in the cold.

'Are you afraid that Mark would think you were chasing him for security now that you're facing huge costs and a possibly vast fine?'

'That's one of the elements of my many nightmares,' she said casually, shrugging. 'Don't worry so much, David. I'll be all right. My sisters have rallied round superbly. Julia hardly ever loses cases. It's just the waiting that gets me down so much.'

'I can imagine,' he said, longing to bundle her up in a thick fur rug and carry her off to some imaginary place where she would never be troubled. 'You look worn out. Why not go home now and try and get some rest?'

'All right,' she said with some of her old submissiveness. 'Thank you for bringing me here. I'll see you soon, I expect. Goodbye.'

David got up as she left and then sat down again on the hard, wooden seat, staring up at the pretty ceiling as he had done so often before. It seemed cruel that Ming should be in such straits when there was nothing he could do to help. He had bottomless faith in his wife, but he had lived with her cases for too long to have any illusions about the legal process and the vagaries of juries.

A black-robed verger appeared and crossed to the far side of the chapel. From behind where David was sitting there was a vast sighing sound and then the first few notes of the organ. Someone had started practising and he sat listening to the *Ode to Joy* with a wry smile at its incongruity. Even if she were to be sentenced to prison it would be for only a few months, he told himself, and she was strong enough emotionally to survive that.

When the *Ode to Joy* was over, he stood up, straightened his jacket and tie and went back to his office.

CHAPTER 23

Determined to get a good night's sleep before the trial, Ming took two of her sleeping pills when she went to bed. They worked admirably and her alarm clock had rung for a full minute the next morning before its urgent clamour reached her brain. She fumbled among the objects on her bedside table, spilling the remaining pills and knocking a book to the floor, until her fingers found the switch that silenced the clock.

With the jangling uncomfortable noise taken over by silence, it was five minutes before Ming remembered why she had taken the pills and ten more before she could force herself out of bed. There was a line of vibrant light between each pair of curtains. Ming pushed herself out of bed and walked bare-footed across the bedroom carpet to the hard, blue linoleum of the bathroom floor. She felt hot, as though the pills had raised her temperature as well as drugging her mind.

She ran herself a cool bath and made a cup of coffee to drink while she washed. When the cup was empty and her body temperature considerably reduced, the fuddled sensation in her mind was beginning to clear and the grits in the corners of her eyes had been rubbed away. By the time she had wrapped herself in a huge, soft bath towel she felt as though she might be able to answer a simple question if it were kindly put. She rubbed herself gently dry, put on a dressing-gown and went to collect the newspaper from her hall mat.

Sitting drinking another cup of coffee at the kitchen
table, Ming tried to read through every page of *The Times* as
carefully as though she were to be examined on its contents.
As she read the first page she found that her eye was merely
skating over the paragraphs and not taking in any information at all, but by the time she reached the foreign news she
had massaged her mind into working order and felt better.

Returning to her bedroom, she opened the wardrobe
doors and looked at the suits and dresses hanging there.
Julia Wallington had suggested that both Ming and Connie
dress conventionally, without too much sophistication and
without trying to look like barristers themselves. Ming
picked out a hanger with a pale grey suit on it, felt the
weight of the material and put it back with a small grimace.

Drawing back one of the heavy curtains, she saw that
not only was the sun bright yellow as it shone down on the
river and the newly green trees but that the sky had that
unmistakable dazzle that presages a warm day. For days the
weather had been typical of April, blustery and freezing
cold one minute and then almost like a June heatwave the
next.

Rejecting all her suits, Ming instead picked out the dark
blue linen dress she had worn to the Wallingtons' house the
previous summer. The dress had a matching jacket, which
would make it warm enough without making her sweat.
With its big, crisp, white collar it looked a little too
summery, but she was prepared to put up with that for the
sake of its coolness. She had had her hair set very simply the
previous day and had planned to make up her face with
more than usual restraint.

When she was ready, with a small, navy-blue hat securely
pinned to her neat hair and a pair of gloves clasped in her
left hand with the handle of her crocodile bag, she went to
examine herself in the long glass by her bedroom door. The
figure that confronted her looked too young. She made a
face at her reflection.

There was no time to change and so she simply added a
little more, darker lipstick and a pair of bigger gold earrings
before slipping on her gloves.

As she closed the door of the flat behind her she knew that she might not have it for very much longer. She also knew that by the end of her trial she might be taken down from the court to a cell to await transport to Holloway prison. With her gloved hand on the brightly polished doorknob, she tried to stop imagining what that would be like. She had never managed to ask Max about life in prison and so she had no information to calm her wildly exaggerated speculations.

Down in the street, she summoned a taxi and asked the driver to take her to the Old Bailey. He drove her along the river all the way to Blackfriars Bridge and then turned up New Bridge Street. Normally Ming would have looked out for the buildings she particularly loved, for the dignified red-and-white ordered symmetry of the Royal Hospital, the squat greyness of the Tate Gallery, the gothic fantasy of the Houses of Parliament and the glories of the Richmond Terraces, but on that morning they all slid past her eyes in a kind of greyish blur.

She noticed nothing of the traffic either, as it held up the cab at junctions and cross-roads. Only the vast, juddering bulk of a brick-delivery lorry that pulled up alongside the taxi at a red traffic light was big and immediate enough to break into her concentration. When the cabbie eventually drew up outside the Central Criminal Courts in the Old Bailey he had to tell his passenger that it was time to get out.

Ming flinched at the sound of the driver's voice and shook her head as though she had just surfaced from under the sea, but she got herself out of the cab, paid the driver and chose an appropriate tip from the handful of change he gave her.

'Cheer up, miss,' he said, accepting the shilling. 'Whatever he's done, he won't forget a lady like you while he's inside.'

Before Ming could do more than smile at the cabbie's assumption, he had banged his nearside window shut, ground into gear and pulled out again into the increasingly thick traffic. Her momentary amusement did wonders for her spirits and she walked more confidently out of the hot, dusty street into the cool but bustling shadows of the court.

Walking up the broad staircase to the courts, she saw that the walls of the circular lobby were covered with historical paintings and the whole place a mixture of far brighter colours than she would ever have imagined from her earlier wait in the main hall downstairs. The sight of those incongruously vivid murals took some of the menace away from the building.

Feeling more in control of herself, Ming found her way to court IV. Mr Ratterley was already waiting outside its doors. He looked her up and down, rather as her father had always done before he took any of his children anywhere out of the house, and then smiled.

'Most appropriate dress, if I may say so, Miss Alderbrook.' He held out his hand.

Ming slipped the glove off her right hand and shook his.

'I'm glad you think so. I'm afraid it's going to be very hot and I'd hate the jury to think I was sweating from fear or guilt,' she said with unwonted frankness.

Mr Ratterley, who was far too experienced in the eccentric behaviour of clients awaiting trials to be surprised by her uncharacteristic directness, merely said:

'Are you nervous?'

Ming took off her other glove, smoothed it carefully against her naked hand and then looked up again.

'When I remember that the trial could end in my going to prison,' she said with great care to articulate her words precisely, 'then I become extremely nervous. But I am not afraid of standing in the dock or answering questions; I won't break down and weep or anything like that.'

'I should hope not indeed. Aha, this must be your sister.'

Ming turned at once and saw Gerry, walking down the corridor with Mike. Ming held out both hands.

'Thank you for coming.'

'I wouldn't have missed it for anything. Mike and I are rooting for you all the way, you must know that.'

'Even though you don't really agree with me?' she said to her brother-in-law.

'Don't be silly. Whatever I think, unlike some others we know about, I believe absolutely in your right to say, write or publish your ideas.'

'Nothing but the office could have stopped him coming today and even then it would have had to be an international disaster,' said Gerry cheerfully. 'Flixe will be here, too, but she's decided to sit up in the public gallery so that no one will notice the rage on her face if the prosecution goes too far.'

Ming managed to laugh at that.

'Now, where do we go?' Gerry asked.

'Mr Ratterley?' Ming suddenly remembered that neither Gerry nor Mike had ever met him and quickly introduced them. He explained that they should wait until Julia Wallington arrived and then go on into the court.

Ming looked round for her and was faced instead with Roger Sillhorne. He was standing about twenty feet away, talking to his lawyer, but his eyes glared at Ming. Hot, suffocating hatred welled up in her.

'Ah, here's Julia.' Mr Ratterley's voice mercifully distracted Ming and she turned away.

Julia was already dressed in her short wig and black gown. The gown flying open over her well-cut black suit and plain white blouse made her look even taller than usual.

'Good,' she said when she had taken in the effect of Ming's clothes. 'Any sign of Connie?'

'Here,' called the familiar voice from the end of the corridor. They all looked round and watched as Connie hurried towards them. She, too, noticed Roger and stared at him contemptuously until his eyes fell. Then she came on to the others and they saw that exhaustion had put deep shadows under her dark eyes.

She also had obeyed Mr Ratterley's instructions and was wearing a simple-looking suit made of blue-and-white flecked tweed. The skirt was plain and straight, but not too tight, and the short, cardigan-like jacket was edged with darker-blue braid. It made Connie look ordinary, which surprised everyone. She had managed to disguise both her

tremendous distinction and the formidable air with which
they were all familiar.

'Did you two exchange notes?' asked Gerry, sounding
amused.

'There wasn't any need,' answered Connie with a gleam
in her eyes that belied the demure convention of her
clothes. 'Ming almost always wears blue-and-white.'

They were all smiling as Mr Ratterley pushed open the
double doors and ushered them into the court, but it
was an effort for all of them. The wood-panelled severity of
the interior was sobering. Ratterley had a word with the
usher, who took Ming and Connie to the dock, where their
warders were waiting for them. At the sight of the uniforms,
Ming felt her insides clench. There was a light singing in
her head and she was afraid that she might not be able to
hear anything that was said to her. Deliberately she looked
down into the court, identifying the various people whom
Julia had said would be there.

Apart from the clerk, who was sitting below the judge's
empty chair, the usher and the policeman who guarded the
door, there was no one except Roger Sillhorne, his solicitor
and Miles Coopering, QC, the barrister they had briefed.
He looked about Julia's age and obviously knew her well
for they were leaning towards each other, apparently
enjoying an entertaining conversation. At one moment
Coopering laughed aloud and even patted Julia's shoulder.

'Doesn't that seem odd?' whispered Connie, who was
also watching them.

'A bit,' said Ming, who had hated to see Julia on such
good terms with the opposition, 'but as soon as it starts, I
imagine they'll forget all that friendliness.'

The doors opened again and a motley collection of
people filed nervously into the room. The first twelve were
led to the jury's benches and the others made to sit at the
back. Ming watched Julia and the other barrister looking
them up and down. Most were men, and most were
middle-aged. Two looked rather like schoolteachers or
perhaps local-government workers; one seemed vaguely
artistic with long hair and a bow tie; three gave nothing

away in their dress and of the rest one appeared to be a great deal richer than the others and much more impatient. He was good-looking in a rather heavy way and made Ming think of the City. He could have been a stockbroker, she thought. Another had a weatherbeaten face and such powerful shoulders and calloused hands that she decided he must be a builder or perhaps a gardener.

The two women were as different from each other as possible: one, perhaps in her late fifties, was dressed in a well-cut dark suit and a good hat and looked quite as formidable as Connie usually did; the other was a motherly woman at least twenty years younger, whose pleasant face was framed in a patterned headscarf. She looked both kind and sensible and Ming felt a tingling hope as she smiled.

'Be upstanding.'

Gerry, standing very close to her husband in the row of chairs behind the barristers, turned to give Ming an encouraging smile, which she did not see because she was looking at the judge. He reminded her irresistibly of statues of Horus she had seen in Egypt. Like the hawk-headed sky god, the judge had hard, punitive-looking eyes. His wig gave him the flat-topped look of a raptor's head and his small mouth was pinched and quite overshadowed by his beak of a nose. He looked irritable, implacable and frightening. To hope for an acquittal began to seem childish.

The atmosphere in the room had changed completely with his arrival. Julia and Miles Coopering had retreated to their own seats and schooled their faces into severity. Even the clerk, who had been chatting to one of the ushers, seemed frozen into a caricature of legal dryness.

Ming's throat tightened and she forced herself to turn her head away from the judge and concentrate on the motherly juror.

The judge lowered himself into his chair and everyone else sat down again. Each member of the jury in turn rose to take the oath. Julia challenged the rich, impatient-looking man and the prosecution barrister challenged the artistic one in the bow tie. They were replaced with one other woman, younger this time and looking like a welfare worker, and another nondescript middle-aged man in a baggy grey suit.

When the court was quiet again Mr Coopering got to his feet, straightened his gown, announced that he was appearing for the prosecution and that his learned friend Mrs Julia Wallington was appearing for the defence in the matter of *R. v. Alderbrook, Wroughton and* The World Beyond.

The formalities over, Mr Coopering began to outline the case he was going to make.

The two women in the dock sat and listened to his description of their magazine and its contents. Having paraphrased the excerpt from *Story of a Lost Love*, Mr Coopering added:

'I do not think I have ever had occasion to read so flagrant a piece of filth in my entire career.'

Ming felt as though her lower jaw had dropped in surprise and hurriedly shut her mouth. She could not believe that a man so obviously educated and sensible could truly subscribe to such an exaggerated statement. Deliberately reminding herself of the friendliness with which he had been talking to Julia, Ming listened carefully.

'And this disgusting story is printed in a magazine, ladies and gentlemen, that is intended to be read by wives and mothers. It is a magazine that might well be picked up by any of those women's children. Think what the effect could be on an impressionable boy of reading an apparently approving account of behaviour that, I must remind you, is a crime in this country, whatever may be the case in France, where the story was first printed.

'The charge against the proprietors of this magazine is that they have published an obscene libel, that is, ladies and gentlemen, material that would tend to deprave and corrupt people who might read it.'

Julia Wallington picked up her pen and wrote a brief note on the big, pale-blue-covered notebook in front of her and then relaxed against the back of her bench. She listened carefully to what her adversary said, showing very little emotion beyond a slightly amused scepticism.

Up in the public gallery, Flixe leaned forward, trying to see the expressions on the faces of everyone involved in her sister's prosecution. It seemed to her outrageous that Ming should be pilloried for such a trivial cause. The smoothness of Mr Coopering's delivery worried her and she wondered how her sister would stand up to being questioned by him.

Ming put up a hand to brush a stray hair off her face and Flixe saw that the hand was shaking. She looked away for a moment and her eye was caught by one of the other spectators, sitting at the furthest edge of the bench. A tall young-ish man, he looked familiar but for a moment she could not identify him. Then he, too, turned and looked her full in the face. Flixe recognised Mark Sudley and her neatly plucked eyebrows twitched.

'Is your name Roger Sillhorne?'

Flixe looked back into the court to see the first witness standing in the box. Rotund and full of self-importance, he bowed slightly as he said:

'Yes, m'lord.'

The judge invited him to sit in the witness box, but Roger chose to stand. Miles Coopering led him to describe the excerpt of *Story of a Lost Love*. When he had finished, Coopering asked:

'Do you believe that it is obscene?'

Julia wrote herself a note, and Ming remembered one of their many long conferences, when she had told her Counsel that they could rely on several eminent literary men and women to support their contention that there was nothing obscene about *Story*. Julia had raised her eyebrows and explained that however eminent they might be, they would be of no help to the defence. It was for the court alone to decide, she had told Ming, whether or not the excerpt tended to deprave and corrupt.

'That is a matter for the court,' said Roger, who had obviously been told the same thing. 'I cannot possibly say more than that I find it distasteful in the extreme and not fit for the eyes of decent readers.'

The judge looked derisively at Miles Coopering. A little

flustered, he picked up his notes and then raised his handsome head again.

'Who are the likely readers of this magazine?'

'Its circulation is composed principally of young married women with children. It can also be found in public libraries and in the libraries of various educational institutions.'

'And so it might be read, for example, by teenage boys?'

'It might indeed. The very people who need most protection from such filth.'

'Thank you, Mr Sillhorne. Please wait there.'

Julia rose as he sat down. She shook out the full sleeves of her gown and turned to the witness box with a smile.

'Is the youth of England more vulnerable now than in earlier generations?' she asked in a voice of gentle surprise.

Roger launched at once into an explanation of how the declining standards of behaviour since the war had sapped the country's lifeblood. England was, he said at one moment, just as much at risk as she had once been from the Nazis, but the new enemy was the creeping fifth column of immorality.

Julia let him talk, rarely asking anything and allowing him to show himself as a man obsessed. She also used his outburst to gauge the jury's opinions. At least two of the men appeared to approve of much of what Roger was saying, while one smiled openly at his increasing hysteria. When she had learned enough, Julia thanked Roger, asked him to wait in case Prosecuting Counsel wanted to re-examine him and sat down.

Miles Coopering declined to ask Roger anything more and called his next witness, a woman in her thirties who described herself as a wife and mother of two children. She had left her only job as soon as she married and spent her days caring for her family.

'Do you subscribe to *The World Beyond*?'

'I have done in the past, yes.'

'Why did you do so?'

'Because of the letter I was sent by my school old-girls' association, which said that the magazine was being published to give women who were at home with children all day some insight into what happens in the outside world. It sounded interesting.'

'Have your children ever picked it up?'

'Yes. My son is thirteen and he wants to be an artist. He has always liked the covers they have on the magazine and often asks what is in it. Until the October issue I've always told him and often showed him articles.'

'And now?'

'As soon as I read the October issue I cancelled my subscription,' said the woman, making a face that suggested some foul miasma was rising from the front of the witness box.

'Why was that?'

'I felt as though I'd crawled through slime, as though I'd never get myself clean again.'

There was so much satisfaction in her voice that Julia was tempted to provoke her into an outburst like Roger Sillhorne's, but that would have given the prosecution far too great an opportunity for a searching re-examination and so Julia restrained herself. She asked only about the witness's education, which elicited the fact that she had passed School Certificate and qualified as a shorthand typist at a secretarial school.

'I see. Thank you,' said Julia in a polite, almost uninterested voice and offered Miles Coopering no opening for any more questions.

Up in the public gallery Flixe was astonished at Julia's lack of enterprise. It seemed absurd to leave the jury thinking that she had no way of challenging the woman's evidence. Flixe also wondered how on earth the prosecution had found her.

Before Miles Coopering could say anything, the judge leaned forward.

'Mr Coopering, I see that it is almost half-past twelve. I think that we should adjourn for lunch.'

'As your lordship pleases,' said Coopering, bowing to the judge.

'Be upstanding.'

'Thank goodness for that,' said Ming as she and Connie

reached the passage outside the court. 'I loathed listening to that woman.'

'I'm not surprised. The whole business is foul. And it's not helped by the heat in there,' said Connie, dabbing at her forehead with a handkerchief.

Mr Ratterley was waiting for them outside the court with Gerry.

'We have time to pop across the road for a bite, I think. Shall we go?'

'All right. I don't feel awfully hungry, but I suppose I ought to eat something. Is Flixe coming?'

'I haven't seen her, Ming, and we have no time to waste. The public gallery has a separate entrance. We may see her outside. Come along.'

Flixe, who had planned to join them, had been waylaid by Mark Sudley before she could reach the stairs down from the gallery.

'It is Mrs Suvarov, isn't it?' he said.

'Yes. And you are Mr Sudley,' she answered coldly. Mark looked taken aback by her obvious hostility.

'Will you . . . ? Could I persuade you to lunch with me?'

'I'm afraid not,' said Flixe. 'I have an appointment.'

'But you will be coming back?' His tone of surprised censure startled Flixe into looking at him more closely. She saw what seemed to be signs of anxiety about his eyes and mouth and began to think that she might have done him an injustice. But he had hurt Ming too much for her to want to eat with him at such a time.

'Naturally. Will you excuse me?'

He stood aside, but as she walked past him, he put out a hand to stop her.

'Is she all right?'

'Ming?' Flixe's voice was crisp with irritation. 'No, she is not all right. She is in an unspeakable situation: feeling guilty towards Constance Wroughton for suggesting they publish the piece in the first place, probably terrified of the consequences, vilely humiliated by being put in a dock as though she were a criminal, and facing being locked up with thieves, prostitutes and murderers.'

Mark dropped his hand and let her go without another word.

When Flixe emerged into the street, she looked about her in case there were any sign of the others. The only possible eating place she could see was a small restaurant almost directly opposite the court. She crossed the road to investigate. There was no sign of anyone she knew.

'Table for one, madam?'

'What?' she said distracted. 'Oh, yes, please.' It seemed the height of absurdity to traipse in and out of every café and restaurant in the district, although she loathed eating alone in public and had not even got a newspaper with her as a shield.

She chose a simple meal and was back in her seat at twenty-past one. The gallery was quite full and she hated to think that the people there had come to gloat over the pillorying of her sister. Flixe felt even more uncomfortable than she had earlier and put it down to indigestion caused by the dull shepherd's pie and soggy cabbage she had just eaten. She heard a latecomer and turned to watch Mark Sudley slip into the back bench just before the court rose and the judge took his seat again.

Full of impotent sympathy, Flixe watched Ming standing by Connie in the dock. For the next twenty minutes she listened to a doctor pronouncing on the deleterious effects on innocent women and children of reading obscene or pornographic literature. Coopering did not make the same mistake again and avoided asking his witness about the obscenity or otherwise of *Story of a Lost Love*.

Julia did not cross-examine the doctor and at the end of his evidence, Mr Coopering said:

'That is the case for the prosecution, m'lord.'

Julia got to her feet once more and called Ming to the witness stand. They had spent much time discussing who was to speak first and had eventually decided that Ming was more likely to arouse the jury's sympathy, particularly if the prosecution could be persuaded to treat her roughly. Ming understood the necessity but dreaded what might happen.

Julia had explained that their best strategy would be to show that publishing *Story* had been for the public good whether or not it was judged obscene, since there was no really permissible way to defend the obscenity charge itself. Ming and Connie had both been horrified to discover that they were not allowed to show that other publications of which no one had complained were more obscene or to bring expert evidence to show that what they had published could not have depraved and corrupted anyone.

The black-robed usher led Ming through the oath and she waited, her hands lying lightly on the brass rail in front of her. Julia thought that Ming looked very young and quite extraordinarily innocent with her lovely face framed in the upturned brim of her blue straw hat. With luck her appearance ought to help keep them out of prison. Julia turned towards her accusers and watched Roger's face flush.

'Miss Alderbrook.' Julia's voice, slow and equable, helped Ming to control her nervousness. 'Could you tell the court why you wanted to publish part of *Story of a Lost Love*?'

'Yes. M'lord, our magazine is written for women who are kept out of public life by their responsibilities to their families. Such women often feel badly cut off from current affairs, new developments in the arts, politics, and so on. We have seen our job as being to provide each month a selection of articles giving them such information.'

'And what information does this particular article provide?'

'Very much background information,' said Ming, beginning to relax again. 'We wanted – I wanted – to give our readers some idea of the background to the Committee on Homosexuality and Prostitution, which will be reporting soon. Homosexuality is a subject of which most women are quite ignorant. If Parliament is to debate the legal position of homosexuals, it seemed to me important that such ignorance should be dispelled.'

'Thank you, Miss Alderbrook.'

Feeling better for having been allowed to put her justification to the court, Ming turned to leave the witness box.

Connie was smiling in approval. The warders in the dock looked impassive and so, when Ming looked towards them, did the jury.

'Just a moment, Miss Alderbrook.' Mr Coopering's voice stopped her and she went clumsily back to the front of the witness box.

'Miss Alderbrook, who was it who wanted to print this translation?'

'It was I,' she said at once, determined to keep Max's name out of the proceedings completely. They had all agreed during the conferences before the trial that any publicised connection with a convicted homosexual could do all of them nothing but harm. 'And it was I who wrote the introduction.'

'Please confine yourself to answering the questions.'

At Coopering's bored, patronising tone, Ming raised her eyebrows.

'Are you married?'

'No.'

'Engaged to be married?'

'No.'

'Do you enjoy reading romances?'

Not certain of the direction his questions were taking, Ming agreed warily, adding:

'And detective stories, and nineteenth-century novels, and ...'

'Nineteenth-century novels such as?'

'Goodness,' said Ming, who for a moment could think of not a single title or writer's name. Then her brain cleared. 'Such as, well, *Pride and Prejudice, War and Peace, Jane Eyre.*'

'Thank you. All books in fact with a strong "love interest" as it is called.'

The direction of his questions had become perfectly clear and Ming tried to think how to extricate herself.

'And a great deal else,' she said feebly. 'The battle ...'

'Is not a fact, Miss Alderbrook,' said Coopering interrupting without mercy, 'that as a spinster with no husband or children to absorb your natural affections you turn to literature to satisfy your starved, er ... feelings?'

'If you are suggesting, Mr Coopering,' Ming began furiously, but before she could get any further she caught her Counsel's eye. Without moving or making any kind of signal Julia managed to express a warning. Remembering that she had once told Ming and Connie that the prosecution would try to portray them as degenerate pornographers, Ming moderated her voice and altered the rest of her sentence.

'If you are suggesting that I obtain some kind of shameful satisfaction from novels, then the answer is no,' she said more calmly.

'I see,' he said and the disbelieving sneer was obvious enough to bring a smile to the lips of more than one member of the jury, although the motherly woman looked distressed.

'Thank you. Do you not think that ignorance of such a distasteful subject is the proper condition for a lady?'

'I do not think that ignorance of any subject whatsoever is the proper condition of anyone who is capable of knowledge,' Ming said with a smile. There, at least, she was certain of her ground.

'Are you then suggesting that no written work could ever deprave anyone?' There was a warm sound of satisfaction in the lawyer's derisive voice and Ming knew that she must pick her words very carefully indeed.

'No, I'm not,' she said and saw Julia's taut shoulders loosen under her black gown. 'There are obviously some deliberately pornographic works that could well corrupt readers.'

'But you maintain that this publication of yours is not one of them? I find that a little hard to swallow.'

'I'm sorry,' said Ming with what she hoped was a charming smile.

'How would you then define pornography?'

Ming was silent for so long that he had to prompt her.

'I would define it as something that had been written to excite in a . . . sexual way,' she said. 'The excerpt we printed in the magazine could not possibly do that. There is nothing in it . . .'

'Have you ever read any pornography?'

'Certainly not,' said Ming without a moment's thought.

'In that case, how can you be so certain that you would recognise it? How can you say that your excerpt is not pornographic?'

After a pause, Ming said carefully:

'In the same way that although I have never read anything that I felt incited me to murderous violence, I am certain that I would recognise it if I saw it.'

'That is hardly relevant, but thank you, Miss Alderbrook.'

Julia declined to re-examine and the judge adjourned the court for the day. Ming and Connie were once more free to leave the dock.

CHAPTER 24

Flixe, who had watched Mark Sudley's face during Ming's stint in the witness box and revised some of her feelings about him, went straight up to him as soon as the judge left the court and held out her hand.

'Mr Sudley, I'm sorry about my brusqueness earlier. I have been very worried,' she said, 'but that's no excuse.'

'I'm not surprised,' he said, shaking her hand. 'It's hideous that she should have to face that kind of salacious impertinence. I ...' He stopped and shrugged. A charming smile crossed his face. 'I wanted to smash my fist in his face,' he added in the voice of a frustrated schoolboy.

'I'm glad,' said Flixe warmly, laying her other, suede-gloved, hand on his sleeve. 'Will you be here tomorrow?'

'Naturally.'

'Then perhaps we could have lunch then. I am sorry about today. Goodbye.'

'Mrs Suvarov?'

'Yes?' said Flixe, turning back.

Mark started to speak, stopped and then shook his head.

'No, it's all right. I was going to ask you to send her my love, but I think ...'

'Quite right. That's the sort of thing you should say face to face.'

'Will she be staying with you tonight?'

'I doubt it. I tried to persuade her to come to us for the whole week but she wanted to be at home. Why?'

'I thought I might drop her a note. I don't want to force myself on her just now.'

Flixe thought of telling him that there would be no forcing and that what Ming needed above all else was to be with someone who cared about her, but then she decided that she had interfered enough. She knew that Ming would never forgive anyone who tried to force Mark into a declaration he was reluctant to make.

'Good idea,' Flixe said casually. 'I must go now. I'll see you tomorrow.'

She walked down the echoing stairs to find both her sisters and Constance Wroughton waiting for her.

'Hello, Flixe,' said Ming in a rather tight voice. 'We thought you must have gone.'

'I'd never do that, sweetie.' Flixe kissed Ming and held her round the shoulders for a moment. 'I thought you did brilliantly when that brute started his idiotic insinuations.'

She was relieved to see a faint smile relax Ming's face.

'That's the worst of looking so young and pathetic,' she said. 'He'd never have dared say those sort of things to Connie.'

'Luckily! I don't know that I'd have managed to keep my temper as you did. I suppose my turn will come tomorrow.'

'Well, who's coming to have tea with me and Connie?' Flixe asked gaily in the pause that followed Connie's bleak statement. 'I must get back to my infants if I'm to prevent a mutiny in the nursery. Thank heavens Nicholas is on the bottle at last!'

'We'd love to,' said Gerry, having looked at Mike who nodded.

'Good. Ming?'

'I don't think so, Flixe. Thank you all the same. I feel completely whacked. I think I'll just go and have a long bath and get to bed.'

Before they could protest, and she could see from their expressions that they were all about to try to persuade her to go with them, Ming signalled to a taxi and gave the driver her address. Having waved cheerfully until the taxi rounded the first corner, she slumped in the deep seat and let her head drop back. She felt drained of all feeling. Even the anger against Roger and her fears for the future had dwindled to a hateful memory.

Back in Cheyne Walk, she got out of the cab, unlocked the front door of the building and pulled herself up the stairs, leaning heavily on the bannisters. She was touched to find a card propped up against the kitchen clock by her charwoman and managed to walk a little more briskly across the room to pick it up. A lurid sunrise provided the background for the gold-embossed message of good luck. Smiling at it, she put it back and went to run a bath.

More than half-asleep in the warm water, she was startled to hear the shrill calling of her front-door bell and lost her balance. Her feet slid off the taps, which had kept them propped up, and her chin sank beneath the water. Realising that half her carefully set hair was ruined, she sat up, shaking the water off her face and feeling for a towel with her left hand.

By the time she had dried, put on a dressing-gown and got to the front door there was no one there. Instead she saw a huge, cellophane-wrapped bunch of red roses. Assuming that they must be from Peter and Flixe, Ming picked up the great bouquet and carried it to the kitchen. It seemed a kind but quite unnecessary gesture for them to have made, she thought.

There was no particularly suitable vase and so Ming simply filled a galvanised bucket with water to keep the flowers wet while she decided what to do with them. She cut off the cellophane and the shiny red ribbon, untwisted the wire that kept the roses in an immaculate fan-shape, hammered the bottom half-inch of their stalks to pulp, and put them up to their necks in water.

It was only when she was gathering up the torn cellophane and wire that she noticed a small white envelope attached to the ribbon. She recognised Mark's distinctive handwriting on the envelope. Shuddering with nervous hope, she ripped it open. Under the address of his old flat, he had written:

I'm with you all the way. Don't let them get you down.
                                        Love, Mark

In her tiredness and anxiety the gesture of comfort broke
through all the careful defences she had built up against the
horror of the trial and against Mark's disappearance from
her life, and she sank down on to one of the red chairs as
though her legs could no longer support her. It was at least
five minutes before she realised that she was clutching a
half-twisted piece of wire so tightly in her hand that it had
punctured the skin. When she had washed the blood away,
she poured out a stiff whisky and water and sat in the
kitchen sipping it slowly and letting herself feel again.

When she had finished the drink, she walked into her
tiny, gilded study for writing paper and her pen and sat
down to thank him:

> *Dearest Mark,*
> *Thank you for your flowers. They are glorious, and it is*
> *just as glorious of you to have thought of sending them. This*
> *trial is a nightmare and it is extraordinarily comforting to*
> *know that you are neither shocked nor ...*

Ming stopped writing and tried to think of a suitable word.
Her brain seemed to have seized up. For a moment she was
tempted to add 'angry', but he had no reason for anger
about the trial, whatever he might have felt about her political articles and their possible effect on his career. She
shook her pen to make the ink flow again.

> *... nor troubled by what we published. Your support – and*
> *affection – mean more than I can say. It would be lovely to see*
> *you. Have you come back to London for good?*
>
> *Love, Ming*

She found a stamp, stuck it to the envelope and then
went into her bedroom to put on some clothes so that she
could post the note in time to catch the last collection that
day. It seemed important that Mark should have the letter
before the end of the trial.

When she got back she made herself some hard-boiled-egg sandwiches and a cup of hot milk with a teaspoonful of brown sugar stirred into it. With the comfort of familiar nursery food inside her, she took a favourite novel to bed and read herself to sleep without needing any pills at all.

The next morning was damp and cloudy, as different from the warm sunshine of the previous day as possible. Ming took a look at the sky and chose to wear her good dark blue suit and a small hat made of even darker felt. She reached the Old Bailey early in the half-acknowledged hope of seeing Mark, but there was no sign of him before her lawyers appeared.

'I had planned to call Connie straight away, Ming,' said Julia when they had all asked about each other's well-being, 'but I think I'll call the schoolmaster first since much of Connie's evidence duplicates yours. Then we'll have Connie and finally the doctor.'

'That sounds sensible. Good luck,' said Ming.

'Thank you. We'll see how it goes. Now take care. You did well yesterday. Don't let anger make you look aggressive or sneering while you listen to our evidence or the cross-examination. The jury need to like you, but you mustn't obviously flirt with them. All right?'

Ming nodded, unsmiling.

'Here's Connie,' she said. 'We'd better go in.'

Julia's first witness was a middle-aged man, who strode into the witness box with his shoulders held very straight.

'Is your name George Dicton?' she asked, looking down at her notes for a second.

'Yes.'

'Will you tell the court what you do for a living?'

'I am a housemaster at Blandfield School in Nottingham.'

'What are your responsibilities?'

'To teach the classes assigned to me and to look after the welfare of the boys in my house.'

'Their physical welfare only?'

'No. My responsibilities include also their emotional and moral welfare. Their spiritual welfare is in the charge of the chaplain. And I teach Classics.'

'That would be Latin, Greek and Ancient History, I take it?' said Julia for the jury's benefit. Most of them looked as though they knew quite well what 'Classics' meant, but she wanted to be certain.

'Yes, with a little Philosophy in the sixth form.'

'You will then be entirely familiar with Plato's *Symposium*?'

Before the witness could answer, Prosecuting Counsel leapt to his feet, saying:

'I object, m'lord, to the introduction of the *Symposium*. M'learned friend appears to have forgotten that the defence is not allowed to bring in any discussion of the comparative obscenity of other books.'

'My lord, I have no intention of doing so,' said Julia with a charming smile. 'My question is designed to establish a quite different point.'

The judge, looking more like a hawk than ever, stared down at Julia from his elevated throne. She stood quite still, her head tilted slightly downwards as though in deference, but her shoulders were held firmly and her spine was rigidly straight.

'I shall allow you a little latitude, Mrs Wallington, but I shall stop you as soon as you stray into doubtful territory.'

'I am obliged to your lordship,' said Julia before turning to smile once more at the schoolmaster. 'Mr Dicton?'

'I am naturally familiar with the *Symposium*.'

'Will you tell the court what is the subject of that book.'

'It takes the form of a discussion of various forms of love at an Athenian dinner party.'

'And what is the conclusion?'

'Make your point, Mrs Wallington,' said the judge coldly. Julia bowed.

Gerry, who unlike either of her sisters had read the *Symposium*, felt thoroughly indignant that the prosecution and the judge knew perfectly well what point Julia was making while few of the jury did.

'My point is that if it is considered desirable for schoolboys to be taught to admire the work of Plato and to consider the subject of the *Symposium* at school it is equally desirable for their mothers to consider it.'

The judge nodded. Julia then quoted three lines of Ancient Greek. The judge looked impassively down but Mr Coopering QC seemed thoroughly uncomfortable.

'Could you identify and translate that for the court, Mr Dicton?'

The witness looked almost as uncomfortable as Mr Coopering and said nothing.

'You must answer, Mr Dicton,' said the judge with no obvious expression in his voice.

'It is taken from Aristophanes' speech at the banquet and it means, roughly: "Boys and lads like that are the best of their generation, because they are the most manly. Some people say that they are shameless, but they are wrong. It is not shamelessness which inspires their behaviour, but high spirit and manliness and virility."'

'And what are the boys and lads to whom he refers?'

Looking briefly at the judge and then at Miles Coopering, the witness licked his lips and then said simply:

'Lovers of men.'

'Thank you, Mr Dicton,' said Julia as she sat down.

Ming and Connie relaxed slightly, but up in the gallery Flixe waited for Coopering to cross-examine the witness.

'It is true, is it not, that ancient Athenian society was based on the existence of slavery?'

'Yes, indeed,' said Mr Dicton, looking more cheerful.

'And when you are teaching your pupils, do you have any difficulty distinguishing between those aspects of Greek civilisation that are to be admired and those – such as slavery – that are barbaric according to our views?'

'None whatever.'

'Would you agree that no pupil studying such a civilisation would be in any doubt as to the proper condemnation of the behaviour extolled by Aristophanes?'

'Certainly.'

'Thank you, Mr Dicton. Please wait there.'

Julia declined to re-examine him and he was allowed to go. She wrote herself another note and then called Constance Wroughton. Connie slowly crossed the court from dock to witness box and was sworn in.

'Miss Wroughton, would you explain to the court why it is that you sanctioned the publication of this excerpt in your magazine,' said Julia.

'Certainly,' said Connie, sounding much more brisk and confident than Ming had done the day before. Julia had been through the few things that she could say to such a question and the importance of explaining to the court that she herself disapproved of homosexuality. Connie had protested at that, reminding her counsel that she would have to swear to tell the truth, and Julia had explained to her some of the facts of legal life.

'I felt that there is a great deal of ignorance about this very sad human condition,' said Connie obediently, 'and that, by publishing a short extract from a most sensitively written book, I might help to remedy that ignorance.'

'Did you hope to force a change in the law relating to homosexual behaviour?'

'Certainly not,' said Connie, managing to sound surprised. 'That is not the business of private individuals. It is for Parliament to decide whether there should be any kind of change.'

Ming saw Mr Coopering writing himself a note.

'May I take it then that what you wanted to do was to alter public opinion on the matter?'

'Not even that. All I wanted to do by publishing this extract is what I have wanted to do with everything we have printed: to inform our readership and to extend their mental horizons, and by doing so make it more difficult for ignorance to thrive.'

A shadow crossed Mr Coopering's face and he altered the note he had made.

'Thank you, Miss Wroughton,' said Julia as she sat down. Her opponent took his time standing up and arranging his gown. As last he looked directly at Connie.

'Do you yourself believe that there should be a change in the law?'

'I don't know,' said Connie, hating the fact that she was having to fudge her strong opinion on the matter. 'I have not read enough to make a judgment. Perhaps when the committee's report is published I shall be able to do so.'

Julia's face relaxed very slightly and the judge sat more comfortably in his throne.

'In that case, would it not have been better to allow your readers to wait until they, too, could read the report? A report after all which will have been compiled by a well-qualified committee consisting of doctors, judges of the High Court, Members of Parliament and ministers of religion.'

'I do not think so.'

'Oh, really? May I ask why not?' The sneering tone was back in Miles Coopering's voice. Ming, taking a quick, side-long look at the jury, thought that she saw in some of the faces a resistance to him and was glad.

'Because factual information such as the results of a committee's deliberations could never convey to a reader as much of the emotional reality of the condition as a novel.'

'Are you telling this court that what you wanted to do was to take into the homes of ordinary, decent English-women the "emotional reality" of this disgusting crime?'

The very slight twitch of Connie's straight dark eyebrows told those in the court and public gallery who knew her that she felt she had been trapped into a legally indefensible corner. She put back her shoulders and lifted her chin to deliver her answer.

'The emotional reality of a human condition that has been known since antiquity,' she said coldly.

'That is mere word play,' said Mr Coopering as he sat down.

When Connie had left the witness box Julia called her next witness, a psychoanalyst. He explained under her patient questioning all the modern theories of the causes of homosexuality.

'Is it possible that any man − or boy − could be driven into that condition by something that he read?'

'I should have thought that highly unlikely,' said the psychoanalyst.

'That sounds as though you think it might be possible.'

'The human condition is so various that one can never state categorically what one person in a million might do.'

Julia allowed a happy smile to widen her generous mouth.

'I suspect my clients would be delighted to achieve a circulation of anything like a million copies of their magazine,' she said. Most members of the jury shared her amusement and Ming thought that she saw a faint quiver on the lips of the judge.

While the court was momentarily relaxed, Julia asked her witness whether opinions on the subject of homosexuality had changed much.

'Enormously,' he answered. 'They change frequently in both directions. In ancient Athens it was considered normal, even admirable. But Justinian believed that it was the cause of earthquakes.'

'A manifestly absurd proposition,' commented Julia.

'Hardly more absurd than some I have heard today.'

'I object!' Mr Coopering was on his feet almost shaking his fists in the direction of the witness. Very smoothly Julia intervened.

'By "today" do you mean, Tuesday, April twenty-fourth, 1957?'

'Good heavens no,' said the psychoanalyst, quickly taking her clue. 'I was using the word as a synonym for "nowadays".'

'Thank you, Dr Gort,' said Julia with a kindly nod towards her antagonist. Mr Coopering sat down again.

Julia's next witness was a bookseller, who had inherited his business from his father. He told the court that he had started to work for his father in 1918.

'Do you remember a celebrated case of this nature in 1932?'

'Yes, indeed. A book called *The Well of Loneliness* was the subject of a case after a campaign in the newspapers.'

'Can you remember what was written about the book then?'

'The editor of the *Sunday Express* wrote that he would rather "put a phial of prussic acid in the hands of a healthy boy or girl than the book in question".'

'What happened to it?'

'After the trial all copies of the book were destroyed.'

Julia noticed both the jury and Michael Coopering looking at her in surprise and she suppressed a smile.

'And what has happened to the book since then?'

'It was republished six years ago and has been in print ever since.'

'Does anyone object?'

'Not to my knowledge. We've had no complaints in the shop and we sell it steadily – in small numbers, but steadily.'

Julia thanked him and Mr Coopering crossly declined the opportunity of questioning him. Before Julia could call her next witness the judge adjourned the proceedings for lunch.

Flixe exchanged a smile with Mark Sudley, who was sitting in the row behind her, and he gestured to the door. Flixe nodded, but it was nearly five minutes before she could get out of the front row. There seemed to be an altercation at the far end of it between an elderly man who wanted to get out and a plump young woman who was muttering angrily and kept dropping things. At last, having picked up her bag and her gloves and straightened her hat, she let him and the rest of the impatient spectators pass her.

When it was Flixe's turn, she murmured an apology and turned sideways to squeeze past. As she went she caught a waft of violet scent that seemed very familiar. The coincidence seemed too much and she wondered if she was face to face and breast to breast with the author of Ming's letters. Allowing her glance to drift downwards, Flixe examined the young woman's hands. Her nails were innocent of varnish and were cut as short as a child's.

Paradoxically disappointed, Flixe went on to catch up with Mark.

'Sorry about the wait,' she said as they were walking downstairs. 'There was a very odd woman holding everyone up.'

'I know,' answered Mark with a look of distaste on his

pleasant face. 'She was there yesterday too, taking rather a lot of satisfaction, I thought, at the sight of Ming in the witness box. Hateful!'

'Yes. I suppose she's just one of those people who enjoy gloating over other people's misfortune. Sad! Where would you like to eat?'

'I don't mind at all. Have you any suggestions?'

'The place across the road is adequate if you're not expecting *haute cuisine.*'

They went across and were given a table in the window. The waiter took their order and left them alone.

'I thought things went better today,' said Flixe to break the constraint that seemed to have seized Mark. His eyes narrowed and his lips lifted into a smile of amusement mixed with mockery.

'So they should since it's been the defence's day,' he said and then he added in a more serious voice: 'But you're right. I do think Mrs. Wallington is doing a splendid job. I've only met her twice before – once at that dance and once at her river picnic – and ...'

'And?' prompted Flixe, adding, in case he was about to be critical, 'She is one of my dearest friends.'

'It's just that on both occasions she seemed a bit ill at ease. I'm not sure I'd have expected her to be so smooth and silky in her professional life.'

Their food arrived and saved Flixe having to comment. She knew exactly what he meant about Julia's mood at the Attingers' dance and understood it, but it seemed inappropriate to tell the young man in front of her that it had been caused by Ming's effect on David Wallington.

'By the way, did you see her last night?'

'Mrs Wallington?' he said, looking up from his whitebait. 'No.'

'Ming, you clot.' Flixe's voice was as energetic and informal as though she had been speaking to one of her sisters and Mark smiled in appreciation.

'No, I didn't think it would be ... sensible.'

'Why on earth not? She's almost been ill with missing you.'

One of the small, hard-fried fish dropped from Mark's fork as he moved suddenly. Collecting himself, he picked it up and ate it, without saying anything.

'You must have grasped that at least,' said Flixe, frustrated by his silence. 'She told me she'd written to you at Christmas.'

'She did,' said Mark, still giving nothing away. 'But she's far too kind to let a friend's resignation from his job pass without comment. She is one of the kindest people I've ever met.'

'Oh, saints preserve us from modest lovers,' said Flixe, trying to rouse him into showing her some real emotions. 'I promised myself months ago that I wouldn't interfere, but if someone doesn't do something you're going to ruin each other's lives. I watched your face yesterday afternoon and it seemed to me that you care a lot for my little sister.'

'I do,' he said, looking at her without either blinking or blushing.

'Then why have you not been in touch with her since the day you cancelled your tea at Searcy's?'

At that question, Mark looked stubbornly at her and shook his head. He said nothing.

'Is there another woman in your life?'

Mark's gaze flew upwards and he looked straight at Flixe. She thought his grey eyes the most honest she had ever seen and at that moment the most severe.

'Certainly not.'

'Aha,' said Flixe, unable to resist a small joke, 'then perhaps you, too, will have been reading romantic novels for, er, emotional satisfaction.'

The stubbornness was banished from his face in a burst of real amusement. Flixe began to think that despite their obvious difficulties he might be perfect for Ming after all. He began to eat the rest of his whitebait. Flixe waited, drinking her soup and trying to gauge what was going on in his mind. When it became clear that he either could not or would not talk, she tried again.

'What is it that's making you so ashamed that you can't talk to her?'

Mark put his knife and fork neatly together and signalled to the waiter to clear away their plates.

'I'm not ashamed of anything ... unless I really have made her unhappy.'

'Aha!' Flixe's exclamation was full of enlightenment. 'I see. I thought you wanted to pump me about Ming's feelings for you.'

'Pumping is not exactly the word I'd have chosen,' he said drily. 'But it is true that I want to know how she really is.'

'And perhaps,' said Flixe, sounding sarcastic, 'whether there is another man in her life?'

'That too,' he said with considerable dignity. 'If she had found someone else who made her happier than I ever managed to do, the last thing I want to do is push in where I was not wanted.'

Then it was Flixe who blushed.

'I'm sorry. I was out of order,' she said. 'As far as I know there is no one else.'

'There's no need to apologise. Good, here's the chicken.'

They ate in silence for a while until Flixe had recovered her composure. She asked him what sort of work he was going to do now that he had left the Civil Service.

'I've joined forces with a man I was at university with. He's a physicist and as a sort of sideline he's been working for some time on the miniaturisation of computers. We're trying to raise the backing to go for it on a commercial basis. I'm advising on the practical uses and will become a ... salesman, I suppose, as soon as we've something to sell.'

'That sounds interesting,' said Flixe, in a voice that made Mark look up, smiling.

'You sound a little like my mother,' he said. 'She thinks it quite frightful that I've thrown up a professional career I'd been building since the war to go in for trade. Do you think that Ming will share your distaste?'

He spoke lightly, but Flixe knew that the question really mattered to him. She had no idea of the answer and told him so, adding:

'Is that why you haven't been in touch with her?'

'Partly.'

'I think you've been rather unfair, because you've left her thinking that you don't care about her any longer. Besides, you must know that she doesn't subscribe to the view that wives should be judged by their husbands' status.'

He looked so surprised that Flixe added:

'Think of the things she's been writing every month, or haven't you read them?'

'Of course I've read them! I've read everything she's ever written, but I hadn't actually picked that out of them, though I do see what you mean.'

'Perhaps I was exaggerating,' said Flixe. 'Do you know, I think that the pair of you have been protecting each other from knowledge that you both need.'

Mark gave up even trying to eat his chicken and pushed the nearly full plate to one side.

'What has she been protecting me from?' he asked.

Flixe tried to say nothing, true to her determination to let them find their own way out of their maze, but the know-ledge of how badly they had lost themselves forced her on.

'From the fact that she is most terribly in love with you; that your apparent rejection of her has hurt her bitterly; that she longs more than anything else to go back to when you asked her to marry you and manage things better this time – and avoid hurting you any more.'

Mark looked as blankly surprised as though she had hit him over the head with her handbag.

'You must have known,' Flixe said when it became obvious that he could not speak. He simply shook his head.

'Then what made you come to the trial?'

'I heard from David Wallington that she needed me,' he said simply. 'I couldn't stay away, but I wanted to find out more before I waded in and upset her. That's why I needed to talk to you.'

'To be perfectly honest,' said Flixe with energy, 'I think that the only thing that would upset her is not hearing from you or seeing you. It's half killed her, you know.'

'And me,' he said after a long pause. 'I . . .'

'Don't tell me. Tell her.'

'I will.'

'Good. Well, since you couldn't manage your chicken, there's not much point in our ordering pudding. Shall we get the bill and go?'

Mark laughed and once again Flixe saw all the charm that had broken through whatever it was that had kept Ming solitary for so long.

'I may be a clot, Mrs Suvarov, but I'm not one of your children.'

Flixe laughed with him and when they had settled the bill they went back to the court in an atmosphere of remarkably good friendship. She tried to make Mark agree to sit beside her, hoping that Ming would look up from the dock and see him there; but he refused and kept to his chosen seat at the back, where he could not possibly be seen from the dock.

Ming saw Flixe as soon as she and Connie went back to the dock. Flixe gave her a discreet victory sign and Ming smiled. Gerry had not been able to take another day away from her university commitments, and Ming found it very comforting to know that one of her sisters was there in court.

She needed comfort that afternoon. Julia's last witness was a doctor, who testified first that he considered that it was on the whole beneficial to society that women should be fully informed about the subject of homosexuality. That was all Julia wanted of him and so she handed him to the prosecution counsel, whose first question was:

'Would you yourself wish to read the excerpt published in the defendants' magazine?'

'No. I find the prospect distasteful.'

Quite without meaning to, Ming looked at the back of Julia's head with an expression of great hurt on her face. Julia knew that the statement might be upsetting her clients but she ignored them. Her brief had been to win the case for Ming and Connie; not to protect their sensibilities.

'May I ask why?'

'Because I dislike the whole subject of homosexuality.'

'Again, may I ask why?'

'You may: I consider it a perversion; injurious to family life and to health; unnatural; sterile and a waste.'

'I see. For once I find myself in complete agreement with one of my learned friend's witnesses,' said Coopering, obviously inviting the jury to enjoy his amusement. Some of them accepted and one even laughed.

'In that case why have you just testified that you consider its publication beneficial?'

'I have already explained that,' said the doctor, sounding irritable. Julia kept her gaze firmly on her own notes.

'Will you please explain again. Some of us are a little confused,' said Coopering.

'I disapprove fundamentally of the physical expression of homosexuality, but I believe that ignorance of the entire subject is not in the public interest.'

'Despite its possible effect on susceptible readers?'

'Yes.'

'In your opinion,' said Mr Coopering, retreating once more to sarcasm. He looked as though he had been faced with the one thing he had never expected and was trying to make the best of it.

'My opinion is what I was asked for,' said the doctor quite mildly.

'Thank you.'

Mr Coopering sat down and Julia got to her feet. Flixe thought that Julia looked slightly nervous and she could not imagine why.

'Can you explain to the court why you believe that ignorance of this subject is undesirable?'

'Anyone who has been in general practice for as long as I have will have treated innumerable hysterical girls and women and troubled boys. From what I have learned of human folly and distress during the years since I qualified as a doctor, I can say that accurate information dispels a great deal of unpleasant and damaging fantasy.'

Julia let him go and then spent a few moments tidying her papers before straightening her shoulders and facing the jury. Some of them were looking overcome with boredom; the housewife seemed depressed and anxious;

but at least five were alert and apparently sympathetic.

'Members of the jury,' said Julia, smiling openly at them without a trace of patronage or mistrust, 'you have heard a great deal of contradictory evidence over the past two days and in a short time you will have to decide what to believe and what to dismiss in order to make up your minds about the truth of this case.'

Even those jurors who had been doodling on their note-pads or fighting yawns with difficulty seemed to sit up straighter and listen properly.

'M'learned friend has asked you to consider the effect of the five thousand words excerpted from *Story of a Lost Love* on a young boy who might pick up his mother's magazine. I would like you to exercise your memories, gentlemen, and your imagination, ladies.'

The efficient-looking woman and the housewife both smiled at Julia.

'How likely do you think it is that any young man or boy would willingly pick up one of his mother's magazines? I am a mother myself and I find it very hard to imagine my son doing any such thing.'

Ming's eyebrows twitched together in surprise. Knowing that Julia's son was only just five, it seemed almost wrong that she should suggest what she had done. But, watching the jury, Ming could see that most of them sympathised with the point.

'Yes, it is an amusing picture, isn't it?' Julia went on. 'I didn't raise it to make you laugh, but because that is really one of the very few points at issue here. You do not have to decide what you think of homosexuality; you do not have to decide what you think of the current laws regarding it; you do not have to decide whether you think the five thousand words my clients published are unpleasant, distasteful, even disgusting. All you have to decide is whether they could corrupt and deprave the people who are likely to read the magazine.

'In a case that took place here just over two years ago, the judge, in summing up, asked the jury to consider who might be corrupted by the book that was then on trial. One of his suggestions of such a person was a fourteen-year-old girl, and he asked the jury whether they believed it right that our literary standards should be based on what might be suitable for a fourteen-year-old girl. In this case, I suppose the question is really, are we now to take our standards from what is suitable for a fourteen-year-old boy.'

Ming saw Michael Coopering making a note.

'If we are,' Julia went on quietly but implacably, 'what then could be considered suitable to be published in a magazine for married women? Nothing to do with child-birth, certainly: that might well upset a young boy. Married love, too, would have to be outlawed; any discussion of women's health and monthly difficulties would be hard to include. In fact, if we are to take our standards from that imaginary boy, all women's magazines would have to be written at a level of, say, the William books.'

There was laughter from the public gallery then and Mr Coopering made another note.

'That is to reduce the proposition to absurdity,' said Julia, once more taking the wind out of his sails. 'But it is an absurd proposition to begin with. Even if our imaginary boy were to take up his mother's magazine and read his way through all the articles that preceded *Story of a Lost Love*, what would happen to him then? You have heard Dr Gort explain that the causes of homosexuality are such that they completely exclude the reading of an article like this. If that is so, it is very difficult to think what other corrupting or depraving effect it could have.

'It might shock them, although that seems hard to believe, but if they were shocked, what would happen to them? Would it be so very dreadful? People are frequently shocked and disgusted by items in the newspapers, but no one suggests that they have been depraved and corrupted by that shock.

'You have heard a witness state that the boys he teaches have no difficulty in distinguishing between those aspects of ancient Greek civilisation they should admire, such as democracy, and those, such as slavery and homosexuality, that they should deplore. If that is true, then they should have no difficulty in making the same distinction in the unlikely event that they read this magazine.'

Julia paused, partly to take a drink of water and partly to give the jury time to absorb what she had said.

'Surely their mothers, too, would be able to make the same distinction? It would be a curious world, members of the jury, if schoolboys were to be allowed to make such a judgment on the subject of homosexuality but their mothers were not.'

For the first time, the housewife on the jury looked positively determined.

'Members of the jury, foreigners often point a finger at us in this country and say that we are a nation of hypocrites. Let us give the lie to such sneering criticisms. In your verdict, you have it in your power to show yourselves as the decent, rational, sensible, unhypocritical and – above all – unhysterical men and women that I know you to be.'

She sat down and Connie for one felt like applauding. Ming had to hold her hands tightly together in her lap to stop them from shaking visibly. She licked her lips, which felt dry and cracked under her tongue.

Miles Coopering stood up.

'M'learned friend,' he said in his rich voice as he bowed to Julia, 'has put in a plea for you to fight the charge of hypocrisy by, in effect, granting a licence to publish an account of utterly distasteful behaviour. Whatever standards may obtain on the Continent, in this country the sanctity of family life remains paramount. Do we really want our homes and families, our children, polluted with the kind of filth that has been printed in the defendant's magazine? I am confident, members of the jury, that you, as right-thinking citizens of this nation, will answer a stalwart "no" to that question.

'In this country homosexual behaviour is outlawed; it is a subject not fit for decent homes. The magazine that included this excerpt is, by the defendants' own acknowledgement, designed to be read in just that sort of home, a home in which young children are learning about the kind of civilised behaviour that is expected of them as they grow up.

Could there be any less suitable setting for a discussion of a disgusting crime?

'Once again, the right-thinking answer is "no".

'M'learned friend has tried to persuade you subtly that the subject of homosexuality is not really so bad by bringing in one of the very few Classical texts that treats of the subject in an admiring way. You will not be deceived by her. Every schoolboy – and for that matter the mother and the sister of every schoolboy – knows that throughout history appalling things have been done and condoned and even admired. All schoolchildren are taught to admire, for example, Queen Elizabeth I; and yet it is well known that in her reign Roman Catholics were burned at the stake and prisoners were routinely subjected to the most barbaric tortures. It is not difficult for any schoolchild to understand which of Gloriana's actions are to be admired and which condemned.

'Mrs Wallington has said that such a schoolchild would have as little difficulty in distinguishing between the activities to be admired and condemned in a modern magazine. But that is a completely different question and there is no connection to be made between historical barbarities and filth such as the article you are asked to condemn.

'And condemn it you must, members of the jury, if the children of this country are to be assured of the clean, honest and secure upbringing they both deserve and need.'

It seemed to Flixe, sitting impotently in the spectators' gallery, that it was enormously unfair that Julia had no opportunity to refute her opponent's speech, to show the jury where he had failed to provide rational answers to her points and where he had glossed over irrefutable truths. Looking down at the judge, Flixe wondered whether he could be trusted to do it for them. She felt very depressed.

'Be upstanding.'

Flixe had been so absorbed in her thoughts that she had completely missed the judge's decision to adjourn for the day. Looking down at her watch she saw that it was almost a quarter to five. He must have decided to let the proceedings overrun the usual half-past-four deadline in order to give the prosecution's closing statement no more weight than Julia's. Her depression lightened a little and she looked round for Mark.

He had already gone. Flixe dawdled, hoping that Mark had waylaid Ming. But when Flixe reached the ground floor, she found only Connie and Ming standing waiting for her.

'Where are the lawyers?' she asked when she reached them.

'Gone. There's nothing more any of us can do now,' said Connie. She took a sidelong look at Ming, who looked ashen-faced and ill. 'What about tea, Flixe?'

'Good idea,' said Flixe, who was also looking at her sister. 'Come on, Mingie. We'll get a taxi.'

She stopped the cab outside Lavell's sweetshop in Kensington High Street and told the others she would follow them on foot.

'No. Do let me come, too,' said Ming, thinking that if she were left alone with Connie she might either burst into fervent apologies or unanswerable questions about what might happen on the following day.

'We'll all come,' said Connie, calmly paying off the driver.

They went into the brightly lit shop together. Flixe made a modest selection of sweets with which to keep her daughters happy and then chose a box of liqueur chocolates for Brigitte, who had uncomplainingly worked much longer hours than usual.

Ming, meanwhile, had asked for a quarter of a pound of peardrops. She had not eaten them since childhood and, remembering the comfort of her previous evening's nursery supper, thought that they might soothe her terrors. They were weighed and poured in a red and cream-coloured stream into a small white paper bag.

'Thank you,' she said to the girl who took her money. Flixe paid for her own purchases and the three of them walked slowly up the hill towards her house.

The children gave them a rapturous welcome and Ming felt warmed by their obvious pleasure when she hugged them.

'Will you sit next to me, Auntie Ming?' asked Fiona, sliding a slightly sticky hand into Ming's.

'And me,' said Sophie, tugging at her other hand. Ming's handbag and the bag of peardrops fell to the floor, spilling their contents far and wide.

Sophie looked nervously up at her aunt, but Ming smiled and bent down on hands and knees to pick everything up. Her nieces joined in, concentrating on the sweets, and Fiona put one in her mouth.

'Don't do that,' said Ming gently. 'It's been on the floor. You mustn't eat that.'

She put out her hand and the child obediently spat the sweet into it. Recoiling from the slimy sensation, Ming hurried to tip the sticky sweet into the wastepaper basket. As she was rubbing her hand on her handkerchief, she recognised the scent of the sweets.

'Flixe!' she said suddenly. 'Smell the peardrops.'

Flixe relieved her elder daughter of the torn bag full of sweets and smelled it.

'Ah, that's what smells like nail-varnish remover but isn't. Well done, Ming!'

CHAPTER 25

The next morning they were all in court again. Connie had decreed that she and Ming should dress in clothes suitable for triumph instead of cravenly wearing some dark colour as though they expected to be convicted. She herself had chosen a new, vivid green coat and skirt, which she wore with a smart black hat, black shoes and handbag.

Ming, unable to forget that they might end the day in a prison cell, had had to battle hard to resist putting on clothes that would have been more suitable for a funeral. Eventually she picked out a simple spring dress and jacket made of light tweed. Although it was grey, it was a silver colour that looked stylish rather than dim, and it made an excellent foil for both her pearls and her pink-and-white complexion. At the last minute she pinned one of Mark's red roses to the left lapel with a pearl brooch her godmother had given her at her christening.

When Ming reached the court Gerry was already in her old place at Mr Ratterley's side, having persuaded a colleague to take her morning lectures, and Flixe was once more in the gallery.

Unknown to Ming, Flixe had a fresh bag of peardrops in her handbag and she arrived deliberately late so that she had an excuse to squeeze in beside the plump young woman who smelled of inexpensive violet scent.

'I am sorry,' whispered Flixe as she sat down. 'I couldn't get a bus this morning; the crowds were so awful. Am I squashing you too much?'

'No; it's quite all right,' said the young woman. 'I've room to move up a bit.'

'I've seen you before, haven't I?' said Flixe, smiling in a friendly way. 'Isn't it interesting?'

'I think it's disgusting, actually.'

Flixe, wondering whether she had been identified, started to cough.

'Oh, do excuse me,' she said during a brief pause. She opened her bag and fumbled in it. 'It's the dust in the streets, I think. Would you like one of these? I find they help a lot.'

The plump girl's brown eyes narrowed into a smile as Flixe held out the bag of peardrops and she took one at once.

'Thanks muchly,' she said with the first pleasant expression Flixe had seen on her face. It improved her, but its eagerness did much to reinforce Flixe's suspicions.

'Be upstanding!'

Standing with Connie between the warders, Ming looked down into the well of the court and saw the squat figure of Roger Sillhorne. He looked so self-satisfied that she was suddenly struck by how much she hated him. The strength of her feeling shocked her. Roger looked up, caught her eye and obviously had no difficulty understanding her expression. He glared back at her, looking as angry – and as disgusted – as she had ever seen him. For once being the butt of someone's anger did not trouble Ming at all. Her own loathing of him took precedence over every other feeling.

As the judge lowered his heavy frame into the great red leather chair, it struck Ming that although she might be facing a prison cell Roger was confronting the possible ruin of his entire career. If she and Connie were to win and the Crown did not take over the costs of the action, as it might very well not, then Roger would have to pay. As Ming knew, he had no money beyond his parliamentary salary.

Into her hatred sprung a little pity for him, which made it bearable.

'Members of the jury,' said the judge, leaning forward

slightly and looking more Horus-like than ever, 'although the issues in this case are very simple, your task is a difficult one. It is your duty to decide whether or not a crime has been committed. In order to help you in making your decision I shall summarise the evidence.

'The prosecution has alleged that the translation of part of a French novel called *Story of a Lost Love*, which was published in the defendants' magazine, *The World Beyond*, is obscene – that is, that it would tend to deprave or corrupt those who might read it. You must decide whether you agree.

'What you must not do is decide whether or not you believe that the magazine article was unpleasant, vulgar or in bad taste. Those are not crimes. Much is published that a great many of us would prefer not to read, but this court has no jurisdiction over matters of taste.

'In coming to your decision you must take no account of other publications you have read which you might consider to be more obscene than this, or indeed less. A comparison with other published matter is not allowed as a defence.

'Learned Counsel for the Defence has argued that the publication of this piece was for the "public good" in so far as it was intended to dispel ignorance of a matter that is now the subject of a parliamentary committee. It is for you to decide whether that is true or not. If it is true then you are entitled to offer a verdict of "not guilty", because the law allows such a defence.

'That is your task, ladies and gentlemen: to decide who is likely to read the publication; whether it would tend to deprave and corrupt them; whether that tendency would be outweighed by the greater public good of increased knowledge of the subject of the article.

'Copies of the publication will be handed to you. You must read them again carefully, taking as long as you want, refer to all the evidence you have heard, and then deliver your verdict. If you have any difficulties with points of law please ask and I shall do my best to elucidate them.'

The three women and nine men shuffled out of their benches, taking copies of *The World Beyond* with them. Once they had gone and the judge had retreated to his room, there was a noticeable relaxation in the court. Julia leaned sideways to exchange some apparently cheerful comments with her antagonist, who seemed happy to smile at her and even seemed to be applauding something she said to him.

Flixe got up from her seat beside the woman who might have written Ming's letters, and found a place beside Mark in the last bench in the gallery.

'What do you think?' she asked.

He shook his head and ran both hands through his floppy brown hair. Flixe thought that he looked as though he had not slept.

'I don't know.'

'I'm going to go down to see whether they'll let me see her. Will you come? Show her, at least, that you don't care what the verdict is?' As she spoke Flixe was surprised to see the expression of drawn anxiety disappear into something that looked almost like happiness.

'She knows how much I care for her and that whatever the verdict is, it will make no difference,' he said with unassailable confidence.

"Ah,' said Flixe, realising that there had been some communication between the two of them after all. 'I'm glad. Well, I think I'll go down. If you're staying up here, will . . . ?'

'Yes?' There was some amusement in the grey eyes that looked so intelligently at her. Flixe smiled slightly in return.

'That unpleasant woman in the front row who seems to have a peculiarly personal animosity towards Ming is here again today. Can you find out who she is?' The amusement in Mark's eyes was replaced by surprise.

'I could try, I suppose. I'll do my best.'

Flixe left and went to find Ming sitting quietly on one of the leather-covered seats outside the court. Connie was walking up and down, but Ming hardly moved at all. Her legs were crossed and she held her gloves and small black patent-leather bag in her lap. She still looked ill, but in her deliberate stillness, Flixe recognised the courage that Peter had always seen.

'Well?' Flixe said as she sat down beside her sister. 'What do you think?'

'Julia told us at one of those conferences before all this started that when a judge gives a clear direction in an obscenity trial the jury tend to do what they're told, but that when he lets them make their own decision, they don't agree. Nothing could have been fairer or more even-handed than the summing-up we've just heard.'

'A disagreement would be better than being convicted,' said Gerry from the other side of Ming. She shook her head.

'In stern principle, perhaps, but not in reality; if they were not to agree a verdict, there would have to be another trial. The expenses of this one are going to be hard enough to meet. A second could ruin both Connie and myself.'

'And it's such a gamble,' said Flixe. 'I've never served on a jury, but friends of mine have and their descriptions of the kind of thing they base their decisions on are terrifying.'

A deliberately ironic smile disturbed the unnatural calm of Ming's face.

'That's very comforting, Flixe. Thank you.'

'Oh, damn!' she said, irritated with her own clumsiness. It was as though all her skills of managing other people had deserted her when she needed them most. 'I'd better shut up.'

Ming laughed out loud then.

'Poor Connie,' she said, watching the tall slim figure loping from one end of the hall to the other.

'It's no worse for her than it is for you,' said Gerry, immediately angry and partisan. Ming turned her head slowly to smile at her eldest sister.

'Yes, it is. She set up the magazine for Max. If we have to close it down, then she'll feel she's failed him twice over. It's not so bad for me – not nearly so bad. There's only me, and all I'd lose would be a ready market for my articles. I'd just have to work harder to get them published elsewhere.'

Gerry looked so taken aback that Ming allowed herself to chuckle.

'I told you, Gerry: I'm not a child, and I'm not afraid any

more; well, not much afraid. Even of prison. Whatever comes will come and I'll deal with it in whatever way I can.'

'Good for you!'

The exclamation had come, most unexpectedly, from Mr Ratterley. He held out his hand. Ming, surprised but pleased, shook it.

'I'd like to retain you as a special adviser to clients facing trial,' he went on. 'I don't know that I've ever seen such good sense or, I might add, good manners. You and Miss Wroughton are a splendid example of ... a splendid example.'

'I'm very touched,' said Ming. 'May I tell Connie what you've said later?'

'If you think,' he was beginning when the doors to the court were opened and the usher beckoned.

'Connie!' called Ming. Smiling at her sisters, she collected Connie and together they walked back to the dock.

'Chin up,' Connie whispered as they climbed into it.

'Good luck, Miss,' said one of the uniformed warders.

Ming was astonished and delighted, but there was no time to say anything in return. The jury emerged from their room and shuffled back into their allotted places. Ming thought that most of them looked satisfied, but could not decide what that meant.

The familiar cry of 'Be upstanding' echoed and for the last time, they stood to await the judge's arrival.

'Members of the jury,' said the usher, standing squarely in front of the jury box, 'are you agreed upon your verdict?'

'We are,' said the foreman, one of the grey-suited, middle-aged men who might have been a schoolmaster.

'How say you?'

Flixe, sitting beside Mark, felt her left hand grasped. She found it difficult to breathe and was astonished by the lack of emotion shown by both Ming and Connie.

'Not guilty.'

Despite her calm, Ming was so overwhelmed by the verdict that she could not concentrate on what was happening all around her. She clutched the rail in front of the dock and felt dizziness rocking her. The judge said something before he retired from the court, but she could not remember afterwards what it was. The warders congratulated her. Connie kissed her. Ming kissed Julia and shook Mr Ratterley's hand once more. Gerry hugged Ming. Roger stared at her for what felt like a full minute.

His dark eyes looked like holes in his white face and his lips were twisted into a death-like grimace. He looked desperate. Then someone walked between them and hid him from her sight.

Somehow Ming reached the doors to the cold-floored hall, where Flixe was waiting. She, too, flung her arms around Ming.

'We must go and celebrate,' said Connie. 'Ming, what would you like to do?'

Everyone heard the invitation but Ming. She was staring over Flixe's shoulder, oblivious of everyone else. Flixe disengaged herself, half-turned, saw Mark, and quickly said:

'Actually, as I told Ming on the telephone this morning, I've prepared a celebration lunch, which is waiting for us at home with Peter. Will you all come?'

As the others agreed, Flixe hustled them away, murmuring a reminder to Ming as they left.

'Mark?' Ming's voice was tentative and slightly husky, as though she had not used it that day.

'Congratulations,' he said, stopping about three yards away from her.

Ming walked towards him with as much effort as though she were wading through seawater over an uneven beach. When she was close enough she put out both hands. Mark reached for them at once.

'Ming.' His voice quivered and, as his hands closed over hers, Ming could feel them shaking too.

'Are you all right?' he asked clumsily. A smile like sunlight on shallow water broke over Ming's face.

'I am now,' she said. 'Mark, let's get out of here.'

Together they left the Old Bailey, looked conscientiously for the others, whom Flixe had spirited into a taxi that was already on its way to Kensington, and walked slowly down towards the river. When they reached Blackfriars, Ming stopped.

'Where are we going, Mark?'

He looked around, as though he had just woken up, and shook his head.

'I don't know – or care very much. Ming, darling, I can't tell you ...'

'Tell me what?' she asked gently. 'You don't have to tell me anything you don't want, but ...'

'I do want to tell you all of it, if you can bear to listen, but what I meant then was that I can't tell you how much I've hated sitting watching you go through all that, quite unable to help.'

'Your roses helped,' she said, cupping the flower on her lapel with gentle fingers. 'They helped a lot.'

Something about the way she touched the rose petals suggested that she really did care. Mark resisted the temptation to sweep her into his arms amid the hurrying lunch-time crowds.

'I'm glad,' he said, making an effort to sound calm and normal. 'Ming, there's an awful lot I want to say to you – and ask you, too – but your sister's expecting you. Shall I take you to her house? We could talk on the way. Or we could meet later if you'd rather.'

'Shall we meet later? I have a feeling that we'll need time, more time than a taxi-ride to Kensington.'

'You're probably right. What time will you ...? No, how can you guess that? Dinner tonight, or do you want to be with your family?'

'I'd rather be with you tonight,' she said simply. 'But I must go to Flixe's lunch now. She's planned it all so carefully for us. Shall I meet you somewhere this evening?'

Not wanting to let her out of his sight until they broke through the misunderstandings of the past few months, Mark was tempted to ask if he could wait for her in her flat. But if she had wanted that she would have said so. He had too much at stake to risk it by snatching at her.

'What about the Ivy again? We had such a good dinner there before the Attingers' dance.'

'Couldn't we go somewhere new?' Ming asked without analysing her powerful need to avoid the places where they had been together in the past. 'I loved it, but it would be nice to go somewhere we've never been before.'

'All right.' There was a look of understanding in Mark's grey eyes and a smile of great affection on his lips. 'We'll start again. What about Stephano's in Dean Street? It's said to be very good.'

'I'll be there at half-past seven. Mark, thank you for being in court today and ... and for being you.'

He touched her face very briefly with his ungloved hand and then turned away to summon a taxi for her. As soon as the cab had driven away Mark walked quickly towards the tube station, feeling young again and half-drunk with excitement. He wondered how on earth he was going to fill the hours until half-past seven and could not stop himself from imagining what she might say to him and how she might look at him.

He spared a glance for the view down the river, which he had always loved. The mixture of dereliction, cranes and building sites, and the wonderful, galleried dome of St Paul's rising above it all pleased him to a degree that seemed surprising. He though that perhaps it was the knowledge of St Paul's survival that gave him such a feeling of comfort: among the innumerable things that are lost to time, mischance, and malice, some endure.

The lunch at Flixe's house was long, lavish and very emotional. Peter Suvarov was at the front door to greet Ming when she eventually arrived and he held out his arms. Leaning against him, she listened to his voice telling her of his pride in her, and she felt the first waves of exultant triumph pound through her. At last she stood back.

'It's over,' she said, meaning the trial. A strange expression twisted his mouth.

'I know,' he said. 'Flixe has told me. If he's good enough for you, I'm very glad.'

'I didn't mean that,' she answered, understanding immediately what he had intended. 'But he is. More than that. I hope you'll like him. That matters.'

Peter's old, beloved smile took the bitterness from his face. He carefully took out the hatpin that held Ming's hat skewered to her hair, lifted the hat away and kissed the top of her head.

'If you love him, I'll like him. Come on, the others are waiting.'

He ushered Ming into the pale, trellised drawing room, where Flixe thrust a glass of champagne into her hand.

'I've telephoned the parents. They're terribly pleased and both send their love. If you can bear it, they'd love to speak to you.'

'I'd better ring. May I, Flixe?'

'Yes, but quick as you can. Julia has to rush back to chambers as soon as we've finished lunch.'

Ming went into the chilly little room where the telephone and shoe-cleaning equipment were kept and asked the operator for her parents' telephone number. Her mother answered.

'Hello,' Ming said, suddenly unsure of her welcome.

'Ming darling, is that you?'

'Mother! Yes, it's me. We won.'

'I know. Flixe telephoned the news. It is such a relief. We both wanted to say congratulations and to send our love.'

'Daddy too?' said Ming doubtfully.

'Yes. He still doesn't understand why you did any of it, and he's still bothered by it, but of course he's as relieved as I am about the verdict.'

'I'm glad. It's a bit much to hope that he'd understand.'

'I think it is. May I give him your love?'

The quick smile on Ming's face made her voice warm.

'Please. And lots of it to you, too. There go the pips. I'd better stop. It's Flixe's telephone. Goodbye.'

'Goodbye, darling. Thank you for ringing.'

Ming returned to the party. Sitting between Max and David Wallington, she did little justice to the hot consommé, cold lobster or iced bombe, and she found she could not talk much. But the pleasure and exuberance of her friends and family were celebration enough.

Connie's face had returned to its customary relaxed amusement and it was only then that Ming realised how different it had become during the horrible weeks of uncertainty. She was sitting between Peter and Tibor Smith, talking as though she had been a prisoner in a Trappist monastery for years.

As soon as Flixe and her elder daughter had cleared the pudding plates, Julia got up.

'It's agony leaving you all,' she said, 'but I have to go.'

Ming got up at once and walked round the table to stand in front of her.

'It's no time for speeches, Julia,' she said, 'and my brain feels like scrambled eggs in any case. But even in this state it knows how much we all owe you. Thank you.'

She leaned forward to kiss Julia's cheek and Flixe was delighted to see that Julia actually put a hand on Ming's shoulder. There was obviously no need to tell Julia that David had actually summoned Mark to Ming's side.

'It was a pleasure to defend you,' Julia said sincerely. She was in such a hurry to get back to her work that she did not see the affectionate, approving smile that Tibor sent her or the pleasure on Flixe's face.

Ming herself was the next to go, wanting plenty of time to have her hair done and wash the smells of the court off her skin before her meeting with Mark.

As she lay in her long bath, letting both the hot water and the knowledge of her new freedom lull her into peace, she kept thinking of Mark and wondering whether they would ever be able to build for each other the security that she had hardly even let herself dream about. For the first time in her life it seemed to be within her reach and completely desirable.

At exactly half-past seven she paid off her taxi outside the restaurant and went in to find him.

He was waiting for her in the bar and stood up as soon as he saw her.

'You look lovely,' he said as he took in the richness of her sapphire brocade dress. 'And older too.'

As he spoke Mark realised that he had chosen his words badly, but he was too experienced to try to mend matters by taking back what he had said.

'That was clumsy,' he said. 'Do you mind?'

Another wonderful smile lit Ming's eyes and her lips curled as she shook her head.

'That I no longer look like a terrified schoolgirl?' she said. 'I'm delighted – and glad that the change shows; it's real enough.'

'That's all right then,' said Mark with an indescribable satisfaction in his voice. 'Come and have a drink?'

'Thank you.'

He took her into the cosy, wine-dark bar and ordered martinis for them both. Then, sitting beside her on the luxuriously cushioned velvet bench, he seemed lost for words. After a while he said:

'Were you very frightened?'

'In general or of the trial?'

'I meant the trial.'

'Yes,' said Ming, looking a little bleak. 'Terrified of the obvious things: being found guilty; being fined more than I could afford to pay; having to sell the flat and beg a room somewhere; having to go back to a dead-end job I hated; perhaps even being shut up in a cell in Holloway.'

The barman brought their martinis. Mark picked his up and drank. Ming picked the olive out of hers and ate it. She looked round, but the only other people in the bar seemed to be completely absorbed in their own affairs.

'And the less obvious things?'

'What?' said Ming, having forgotten what she had said. 'Oh, I see. All sorts of things.'

She turned her martini glass round and round on the table in front of her. Mark waited. After a while she looked frankly at him.

'There were times when I woke at four in the morning and I couldn't get to sleep again when I thought that the trial was the price I was paying for having been such a coward for so long.'

'You've never been a coward.' Mark's instinctive protest

told Ming a great deal about his feelings. If they had been alone she would have hugged him.

'Oh, yes, I have. I've stopped myself doing and saying innumerable things because I thought they might make people angry. I've been afraid of other people's anger for years and years. It seemed somehow inevitable that I would be punished when I eventually did break silence.'

Ming picked up her own drink and sipped it, shuddering slightly as the barely diluted spirit hit her palate.

'But the nightmare's over now,' said Mark, gripping her free hand as it lay on the velvet bench. 'I'm beginning to think that all our nightmares might be over.'

Ming turned her blonde head so that she could look at him properly. The lighting was so discreet that his face was shadowed, but she could see the gleam of his eyes and the confidence of his smile. Smiling herself, she asked:

'What was yours, Mark?'

'That you might be kind to me.'

Of all the things Ming had thought he might say that was the last she would have expected. She peered at him in the romantic gloom, her head on one side.

'I don't understand. When were you afraid of that? And why?'

'Your table is ready, sir.'

'What?' Mark looked towards the voice that had interrupted them, saw the waiter's white coat and dropped Ming's hand at once.

'Thank you,' he said. He stood up. 'Ming?'

She got up off the purple velvet banquette and preceded him into the dining room, wincing a little as the brighter light hit her eyes. Almost every table seemed to be filled and as she stood there, she felt as though all the other diners broke off their conversation and looked at her.

The waiter led them to a table against the mirrored wall about half-way down the restaurant. As they sat down, another waiter brought their first course of hot crab soufflé and then reached for the bottle that had been chilling in an ice-bucket and poured them each a glass of wine.

'I ordered for us both,' said Mark, watching her. 'It seemed easier. Do you mind?'

Ming shook her head. Laying down the knife and fork she had just picked up, she said abruptly:

'Why, Mark?'

'I thought that was what your Christmas letter meant,' he said with a small shrug. 'It sounded as though you were offering to do whatever I wanted simply out of kindness. The thought was unendurable.'

'Oh, dear. Yes, I do see. Mark . . . I . . .'

'Don't worry about it now, but tell me something.'

'Can I ask you something first?'

Surprised and a little worried, Mark nodded.

'Why did you resign?' asked Ming, sounding breathless.

'I'm surprised that you of all people need to ask that.'

Ming's legs started to tingle and the olive and the martini she had just swallowed felt like a cold curdled mess in the pit of her stomach. All the delight and certainty that she had felt since he had stroked her cheek drained out of her.

'I'm sorry,' she said and put a hand up to cover her eyes.

She felt Mark's hand on her wrist, pulling her arm down to the table again with urgent strength.

'Ming, what is it? What have I said?'

She looked at him with huge, dark eyes. There was no light in them at all and her lips quivered slightly.

'I never meant to damage you, Mark,' she said slowly. Her tongue felt thick and clumsy, and it made the words difficult to articulate. 'I do seem to cause dreadful trouble. Whoever it is, is right about that at least.'

'What on earth are you talking about? You haven't damaged me. Ming, don't look so tragic. I just thought that you'd understand. After all, you put it so neatly in your article. I agreed with everything you wrote about Suez. And feeling like that, I decided that I had to resign. That's all. There's nothing to frighten you about that.'

Relief made Ming feel almost as sick as she had before his explanation.

'I thought it was because of me,' she said after she had drunk some wine. 'I thought they'd sacked you because of what I'd written. It was all part of the same nightmare ... all my old terrors of making people angry translated into adult punishments. And although they should have been mine, both punishments were visited on other people.'

The waiter came back, saw that both of them had hardly touched the food on their plates and backed away.

'We'd better eat,' said Ming, noticing his unspoken reprimand.

Mark looked into the mirror behind her and saw what she had seen. He picked up his fork.

'Oh, Ming,' he said before he ate anything. 'I seem to have made you dreadfully unhappy this past year. I'm sorry.'

Her eyes did lighten then and she smiled at him.

'That makes two of us. It was David Wallington who showed me how bloody I've been to you. It wasn't deliberate cruelty, Mark. None of it was. It was only because ...' She broke off, noticing that several of their neighbours were listening avidly.

'I never thought it was deliberate. But you are right. We'd better eat.' He, too, saw the interested faces all around them.

When they had finished their first course, the waiter substituted plates of veal cooked in marsala, and handed them their vegetables.

'I do like your magazine, you know,' said Mark in a more conversational tone of voice.

'Really?' Pleasure showed in Ming's smile. 'I wouldn't have thought it was exactly your thing.'

'Perhaps not. And perhaps before Suez I didn't sympathise quite so much with your desire to explain and reveal things to the powerless.'

'But now?'

'Now I've begun to think that secrets may be over-rated – and power too.'

'You're surely not saying that governments should not have any secrets from their own citizens?' said Ming, thoroughly interested. 'That's hardly practical in a world where we still have plenty of enemies.'

'No, it's not practical. And the government must be allowed to govern. I suppose it's a bit like your statement about pornography at the trial.'

Ming nodded. 'We all know exactly where we would draw the line between the acceptable and the unbearable, but everyone's line is different.'

'Tricky, isn't it?' said Mark, swallowing the last of his veal. 'That's why I got out. Pudding?'

'No, thank you. That was wonderful.' She thought of suggesting that they went back to her flat for coffee, but just as she was about to speak she caught the eye of a woman sitting at the next table and raised her eyebrows. The woman flushed and looked away.

'I think I'd better get the bill.' Mark's voice was full of amusement and she knew that he had understood both her intention and its frustration.

Ming's own smile widened and she bent her head in the familiar gesture of graceful acquiescence. It was not until they were sitting side by side in a taxi that she asked:

'Will you come in for a moment when we get there?'

Mark took her hand in the darkness and did not speak for a moment. At last he said with some difficulty:

'I suppose that the thought of your being kind to me still fills me with a kind of horror.'

'It need not. I can promise you no kindness at all.'

He looked down at her.

'Then I'd like to come in very much,' he said.

As she opened the door and stood aside he stepped across the threshold.

'Coffee?'

'Thank you.'

She made it and carried it to the drawing room, where he stood looking at the painting of the cool, empty northern seascape.

'It's beautiful, but awfully lonely.'

'I know,' she said as she put down the tray and waited for him to take her in his arms. But he did not. After a while she poured their coffee and began to understand that he was not going to make any move at all. He was leaving her absolutely free to decide what she wanted. He had told her everything about his love for her without asking for anything in return.

Here, she realised, was a man who was not demanding that she yield to him in any way at all. When she had tried to do that physically he had rejected her. What he was asking was much more difficult than a surrender: he wanted a treaty with an equal.

'I'm beginning to think,' Ming said slowly as she watched his serious face, 'that you are the first person I have ever known who has treated me as an adult.'

Mark's face creased into a smile. He drained his cup and held it out for her to take.

As their hands briefly touched Ming felt a tremendous pull towards him. She wanted him to hold on to her, to touch her, to make love to her and to answer the questions she longed to ask and could not: do you love me best of all? Will you forgive me whatever I do? Will you swear never to leave me? Will you make me safe for ever? She knew that if she had not let herself love him the questions need never have been asked, just as she knew that, loving him, she could never expect him to answer them.

Peter Suvarov's words came back to her: 'Being prepared for really swingeing hurt.'

She put down her own cup on the tray with Mark's and went to stand in front of him, putting her hands on his arms. He bent his head and she felt the soft resilience of his lips on hers and the strength of his hands on her back. Her breathing quickened and she could feel his heart slamming against his ribs. Her lips opened and she let herself lean against him. Mark's arms tightened. At last he lifted his head.

'This is different from the last time, isn't it?'

'Quite, quite different,' said Ming. 'Then I was trying to pay a debt.'

'And now?'

'Now, I only want to love you.'

CHAPTER 26

They woke early next morning, soon after six, and lay side by side in an ecstasy of freedom. For the first time since Mark had asked Ming to marry him more than a year earlier they were able to be completely honest with each other. Because they had shared them, their feelings were no longer the stuff of nightmares.

At one moment, Ming leaned sideways to kiss Mark as he lay with his eyes closed. She thought that he looked wonderful propped up against the banked-up pillows with his splendid shoulders rising above the bedclothes. All the strength that he usually disguised was plain to see, even though he was quite relaxed. There was stubble on his chin and grey-brown arcs were smudged under his eyes, but he seemed desperately attractive, very male, and utterly familiar. The misery they had caused each other in that room could be forgotten at last.

He slid an arm under her back and held her close. The curtains had not been properly shut the night before and the pale, early sun poured through on to the foot of the bed, lighting the crumpled white linen bedspread and the pale green blankets. Their clothes were hanging over the back of a damask-covered elbow chair but the rest of the room was impeccably tidy and very pretty.

Ming had cut down some of his roses and arranged them in a pair of silver vases on her dressing table, where they were reflected endlessly in the triple glass. Their dark red seemed oddly strong against the pale greens, creams and delicate pinks of the room, but their scent was heady and sweet.

'Mark,' said Ming, taking courage from the feeling of his shoulder under her cheek.

'Mm?' He sounded lazily happy and half-asleep, but Ming was determined to tell him everything.

'Yesterday you talked about your fears of what I might do, and I let you do it, which I think was rather unfair,' she said, waking him fully. Before he could protest, she went on: 'Most of what went wrong with us was my fault, not yours.'

'I don't think fault comes into it,' he said, stroking her warm cheek with his right hand. Her fine hair was tousled, which he liked better than the ordered waves of the previous evening.

'Perhaps not. But I was muddled too. Can I tell you about it?'

'If you want to. But there's no need, Ming. We're here with each other again. Isn't that enough?'

'I'd like you to know,' she said carefully. 'You see, I used to tell myself sometimes that the reason I could never love anyone was because of what happened to me in the war. I knew that it had left me with a terror of being in anyone else's control, but ...'

'What happened?'

Mark's voice sounded rough. A little surprised, Ming pulled away to look at him and then relaxed again as she saw his eyes. For a long time he had hidden all but the most manageable emotions. His new readiness to reveal them moved her. As she watched the strength in his face yielding to anxiety, she could think of nothing except how much he mattered to her.

'Ming?'

'It's shamingly trivial compared with most people's stories,' she said when she could speak again. 'You know I went over to France? Well, on the way back to London I was picked up by some people who were working for ... against us.'

Mark's hand gripped hers suddenly, but he did not speak.

'All that happened was that my hair was pulled, my face slapped a bit and my arms twisted,' she said quickly to comfort him. 'But it was vile. For a long time I ... But there's no point talking about it now.'

He moved closer to her so that their shoulders touched again.

Ming, I wish I'd been able to ...' He broke off, shaking his head. 'I wish that I could take away everything that has ever hurt you, but that's childish. We are what we are because of what has happened to us.'

'I know that now,' said Ming. 'Besides, I've learned rather painfully and unforgivably slowly that it wasn't what happened then that stopped me from understanding how much I loved you.'

'No?' Despite the brevity of his intervention, his voice was full of compassion. 'You don't have to tell me anything, Ming.'

'It was my terror of what would happen to me if I let myself love you and then you stopped wanting me, if I lost you as I always seemed to lose the people I loved.'

The difficulty of her confession almost broke Ming's self-control, but her need to make him understand at last forced her through it. He put both arms around her and cradled her head against his shoulder. She felt his chin on her head, comfortingly solid.

'Barring accidents, you're not going to lose me without a great deal of trouble. I'm a dogged sort of chap, you know.'

'You sound wonderfully British, Mark,' said Ming, laughing again. Later, as she sat up, she said: 'I'm glad you're dogged. I'd better do something about breakfast.'

'Let me do that,' he said. 'I'm quite good at bacon and eggs, too.'

Ming looked at him suspiciously but she was disarmed by the conscious wickedness of his smile. It seemed as though everything that had gone wrong between them in the past could be mended with ease now, and that however important the feeling between them they could take it lightly and laugh.

'That would be lovely. I shall go and have a bath,' she said graciously, adding in a less stately voice: 'and if there's a brown frill around the edges of the eggs I'll personally book you in for a cookery class.'

'Sounds like a challenge, Ming! I'm a dangerous man to put on his mettle. It brings out all my worst stubbornness.'

She shrugged herself into her pale green cotton dressing-gown and knotted the sash round her waist before going to run her bath. When she came back into the bedroom, she sat on the edge of the bed. There she took his face between her hands and kissed him.

'I love you for your stubbornness.'

He lay, looking up at her and wanting to tell her how much he loved and needed her, but he wanted to make her laugh, too. She had a wonderful laugh, rare but chuckling and lovely to hear.

'Only for my stubbornness?' he said, sounding theatrically sad.

Ming took her hands away from his face, laid them side by side on his chest and shook her head. Her lips were severely still, but she could not prevent the gleam in her deep blue eyes or the slight quivering of her nostrils.

'It's a rather unattractive attribute for you to have chosen from my armoury of charms,' he said, feeling the effort she was making to keep her face serious. 'My profile, for instance,' he added, turning his head sideways on the pillow and fluttering his brown eyelashes over his grey eyes.

Looking at his slightly blunt nose and firm chin silhouetted against the white linen, Ming could not hold on to her frown any longer. As she laughed, he sat up and swung her back across the bed. With his hands on her shoulders he gazed at her face. To him it was infinitely more beautiful in its broad, unqualified amusement than in the calm, untouched perfection she showed most people.

'God! How I love it when you laugh,' he said and then suddenly sat up and listened.

There was an ominously liquid sound coming from beyond the bedroom door.

'Oh, no! The bath,' said Ming and ran to mop up the

growing pool of water on the bathroom floor.

Twenty minutes later she was sitting at the kitchen table watching as Mark slid a perfectly fried egg between two rashers of bacon and two halves of grilled tomato onto a warmed plate. A pot of coffee stood in the middle of the table beside a rack of hot toast.

'I have to admit,' she said, watching him from under her eyelashes, 'no brown frills.'

'I'll forgive you for the slur.' Mark poured coffee for them both and handed her the sugar bowl. 'Ming, I ... Can we choose a date?'

'For a wedding?' Ming smiled at him and reached across the table to him. He took her hand. 'Yes, let's. I ought to talk to my parents first, I suppose. Some time in the summer?'

'Oh, no! Must we wait that long? Can't I whisk you off now? No, I suppose you're right. June?'

'How about July? That should give us enough time to get everything sorted out. Where shall we live? Do you have to stay in Oxford?'

'Not for much longer. In fact July would be a good month, because I'm supposed to be setting up a London office for the firm in the autumn. Where would you like to live, Ming? Here to start with? Or would that be taking advantage of you?' Mark stirred a spoonful of sugar into his coffee and drank.

Ming shook her head, tucking a stray curl behind her ear. 'I'm very fond of this flat, and I'd love to stay – if it wouldn't cramp your style.'

'I love it too,' said Mark, looking around the comfortable kitchen with its red-painted Windsor chairs, the pale grey floor and white cupboards and the big practical red dresser full of an odd but pretty mixture of unmatching china. 'I feel at home here. We can always move later if we need more space.'

'Good, that's settled. I suppose I'd better go and ring up my parents before Flixe jumps the gun. We'll have to go down and stay. Shall you mind?'

'No. But oughtn't I to talk to your father first?'

Ming laughed. 'Mark, my love, I'm thirty-two – not in my father's gift any longer, even if I once was.'

'That's a relief I must say. It would be pretty hard to answer any questions about how I intend to keep you in the manner to which you are accustomed.'

While Ming was telephoning her parents, whose obvious relief made her smile, the post arrived. She handed the receiver to Mark when her mother asked to speak to him and went to collect her letters. When she came back into the kitchen, Mark said:

'Your mother was charming. She's invited me for this weekend. I said "Yes". Was that all right?'

'Fine,' said Ming in an abstracted tone of voice. At once Mark got up out of his chair and went to stand beside her.

'What is it?' The morning's mockery had gone from his voice but all the warmth was still there. 'Ming, what's happened?'

She shook her head and ripped open the top envelope. When she had read the few lines, she handed him the letter.

Ming, are you satisfied now? Having forced one man out of his job and his home, you've now managed to ruin another. Wasn't it enough for you to make them both unspeakably miserable? Does it give you pleasure to strew unhappiness among the people who are misguided enough to admire you? Well I for one have never been misled by your sugary voice and your little bones and your expensive clothes. I have always known you for the bitch-destroyer that you are.

'What on earth?' Mark's furious voice whipped through the sickening hurt in Ming's mind. 'Who's it from?'

Ming shrugged her slim shoulders.

'I've no idea. It's one of a series. They've all been a bit like that, if not quite as ... quite as explicit.'

'Who is the man you forced out of a job?' Mark seemed genuinely puzzled, and Ming smiled. There was sadness in her eyes as well as amusement and a faint, ineradicable fear.

'You, my dear. Your departure from the Civil Service gave

whoever it is a lot of scope. It's one of the reasons why I so hesitated to get in touch with you again after your resignation.'

Ming picked up her cup and drank a mouthful of coffee, making a face as she realised that it was nearly cold. When she looked at Mark again she saw that he was still angry. She felt that she ought to have known that the heavenly peace and security of the morning could not last, and she hated her correspondent for breaking into it so soon.

'Did you think that it was me? That I would do something like this?'

Ming shook her head. For a minute she could not speak at all.

'These letters have come once a fortnight for about a year,' she said at last. 'When they started to refer to you by name and to accuse me of not only hurting you but ruining your life, I . . .'

'When was that?'

'By about October or November, I think,' said Ming, surprised by the sharpness of his question. 'I never believed that you were writing them, but then, when I was so distressed by the mess I'd made of things with you, for a time I was terribly afraid.' When he said nothing, she added quietly: 'You do see the difference, don't you?'

At that question, he managed a smile again.

'Yes,' he said. 'Of course I see the difference. It's not sensible to feel ... bothered by it, because how could you possibly have known that I wasn't like that.' He pointed to the letter lying on the kitchen table.

Ming went to fetch a glass of water. She ran the tap into the sink until the water felt really cold. The bite of it against her teeth seemed to help.

'I hate hurting you,' she said. 'But at this stage pretending would have been worse.'

'I'm glad you didn't pretend.'

Ming swung around so fast that she had to hold on to the sink with her free hand.

'Really?'

'Yes. Now, we've obviously got to find out who is writing

this rubbish and get it stopped. Have you no clues at all?'

'Flixe,' said Ming with a slightly derisive note in her voice, 'believes it is a woman smelling of violet scent with a passion for nail-varnish remover – or peardrops.'

'Now I understand.'

Ignoring the letter on the table, Mark joined her by the sink and put a comforting arm around her shoulders.

'Your sister asked me about a woman who was in the Old Bailey gallery every day. She must be the suspect.'

'Mark, what are you talking about?' Ming put the empty glass down on the draining board.

'Your sister spent most of the second morning of your trial talking to a peculiar woman and feeding her pear-drops. When she – Mrs Suvarov, I mean – left the gallery while the jury were out she asked me to find out who the woman is. That must be why.'

'And did you find out who she is?' asked Ming, almost reluctant to have her enemy identified after so long.

'Her name is Veronica Dickenden,' he said. 'She's in her late twenties, I imagine, rather plump, adequately dressed, poppy brown eyes, slightly down-at-heel shoes and a lot of rather slapdash make-up.'

'I see,' said Ming, understanding at last how the writer had discovered so much about her.

'Do you know her?'

'Not really. She's Roger Sillhorne's secretary: the one who took over after me. What an anticlimax!'

'Why that?'

'I've spent so long being terrified that someone I cared for hated me and to discover the writer is a comparative stranger makes all the anguish seem ridiculous ... wasted.' Ming blinked, as though she could not see very well. 'I'm slightly puzzled as to why she should have been quite so angry with me.'

'From what you've told me there's no actual proof that it was her.'

'No,' said Ming with a smile at his caution. 'But it seems oddly convincing. I shall have to find out for certain. I'd better see her.'

Ming went to put on the kettle so that she could make a new pot of hot coffee.

'It's none of my business, Ming,' said Mark, 'except that everything that bothers you is my business; but mightn't it be better just to ignore her?'

'If I do, she might never stop. No. I must do something about it.' She smiled at him suddenly. 'For my sake as much as to stop her. I've cowered away from it all for too long. A confrontation is necessary.'

'Perhaps she might stop anyway, now that the case is over.'

'You sound remarkably optimistic, Mark. There's ...'

'Who wouldn't be optimistic in my place? Last night was the summit of my dreams, and this morning you have given me everything I ever wanted.'

'I'm glad.'

'And happy?' He stood up and held out his arms. Ming went to lean against him.

'Very happy,' she said. 'I suppose you'll have to go back to Oxford now. When will I see you?' Ming revelled in the freedom he had given her. Never before had she felt able to ask him a question like that; she had always waited for him.

'At the week-end. Shall I meet you at your parents or half-way?'

Ming made arrangements to collect him on her way to the Cotswolds on Friday evening and then said goodbye, far happier than she had ever expected to be. At the front door Mark stopped and turned back.

'Wouldn't you rather I saw this woman for you? If she's been writing that sort of stuff, who knows what she might actually say? I'd hate you to be faced with the sort of foulness she might produce.'

Ming thought for a while and at last smiled her most glorious smile as she shook her head.

'This is something I have to do, and it's something that I can do now. You've given me all the protection I need. Goodbye, Mark. 'Til Friday.'

'Will you telephone and let me know what happens?'

She nodded. He kissed her once more and left.

When he had gone, Ming tidied up her bedroom, smiling whenever she thought of the things he had said to her and the answers she had made. Armoured in happiness, she sat down at her desk to write a short note:

Dear Veronica, After yesterday's verdict, I very much want to make peace with Roger, but I am not quite sure how. Would you help me? I shall be having coffee in Brown's tea shop at half-past eleven. Will you meet me there?

It seemed a little unfair to use the woman's loyalty to Roger Sillhorne to cheat her into meeting Ming, but she could think of no other way of achieving the confrontation she wanted. She took the note to the familiar door into the House of Commons and asked one of the policemen on duty to get it delivered for her.

Twenty minutes later as she sat, taking as long as possible to drink her coffee, she saw Veronica arrive. Ming lifted her hand and watched Veronica identify her, pause for a moment in the doorway and then deliberately pick her way through the crowded tables.

'Thank you for coming,' said Ming, rising politely to shake hands. She could not help noticing the familiar violet scent and felt slightly sick. 'What will you have? Coffee, hot chocolate?'

'I'd rather have tea.'

Ming ordered it and waited until Veronica had poured her first cupful before she said anything. While she had waited for the girl to arrive she had practised several different opening gambits, none of which seemed quite right.

'I've been thinking,' she said at last, 'for over a year how much I wanted to talk to you.'

'Really?' Veronica's untidy eyebrows were raised and her voice sarcastic.

'Yes. At first I wanted to protest and explain how wrong your accusations were, and then later when I had learned to hate you I wanted some sort of revenge. Now I think that I ought to thank you.'

Veronica, who had been lifting the thick white cup to her

lips, stopped and put the cup clumsily back into its saucer. Ming watched the rich, brown tea slop from side to side, spilling over the edge of the cup.

'I don't know what you're talking about.' Veronica bridled like a pantomime villainess protesting innocence.

Ming felt certainty driving out her residual doubts. She laughed in deliberate provocation and discovered that she was enjoying herself.

'Did it never occur to you that we'd be able to find out who was writing the letters?'

'What d'you mean?' The high colour in Veronica's cheeks intensified.

'There's your scent for a start,' said Ming, still noticing it even over the smell of tea and coffee, and sugary buns, and the cigarette smoke that hung like a fog over the restaurant. 'And the typewriter. and even your fingerprints. Didn't you think of them?'

'No one's ever taken my fingerprints.'

'But they are identifiable and will be all the proof anyone needs.'

The woman's vivid blush faded into an ugly mottled look, reminding Ming horribly of a slice of mortadella. Veronica's hand shook as she raised her teacup to her lips and drank noisily.

'But I'm not interested in official proof,' Ming went on implacably, 'so much as in knowing why you went to all that trouble to find out about my circumstances, my friends and my family, in order to write those letters. I want to know what it was you thought I'd done to you.'

There was a pause and then Veronica put down her cup again and looked at Ming. The malice was quite obvious in Veronica's protuberant brown eyes.

'All right then, I'll tell you.' There was satisfaction now in the unintelligent voice. 'I hated you because of what you'd done to him. You made him twisted and cruel.'

'That's absurd,' said Ming without even pausing to consider her words. 'Roger's character is no responsibility of mine. I take it that you do mean Roger.'

'Oh, yes, it is your responsibility. Before you made him so

miserable, he was kind. Then afterwards he was ...'

'Before? Do you mean you knew him before you went to work with him?' Curiosity had got the better of Ming's determination to ask only directly relevant questions.

'You know that perfectly well,' said Veronica, almost spitting as she forced out the words in anger. 'I lived in the constituency. You've seen me there often enough, even though you never took any notice of me. Too stuck up and pleased with yourself. We were old friends. That's why you pretended never to know me, wasn't it? You'd always been jealous of us.'

Ming was not at all sure how much to believe, but she was certain that she ought not to encourage the fantasies by asking any more questions.

'I can only say that I am very sorry if he changed after I left his office and I am sorry that you were hurt, but ...'

'Hurt? That's a pathetic little word for what you did to me.' Veronica's voice rose alarmingly, but then she seemed to take control of herself again. 'I always read his letters to you, you know,' she added.

Remembering some of the things Roger had written about the woman sitting opposite her, Ming began to understand something of her bitterness.

'How?'

'He used to leave them on my desk for me to stamp and post. He never used to seal them up. I always had to do that, too. He must have meant me to read them, you see.'

Ming wondered why it was she and not Roger who had always been the target of Veronica's fury, but it did not seem politic to pursue the point.

'Well, it has to stop,' she said, unaware of quite how determined – or how commanding – she sounded. 'You have had a good run for your money.'

Ming picked up her bag and gloves and stood up.

'Why did you say you ought to thank me?' Veronica asked suddenly before Ming could go.

'Because you have taught me a great many valuable lessons.' Ming smiled. 'In trying to punish me for what you thought I had done to you, you and Roger have simply shown me that I am stronger than I ever thought I could be, and that most of the fears that used to rule my life are unimportant. You have done for me what none of my friends could do. You see, Veronica, I do not care what you think of me. Your hatred has no relevance at all. Your letters have set me free. Thank you.'

Ming bowed slightly and threaded her way between the tables and out into the clean air of the street. She no longer felt either afraid or guilty and the memory of Connie's lecture in Egypt no longer burned. Ming had learned to say what she thought, she had upset people, she had caused trouble and she had survived to do it all again if necessary.

CHAPTER 27

Ten weeks later Ming and Mark were married in St Margaret's, Westminster. She had yielded to her mother's plea for a big conventional wedding, although she thought the idea absurd and the weeks of argument and arrangements quite unnecessary. The entire fuss seemed irrelevant to the real things that she and Mark had already said to each other. If it had not been for her sisters and Julia Wallington, who all urged her to go on with the circus, she might have cancelled all the arrangements and exchanged the church for a register office.

Gerry's view was that a wedding provided a good excuse for a more lavish party than anything else and that the white dress and veil could be ignored as archaic props. Flixe thought that the whole occasion could be so splendidly theatrical that she could not understand why Ming did not revel in it. Julia added no direct persuasion, but simply described her own marriage before the registrar. She made the story funny, but her description was enough to persuade Ming of the advantages of a full-blown wedding. David added his persuasion by offering to arrange the reception on the terrace of the House of Commons.

But it was Mark who, after their second weekend with Ming's parents, produced the clinching argument.

'What does it matter? It's quite true that nothing we do or say can change the real things we've already said, but why not let them have it since they want it so much?

They've done their best for you all your life. It's little enough in return, Ming, and you could make them both so happy. Why not?'

Ming, who had been practising her new-found determination and refusal to please people for the sake of peace, capitulated at once.

Emerging from the church into glorious sunlight on her husband's arm, she was glad. She had not expected to enjoy the service, but as it unfolded she had been caught up in it and forgotten all her doubts. The familiar, sonorous words of the 1662 prayer book carried their own conviction and her senses responded powerfully to the rest.

The heavy scents of the white Bourbon roses and yellow and white lilies seemed to mingle with the singing and the organ and the tumbling clangour of the bells. The feeling of Mark's hand, firm and superbly confident in her own, reminded her of the physical reality of what she was doing and as they walked side by side down the aisle she felt buoyed up by the happiness she saw on the faces of her friends.

'Nearly done, darling,' Mark whispered as they stood in the warm sun ten minutes later, waiting amid their relations to be photographed.

Amanda Wallington and Fiona Suvarov, the two bridesmaids, looked enchantingly pretty in butter-coloured organdie with cream and yellow roses in their dark hair. A sudden hot wind blew their full skirts up above their waists and they shrieked with one voice. They gave the photographer the only relaxed picture of the afternoon. Both bride and groom were laughing as they leaned forward to help hold the skirts down and the rest of the group stood out of line, watching what was happening like human beings instead of standing like waxworks.

When the photographer had released them, they crossed Margaret Street and walked into the shadowed coolness of the Houses of Parliament, followed by a stream of family and friends, to emerge under the green-and-white awning on the terrace.

With all her new decisiveness in view, Ming refused to

stand by the entrance to the tent to be greeted.

'It only holds everyone up and makes them hot and cross without a drink. Let them come into the tent, get their champagne and if they want to talk to us they can cross the terrace and find us at the far end. Coming?'

'Brilliant idea, darling,' said Mark, putting his hand under her silken elbow. 'Fanny? Mother?'

Beaming at him, Ming's mother took his other arm, leaving her husband to escort Mark's widowed mother. They took charge then and made Ming stand in the middle of the line. That at least she was prepared to let them do.

She looked, as Mark had told her, adorable in a dress made of thick ivory silk. It had a deeply cut v-shaped neckline, a slim bodice and a spreading bell-like skirt. The elbow-length sleeves echoed the shape of the skirt, and the whole dress was of immense simplicity, its only ornament a row of silk-covered buttons down the centre of the bodice. With Connie's splendid tiara and her own brooch and earrings, she looked not only pretty but distinguished too.

People processed in front of her, kissing her, shaking her hand, telling her how well she looked, how glad they were that she had married Mark, how much they hoped she would be happy. She introduced her friends and relations to him and listened to the names of his, smiling, leaning forward and shaking hands, but when at last the line of guests had dissolved into a noisy, jostling muddle, she heaved a huge sigh.

'I need a drink,' she said, shocking Mark's mother, who found it hard to connect the bride's delicate looks with her unlikely strength of character. Ming's own parents found it hard, too, but were so pleased with Mark for marrying her that they managed to ignore it.

Mark presented her with a brimming glass of champagne and a smoked salmon sandwich, and drew her away from the others.

'Tuck in, darling,' he said with the mocking smile that she had come to love.

'Do I look fearfully greedy?' she asked with her mouth full.

'Fearfully! But I love it.'

She laughed, swallowed the last of the sandwich, drained her glass and squared her shoulders.

'That's better. I suppose we ought to plunge into the throng.'

'Probably. Do you want to go as a team or separately?'

Ming looked down at the diamond-encrusted antique watch he had surprisingly given her that morning.

'We've only got forty-five minutes before the speeches; we'll get round more of them if you take one side and I the other.'

'Good idea. I'll meet you at the cake, then. Synchronise watches and don't forget to eat sometimes.'

'I won't, Mark.' Ming reached up to kiss him behind the ear and whisper that she loved him.

She waited for a moment, watching Amanda and Fiona forgetting the glory of their long, sashed dresses and tearing about with Jonathan Wallington and Sophie as though they were in the middle of a playground.

'That's a very wonderful dress, my dear.'

Ming started and looked round to see Max standing a few feet away, smiling at her. She walked straight over to him and kissed him.

'Thank you. I spent a lot of time resisting the temptation of frills and pearl embroidery.'

'You were wise. Happy now?'

'Very. I can't think why I made so much fuss for so long. It's really remarkably easy when you've taken the plunge.'

Max's eyebrows arched up over his cool blue eyes.

'It won't always be, you know.'

'I know that; but it was getting to this stage that always frightened me so much. I think we'll manage.'

'I think you will. He's a nice man, Ming, and funny, and I think a good one, too – they're not often all three.'

'I'm glad you like him, because we'll all be seeing a lot of each other when the magazine really gets going.' Ming watched Max's face change and said slowly: 'What haven't you told me?'

'I hadn't meant to say anything until you came back

from the honeymoon,' he said, sipping champagne, 'but I've decided at last. I'm going to live in France, down in the Alpes Maritimes.'

'Alone?' she said, too worried to be tactful. Max shook his head and a charming smile caught the edges of his lips. She kissed him once again.

'Oh, well done, Max! I hope you'll be very happy.' He nodded and let her go.

'But what about Connie?'

'She'll be all right,' said Max calmly and then he added, not calmly at all: 'I feel almost unbearably guilty, but it is an artificial arrangement as things stand. I can't make her happy – or she me. If I stick it out from gratitude I'm going to hate her in the end, and that'll do no one any good. This way, we've a chance of staying friends. Cold-blooded, I know, and I know it wrings your soft heart. But it is practical, Ming.'

After that exchange Ming was not surprised to find Connie looking almost grim, but she was talking to Flixe and Peter and so Ming had no chance of talking to her properly. They exchanged a brief word and Ming went on through the richly dressed crowd, seizing a tiny sandwich whenever someone offered her a trayful, and trying to think of something appropriate to say to everyone who congratulated her.

By the time she had reached the podium where her wedding cake stood between two obelisks of cream and yellow flowers, she was both tired and almost voiceless. The air inside the striped tent was hot and smoky, and the conversations all around her had become a kind of pulsating roar. She croaked a greeting to Mark and then David Wallington, who was to propose the toast to her, and asked for a glass of water.

'Ladies and gentlemen,' he said when she was ready and the cheerful crowd had shuffled and muttered into silence, 'I have always though it the duty of a best man to describe the bridegroom to those of the bride's friends and relations who have never met him and my toast gives me the opportunity to do the same for the bride.

'Having first met her only seven years ago, I cannot tell you any sentimental stories of her childhood or describe how charming she looked in her bath. But I can tell you something of the sort of woman she has become.'

He turned and put his arm lightly around her shoulders for an instant.

'There's no need for me to describe her looks or her sweetness, because those are manifest. But those of you who don't know her may not know of her courage or her wits or her brains.'

He went on to give a brief account of what Ming had done in the war, her developing career in the Houses of Parliament and her recent essay into journalism.

'When her honesty and determination led her into conflict with an archaic law and landed her in court, she did not falter,' he went on. 'And that is typical of her. Whatever life may throw at her and Mark in the future, she will be equal to it.

'Today, as any of Ming's legion of friends will tell you, he is the luckiest man alive.'

Tibor, standing very close behind Julia Wallington, refilled her glass and whispered:

'What about you, Julia? Do you agree?'

She looked over her shoulder at him and he was struck by the new peace in her dark eyes.

'Yes. I do agree. David and I had a long, long talk last night. But hush now, Tibor.'

'Ladies and gentlemen, I ask you to raise your glasses to the bride.'

A moment later David had walked down from the podium to join Julia, who smiled at him and touched his arm.

Watching them unobserved, Tibor thought that Julia was safely through yet another storm. There would be others, he was sure, but for the moment she was happy. He was about to refill his own glass when he felt four sticky hands on his striped trousers. Looking down he saw that his god-daughter and fellow bridesmaid had grabbed his legs.

'Me and Fiona are bored, Uncle Tibor. Come and play!'

Not particularly interested in hearing what the best man had to say about Mark, he went with them beyond the confines of the tent where they clearly felt they could make as much noise as they wanted. Breathing deeply in the fresher air, he pulled a small brown book out of one pocket and the stub of a pencil from the other, and sat down to draw quick, clever sketches of them as they ran and tumbled over the terrace, messing up their dresses and their specially dyed satin dancing shoes.

In a short time Gerry joined him, sitting down beside him with a sigh.

'I do find weddings tiring,' she said. 'D'you mind being interrupted?'

'Not at all,' he answered, looking up from his drawing. 'Are the speeches done?'

'Yes, Ming's gone to change with Connie. It'll all be over soon.'

As she had passed Connie on her way to the room David had organised for her, Ming seized her hand.

'Come and help me dress, Con,' she said.

A little surprised but willing enough Connie followed her and then sat in a chair watching as Ming untangled the tiara from her carefully arranged hair and undid the twenty tiny buttons down the front of her dress.

'Shall I help?' Connie asked. Ming shook her newly free head.

'No need. It was company I wanted, not a substitute for a lady's maid,' she said, laughing. Then she sobered up. 'Max tells me he's leaving England.'

Connie's face darkened. She took a cigarette from her bag and lit it, drawing the smoke deep into her lungs.

'I always expected it,' she said, tilting her head back. 'But that doesn't make it any easier.'

'Does he know how much you care for him?'

'Of course. He kindly said that he didn't want to exploit me any longer when he couldn't give me anything back.'

There was enough bitterness in her voice to make Ming choose her words with care.

'He must have worried a lot about taking so much from

you.' She heaved the heavy mass of silk over her head and laid it across a chair.

'Possibly. But I wanted to give it and not being able to any longer leaves me very stuck.'

Ming slipped into the skirt of her pale blue suit and reached for the cream open-necked blouse.

'Stuck?' she repeated.

'Stuck with an empty house, an empty life, and a magazine I don't want. Well, not stuck with that because I can stop it straight away.'

'But you won't!' exclaimed Ming, pushing the blouse into the top of her skirt. She watched the other woman's face. 'Connie, you can't.'

'Of course I can. Our contract says that either of us can shut down at once provided we pay the other one's debts. With both of you gone what's the point in carrying on?'

'Connie, you're mad! It's well on the road to success. We've had huge publicity over the case and all those letters of support. People we couldn't have dreamed of approaching are prepared to write for us now. We've a chance really to make something of it. You can't give up now.'

'We?' said Connie rather distantly.

'Yes. You didn't really think that I was going to desert, did you?'

'I rather assumed that you'd stop now that you've opted for the safety of marriage, yes.'

Ming's face broke into one of her nicest smiles. She shrugged her shoulders into her jacket, arranged the collar of the shirt and pulled a simple straw hat on her head. There were two white roses pinned along one side of the crown.

'I don't think there's anything safe about marriage. It's the single life that is the safe one – as you know.'

'I?' Connie ground out her cigarette with unnecessary force.

'Yes. Occasionally lonely, but much, much safer. Come on, Connie, you know that as well as I do. You chose the security of power and freedom. I'm going for the big gamble.'

The dark eyebrows flattened and Connie's fine mouth curved at last.

'I do know what you're talking about actually,' she admitted.

'I know you do.' Ming looked at her watch again. 'Help. Connie, there isn't time now to sort out about the magazine. Will you promise not to do anything fatal until I get back from Italy?'

There was a pause.

'Promise, Connie?'

There was a knock at the door.

'Are you ready, Ming?' called Mark from the other side.

'Promise me, Connie!' It was no longer a question.

'All right,' she said. 'I'll wait until you get back to make the final decision, but I can't promise to keep it going. After all, what I should be doing is cultivating my garden.'

'Ming? Are you there?'

'I'm here,' she said, giving Connie a quick, amused smile before turning to open the door.

Mark stood there tall and broad-shouldered, smiling at her with an expression in his eyes that seemed to answer all the questions she could never ask him. Delight spread all through her.

'And I am ready.'